Light blinded them. When Galen and Raffi could see again, the candle was a bubbling, hissing pool of wax and molten metal on the seared floor. There was a shocked silence, and then Alberic began to laugh. The tiny man wheezed and giggled and cackled; jumping from his chair, he cavorted around the candles, catching Sikka's hands and kissing them, then dancing away. His own people watched him in amusement; Raffi stared; Galen stood stiff with distaste.

At last, breathless, Alberic slumped over the arm of his chair, clutching his side. "Oh, this is wonderful!" he managed. "Superb. Beyond belief. To rob a Relicmaster!" He lifted the box and rubbed it as gently as if it had been a bird; then his head turned, and his eyes were cold and crafty.

"This is the arrangement. I want the Sekoi. You have power, contacts. You'll find him for me and get him here alive. And then I might, I just might, give you your box of flames back."

FIREBIRD
WHERE FANTASY TAKES FLIGHT™
WHERE SCIENCE FICTION SOARS™

CATHERINE FISHER

RELIC MASTER ^PART 1

The Dark City & The Lost Heiress

FIREBIRD

AN IMPRINT OF PENGUIN GROUP (USA) INC.

FIREBIRD
Published by the Penguin Group
Penguin Group (USA) Inc.
375 Hudson Street
New York, New York 10014, U.S.A.

USA / Canada / UK / Ireland / Australia / New Zealand / India / South Africa / China
Penguin Books Ltd, Registered Offices: 80 Strand, London WC2R 0RL, England

For more information about the Penguin Group visit www.penguin.com

The Dark City
Published in the United Kingdom by Random House Children's Books UK, 1998
First published in the United States of America by Dial Books,
an imprint of Penguin Group (USA) Inc., 2011
Copyright © Catherine Fisher, 1998

The Lost Heiress
Published in the United Kingdom as *The Interrex* by Random House Children's Books UK, 1999
First published in the United States of America by Dial Books,
an imprint of Penguin Group (USA) Inc., 2011
Copyright © Catherine Fisher, 1999

Published by Firebird, an imprint of Penguin Group (USA) Inc., 2013

THE LIBRARY OF CONGRESS HAS CATALOGED THE DIAL EDITION OF *THE DARK CITY* AS FOLLOWS:
Fisher, Catherine, date.
The dark city / by Catherine Fisher.
p. cm.
Summary: Sixteen-year-old Raffi, Master Galen, and a mysterious traveler, Carys, enter
the ruined city of Tasceron seeking a relic that may save the world, while evading the Watch,
a brutal organization opposed to the Order to which Raffi and Galen belong.
ISBN 978-0-8037-3673-3 (hardcover)
[1. Fantasy. 2. Apprentices—Fiction. 3. Antiquities—Fiction.] I. Title.
PZ7.F4995 Dam 2011 [Fic]—dc22

THE LIBRARY OF CONGRESS HAS CATALOGED THE DIAL EDITION OF *THE LOST HEIRESS* AS FOLLOWS:
Fisher, Catherine, date.
The lost heiress / by Catherine Fisher.
p. cm.
Summary: Even though the city of Tasceron and its Emperor have fallen,
when Master Galen and his sixteen-year-old appentice, Raffi, hear a rumor that
the heiress to the throne still lives, they must try to find her and keep her safe.
ISBN 978-0-8037-3674-0 (hardcover)
[1. Fantasy. 2. Apprentices—Fiction.] I. Title.
PZ7.F4995 Lo 2011 [Fic]—dc22 20100038156

Firebird ISBN 978-0-14-242687-6

Printed in the United States of America

1 3 5 7 9 10 8 6 4 2

Designed by Nancy R. Leo-Kelly

The Dark City

To Stephen Herrington
for the idea

Contents

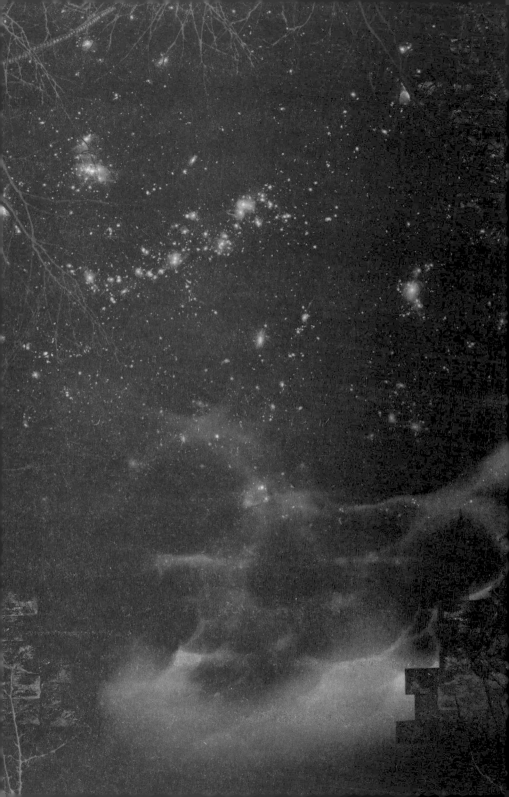

The Box of Flames

1

*The world is not dead. The world is alive
and breathes. The world is the whim of
God, and her journey is forever.*

Litany of the Makers

THE SEVEN MOONS were all in the sky at once. Tonight they made the formation that Galen called the web: one in the center—Pyra, the small red one—and the others in a circle around her. They glimmered over the treetops; it was a good omen, the sisters' most perfect dance.

Raffi stared up at them with his arms full of wood. As an experiment, he let his third eye open and made tiny purple filaments of light spray from the central moon to all the others, linking them in a flaring pattern. After a while he changed the color to blue, managing to hold it for a few minutes, and even when it faded, a faint echo still lingered. He watched it till his arms were tired, then he held the wood more carefully and turned away.

That had been better than last time. He was getting quite good at it—he ought to tell Galen.

Or maybe not.

Gathering up more of the crumbling twigs, he moved through the dark trees resentfully. It was no use talking to Galen. The keeper was in one of his bitter moods; he'd only laugh, that short, harsh laugh of contempt.

The wood was very dry, rotting on the forest floor. Huge ants scurried out of it, and the armored wood-grubs that chewed slowly. He flicked a shower of them from his clothes.

The forest was quiet. Two nights ago a pack of woses had raged through here, tearing great holes in the leaf canopy; the wreckage still lay under the oaks. In the green gloom of the night, insects hummed; something whistled behind him in the wood. It was time he was getting back.

He pushed through hanging ivies and across a clearing deep in bracken, alert for snakes and the venomous blue spiders, but only shadows shifted and blurred among the trees, too far off to see or sense. He'd come farther than he'd thought and in the shafts of moonlight, red and pale and rose, the path looked unfamiliar, until the trees ended in a bank of dead leaves. He waded through them to the hillside, seeing the vast black hump of the cromlech and Galen's fire like a spark in its shadow.

Then he stopped.

Somewhere behind him, far behind, something had tripped one of the sense-lines. The warning tweaked a tiny pain over one eye; he recognized it at once. The lines were well above ground; whatever it was, it was big, and coming this way. He listened, intent, but only the night sounds came to him, the insect buzz and the flittermice, the crackle of the fire.

Scattering wood, he ran down quickly.

"What's the matter?" Galen sat carelessly against the slabs of the tomb, his coat tugged tight around him. "Scared of moths now?"

Raffi dumped the wood in a heap; dust rose from it. "One of the sense-lines just snapped!"

The keeper stared at him for a moment. Then he turned

to the fire and began piling the wood onto the flames. "Did it now."

"Don't do that! Someone might be coming!"

Galen shrugged. "Let them."

"It could be anyone!" Raffi dropped to a crouch, almost sick with worry, the strings of purple and blue stones he wore around his neck swinging. He caught hold of them. "It could be the Watch! Put the fire out at least!"

Galen paused. When he looked up, his face was a mask of flame light and haggard shadows, his deep eyes barely gleaming, his hook nose exaggerated like a hawk's. "No," he said harshly. "If they want me, let them come. I've had enough of skulking in the dark." He eased his left leg with both hands. "What direction?"

"West."

"From the mountains." He mused. "Could just be a traveler."

"Maybe." Raffi was preoccupied. Another line had twanged in his skull, closer now.

Galen watched him. "So. Let's put my pupil through his paces."

"What, now!"

10

"No better time." He turned his lean face to the fire. "If it is an enemy, what might we put on the flames?"

Raffi, appalled, rubbed his hair. He was scared now; he hated Galen in this mood. "Bitterwort. Scumweed, if we had any, goldenrod to make him sleepy. Shall I do that?"

"Do nothing, unless I tell you. Say nothing." Sharply, Galen raised his head, his profile dark against the smallest moon. "Have you got the blue box?"

Raffi nodded; he clutched it, in his pocket.

"Use it only if the danger is extreme."

"I know, I know. But—"

A twig snapped. Somewhere nearby a were-bird shrieked and flew off through the branches. Behind it, Raffi caught the snuffle of a horse.

He stood up, heart thumping. Behind him the cromlech was black and solid, the rock face gnarled under his palms, hollowed by a thousand years of frost and rain. Lichen grew on it, a green powder over the faint carved spirals. It felt like a great beast, fossilized and hunched.

Galen pulled himself up too, without his stick. His

long hair swung forward, the tangled strings of black jet-stones and green crystal catching the light, the heavy cowl of his coat high around his neck.

"Ready?" he breathed.

"I think so."

The keeper gave him a scornful glance. "Don't worry. I won't risk your life."

"It's not mine I'm worried about." But Raffi muttered it sullenly under his breath, feeling for the powders and the blue box.

A horse came abruptly out of the wood.

It was tall, one of the thin, red-painted kinds they bred beyond the mountains, and the sweat on its long, skel-etal neck made it ghostly in the sisters' light. It walked forward and stopped just beyond the flicker of the fire. Staring into the dark, Raffi could just make out the rider: a dim, bulky figure muffled against the cold.

No one spoke.

Raffi glanced into the trees. He couldn't sense anyone else. He tried to look into the wood with his third eye, but he was too nervous; only shadows moved. The rider stirred.

The Box of Flames

"A fine evening, friends." His voice was deep; a big man.

Galen nodded, his long dark hair swinging. "So it is. You've come far?"

"Far enough."

The horse shifted, its harness clinking softly. The rider urged it a few steps forward, perhaps to see them better.

"Come to the fire," Galen said dangerously.

The horse's fear was tangible, a smell on the air. It was terrified of the cromlech, or perhaps the invisible web of earth-lines that ran out from it. The man, too, sounded tense when he spoke again. "I don't think so, keepers."

Galen's voice was quiet as he answered. "That's an unlucky title. Why should we be keepers?"

"This is an unlucky place. Who else would be living here?" The rider hesitated, then swung himself down from the saddle and came forward a few steps, unwinding a filmy, knitted wrapping from his face.

They saw a powerful, thick-set man, black-bearded. A crossbow of some sort was slung on his shoulder. He wore a metal breastplate too; it gleamed in the light of the moons. Dangerous, Raffi thought. But nothing they couldn't handle.

The stranger must have thought the same. "I bring no threat here," he went on quickly. "How could I? There's no doubt an armory of sorcery aimed at me as I stand." He held up both hands, empty; a jewel gleamed on the left gauntlet. "I'm looking for a man named Galen Harn, a Relic Master." He glanced at Raffi, expressionless. "And for his scholar, Raffael Morel."

"Are you now," Galen said bleakly. He shifted; Raffi knew that his leg would be aching, but the keeper's face was hard. "And what do you want with them?"

"To pass on a message. West of here, about twenty leagues, in the foothills where the rivers meet, there's a settlement. The people there need him."

"Why?"

The rider smiled wryly, but he answered. "They found a relic, as they were plowing. A tube. When you touch it, it hums. Small green lights move inside it."

Galen didn't flicker, but Raffi knew he was alert. The horseman knew too. "It seems to me," he said ironically, "that if you should see this Galen, you might tell him.

14

The Box of Flames

The people are desperate that he come and deal with the thing. None of them dares go near it."

Galen nodded. "I'm sure. But the Order of keepers is outlawed. They're all either dead or in hiding from the Watch. If they're caught they face torture. This man might suspect a trap."

"He'd be safe enough." The rider scratched his beard and tried a step forward. "We need him. We wouldn't betray him. We're loyal to the old Order. That's all I can say, master. He'd just have to trust us."

Take one more step, Raffi thought. In his pocket his fingers trembled on the blue crystal box. He'd never used it on a man. Not yet.

The rider was still, as if he felt the tension.

Suddenly Galen moved, limping forward out of the tomb's shadow into the red and gold of the firelight. He stood tall, his face dark. "Tell them we'll come. Bury the device in the earth till we get there. Set a guard and let no one come near it. It may be dangerous."

The rider smiled. "Thank you. I'll see that it's done." He turned and climbed heavily up onto the horse; the red beast circled warily. "When can we expect you?"

"When we get there." Galen stared at him levelly. "I'd ask you to stay the night, but outlaws have little to share."

"Nor would I, keeper. Not under those stones." He turned away, then paused, glancing back. "The people will be glad to hear this. Depend upon it: You'll be safe with us. Ask for Alberic."

Then the horse stalked cautiously into the wood.

They both stood silent a long time, listening to the faint crackle and rustle, the distant charring of disturbed birds. The sense-lines snagged, one by one, in Raffi's head.

Finally, Galen moved. He sat down, hissing through his teeth with the stiffness of his leg. "Well. What do you think of that?"

Raffi took his hand off the blue box and collapsed beside him. Suddenly he felt unbearably tired. "That he's got guts, coming out here."

"And his story?"

"I don't know." He shrugged "It sounds true. But . . ."

"But. Exactly." The keeper sat back, his face in shadow.

"It could be a trap," Raffi ventured.

"So it could."

"But you're going anyway."

The Box of Flames

Galen laughed sourly. A sudden spark lit his face, twisted with pain. "I used to know when people lied to me, Raffi. If only they knew!" He glanced across. "We both go. Someone has to deal with this relic."

Uneasy, Raffi shook his head. "There may be no relic."

Galen spat into the fire. "What do I care," he said softly.

2

*This is how the world came to be. The
Makers came from the sky, on stairways
of ice. Flain opened his hands and the
land and sea were there, the soil and salt.
He set them one against the other, erod-
ing, in conflict forever. Out of stillness he
brought movement, out of peace, war.*

*Soren called out the leaves and the
trees. She walked the world, and seeds
fell from her sleeves and the hem of her
dress. The Woman of Leaves clothed the
world in a green brocade.*

*It was Tamar, the bearded one, who
brought the beasts. Down the silver stairs
he led them, the smallest a night-cub that
struggled in his arms.*

*All the sons of God watched them
scatter.*

Book of the Seven Moons

THE JOURNEY TO THE SETTLEMENT took five days. On his own, Raffi could have gotten there in four, but Galen's limp slowed them down. The keeper's leg was long healed, but it was stiff, and he walked grim and silent with a tall black stick. Even when the pain must have been bad after a long day's tramp in the rain or cold, he never talked about it. Raffi was used to it all: the keeper's brooding, his sudden outbreaks of foul temper. At times like these he kept quiet and wary and out of reach of the black stick. Galen had been hurt too deeply. The explosion had damaged more than his leg—it had scarred his mind. Toiling up the steep rocky path, the pack heavy on his shoulders, Raffi watched the Relic Master scramble ahead of him, slithering on scree. Galen was almost as unstable. And now this message.

If it was a trap, Galen wouldn't care. Raffi knew that sometimes he wanted to get caught, that he took deliberate risks, carelessly, proudly; like in the summer when they'd walked out of the forest into a village and taken a room and stayed there for three days, sleeping on comfortable beds, eating outside in full view of everyone. Galen hadn't cared, but for Raffi it had been three days of terror. The villagers hadn't betrayed them. Most had looked the other way. They'd been so lucky, Raffi thought, stumbling over a stone. Everyone knew there was a reward for the capture of any keeper. Two thousand marks. They'd been incredibly lucky.

"Come on!" Galen was standing on the top of the ridge. His voice was a growl through his teeth. "You can go faster than this. Don't think you need to slow down for me."

Raffi stopped, wiping sweat from his hair. "I'm not. The pack's heavy."

Galen glared at him. "Then give it to me."

"You've had your turn."

"Do you think I can't manage another?"

"I didn't say that!" Raffi spread his hands. "I just—"

"Save it! And move. We want to get to this place before night." He had turned and gone before Raffi could answer.

Looking at the empty sky, Raffi felt furious and hurt and reckless. For a cold moment, he told himself he would leave tonight, just take his things and go home. There were no Relic Masters now, the Order was broken. And Galen could look after himself with his scornful, bitter jealousy. But even as he raged, Raffi knew it all meant nothing, and he took the blue crystal box out and glared at it. Curiosity would keep him here. There was so much he had to learn. And he'd felt the power surge in him, and now he could never be without it.

THAT AFTERNOON they sat on warm stones on a hillside, looking down, at last, on the settlement.

"Well," Galen said acidly. "Well, well." He drank from the water flask and passed it over; Raffi took a cold mouthful thoughtfully. They had expected a village. And indeed there were houses, barns, outbuildings. But mostly, this was a fortress.

The central building was ancient; maybe even from the time of the Makers. The sides were strangely smooth and pale, the signs of old windows clear, now clumsily bricked up to slits. There were about six levels. On the higher ones balconies hung out precariously; most were ruined, but Raffi could see bowmen on one, tiny moving figures. The roof had partly collapsed, and been mended with hurdles and thatch.

"What do you think?" He passed the flask back and chewed the hard bread. "Safe?"

"Not safe." Galen stared down moodily. "Those who have the nerve to live in a Maker-house are no ordinary villagers. Since the Emperor fell the land has gone wild. Robber-gangs, warlords, each one fighting the others. I'm sure this is the castle of one such."

"And we're going in, blindly."

Galen gave a sour grin. "Going in, yes. Blindly, no."

The stones were warm in the autumn sun. Raffi leaned back, feeling better somehow. "Sense-lines?"

"Around us both. Powders. And if all else fails, the box."

Raffi shook his head. "If there are too many of them, that won't save us. It might be better not to go in at all."

"Curiosity, Raffi. Always my downfall." Galen was rummaging in the pack; now he brought out a small black tube and held it in both hands lovingly. He spoke a prayer, and made the sign of humility. Then he put the tube to his eye and looked down.

Like the blue box, it was a relic, a holy thing the Makers had left. They had found it in a farm north of the forest two years ago; the woman of the place had sent for them secretly, terrified the Watch would find out. Galen had blessed the farm, spoken prayers over the house, and taken the relic away. He had a secret place to keep them, a cave in the hills. Once, coming back there, they had found signs on the walls, as if some other member of the Order might have sheltered there. But the marks had been rain-washed, unclear. No one knew how many of the Order were even alive.

Galen gazed at the tower for a long time. Then he handed the tube to Raffi, who stared. "Me?"

"Why not. It's time you did."

Nervous, Raffi took it. It was warm and miraculously smooth, made of the Makers' strange material, not wood or stone or skin, the secret no one knew. He muttered a prayer over it, then raised it and looked in.

Despite himself he gasped.

The fortress was huge, close up. He saw the weeds growing from it, the cracks in the walls. The door was bricked up, a small black slot where two men loitered, talking. He moved the tube carefully; noted the deep pits, the spiked ditch, the strong fence with the walkway behind it.

"Whoever they are, they're well-defended."

"Indeed." Galen's voice sounded amused. "Now touch the red button."

He felt for it; the tube stretched itself in his fingers, the focus blurring quickly to his eyesight. Houses and a row of stalls, their goods hanging in the wind, tawdry and cheap. Dogs in the mud. A crowd of women washing clothes in tubs. Smoke. He followed it up, high into the sky, until the small moon Agramon flashed briefly across the glass. For a moment even that looked close, the smooth faint surface, with tiny formations glinting.

The Box of Flames

"That's enough!" Galen's hand clasped around the tube; Raffi let go reluctantly. The Relic Master folded it into its wrappings, pushed it deep in the sack, and stood up.

Suddenly he looked dangerous, his gaunt face tense, his eyes dark under deep brows. "Come on," he said grimly. "Let's go and ask for Alberic."

IT WAS NIGHT when they reached the gates, and the buildings glimmered behind the palisade. The men stationed outside had a lantern; they were playing dice, but they stood up soon enough.

Galen ignored them. He strode past without a word, through the open gates, and no one challenged him. Hurrying behind, Raffi glanced back; the men were whispering. Planning to shut us in, he thought.

They walked together between the dark houses, through the mud, the soft pools of water and dung. The stench of the place was appalling. Filthy children watched them from doorways, silent and unsmiling. The buildings were squalid and patched, the wood rotten and green with age. As he squelched through the muck, Galen muttered, "Anything?"

"People watching. Just curious." The sense-lines moved about them, invisible, fluid. Raffi held them with some distant part of his mind, easily, from long practice. It had been the first thing Galen had taught him.

The fortress loomed up. Noise and smoke drifted out from it, laughter, the yells of an argument. In the ruined windows, faint lights glimmered; the strange smooth walls were dappled with moonlight.

At the doorway, the entrance Raffi had seen through the glass, three men waited. Their weapons were in their hands—long hooked knives. They watched Galen come with a mixture of fear and something else, something disturbing. Warnings rippled in Raffi's skull. "Galen . . ."

But Galen had walked right up to them.

"My name is Galen Harn. I'm looking for Alberic."

Whatever else, they weren't surprised. One grinned at the others. "We've been expecting you, keeper. Come with me."

Inside was dark, a maze of rooms and passages. Voices echoed ahead, or from behind closed doors;

smoky torches guttered on brackets. The air was fetid and smelled worse than outside. As they walked down a long corridor, men squeezed past them, a few slaves, two girls giggling behind Raffi's back, sending the sense-lines rippling. Looking up, he saw something on a wall, marks under the dirt, a symbol he knew. Next to it was a grid of buttons and numbers by a door. Galen stopped too and made the humility sign; Raffi knew he longed to touch it. "This is a relic," he said to their guide. "It shouldn't be left here."

The man shrugged easily. "That's up to Alberic."

"Don't you fear it?"

"I stay away from it, keeper. The whole castle is old."

"Where does this door lead?"

"Nowhere. There's a square shaft behind it, empty. Goes right down." He leered. "Alberic uses it as a burial pit. Knee-deep in skeletons."

He wasn't joking. Raffi glanced at Galen, but the keeper's face was dark and grim. Putting his hand in his pocket, he let the touch of the blue box comfort him.

They came to some stairs leading up, wide but dingy. Raffi's eyes smarted from the smoke; he stumbled on greasy bones and other rubbish in the thick straw. Gnats whined around him; fleas too, he didn't doubt.

The stairs rose up. Ahead in the dark, Galen climbed them steadily, his black stick tapping. Something was cooking somewhere, a rich, meaty smell that tormented Raffi like a pain. He wondered if they'd get any of it. He couldn't remember when he'd last eaten meat.

Finally they came to the top, a long, dim room, full of smoke. The floor was made of wooden planks, sanded smooth; it spread before them, an empty expanse.

Their guide stood still. "Go on," he said curtly.

Through the smoke they saw a group of four people waiting for them, sitting and standing around a fire at the far end of the room. Galen glanced across. "Well?"

"It doesn't feel right."

The keeper shrugged. "Too late." He stalked forward; Raffi followed him down the hall, his heart hammering with nerves.

Talk hushed. The men and woman waiting stood up, all but one, the man in the center. As Raffi came closer, he saw to his astonishment that the man was tiny, his feet resting on a box, his body far too small for the great cushioned chair in which he sat. His face was narrow and clever, his hair stubbly; he wore a gold collar and a green quilted jacket slashed with red.

Galen stood still, and looked down at him. "I was told to ask for Alberic," he said gravely.

The dwarf nodded, his eyes sharp. "You've found him," he replied.

3

*Though the Makers are gone, their relics
remain. Let the keepers seek them out.
For the power in them is holy.*

Litany of the Makers

IT WAS A TRAP.

Raffi knew that, as soon as he saw Alberic. He had a sudden vivid sense of the empty room behind him, the stairs, the maze of corridors, the gate and spikes and ditches. It was a trap, and they were well inside it.

But Alberic only grinned. "So you're Galen Harn. You took some finding."

Galen said nothing. His face was stern.

"And a pupil!" The dwarf's shrewd eyes glanced over Raffi. "Bursting with sorceries, no doubt."

Someone sniggered behind him. Alberic leaned back into the cushions, the candlelight soft on the silk of his jerkin. "Sit down, please," he said amiably.

A big, black-haired man lifted a gilt chair from the wall and thumped it down in front of Galen. As he straightened up, he smirked at them and they recognized the horseman from the forest. He still wore the breastplate; close up it looked thin, pitted with rust.

Galen ignored the chair. Someone edged a small stool toward Raffi, and he gave it a longing glance but stayed standing.

"We came here," Galen said ominously, "because of your message. A relic . . ."

"Ah yes!" The small man put his tiny fingers together and grinned over them. "I'm afraid there might have been a slight misunderstanding there." He gave the briefest of nods. The sense-lines snapped; Raffi found himself being shoved onto the stool by a girl in snaky armor, and glancing around he saw they had forced Galen to sit too, the black-bearded man and another standing over him.

For a moment the keeper's eyes were black with fury. Then he seemed to control himself; he leaned back, thrusting his legs out.

The Box of Flames

"You seem determined to make us comfortable."

"It's not that. I don't like looking up."

They stared at each other. Finally the dwarf's grin widened. He spread his hands. "It's like this, keeper. I'm the power here. My body may be puny, but my brain's sharp, sharper than any, and my lads and lasses here know Alberic's plans and Alberic's cunning bring the most gold. This is Sikka, Godric, whom you've already met, and Taran. My rogues, my children."

He blew a kiss at them; the girl Sikka laughed, and Taran, a man in a dirty blue coat, gave a snort of derision. Carefully, Raffi moved his hand an inch toward his pocket.

"Gold." Galen nodded. "So you're thieves, then."

There was a tense silence. Raffi went cold all over. Then Alberic shook his head. "For a wise man you have a blunt tongue, Galen. As it is, this time I'll let you keep it." He leaned over and poured himself a drink from a delicate glass container on a round table beside him, lit by tall candles. The goblet glittered; it was crystal, almost priceless. Raffi tightened his dry lips. Slowly Alberic drank, leaning back on the plump cushions.

"The relic," Galen growled.

"There is no relic. At least—" The small man sat up, looking around in mock surprise. "I don't think so. Is there?"

The girl laughed. "You're a cruel man, Alberic," she said, coming around and gripping the back of his carven chair. She stared at Galen in amusement. "Did you really believe that we'd have a terror of relics, like the old fools in the villages?"

Galen said nothing; it was Alberic who answered. "Oh no," he said softly, watching the Relic Master. "Oh no, my pet, he's a deeper one than that. Very deep. I think he knew what he was coming into all along. I think he knew very well . . ."

For a moment the dwarf's voice was so thoughtful that Raffi had the sudden sense he had guessed Galen's bitter secret, and his anxiety sent the sense-lines rippling, so that he had to fight to hold on to them. Alberic watched silently, head on one side. Suddenly his voice was sharp. "Let me see some sorcery, keeper. I need to know you're who you say you are, not some spy of the Watch."

Galen's hands tightened, the fingers clenching on the chair. Raffi saw them uneasily.

38

The Box of Flames

"I don't do sorcery—as you call it—on the orders of anyone." His face was proud and his dark stern eyes held Alberic's. "I'm a Relic Master of the Order of keepers, and the power I have is holy. Not for fireside tricks."

Alberic nodded. "But the Order is finished," he said sweetly. "Broken, outlawed. Dead."

"The power remains." Galen leaned back in his chair, legs stretched out. He had the look of a man playing chess, playing for his life, on an invisible board.

"To open and close," Alberic murmured, "build and destroy, see forward and back."

Raffi looked surprised; Galen didn't. The dwarf grinned at them. "One of your Order was once . . . in the way, on one of our raids. Unfortunately some of my rogues were a little enthusiastic. The only thing he had worth stealing was the Litany of the Makers, written in code on parchment. I worked it out and read it. An amusement for the long winter nights . . ."

Galen said nothing, his eyes cold with anger.

"The boy, then!" Alberic waved at Raffi. "Let the boy do something. You don't object to that?"

Galen shrugged. "If he wants to. He knows little. A

few effects of light that might amuse you." He turned a cold look on Raffi. "Do your best for our audience."

Reluctantly Raffi stood up, catching the hidden message. They all stared at him, and he felt nervous and furious with Galen. But then, he'd had no choice.

He stepped out and pushed the stool away with his foot. Then he raised both hands, spoke the words in his mind, and let his third eye open, the eye of the Makers.

In the air he made the seven moons, each hanging from nothing, the small red Pyra, pitted Cyrax, the icy globe of Atterix, all the sisters of the old Book. They glowed in the dark room, and beyond them he glimpsed Alberic, watching intently, his face bright with the dappled lights.

"Very pretty," the dwarf murmured. "Most pleasing."

But he hardly seemed impressed. Uneasy, Raffi set the globes spinning. They moved in long ellipses, made the complex orbits of the moons, each leaving a glinting thread of light that interwove into a net of colors, purples and reds and blues. And each had its own note of music that hummed, building into harmonies that rose and gathered in the dim hall, an underthrob of sound like the voices of strange beings. He was sweating now, and there was a pain behind his eyes, but he kept the moons spinning till the wordless song rose to a crescendo of exquisite beauty, and then he let it fade, slowly, into silence. The moons became ghosts of light. Then they were gone.

"Charming," Alberic said drily.

Sweating, his head thumping, Raffi glanced at Galen. He hadn't moved but sat still, arms folded. "Is that enough for you?"

"Certainly. No Watchman could do that. With such a pupil you must be who you say you are."

"You never doubted that."

Alberic grinned. "No."

"So what do you want? We're not worth robbing."

There was silence. Wearily Raffi sat down; no one took any notice of him. He slid his hand into his pocket and gripped the blue box. The tension in the room was taut as a rope; he could feel it tighten his nerves.

For the first time Alberic didn't seem amused. He drank from his glass and flashed a glance at the girl, Sikka. She nodded, her long plaited hair swinging.

The small man put his glass down. "Revenge. I want revenge."

"On us?"

Alberic smiled dangerously. "Don't pretend to be stupid." For a moment he fingered his golden collar, then he looked up and said fiercely, "You called us thieves. Indeed we are. What does a thief hate most, wise one?"

"To be robbed." Galen's voice was somber, his hawk-face a mask of shadows.

"Indeed." Alberic looked at him, impressed. "Let me tell you about it. Two months ago, a wandering Sekoi came to this place. He was one of the ones who tell stories: a lazy, mocking creature. Brindled gray and brown. A zigzag under one eye."

Raffi edged closer. Any mention of the Sekoi fascinated him. He had only seen a few of them, years ago when he'd been too small and had run away, thinking they would eat him. The Sekoi were the others, the different race. They were taller than men, and thin, their sharp faces furred like cats, their long fingers streaked in tribal markings. People said it was the Sekoi who had made the cromlechs, eons ago, before the Makers came. They had stories about that time, or so Galen said. The Order had had texts of a few, laboriously copied in the great library in the tower of Karelian. All dust now.

"He fooled us," Alberic said waspishly. "Hung around, played with the children. We threw him out but he came back. He prattled, dreamed, sang foreign songs. We thought he was harmless."

"The Sekoi make an art of that," Galen muttered. He was looking at the jug of wine. Alberic noticed, and grinned.

"As you say. All the time he was learning about us, where the strongrooms were, who held the keys, what the raids brought in." He shook his head. "There was plenty of that, believe me. Gold, silver, clothes, wool, wine. This place is well stuffed."

"I can believe it." Galen leaned back, pushing the long hair from his face. "And so he robbed you."

The dwarf glared. "He gave a performance. Down in the courtyard. None of us had seen a Sekoi work." He leaned forward. "No disrespect to you, boy, but he was astounding. He told a story, and the things he spoke of appeared, and I was inside the story, we all were; it happened all around us. It was some tale of castles and battles and gods who rode from the sky on silver horses, and believe me, keeper, I lived every minute of it! I felt the rain, the sparks from the swords, had to run out of the way in case I was crushed." He leaned back, remembering. "It was no illusion. It was real. Some of my people were injured in that dream. Two never came out of it."

"And when it ended?"

Alberic's eyes were hooded with wrath. "The fires out, the courtyard dark, the guards asleep. And the strongroom door wide open."

"What did he take?" Raffi asked eagerly.

"Gold. What do they ever want? A box of gold marks. A fortune!"

"You want it back."

"I want him!" Alberic leaped up suddenly, shoving Godric aside and prowling, a tiny, hunched figure, among the candles. "I want that filthy dream-peddler! What I'll do to him!" He spun, his eyes bright. "And then with him! Imagine the work he could do for me, the use he'd be to me. I want him brought back, relic-man. And I want you to get him."

44

The Box of Flames

Galen sat still, his black hair and clothes making him a figure of darkness. Raffi knew he was tense, uncertain.

"Why me?"

"You have ways. I'm known, so are my people. None of us can travel that far. The Watch . . ."

Galen laughed bitterly. "The Watch! They want me more than you. No, you can find the creature yourself, thief-lord. He may well be sharper than you are." Then, abruptly, he looked up. "Why did you think I would go?"

"Because of our hostage."

"What hostage?"

Alberic grinned at him. "The boy."

Raffi felt the sense-lines leap; danger surged in the room like a tide. "Galen!" he gasped, jumping up.

The stool smacked behind him. The blue box was in his hand. Weapons glinted; Godric's sword unsheathed with a sharp snick; Sikka caught hold of him so that he yelled and jerked the box up, his thumb stabbing the small round control.

The box throbbed. A blast of light scorched out from it, searing the floor at Alberic's feet so that the dwarf leaped back with a yell, the planks blackened and smoking. Shock forced Raffi back; the box jerked out of his hand and he grabbed for it but Alberic already had him, a knife jabbed in his ribs, one skinny hand gripping his hair so that he yelped in pain.

Through watering eyes he saw their astonished faces, the crisped ends of the straw stinking and curling. In front of him, Galen was holding the box level, his eyes bleak.

"Now that," Alberic said slowly, "is a relic worth having." He turned the knife in Raffi's side. "Even if you get out, the boy won't."

"Let him go."

"I might. If you give me that box." The dwarf stared at it greedily.

"Never." Galen was steady, without expression.

Alberic shrugged. "Your choice, keeper. Keep the box; lose the boy."

4

*It is vital to remember that the powers
the Order claim to have are a complete
illusion.*

Rule of the Watch

Journal of Carys Arrin
Atelgarsday
3.16.546

Two days ago, at last, I found the cromlech.

As I wrote in my last report, the people of the forest hate to talk to strangers; finding anything out is difficult. I'm still traveling as a pack-merchant, so bribes have been easy to give, but it's cost me a great deal in fabrics, buttons, agricultural tools. (NB—Claim the money for this when I get back.) The forest is an eerie place, and most of our charts of it are wrong. The old superstitions of the Order hang around here; also a number of fugitives and vagabonds. Other areas are empty. Once I traveled for three days down airless green paths, slashing my way through, and saw no one. Jekkles have attacked me twice—once scaring the pack-beast almost berserk. Fire seems to keep them off. There are also blue spiders that bite; as I write this my hand is swollen and black, but I killed the thing fast enough to save my life.

Once I'd found it, I watched the cromlech for three hours. No one came near it. Finally, wary for traps, I crawled out, gathered the pack-beasts together, and picked my way down. The slope was steep and rocky. Night was coming; strange mists and veils of murk clung around the rotting tree-stumps, and the enormous stones stood like shadows. As I clambered down to it, my whole skin prickled. The foul witcheries of the place hung on the air.

Someone had been living there, that was clear. There were fire-marks, a pit dug for rubbish, a lot of footprints. But the ashes of the fire were about a day old, and had already been scattered and scratched at by some animal. The Relic Master had gone.

There was no chance of following straight-away—twilight was closing and only four of the moons were up. Warily I wandered around, searching the ground carefully. The place is all humps and hollows; a green ditch surrounds the stones, and as I crossed it I thought I felt a whisper of power. Galen Harn and his boy were here. I'm close to them.

But there was one thing that puzzled me. In the soft mud near the forest fringe I found hoof prints. They came near, but stayed outside the ring. The horse had trampled the ground as if it had stood there and been restless for some time. Then it had gone, back among the trees.

Could Harn have gotten hold of a horse? Could it carry both of them? In one way it would make tracking them easier, but they would move fast then, faster than me.

Don't make problems, old Jellie used to say. Think things out, be clear, and always watch your back. I remembered that when I turned around.

The cromlech is huge, close up. One great lintel-stone balances on three others, the whole thing black against the sky. It must be thousands of years old. I don't know if there are any bodies buried under it, but there are carvings; spirals and strange zigzags, powdered with lichen. It seems impossible to me that the Sekoi could have put these up. There are so few Sekoi, and they always seem so lazy.

I didn't spend the night by the thing, but up in the wood, and I wasn't comfortable. Noises whispered among the branches; a faint breeze made the beasts restless, and endless insects plagued me. Once when I sat up and looked down the slope, I had the feeling the stones were looking back. (None of this will go in the report. I don't want to look a fool.)

At first light I set off. The horse-tracks were lost in marsh, but they started to lead west, so that's the way I'll go.

Atelgarsday, evening

I'm writing this in a village called Tis. At least I think that's what they call it. No one here has seen Harn or the boy Raffael, but I've found out one thing—we're not the only ones looking.

A woman here told me that about a week back, a horseman came through. He was asking for a man named Galen Harn, and even knew what he looked like—dark, hook-nosed, a limp.

The Box of Flames

No one could help, and he went off east.

I'm assuming this is a stranger to the Watch, not one of us. So who? It's clear to me he's already found them—the horse-tracks at the cromlech must have been his. A red horse. Painted. They may have gone with him somewhere—if there was word of a relic, the sorcerer would have been drawn to it, undoubtedly.

After careful questioning and a lot of bribes, I've found out the names of a few likely villages, and one nest of bandits. That might be the best bet, as not many villagers have horses. It's west of here, an old Maker-ruin, a lair of thieves. The villagers say the warlord is called Alberic, and if he's the one on our files, then Galen Harn might well be in more trouble than he knows.

And my job might already be done for me.

5

*The Wounded City—who can see to the
edge of it?
Who can feel the pain of its loss?*

Poems of Anjar Kar

GALEN HESITATED.

Raffi waited without breathing, hating him, desperate for him to give up the box, then not to. He was numb, dizzy with fear.

Galen lowered his aim.

With a snicker of triumph, Alberic loosed his grip on Raffi's hair and held out one small palm. The Relic Master dropped the box into it heavily.

"Thank you." Alberic smirked. "For a moment I thought you wouldn't."

Raffi tugged away across the room, weak with relief. For a moment he had thought the same, and that made him angry. "You should have used it!" he snapped.

"He was too close to you."

"But just to give it to him!"

"Would you rather be dead?" the keeper asked quietly.

"He wanted me as a hostage. He wouldn't have killed me."

"He wanted the box more." Galen glared at him. "We have other weapons, Raffi. Keep your mind on them."

Simmering, Raffi watched Alberic. He had climbed back into his chair and was fingering the box avidly, exploring it by touch. When he looked up his eyes were alert. "So what's wrong with it?"

"Wrong?"

"You wouldn't have given it to me otherwise." He lifted it and pointed it straight at them. Raffi went cold.

"Be careful," Galen said calmly. "It's dangerous."

"That's what I want."

"And unstable. We have no way of knowing how much life is left in it, but it's already hundreds of years old. Maybe very little."

"And maybe a lot." Alberic swung the box and aimed

it at a tall bronze candlestick by the window; Godric and Taran scattered instantly. "Chief!"

"Be quiet." Then he fired.

Light blinded them. When they could see again, the candle was a bubbling, hissing pool of wax and molten metal on the seared floor. There was a shocked silence, and then the tiny man began to laugh. He wheezed and giggled and cackled; jumping from his chair, he cavorted around the candles, catching Sikka's hands and kissing them, then dancing away. His own people watched him in amusement; Raffi stared; Galen stood stiff with distaste.

At last, breathless, Alberic slumped over the arm of his chair, clutching his side. "Oh, this is wonderful!" he managed. "Superb. Beyond belief! To rob a Relic Master!" He lifted the box and rubbed it as gently as if it had been a bird; then his head turned, and his eyes were cold and crafty.

"This is the arrangement. I want the Sekoi. You have power, contacts. You'll find him for me and get him here alive. And then I might, I just might, give you your box of flames back." He stretched over for the wine and took a long drink, then climbed into his chair and sat.

Galen said nothing. His look was dark.

Alberic shrugged. "Think about it. In the meantime you can try my hospitality."

Godric came forward and led them to the door, but just as they got there the sly voice behind them said, "It doesn't sound very inviting, does it? But one thing might interest you, Relic Master. The Sekoi was headed for the city. The city of the Makers. Tasceron."

Galen stood stock-still, as if the word had frozen him. Then, without turning, he stalked out of the room.

ALBERIC'S HOSPITALITY TURNED out to be a locked room, as filthy as the rest of the building, with one threadbare mattress and a window that let in a drizzle of rain and moonlight. Galen sat moodily in a corner, his knees drawn up and his arms resting on them, staring at nothing.

Raffi left him alone. He swept all the filthy straw and dung into one corner with his foot, tossed the mattress after it, then dragged their pack over, and the two plates of food a hand had just banged in through a grille at the base of the door.

He looked them over anxiously. "There's some sort of meat. It looks all right. The bread's stale. Cheese." He tasted the clear liquid in the wooden cup and scowled. "Water. He's not stripping the apple tree for us, is he?"

Galen made a meaningless murmur. Raffi began to eat hurriedly. He was hungry—he was always hungry—and even the stale bread could be moistened with water and broken up. With a few withered shar roots and herbs from the pack it was almost tasty.

Swallowing a mouthful, he muttered, "So what do we do?"

Galen looked up. In the dim cell his face was haggard. "We agree."

"Just to get out of here? I mean, he'll never give it back."

Galen stirred. He reached into the pack and tugged out the stub of candle, clearing a place in the dust for it. Then he fumbled for the tinderbox.

The blue flame crackled, flared up. When it was steady and yellow, Galen lifted a cup of water and drank thirstily. "Maybe. Maybe not. The spirit of the Makers is in the box. It won't rest with Alberic. It will want to come back to us."

"Then we needn't bother about this Sekoi?"

Galen put down the cup and picked at the food. He had a strange, intent look. "I think I want to bother."

Raffi stopped picking up crumbs with his finger and stared. "You want to run Alberic's errands?"

"My errands."

"But you heard him! We'd have to go to Tasceron!"

Galen smiled then, a wolfish, secret smile. "Sometimes, Raffi, the Makers send their messages through the people you'd least expect. I knew I had to come here; now I know why. I can't hear them any other way, so they speak through Alberic. I knew, as soon as he said it."

Appalled, Raffi ate the rest of the crumbs without tasting anything. Tasceron! Galen was mad.

All his life Raffi had heard about the burning city, the city of the Makers, far to the west. It was vast, a web of a million streets, alleys, bridges, ruins. No one knew half of Tasceron; no one was sure who had built it or when, or what most of the structures were for, the immense marble halls, the squares with their dry fountains. Under the city were said to be tunnels, buried rooms, untold secrets. It was where the palace of the Emperor had been, and the temples of the great relics, and most secret of all, the House of Trees. All lost now, leaving only stories and rumors. The Emperor was dead, the temples destroyed. And the Watch guarded Tasceron, their tall black towers rising among the smoke and stench.

"Suicide," he muttered.

Galen was eating calmly. "No," he said. "I've been thinking of it for some time. In Tasceron something may have survived. Maybe even others of the Order."

Raffi scrambled up and paced about. Then he kicked the wall. "We'd be caught! There must be Watchmen everywhere; how long do you think we'd last? You can't see there, can't even breathe . . ."

Galen looked up sharply. "I'm not mad."

They stared at each other. Slowly, Raffi sat down. "I didn't say that."

"You thought it. You've been thinking it for months. Since the explosion."

Raffi was silent.

Galen gripped his strong fingers together and tapped them against his lips. Then he said steadily, "Since I lost all my power."

There, it was spoken, as it hadn't been spoken in the long summer, since the relic-tube had blown up as Galen was examining it, breaking his leg and his mind, leaving him lying silent for a week, eyes open, unspeaking. He had never said how it felt; Raffi had never dared ask. Now, picking up the empty cup and rolling it in his hands, Raffi knew it was coming.

"For a moment," Galen said, "in that room, I thought Alberic had guessed. But you reassured him." He leaned back against the dim wall, tugging the long hair out of his collar. "I'm empty inside, Raffi. Since the explosion, my mind has been silent. No echoes, no colors, no spirits. I can't move out of myself. I've lost the power and I have to find it again." His voice was raw with pain, with the pent-up agony of months. "I can't . . . exist like this! The trees, the stones, I can't feel them. They speak and I can't hear. Even the relics, the gifts of the Makers themselves—even when I hold those, Raffi, I feel nothing. Nothing!"

Embarrassed, hot with pity that was almost anger, Raffi rocked the cup. He had known this would come out, all Galen's torment. For the last few months the keeper had been a tangle of rage and bewilderment: trying trances, starving himself, storming off into the forest for days, punishing them both with prayers and chants and penances. And never talking about it. Until now.

Because the power was gone. Although he'd only gained a little of it, Raffi guessed the horror of that. The Order had the skills to contact all sorts of life. And in the relics, they touched traces of the Makers themselves, who had come down and lived in the world, built and formed it, and then gone, no one knew where.

It would kill Galen, that loss. Or drive him insane.

"You think there'll be some sort of cure in Tasceron?"

"There must be!" Galen limped around the cell with a pent-up, feverish energy. "There must be some of our people left, someone who could help me! I've got to try anything!"

Crouching, he put his hand on the rocking cup. Raffi looked up; the keeper was watching him, eyes dark. In the candlelight his face was edged with pain, gaunt. "I'm sorry to have to take you into more danger. But I'll need you."

Raffi shrugged. "I made a promise. To go where you go. Into darkness, into light, remember?" Uneasy, he looked away.

THEY SLEPT ON the floor, cold and unbearably hard after the bracken of the forest. For a while Raffi lay awake, listening to the keeper's steady breathing. He knew Galen was desperate. But Tasceron! He'd have to go with him, if only to try and keep them both alive, but he didn't know enough, he was only at the fourth Branch. It wasn't fair, he thought bitterly. And the fires burned under Tasceron, had burned for years. How could any of the Order have survived?

He must have slept, because a long time later someone was shaking him out of unreachable dreams; he groaned and rolled over stiffly. He was soaked with drizzle, the room cold with an early-morning light.

Alberic stood in the doorway, burly men behind him. He wore a silk tunic trimmed with dark fur and small boots that must have cost the shoemaker an immense amount of trouble.

"Mmm." He glanced around the cell. "The guest room could do with a little more work. But then, most of our guests don't leave. What about you?"

Galen stood up, tall and grim. "We've decided. We'll find your Sekoi."

Alberic grinned slyly. "Oh, excellent," he murmured. "I knew you would."

The Bee's Warning

6

The agent must carry out a proper surveillance.

Rule of the Watch

Journal of Carys Arrin
Cyraxday
4.16.546

It was a light of some sort. Nothing like I've
ever seen before. Something utterly, brilliantly
white, and it flashed out from the top window
of the fortress, facing east, two hours after dusk.

If I hadn't been watching the place closely I
might have missed it, though both the pack-beast
and the horse skittered and stamped in fright.
For a moment I was afraid they'd be heard, but I
needn't have worried; all the animals in Alberic's
pens were just as terrified; the clamor of geese
and the barking of all the dogs came up clear
through the drizzle.

I got to the fortress this afternoon, and
camped on a rocky knoll above it. It's sheltered

here. Two great pines sprout out over the cliff; by climbing one I'm well hidden and have a good view of Alberic's defenses. (A separate report on these will go to the Watch as soon as I find someone to take it.)

At first there were a lot of people about; as it got dark and the weather closed in, they went indoors. A fine, gray drizzle fell, but I was well sheltered. After the light flashed out, I lay along the branch and thought about it. First, it had to mean that Galen Harn was inside the fortress. Only he could have done that, or his scholar— though according to our information Raffael Morel has only been with him for four years, since Harn took him from his father's farm.

And they must have used a relic. This was no wood and water mumbo jumbo, no sacred trees or spirit journeys. This was something brimming with power, blinding. Something of the Makers.

For a long time I waited, fidgeting with curiosity. What was going on in there? Harn and Alberic must be in some plot together, brewing something against the Watch. If only I could have gotten inside!

Ten minutes later, the light came again.

The Bee's Warning

I was ready this time, and it may have been nearer the window, or simply stronger, because the ray was breathtaking—pure white, so that in one instant I saw all the roofs of the buildings below lit in a sudden stark glare; squalid walls and rain and a pig lying on its side in a sty. Then blackness.

It seemed to shock the people of the fortress just as much—they came running out of all the doors and clustered, staring up.

Nothing else, all night. I ate cold food and put the beasts in shelter, then lay on the branch and watched. Three moons shone on the thieves' tower—even in the dappled moonlight the pale walls gleamed. Whoever the Makers were, they could build. An owl is hooting in the wood; the wet branches stir around me, dripping on this page.

Tomorrow, if nothing else happens, I'll have to try and get inside. This might not be too difficult. My face isn't known—after all, this is my first real mission, first time outside the Watchhouse. And according to what I've heard, Alberic's tower is a nest of cutthroats, poachers, thieves, renegades. People come and go there all the time, with no real rules except Alberic's orders. Maybe no one will notice one more vagabond.

Especially if she is a girl.

Karnosday, early

No need. They're coming out. Two figures have just left the gate, and they look like Harn and the boy. They must be in some plot with Alberic—he'd never let them go otherwise. It'll take me a while to get down the hill and after them. But this is luck, real luck.

Dead or alive, say the orders. And I won't lose them now.

7

*The Order will survive. They can never
kill us all. Underground, well hidden,
we have knowledge that can outlive the
world.*

Reputed last words of Mardoc
Archkeeper, from the rack

"ARE YOU SURE?" Galen stood on the grass under the oak and stared back at the misty country they had crossed.

"Not sure." Raffi shrugged, uneasy. "Just a feeling. As if someone touched me and drew back. It may have been nothing."

"Unlikely." Galen hadn't moved; shading his eyes from the rising sun, he stared east. "It could have been an animal."

"Do you think Alberic is having us followed?"

Galen came and sat on the wet grass. "I doubt that."

"But he knows we could go anywhere!"

"He has the box."

"Yes, and that was a big mistake."

Galen gave him an icy glare. "If I want your opinion, boy, I'll ask. The box is nearly dead. And he's greedy but wily. He'll keep it for himself, a personal weapon to keep his rabble in order. He won't risk wasting it."

Raffi simmered, his back against the ridged oak bark. Galen was right. He was always right. Except about Tasceron.

"Well," the Relic Master said grimly, "if you think someone's following, you'd better look back." He looked resentful. "Take your time."

Raffi sat back, tried to relax, breathed in the cold damp. Under his palms he felt the crushed stalks of grass. Slowly, his third eye opened. He looked back along the paths of the last day and night, felt the stir of small animals along the hedgerows, the giant ant-castle where the track crossed the stream. He tasted the dreams of the sleepers in the village they had skirted, smelled the great silent strength of the trees, the leaf-rot, the strange night-walkers among them. Along the waterlines he went, and the earth tracks, back, far back, as far as he could reach, and all he felt at the edge of the land was the sun, a red heat, a blaze that rose with a searing pain out of the steams of the valley.

His lips opened; no words came.

Galen grabbed his arm. "Stop it. You're burning."

Raffi dragged himself back, such a long way. Opening his eyes, he felt drained; he was sweating, dizzy.

"Don't look into the sun!" Galen was angry. "How many times have I told you that! Was there anyone?"

"I don't know," Raffi said faintly.

Galen stood up and limped around. "If only I could see!" he cried, raging, banging down his stick.

"Don't shout," Raffi moaned.

Galen glared at him, then nudged the pack with his foot. "Drink something. It helps."

Feeling a failure, Raffi got the water out and drank thirstily. It ran down his chin; he dragged the cool drops over his hot face. He was tired and wished they would stop; it was dangerous to travel in the day.

A few minutes later Galen came and stood over him. "Not your fault," he said gruffly. "Not enough practice."

"Not your fault either," Raffi said quietly.

The keeper jabbed the turf with his stick. "Isn't it?" He looked up, out ahead. "Come on. Let's find somewhere to lay low."

IT WAS STILL EARLY, and the fields were waist-deep in damp mist. Walking through them seemed more like wading; browsing flocks of tiny birds rose up in clouds before them. This was someone's pasture, lush and green, the hedgerows thick with leaves and bines, the trees already losing their leaves. A herd of tawny cattle wandered in the fields beyond, staring, chewing, at the passing strangers.

Raffi chewed back at them. It was easy country to walk, low and firm underfoot. Lanes and small tracks crisscrossed it; gates were in good repair. It was a different world to the forest. But the people also made it dangerous.

Climbing down a hedge bank into a deep hollow lane, he saw that Galen had stopped. The Relic Master stood tall among the white flowers of the hedge, the pack on his back, listening. Then he turned. "Anything?"

"Someone ahead. Near."

As Raffi said it, she came around the corner of the lane: a large woman, wrapped in rough shawls, avoiding the puddles. She carried a small sack in her arms; it seemed heavy as she put it down and straightened wearily. Then she saw them.

"Be careful," Galen whispered.

"You don't need to tell me that!"

There was no way of avoiding her. The lane was deep, the hedges high on each side, spiny and tangled. They walked on quickly, Galen's staff sticking in the soft ground.

The woman waited, hands on hips. She probably had some weapon, Raffi thought. He put his head down and tried to look pitiable. As he was wet through and tired, that was easy.

"Fine day," Galen said quietly as they came up to her.

The woman nodded; she looked at them both with a shrewd interest. "For traveling, it is. Have you come by the village?"

"A different way." Galen rubbed his chin with the back of one hand, then he stopped, digging the stick in and leaning both hands on it. His long strings of black jet and green crystals swung in the pale light. "Can you tell me about the pathways hereabouts?"

She didn't seem afraid. "I could. Where are you going?"

He hesitated. "The coast."

"It's four days' walk." She turned slightly, but still watched them both. "You should keep heading west. Make for that stone on the ridge up there." She pointed, and far off Raffi saw a tiny pillar on the skyline, dark against the clouds. "From there the track goes on, clear over the chalklands. Lots of old tombs up there—Sekoi country. I wouldn't pass it at night." She scratched her neck. "But you may not mind."

If that was a hint, Galen ignored it. "Where do we cross the river?" he asked.

She laughed shortly, then looked at him carefully. "Well upstream. Almost at the top of the valley. Half a day's tramp."

"Isn't there a nearer ford? Or a bridge?"

For a moment she said nothing. Then, strangely, "Oh, there's a bridge, master. At the bottom of the gully. But no one can cross it. Take my advice and keep away from it."

Raffi felt Galen's interest. "Why?"

Instead of answering, she said, "We all fear the Watch, stranger, don't we?"

"Indeed we do," Galen said very quietly.

"Then listen. The bridge is a thing of the Makers. Many have tried to cross it and can't, that's all I know. Go upstream." Then she almost smiled. "I see I'm wasting my advice."

Galen looked at her steadily. "Thank you."

"Take care. If you were one of the old Order I might ask for your blessing."

"If I were one of the old Order I would give it."

She nodded briefly, then picked up her sack and trudged past Raffi. He moved aside for her; saw her glance at him, sharp and interested. She knew who they were. But none of them would say anything, just in case.

At the end of the track she turned. "Keep that boy of yours fed," she called. "He looks half starved."

Then she was gone, brushing through the wet sprays of hawthorn, so that the drops fell in a glinting shower.

Raffi glanced at Galen. "So."

Galen tugged his stick out of the mud. "Let's go and see this bridge."

Raffi sighed. "I knew we would."

At the end of the track was a field path, and then a tiny stone-lined gully, leading down to the left between dripping trees. The going was steep; the wet stones slippery and so overgrown that Galen had to slash away the weeds.

"Not many use this," Raffi gasped, slipping.

"They did once." Galen snapped a branch with an effort, muttering the prayer that would calm the tree. "It's cobbled. That was done for a reason."

As they went down, Raffi felt the age of the rutted way. It became a green tunnel of leaves; great ferns and banks of cowflax and horsetails, meadowsweet and tiny carpets of purple flowers that climbed and sprouted between the stones.

Crouching, pushing the wet leaves aside, he found that both sides of the track were walled; Galen was right, it had once been important. But now it was dim and dripping with rain from the trees overhead, so that small runnels of water slid down through the red mud and over the stones where Raffi's feet slithered and splashed.

Down they went, into the valley's depths. The air became sticky, clammy with pollen; small flies droned in the clumps of white umbrels, their sweet stench pungent. Below him, Galen was flecked with light, gold tints of sunlight on his back as he passed through a brighter patch. "Coming out," he muttered.

Raffi scrambled down, one ankle aching. At the bottom, balanced on two stones with the water trickling between, he turned and looked back up the green hollow. It dripped silently. If anyone was following, he'd have to come down the same way. For a moment he thought, then crouched to the stone under his boot and, putting a finger in the wet mud, drew a design carefully on it. A black bee, gatherer and storer—one of the signs of the Order. He threw a handful of clotted leaves to cover it. Now we'll see, he thought.

The hollow widened onto the riverbank, a steep incline of red mud, the exposed roots of great beech trees sprawled over it like a natural stairway. Galen was already climbing down. Beyond him, Raffi saw the bridge.

It was a bizarre structure. Low, only inches above the

water, and made of chains; black, seemingly wooden chains that had splintered and split in places. Planks hung from them, looking half rotten. On the two heavy posts rammed into the shore were carvings—faces, grotesque and snarling—and a few snags of cloth and feathers hung from poles nearby.

Jumping down, Raffi stood by Galen. "People are still afraid of it."

"I'm not surprised."

The river was sluggish and choked with weeds and sedges; mist hung over it, so that the bridge led into gray uncertainty. Thick green weed trailed under the surface like hair.

Raffi swiped at mosquitoes. "It's becoming a swamp."

"What about the bridge?" Galen asked coldly.

Sighing, Raffi tried to sense it, but it was just mist and drift, and he was tired. "Can't we sleep?" he muttered. "The sun's up, we've been walking all night. No one's likely to come here."

"We stop when I say!" Galen shrugged the pack off and threw his stick on it. He walked to the bridge and put a hand on each of the black posts and stood there a moment, looking into the mist. Raffi knew he was straining to feel something. Anything. When he spoke, the keeper's voice was harsh with defeat.

"I'm crossing. Stay here. If I call you, come."

"Look." Raffi hesitated. "Shouldn't I . . . ?"

"No! I'm still the Master."

Galen edged forward cautiously. The black chains tightened; the bridge creaked and swung, but it seemed strong enough to hold him. He walked on, step by step, avoiding the broken planks, merging into the mist that rose from the stagnant water. Slowly it closed around him, and he was gone.

Raffi waited, anxious. The river rippled quietly, stinking of rot. A snake slithered between reeds and flicked away. Nothing else moved. The silence was intense, suddenly eerie. Raffi came to the end of the bridge and gripped the posts. "Galen?"

Before he could call again he caught a movement in the mist. Galen's dark figure loomed out of it, walking carefully. When he looked up, he seemed astonished.

He stared at Raffi strangely. Then he stepped off the bridge and stood in the mud. He looked around.

"What happened?" Raffi demanded. "Why did you come back?"

"See for yourself."

"What?"

Galen sat on the bank. He seemed bewildered and amused about it. "Go on. Take a look."

Raffi stared, then turned abruptly and walked out onto the bridge. He went quickly, jumping the splintered boards, avoiding the gaps in the rail. When he looked back, the bank was lost in mist. Mist drifted all around him; a waterbird croaked in it.

Ahead of him, as the bridge swayed, he saw something. Trees on a bank, beech trees, high and green. One plank went soft underfoot; he stepped over it quickly and looked up. The bank loomed out of grayness.

Raffi stopped dead in astonishment.

Galen was sitting by the pack, legs stretched out. He waved a long hand. "So," he said sarcastically. "What happened? Why did you come back?"

"I didn't! I went straight across!"

The keeper laughed grimly. "So did I, Raffi. So did I."

8

"Now," Flain said, "we must have a messenger to go between us and God."

The eagle said, "Let it be me." But the eagle was too proud.

The bee-bird said, "Let it be me." But the bee-bird was too vain.

The crow said, "Let it be me. I'm dark, an eater of carrion. I have nothing to be proud of."

So Flain chose the crow, and whispered the secrets to it.

Book of the Seven Moons

IT WAS AMAZING. And infuriating. Three times now, Raffi had crossed the bridge. Each time he came back to where he'd started from.

"It's impossible," he muttered. "I mean, it's not circular, it doesn't turn! I don't understand!"

Galen sat on the bank, legs crossed. He had pulled some orange fungi from the bole of a dead tree; now he was frying them in the small pan over a carefully smokeless fire.

"What have I taught you?" he said. "Understanding's not enough. Understanding is from outside; merely a function of the mind."

Raffi sighed. "I know."

"To enter, that's the secret. To become the bridge, to crawl into its sap, to sway with it, to rot over centuries as its heartwood rots. When you are the bridge you will know what the bridge knows. It takes time. A lifetime. And skill."

Sullenly, Raffi sat down. Galen gave him a sharp glance.

"You know it but you don't apply it. You're lazy. Now think. How could the bridge be like this?"

Raffi was scowling at the sizzling mushrooms, counting the pieces. He said, "It could be a device of the Makers. Though it doesn't look that old."

Galen nodded, shaking the pan. Pig fat spat and crackled. "Possible. The entire bridge a relic. It could be older than it seems. The wood is from no tree I know. What else?"

Raffi swallowed. "Aren't they ready yet?"

"Concentrate. What else?"

He forced himself to think. "A protection spell. Someone who lives on the other side."

"Also possible. Here, take some now."

Raffi jabbed his knife in and dragged out one slice carefully, waving it, eating it before it cooled so that it burned his mouth. He gulped down three more without speaking, then paused, with another on his knife.

"What about the Sekoi?"

"No." Galen chewed slowly. "Not this. I have a feeling this is one of ours."

"Ours."

"The Order."

Raffi sat up. "Someone alive?"

"Maybe." Galen stared at the bridge, his eyes deep and dark. "There were men in the Order once with great skills, boy. They knew the mightiest relics—handled them every day. The power of the Makers lingered in them. They knew strange things—things that have never been written, maybe even the secrets of the Makers themselves. An old man once told me that when the Makers departed the world, they left behind a certain book of their deeds wrapped in black cloth. Only one man knew the script it was written in. The knowledge was taught, from one Archkeeper to the next, till Mardoc was betrayed. Maybe someone still knows it."

He stood up abruptly, emptied the fat from the pan,

and swirled it in the river, leaving a greasy trail. Then he tossed the pan down next to Raffi. "Pack up. You can carry it."

"But where?"

"Over the bridge, where else?" Galen dragged his stick up and gave a sudden, sidelong grimace. "I may have lost my powers, but I still have my memory. Words may be enough, if you know the right ones."

At the bridge end he took some red mud and crouched, making two images on the carved posts, waving Raffi back so he couldn't see what they were. Then he pushed the tangled nettles back over them. Sucking the edge of one hand, he stood up.

Raffi watched. A tingle of excitement stirred in him. Already he could sense something new; it leaked from the hidden signs like a faint aroma.

Galen stood on the bridge and began to murmur. It was an old prayer, one Raffi had heard only once before, littered with the ancient half-understood words of the Makers. The keeper's deep voice hoarsened as he spoke them; the air lightened, as if something in the mist curled up, retreated. Raffi came forward quickly.

The Bee's Warning

Galen fell silent, listening. "Well?"

"It feels as though something's changed."

"Then I was right. Stay near." They stepped out onto the bridge; it slipped and swayed under them. Mist swirled over the sedges; Raffi gripped the worn wooden chains, feeling the whole shaky contraption rattle under him. But this time it was different. As they crossed he saw trees loom out of the damp, not beeches but oaks—old, squat, hollow trees—and holly, and thorn, crowding right to the bank.

"You did it!"

Galen nodded. He stopped at the rotting end of the bridge and looked around. "But this isn't the other bank. It seems to be some sort of island in the river. Tiny. And overgrown. No one's been here for years."

The disappointment was hard in his voice.

Crushing foxglove and bracken, they pushed their way in. The island had a silence that made Raffi uneasy. No birds sang. Above the gnarled branches the sky was blue, pale as eggshell. He realized the morning was half over.

Galen stopped. Before them was a house, or it had been, once. Now only a few fragments of wall rose among a thicket of elder; red wall, made of mud brick. A single window with a black shutter hung open. Trampling down nettles, Raffi clambered up and looked inside.

The room was a grove of trees. Oaks had splintered it; over the years its outline had faded under ivy, swathes of fungus on rotting wood. Half a chimney still rose up, weeds waving from its top.

A crash made him jump; Galen had forced his way in, through a cloud of seed and gnats.

Raffi followed. "Was it ours?"

"I should think so."

"But why the protection spell? There's nothing here to protect."

Galen threw him a scornful look. "That's what we're meant to think. Go and get the pack."

When he'd dragged it in, he found Galen kneeling at the hearth, brushing earth and worms from flat red bricks that were smashed and broken. The keeper eased his filthy nails in and forced one up; it moved with a strange hoarse gasp.

The earth underneath was smooth. Galen tugged the next stone out.

The Bee's Warning

"What are you looking for?"

"Anything. The spell was strong. Something's here worth guarding."

"Relics!"

"Almost certainly." Another tile came out and left a dark gap. Raffi crouched down quickly. He had felt the shock of power, faint but unmistakable. "Something's in there!"

Galen widened the hole, reached in, and seemed to scrabble and dig with his fingers. He paused, then he pulled his hands out in a shower of soil.

He was holding a small packet, wrapped in layers of waxed cloth. Shuffling back, he turned and carefully laid it on a flat stone.

"Is it dangerous?" he asked without looking up.

"I don't think so." Raffi felt inadequate, the old feeling. "I don't really know."

Galen shot him a glance. Then he unwrapped the packet, his fingers working eagerly. Raffi knew he was taking a chance.

The cloth opened. They saw a small glass ball, and a piece of rough parchment made from some thin bark.

This had rotted and, even as Galen opened it, infinitely carefully, pieces flaked off. Then it split, and he hissed with frustration.

The writing was faint, barely a scrawl, and some words had gone. Galen read it out grimly.

Kelnar, of the Order of keepers. To any others of the Sacred Way who still live and . . . come this way. The Watch . . . from the chalk hills. The Archkeeper Tesk died yesterday, they took him. They know I'm here, I have to go to find . . . I have little time. Understand this. I have seen the Crow. The Crow still lives in the dark places of Tasceron, in the House of Trees, deep underground, guarded with spells. I cannot say. . . .

Galen frowned. "This bit's very broken. I can just get words: *hollow, sacred, the messenger.* Then, *Find him. Find him. Prayers and blessings, brothers. Strength of the rock, cunning of the weasel be yours.*"

He looked up. "That's all."

Carefully, he sifted the tiny scraps that had fallen, trying to find more.

"The Crow!" Raffi breathed the words in awe. "Still alive!"

100

The Bee's Warning

"Tesk died twenty years ago. That dates it."

But Raffi could see the news had shaken Galen, stirred him deep. He wanted to ask more, about what it meant, but instead he picked up the ball carefully. It was cold, heavy, quite transparent. He turned it in his fingers. Nothing came from it now. It was silent.

Galen took it from him. "A relic. But of what?" He muttered a prayer over it, a brief blessing. "Once I saw an image of the Crow carrying such a glass ball in his mouth. A most secret sign. But what it means, I never learned."

"Did you know him?" Raffi asked.

"Kelnar? No. Not even the name. But the Order was great when I was a scholar. There were hundreds of keepers."

"I wonder what happened to him."

Galen scowled. He wrapped the ball back in the waxed cloth and, picking the letter up, read it again. Then he crushed it in his strong grip. Fragments of desiccated parchment gusted in the river breeze.

"Dead," he said softly. "Like all of them."

THEY DECIDED TO SLEEP on the island. With the spell on the bridge, and on the second bridge that led through a great bank of nettles to the far shore, there was nowhere safer. Raffi was too tired to think about what they had found. He drank hot tea made of nettle leaves and curled up hastily in a blanket in the shelter of the ruined wall.

His dreams were strange. He found himself walking endlessly over a grassy plain; a great city lay before him, its spires and towers rising over the horizon, but he could never reach it, never get any closer. And behind him his shadow stretched, long and black, and it danced and capered with glee, he knew it did, but every time he turned and looked at it, it kept still. Walking on, he felt the evil dance break out again behind him. There was nothing he could do about it.

When he woke, he lay with his eyes closed, sleepily, trying to remember. Dreams were important. Perhaps someone was following them. The Watch, he thought, in sudden terror. Or Alberic. But whoever it was, the bridge would stop him. Relieved, he knew that was true. No one else could cross that.

The Bee's Warning

When he sat up, the sky was dim—the sun had set into red streaks toward the west. Cloud was building there, a sullen bank of weather; gnats and humflies gathered in twisting columns among the sedges.

He made the fire, boiled water, found some roots and a solitary duck's egg. When Galen woke they said the long chant of the day solemnly, sitting under a willow, their hands spread. Then they ate. Galen halved the egg, though it was his by right. Spitting out some shell, he said, "We'll stay here tonight and go on in the morning. It'll be more dangerous, but we shouldn't cross the burial hills at night."

"Good," Raffi muttered, his mouth full.

Galen sat back, folding his arms. Then he said, "Who is the Crow, Raffi?"

Raffi swallowed hastily. But he knew the ritual; the Litany of the Makers had always fascinated him.

"The Crow is the messenger. In the beginning the Crow flew between the Makers and God. He carried their words, written in gold letters. He spoke their words to God. Later, when the Makers left Anara and went to the seven sisters in the heavens, the Crow brought messages from them to the keepers and Relic Masters of the Order."

"Is the Crow a bird?"

"The Crow is a bird and not a bird. He is a man and not a man."

"Is the Crow a voice?"

"He is the voice of the Makers."

Galen nodded. "Good. I've neglected the Litany with you lately."

"Knowing the answers is one thing," Raffi said. "I'm still not sure what they mean."

Galen stirred the fire and laughed harshly. "Wise men have spent their lives on them. A four-year scholar knows nothing yet. The Crow is a spiritual being. He can take many forms. He's real."

"Have you ever . . . seen him?"

Galen looked up, surprised. Then he shrugged. "I was no older than you when the Order was destroyed. Such visions were far above me. What I've learned since then has been from Malik, my own master, from the Book, from the few of the Order I've met. The great visions are shattered, Raffi. Our knowledge is in pieces, in the ashes of burned libraries. Only in Tasceron might there be someone who knows the answers."

Raffi looked up at the moons; Atterix and Pyra, almost together. "The man who wrote that letter—he says he saw the Crow."

"A lot can happen in twenty years." Galen's eyes were shadows, but as he shifted, Raffi saw them glint strangely. "And yet the Crow is immortal. If we could find him, speak to him . . . If he could take our message to the Makers . . . If the Makers would come back . . ."

He was silent, choked with the joy of it, and Raffi too, hearing the ripple of the sluggish water, the splash of a bird settling for the night. Then, with a hiss of pain he snatched his hand up.

Galen looked over. "What's wrong?"

"A bee sting!"

A small red lump was swelling on his wrist. He put it to his mouth, sucking at the pain.

"At night?"

Raffi let the throb subside. Then he said, "It's not a real bee. I put the sign of the bee on a stone at the bottom of that track we came down. Someone just stood on it."

9

The Watch is unsleeping. Never relent in the search; never turn back.

Rule of the Watch

Journal of Carys Arrin
Larsnight
7.16.546

I've lost them.

And this is so infuriating I can hardly get the words down, but what stopped me was a spell.

There's no other word for it. Every time I tried to cross that bridge I found myself back where I started! It seems to be some sort of power field to confuse the mind—I can't believe that it actually changes matter in any way or that the bridge can have only one end. In all my training, the Watchleaders insisted that the powers of the Order were an illusion—I can see fat old Jeltok now, banging his cane on the table. Well, it's an illusion that's worked on me.

Galen Harn had crossed. I found traces of a

campfire on the bank and scraps of food—fungus of some sort. Maybe they brew a concoction of this and drink it to counteract the spell. Too risky to try without knowing more.

In the end I had to give up. Even leading the horse into the swamp would have been useless—the whole area was thick with seedbeds and alder; soft, probably deep. I almost screamed with frustration, and kicked the black rotting chains of the thing with hatred.

What makes it worse is that they're traveling by night. Harn is cunning. He's been hunted all his life; he knows how to blend with the leaves and the land, though I don't believe that non-sense that the keepers can turn into trees and stones.

It was well after dark when I turned back from the bridge and though I'd slept a little, I was tired. Yesterday I sold the pack-beast and most of the goods in a village beyond the fields—speed is more important now. But I kept the horse, and that's one advantage. They're on foot.

I rode the horse back up the stony gully and turned east, quickly crossing the fields in the dark. My plan was to follow the river upstream until I could cross it. The wind was chill and the stubbly ground uneven; worst of all it rose constantly, and the river ran below in a steep cleft with ash and elder springing out of the sides. There was no way down—I just had to keep going, farther away from the bridge all the time.

Furious, I strapped my jerkin tight and kicked the horse on; we galloped now, leaping small walls and hedges, four moons watching us through cloud. Down lanes bordered with stone walls, past a dark farmhouse, skirting tangled copses; the search for a track seemed endless. It was almost light before I found it. A narrow, beaten trail. It looked as if animals had trodden it; it led into a dark stand of juniper and fireberry bushes, and smelled of night-cat.

The horse didn't like it. Neither did I, I suppose, but time was pressing and I was angry and a bit reckless. So I rode down. I can see old Jellie shaking his head now.

It was dark among the trees, the branches low and tangled. I had to dismount, slashing them aside, leading the horse. Uneasy, fly-bitten, and scratched, we scrambled down, tread muffled on a springy mattress of needles, the winter's shriveled berries. The track dropped steeply and the horse kept whickering, the smell of its fear sharp on the air. I swore at it, then swung my crossbow out and racked it hastily. In the undergrowth a twig had cracked.

I stopped, raising the bow. The copse was dim. Ahead, somewhere below, I could see a pale daylight, but here the trunks crowded, silent.

I heard it before it leaped and squirmed around; the yowl was in my face, past me, then the lithe black shape had fastened onto the horse; it reared, screaming with terror. I aimed too fast; the bolt shot wide, crunched in an ash-bole. Then the horse was gone, in a heedless bloodstained panic, the night-cat streaking after it like a shadow.

Furious, I scrambled down the track, all hope gone. I'd seen what a night-cat could do—there'd be no chance of riding back to the bridge. And I was scared, believe me. But I needed the food and money in the saddlebags. Everything was on that wretched horse. Then as I came out of the trees, I fell smack over something lying in the path, and stared at it, on hands and knees.

The Bee's Warning

The night-cat lay sprawled, mid-jump. One paw was flung up, the snarling mouth wide in the agony of its death. It was still hot. Fleas jumped off it. I reached out cautiously and touched it. The great head slumped; blood clotted the black fur, just congealing. A crossbow bolt stuck out of its neck.

I rolled under the nearest bush, racked the bow hastily, and reloaded it. I'd missed the cat. This was someone else's work. And they'd be back for it. Steadying my breath, controlling, I waited for them under the leaves. Always see what you're up against, Jellie used to wheeze. I'd never believed he'd been a field agent, not then, but his captures were listed in all the Watchtowers, so he must have been thinner once.

Two minutes later a blackbird screeched and flew off. I heard voices coming up the path from the river. Putting my eye to the sight of the bow I watched them come, two men, shouldering through bracken, my sweating, nervous horse dragging behind.

I could have killed them both. Or maybe one; the other would have gone before I could reload, and then it would have been cat and mouse, and I had no idea who else might be around. Safer to wait.

They stood over the cat, laughing, more than pleased with themselves. The bigger one gazed up the track. "The rider might still be alive."

"Maybe."

"Should we look?"

The smaller one laughed and shook his head. "Not me. Cat's had him. Or he broke his neck coming off. This horse is worth at least fifty marks, never mind the stuff in the bags."

"What if he turns up?"

They looked at each other. Then they laughed again.

I had to take my finger off the trigger, force myself to be calm. I get angry too easily, and an agent needs control. They didn't know I was Watch. I could have gotten up and told them—they might have backed off. Or might not. Bitterly I lay where I was, deep in leaves, woodbugs crawling over me. And all the time Galen Harn was slipping away.

They were in no hurry. They skinned the cat on the spot, taking the soft thick pelt, the teeth, the paws, some of the innards. Soon the air stank of blood; flies buzzed in clouds over the carcass. Finally, well into the morning, they gathered up their packs, loaded them onto the horse, and set off, down toward the river. They talked loud and easy, but their bows were ready.

Stiff and filthy, I watched them go, then got up and followed, silent, from bush to tree. I may not be one of the magical Order, but even as kids in the Watchhouses, we played this game. No one caught me then. Or now.

It took over an hour to reach the farm. I smelled it first, the tang of cattle over the marshy ground; then I saw the low rise of the roof, close to the water. The river was narrower here, still sluggish but shallow; I could see cows knee-deep in it on a bank of shingle. I could have crossed. But I wanted the horse.

The men tied it up and went inside.

Flat behind low scrub, I looked the place over. Not a village, as I'd feared, but a house, isolated. Maybe fewer than ten people. Abruptly the door opened; the two men were back, women with them, an old man, children. They fed the horse an apple, walked around it, slapped its legs admiringly. A small girl in a tattered dress was lifted onto its back.

There were dogs, of course. Two. I was downwind, which was just as well, but they terrified me. Dogs you can never trust. Then I saw the saddlebags were open. Bit by bit, my food supplies went into the house. I saw them holding up my clothes, surprised, and managed a sour laugh. I was small, even for a girl. What were they thinking now?

Finally, when I'd almost wriggled away and given up, they all went in. I slid forward quickly, through the marshy tussocks. Frustration broke out—suddenly I was reckless and fierce. I'd lost so much time; if I was to act it had to be now, before they came back!

With the thought I was up, running, head bent low, into the muddy yard. The horse whinnied; I slashed the rope and was on its back kicking my heels in hard; we were halfway through the gate when the shouts erupted. I didn't look back but drove the beast hard, mud splashing high, cows scattering. Barking and yells and the whistle of a shot smacked from somewhere, but we were slithering down the red bank into the water; I shouted and kicked anxiously.

The river was sluggish; boulders choked the peat-brown water, the shingle underneath soft and treacherous. The horse sank in it; a splash and a bark behind warned me, and turning I saw a dog close, its white teeth snapping at the horse's tail.

That probably helped. The horse kicked. Then its hooves grounded in firm soil; I felt it and whooped with delight as we raced over the grass and into the tree cover beyond, a steady joyous run with the wet mane flicking drops into my face like diamonds. Defiant, I sat up. Another bolt splintered bark a meter to my left, but by then I was too reckless to care, and in seconds the trees were around us, and I had to slow the horse.

It took me an hour to calm down.

When I did, I was tired and hungry, and suddenly cold. The wood had petered out; I found myself climbing the slopes of a high bare landscape of chalk, the turf cropped low, and the huge sun in a furnace of gathering cloud. Rain began, drizzling lightly. There was nothing to eat, and no shelter.

Coming carefully over the skyline, I sat still, watching the clouds gather. The empty country stretched out below; dark, smooth green slopes. Pulling the bags off, I let the horse rest, pulled out this book, and wrote. I'm lucky to still have it.

Harn must be far from here by now. He must be out in the middle of these downlands, somewhere. I sit silent, writing, and the horse crops the grass. The tearing of the stalks is loud in the drizzle.

10

*Flain the Tall built a tower, and he
called it the House of Trees. This was
because the trees gave their wood for it
freely, without pain. All the trees of the
wood offered a branch, and the House
was fragrant with calarna and yew
and oak, pale willow, red hazel, dark
mahogany.*

*"This," he said, "will be the court
of the Makers; without guile, without
hardship."*

*And the battlements were living
branches, woven tight in a web.*

Book of the Seven Moons

"WHAT ARE THEY?" Raffi whispered.

"Burial places." Galen didn't turn. He was staring out at the strange country before them, the short grass, the hard white stony track that led away so clearly they could see it mount the ridge and vanish over the top. The sky was immense, Raffi thought, pale blue, as if he could brush it with his hand.

"But are they safe?"

Galen glared at him. "Don't fear the dead. They're not our enemies." Carefully he poured the last drop of red wine into the cleared circle of chalk; it sank into the dry rubble, as if the ground was thirsty, and the small ring of pebbles seemed charged for an instant with clarity. Far ahead the green downs brightened.

They had stayed on the island a day and a night, resting. Nowhere else was safer and, despite Galen's restlessness, he knew they'd needed it. Raffi had fished, mostly. Galen had eaten little and then gone off on his own, and hours later Raffi had come across him sitting in the ruined house, deep in trance, his fingers moving over the black and green awen-beads.

Uneasy, Raffi had retreated to the fire and eaten the rest of the fish. He knew Galen like this. He just had to wait, sleeping on and off, sitting up to stare anxiously into the dark.

At last, late on the second night, the keeper had stumbled through the nettles, thrown himself down, and slept. Raffi sat up and looked at him. He was exhausted, soaked with sweat. Tugging the blanket over him, Raffi curled up in his own worry. Galen was killing himself. The constant struggle, the useless desperate search for his lost power was driving him to madness. They had to get some help! And with Galen's magic gone, all their defenses against the Watch had dwindled to his own sense-lines, frailer the farther he sent them.

Rubbing the bee sting, he wondered what more he could do. Someone had followed them down that path. That overgrown, unused path.

NOW, HIGH ON THE DOWNS, he thought of it again. "I don't like traveling in daylight."

"Maybe, but the woman is right. Here, daylight is best." Galen had shouldered the pack, his long hair tied back in a knot of string. "Keep the lines out."

"You don't have to tell me that!"

Abruptly Galen caught up his stick; Raffi jerked back but the Relic Master gave a sour laugh. "Come on."

They walked all morning, quickly, not speaking. The track climbed the smooth slopes easily, the grass green and short, spattered with rabbit dung. Distant flocks of fat sheep grazed.

On the top of the ridge they lay low, till Galen was sure no one was near; they crept over, not straightening till they were well below the skyline. The stone they had seen from the valley leaned beside the white track, glinting with quartz.

"Sekoi," Raffi said, seeing the carved spirals.

Galen grunted, walked around it. Then he touched it, feeling for the bands of energy, but Raffi knew by the way he turned away that he had failed.

"What's that?"

It was a small red flower, lying propped against the stone. Galen picked it up. "Not from here. It's been brought."

"Alberic's Sekoi! He's come past here—and not too long ago. It's still fresh."

Galen nodded, then tossed it down. "Then I hope the creature puts on speed. I want Tasceron, not him."

It was a bare place, green to the world's end, and the sky blue and empty. Trudging, Raffi felt exposed, open to attack, and through the eyes of the one circling hawk high up he managed to see himself briefly, a tiny dusty figure, hot and tired and thirsty, moving with infinite slowness over the green hollows. The bird swooped and swerved; giddily he came back to himself, stumbling over a stone.

Then they came to the tombs. A few loomed up, huge,

on each side of the track, smooth humps of grass, some with ditches around them, one with a rowan tree sprouting from the top. For each Galen spoke prayers, chanting under his breath, mile after mile. It was a dry country, incredibly still, with only a sudden arrowbird darting up to break the crisp silence.

Raffi trudged on. The tombs oppressed him; their silence was a weight on his shoulders. He wondered if Galen felt it. Unlike the cromlech, these kept their dead, and passing one he saw for a moment the hidden dark chamber under the grass, the scrawled spirals on the long bones.

Ahead, a ridge rose up. To the left of it a single tree-clump stood, dark tops moving in the breeze. Rooks flapped and cawed above it, a black, restless colony.

Galen stopped. He looked up at the trees, his face stern. Then he stepped off the track. "This way."

Raffi stared. "Why over there?"

"Where I go, you go." He hadn't slowed. Raffi had to hurry to catch him.

"But why?"

"Because I say so."

"That's not enough. It's not enough!" Suddenly angry, Raffi grabbed his sleeve and forced him around. Galen stared at him, eyes black. Raffi forced himself not to step back. Then he said, "I have to look after us both. I have to read the signs, as well as I can. You can't do it. You wouldn't know, if anything was wrong." He let go of the keeper's sleeve and said quietly, "You have to let me warn you, Galen."

Galen didn't move. It was the truth, but Raffi knew he felt it like a blow to the face.

"So what is wrong?" he growled.

"The tombs. They're watching us."

"And the tree?"

He shrugged. "It feels strange."

Galen stabbed the ground with his stick. Then he said, "Listen. Yesterday, I had a dream. The only dream I've had for months. Faintly, in all the pain and the darkness, I saw this place. Those trees up there. Nothing else."

Raffi was silenced. He knew the importance of dreams, knew that Galen would clutch at anything that might help him.

"I can't ignore it, Raffi."

The Bee's Warning

"No," he mumbled unhappily.

They climbed up. The turf was springy, studded with yellow gorse-bushes. Warm, Raffi loosened the fastening of his dark green coat for the first time in days. The slope was steep; Galen stumbled once and picked himself up stubbornly. The dark grove hung above them, the rooks clamoring, disturbed. Anyone for miles would hear them. Catching his breath, Raffi stopped and looked back.

The downs stretched endlessly to the horizon. Great cloud banks hung, hazed with sunlight; white darkening to ominous gray, their slow rain-curtains dragged across the green land.

He turned and walked into the gloom of the trees. Yet as he passed the outer trunks he realized that this was not many trees, but one, immensely old, its trunk fibrous and dark, centuries old, maybe even older than the barrows.

Coming closer, they saw the central trunk was hollow; split wide enough for a small room. Trunk upon trunk had grown out of it, root upon root; the bark was ridged and scored, and Raffi guessed that six or seven men couldn't have joined hands around it. And yet it was alive. His feet sank in a thousand years of needles.

Around it, almost lost in gloom, stood three stones that might once have been some cairn or building. Pieces of rag hung from the branches. On one a piece of quartz swung and glinted in the sun.

"The Sekoi."

"Again."

Galen was bent under the thatch of branches. He put his hand on the central trunk. "How old this is. The secrets it knows. If I could . . ." He stopped himself. Then he sat down, closing his eyes.

"Galen," Raffi said anxiously. "How long are we going to stay here? We should get on!" There was no answer. Shaking his head, he sat down himself, against one of the outer trunks.

By late afternoon he was still there, watching the rain come. The gray curtain swept toward him over the downs, it swallowed the barrows and was on him, the first drops pattering in the thick green growth above, but none of it came through to him; the great yew was like a hut, its central trunk and pillars, its meshed roof. With the rain came the darkness, early. The rooks cawed and settled into a cowed silence. Nothing but the pattering of drops dis-

turbed him. Glancing back stiffly he saw Galen still meditating, a shadow.

There was no way of lighting a fire; they were so high
up it would be seen, and besides, he felt the tree wouldn't
like it. Sitting there, against its back, he knew its hollows
and veins and ridges; his fingers buried themselves in the
woody debris, the crumbling rich stink of needles and
grubs and tiny wriggling things that it nurtured. Nothing grew under here; it was too dark, but the tree's roots
spread far out under the ground, he could feel them, widening to the nearest tombs, groping deep in the chalk, to
the hidden waterlines, the fractures and fissures of rock,
the strange magic that moved there. And the tombs clustered around it; he saw that now. The Sekoi had put their
dead here, to watch with the tree.

And deep in his mind the tree said to him, *Raffi, get up
and come in.*

He turned, thinking he'd misheard, but Galen was
standing, looking at him, and though his face was in
darkness there was something about him that gave Raffi
a shiver of fear.

"What did you say?"

"I didn't say anything." The Relic Master stared at him in the gloom. His voice was dull with weariness.

"I thought . . . you said, 'Get up and come in.'"

Galen stiffened; then he got down in the soft mulch and grabbed Raffi's hood and hauled him closer. "It spoke to you!"

"I don't . . I'm not sure."

But Galen breathed out harshly. He turned to the inner trunk, the seamed split. "Sit there," he hissed, pushing Raffi down.

Don't fear me, the tree said, and its voice was old, textured like wind and rain on stone, the knock of a hammerbird in wood.

"It says not to be afraid."

"Afraid!" Galen had the threaded stones off his neck; he snapped the string, tipped them out, his long fingers arranging them hurriedly into patterns Raffi didn't know. Then he looked up, and his face was sharp and eager and desperate all at once. "Ask it to come out. To show itself. Tell it I can't see, or hear. Get it to come!"

Raffi barely knew how. Then training took over; he made a space in his mind, opened the third eye. *Please come out,* he asked, over and over. He knew it was close, and could hear him.

Galen crouched at his shoulder, his hand gripping tight. When Raffi looked now he saw rain, glinting on the trunk, dripping in places from above. The yew was huge; one edge of the split a bent contorted angle of wood, but as he looked closer he saw that he was mistaken, that it was a man, an old man in russet flaking, shapeless clothes, his eyes deep as knotholes, turning toward him.

Galen's fingers shook him.

"Has he come?"

Raffi nodded, silent.

The yew-man smiled at him and nodded too. *I've come, keeper.*

"He can't hear you," Raffi muttered, his throat dry.

How is that?

"There was an accident; he was hurt."

Glancing up, Raffi saw Galen's wild excitement. "Go on! Ask him! Can he help me!"

"There was an accident," Raffi said again, stumbling for words. "The keeper has lost . . . He can't enter the land now, or hear it when it speaks to him." He felt torn with awe at the yew-man's eyes, and embarrassment at Galen having to hear this.

The yew-man, too, seemed fascinated. He turned his brown old gaze on Galen, moved a fold of cloak to show two gnarled hands clasped on a root.

That must torment him. There is no loss as great as that.

"Yes . . ." Raffi wondered if Galen could hear. "Can you help? The yew is a tree of poison and healing. Do you have some way . . . ?"

No. The old man shook his head. *Only the Makers can give back what they have taken.*

"But the Makers are gone."

Tormented with impatience, Galen hissed, "What does he say about the Makers?"

But Raffi waved him back.

Yes, they are gone. The old man sighed. *I remember them, long since.*

"Remember them!"

I'm old, child, older than anything here. I guard the bones of the cat-kings, but before them all, I was. And when the Makers came and walked on the grass I saw them when they were young, Tamar and Therris and Flain. Even Kest, whose sorrow burns us all. They could have helped your master.

"But . . ." Raffi grew dizzy; he shook his head, stunned.

"Hold on to it!" Galen's voice snapped. "Hold on!"

"The Makers are gone. We can't speak to them. The only messenger was the Crow."

The Crow is still here, the yew-man said calmly.

"Here!"

In this world. In this body. The Crow lives, for without him the world would die. The voice became slurred, a harsh gabble of sound, then clear again. *Stone and tree miss the keepers. Other men do not speak to us. We do not know how to speak to them.*

The tree blurred before him.

"Hold on!" Galen muttered.

Sweating, dizzy, Raffi gripped his hands tight on the old man's. "Where is the Crow?"

In Tasceron. In you. In your master, if he knew it.

"But where?"

The answer was harsh and garbled; the sound distorted as if down tunnels and veins, deep in the earth. His hands clasped a wooden knoll. He felt sick and retched, choking.

"Hold it!" Galen was yelling.

"I can't! He's gone! He's gone!"

Sweating, he was hauled up, dragged out from the tree on hands and knees. He collapsed in the grass, sick, shivering uncontrollably, his head throbbing with flashes of light and pain. After a while he realized Galen was holding him. Rain had soaked them both.

"Sorry."

"You did your best."

The keeper eased him against the tree, dragged the pack over, and pulled the blankets out. "Get these around you. It's aftershock. We should have a fire."

"Not safe."

"What did he say, Raffi?" Galen clutched him on both arms, as if he couldn't bear the suspense. "Can he cure me?"

Raffi shook his head. He looked away from the keeper's face.

"He remembered the Makers. He said . . . only they can give back what they've taken. He said the Crow is in Tasceron. And in us, if we knew it."

"In us?" Then Galen stopped.

Another wave of nausea shuddered through Raffi. "What's wrong?" he croaked.

Galen had leaped up. He was looking down the hill, into the dark, and there was something in his look that made Raffi feel for his sense-lines.

They were all in shreds.

He staggered up and stood there, the blankets falling.

"Why don't you come up," Galen said grimly, "and see us from a little closer."

A dim shape was down there just beneath them, crouching on the dark turf.

"Come on!" Galen's voice was murderous.

The figure stood up, small and indistinct. Then the tiny moon, Pyra, came out. The light from it, ruby and warm, flickered over the girl.

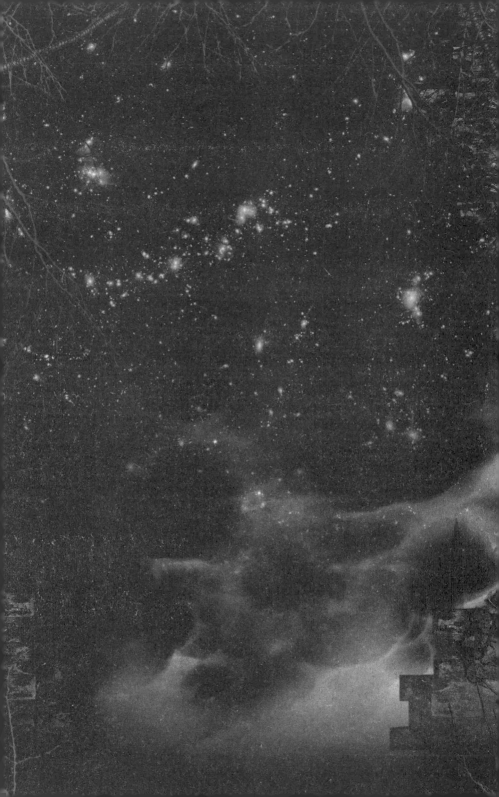

The Watch, Unsleeping

11

Once you believe, you are lost. Anything you see or hear can be twisted against you. The Order are masters of nothing but falsehood.

Rule of the Watch

SHE CAME A LITTLE CLOSER, then stopped.

"Is he all right?"

Galen glared at Raffi. "Is there anyone with her?"

Bewildered, Raffi groped for knowledge. "Only a horse, somewhere."

The girl stared at him in surprise. "You can hear it?"

He shrugged, uneasy.

She was small, wearing dark blue and gray trousers and jerkin, her hair a shiny nut-brown cut against her cheek. She seemed remarkably unconcerned.

As no one said anything, she went on, "My name is

Carys. Carys Arrin. I'm traveling west from here. Are you sure you're all right?"

Raffi was surprised. It was a long time since anyone had asked him that. "Fine," he said weakly.

"Why were you watching us?" Galen's voice was cold; Raffi felt the tension behind it. For a moment he felt sick again, and sat down abruptly.

"He's ill," the girl remarked accusingly.

Irritated, Galen glanced down. Then he hauled Raffi up and turned, his hawk-face dark against the rainy moon. "Come under the tree. We can talk."

Without waiting to see if she followed, he led Raffi in and sat him against the hollow trunk, tossing the blankets to him. Sensing the tree behind him made Raffi feel better, as if the strength of the wood and the spirit of it gave something back to him. His head cleared, and he looked up.

The girl stood hesitating under the thatch of branches. As she crouched he noticed the crossbow for the first time; it was wound back and loaded, he could see the bolt from here. She laid it on the dusty needles, but her hand stayed near it.

"I wasn't watching you. At least, not at first." She

glanced curiously around at the enormous bulk of the yew. "I saw the trees and came up to see if I could shelter here. The rain's getting heavy."

Galen said nothing. He was still standing, his head bent under the low roof of twigs.

"Then I heard you talking." She shrugged. "I crept up. I wanted to see who you were. You have to be careful, traveling alone." Her fingers tapped the smooth shaft of the bow.

"Indeed you do," Galen said. He sat down. "That goes for us too."

She looked at him shrewdly. "I'm no threat to you. I think I know what you are." As neither of them moved or spoke, she shrugged again. "All right, I won't say it. But no one else could have . . . It was very dark under here, but I'm sure I heard him . . ." She glanced at Raffi and shook her head, as if she couldn't get the words out.

"The tree spoke to him." Galen's voice was hard. "Is that so difficult?"

"For some." She gave him a half smile.

After a moment he said, "Why travel alone?"

"I was with two friends of mine, but they turned back

at the last village. They'd heard stories about the Sekoi tombs on the downs, and that scared them off." She glared at her feet fiercely. "We had a terrible row and I stormed away. Told them I'd go on by myself. Then the rain came. They may be looking for me; but I doubt it. They had all the courage of jekkle-mice." She looked up suddenly. "You haven't got anything to eat, have you?"

Raffi's hopes plunged. Galen shook his head. "No. So where is it you're so eager to get to?"

For a moment she was silent, as if weighing him up. "I'm looking for my father." Her voice dropped. "The Watch took him."

Raffi peeled himself off the tree. "The Watch! Why?"

"Oh, you do speak, do you?" For a moment a laugh glinted in her face; then she turned it into the shadows. "I don't really know the answer to that. I wasn't there. When I came back to the village where we lived, he was gone. The Watchmen had come in the night—six of them, all armed, on black horses. They had broken the door down, dragged him out and taken him. It was so sudden . . ." Her voice was quiet; the rain outside hissed harder. Drops fell on Raffi's shoulder. "There was talk later that a man and a woman—travelers—had come to the house two days before. My father gave them a room, for one night. They paid him. There was nothing wrong with that. But if they were keepers . . ."

They were silent a moment. Raffi knew the Watch wouldn't have hesitated.

Carys looked up. "They came west, but I've lost the track. You would know, keeper. Where might they take him?"

Even Raffi wondered. But Galen said bleakly, "They want information. They'll get it out of him, then kill him. It's useless."

Stubbornly she shook her head. "I'm not giving up! Where?"

In the darkness of the tree the three of them had become dim shapes to one another. Galen's voice sounded strange. "I don't know. Maybe to Tasceron."

"Tasceron! Does it still exist?"

"It exists."

The rain was lessening. Slowly it pattered into silence, but the slow drops still fell here and there through the thick growth, branch to branch, steady and relentless, and the scents of the wet night rose in the after-storm hush.

Carys looked at them curiously. "Is that where you're going?"

Galen laughed harshly. "Us! It's the last place we'd want to go."

The girl was silent a moment. Then she said, "Look. Will you let me go on with you? I don't like being on my own. Not out here."

For a long moment the Relic Master watched the darkness outside. Then he said, "Until we reach a village, or a place you'll be safe. But we've no horses. We walk."

"So can I." Carys knelt up eagerly on the crushed needles. "Thank you. So now I won't need this." She lifted the bow.

"Maybe," Galen said stiffly. "Maybe we're not so safe as you think."

"I think you are." She stood up against the sky. "I'll bring my horse up." Then turning, she said, "You didn't tell me your names."

Galen looked into the dark. "Galen Harn," he said, his voice quiet. "And Raffael Morel."

When she was gone he looked across. "Well?"

Raffi pulled the blankets tight. He felt better now, but

tired. "She seems all right. And she's on her own. She won't be any threat."

"But is she telling the truth?"

"I don't know!" His throat was dry; he swallowed a few drops of rain from the ends of his fingers. "I don't know how to tell."

Galen was silent. "Once I knew when people were lying to me."

Raffi winced. The keeper turned on him suddenly as the horse harness clinked in the dark. "One thing. She's not to know about what happened to me. Understand? She's not to know!"

Sadly, Raffi nodded.

Journal of Carys Arrin
Agramonsnight
9.16.546

> The boy's asleep. Harn has drifted into some sort of trance; he sways and murmurs prayers in the dimness. I'm taking a chance but this book's small and easy to hide. It may be my last chance to write for a while.

First of all, the tree. I was lying out in the long grass—it was dark, but it seemed to me the boy was speaking to the tree and it was answering. I heard no words, but there was a sort of . . . tingle. I know this is heresy and I know it can't be real. But why make an illusion if they didn't know I was there? And the boy believed it.

I heard one thing that puzzled me. The boy distinctly said the Crow was in Tasceron. I remember the stories of the Crow from my training, but I'd always thought it was a figure of myth, a bird that talked. The bolt was on the crossbow; I had it aimed right at the middle of the keeper's back—but those words stopped me. After all, dead or alive are the orders. And they know something about this Crow. It may be the name of someone real, high in the Order, like an Archkeeper. A code name. It seemed worth a risk to find out.

So I let them see me. Harn is wary; he asked a lot of questions. I told them a story that would get them on my side, make us all enemies of the Watch. I was surprised how easy they were to deceive. The boy looked ill; they both seem half starved.

(Note for Jellie—the psychic defenses the

records mention can't exist. I'm certain they didn't know I was there.)

I'll try and stay with them as long as possible—to Tasceron, because I'm sure that's where they're going. I know the city is enormous, but if they find this Crow I'll be with them. To catch Harn and his boy would be good, but someone higher, a real chance to get into the secrets of the Order—that would make old Jeltok sit up. He always said I'd never make an agent.

I'm hungry, and the rain's started again. On foot we'll be slow. But they won't get rid of me now.

12

*Tamar called the Sekoi to him and
said, "We have brought life to the world,
new trees, new animals. What gift have
we for you, tall people?"*

*The Sekoi spoke among themselves.
Then they said, "We ask no gifts of you.
You are not our Makers. We were here
before you. We will be here after you."*

*And Tamar was angry with the Sekoi,
and turned them away.*

Book of the Seven Moons

FOR TWO DAYS THEY TRAMPED the endless downs. They lived on water and whinberries and dried fish from the pack, and Raffi took it in turns with Carys to ride on the horse, which he enjoyed. Galen bluntly refused, and limped ahead.

Over the slow miles of chalk, Carys talked. She told him about her village, the school there, the ruined keeper's house beside it, and about her father, a small, shrewd man with red hair, though Raffi noticed if he asked too many questions she fell silent after a while. She must be worried sick, he thought guiltily.

The Sekoi tombs still bothered him. They were watchful, and eerie at night. Galen was silent most of the time. After the night at the tree he hurried them on, and Raffi knew that the promise of Tasceron tormented him, the lure of the Crow, of the cure he might find. He pushed them on all day till they were worn out, but even at night Raffi woke to see the keeper sitting up in the moonlight, turning the pages of the Book, while the were-birds moaned over his head.

"What's wrong with him?" Carys whispered once.

Alarmed, Raffi shook his head. "Nothing. And quiet, he'll hear."

"So? You seem scared of him."

He shrugged. "No. It's just . . . we've been through a lot."

"He doesn't treat you very well," she said archly.

"He doesn't treat himself very well."

"That's no excuse."

She had plenty to say and said what she thought. She made him laugh, and he hadn't done that for a long time. He realized how he had longed for company of his own age—at home there had been seven others. Though he'd missed them bitterly at first, he'd gotten used to Galen's morose silence. Or thought he had.

The Watch, Unsleeping

"How did you come to be a scholar?" she asked as they half slid down a slope of slippery grass, coaxing the horse. Galen was ahead, far below. Raffi pulled a face. "I lived on my mother's farm. There were eight of us."

"No father?"

"He'd died. Galen turned up one night, about four years ago." The sun broke through as he said it, and he had a dream-flash of his mother turning from the door, her eyes full of surprise, the man's gaunt shadow behind her. "He stayed three days. I remember how he watched all of us. He scared us a bit."

Carys grinned. "I'm not surprised."

"No . . . Then he picked me. He didn't say why. Just caught my arm one day and made me sit down and talk to him. Asked me about my dreams. Looked into my mind, my spirit-web."

Carys stumbled over a tussock. She brushed hair from her eyes. "He can do that?" she asked, her voice strained.

"Yes. At least . . . Well, sometimes." Raffi looked up at a wan yellow cloud blotting out the sun. "He asked me if I wanted to go with him."

She looked at him sidelong. "That's all? No payment?"

"Payment! Keepers have no money. My mother was honored, and I think a bit relieved. It's hard to feed eight. And as for me . . ." He shrugged. "I knew it would be dangerous, but that was exciting. And I wanted to learn. The Litany, the mind-webs, the opening and closing, all the rites and the Branches of power. I wanted that. I still do. I haven't learned half of it yet. They knew so much, Carys, these people! Before the Watch destroyed everything."

She was silent, nodding.

"The Watch are always after us. A while back I had a feeling they were on our trail. It's petered out now . . ."

"Raffi!"

Galen's yell was urgent. He was rigid, staring up at the sky.

Raffi raced down. "What is it?"

"That!"

Before them the sky was sour, a hissing yellow haze. It seemed to shift and swirl as if some enormous insect swarm blew toward them on the rising wind.

"Fireseed!" Carys breathed, beside him.

The Watch, Unsleeping

Galen nodded. "You've seen it before?"

"Heard of it."

So had Raffi, and the sight filled him with terror.

Once he had seen a man who'd only just survived a fireseed storm, his face burned and horribly scarred. Most weren't so lucky. Early in autumn, when the weather began to chill, the firepods exploded, the round spiked seed drifting, sometimes for days, in great poisonous clouds until they sank and grew into the dull reddish plants that were so common. There was nothing dangerous about the plants, but the seed would sear through the flesh it touched, the acid on the soft spines burning through leather and clothes. Kest's work. Like all the other evils.

Galen glanced around. There was no shelter. Only a few Sekoi barrows studded the turf.

The yellow cloud billowed.

"Run!" Galen turned. "Get on your horse, girl. Get out of here!"

He scrambled back up the slope; Raffi raced after him, grabbing handfuls of grass to haul himself up. Carys galloped ahead; she reached the ridge top and stared around hopelessly, the horse whickering with fear.

"Nothing! Not for miles!"

Galen pulled Raffi up. "The tomb. The nearest! Inside it!"

Despite the crackling cloud looming down on them, Carys paused. The horse pirouetted in terror. She had a sudden urge to gallop before the storm, away, abandoning them. But it was already too late. Scowling, she urged the beast toward the barrow.

Raffi was nearly there, Galen limping behind him. As she raced after them the storm swirled over her; glancing up she caught her breath at the yellow mass of seeds, billions of them, clotted like a rustling curtain. Something stung her face; she screamed, rubbing at it, jerking her head down on the horse's sweating neck.

The sky crackled around them. Galloping past Galen, she swung herself off. The barrow was a huge green swelling in the storm.

"How do we get in?" she screamed.

Seeds gusted around them, scattered on Galen's hood. He scrabbled at the edge of the mound, the row of sealing stones, tearing them away. She pulled too, and Raffi; something slid and rumbled, small stones falling in a dusty heap.

A black slit opened in the tomb like an eye. Raffi was gone, burrowing in, the pack dragged after him. "Now you!" Galen yelled.

Seeds fell on her shoulders; she squirmed and beat them off. "My horse!"

"We can't save it! Get inside!"

Pain stung her cheek. Desperately she dragged the maddened horse still; tore the small bag from the saddle. Then she was down, worming into the tiny black hole, stinging seeds kicked from her legs. Hands hauled her in. Galen's head and shoulders scrabbled through; then he was in, piling rocks in the entrance, and she glimpsed for a moment the air outside thick with poisonous flying drifts. The last stone blocked the gap.

"My poor horse," she whispered in the dark.

"Can't be helped." Galen's voice sounded hollow; it echoed around them. Raffi realized his skin was stinging; he rubbed his forehead and his fingers were burned, so that he hissed with the pain.

"Don't touch it," Galen's voice said. A sputter and crack came from the tinderbox; then a small flame lengthened to yellow. Galen's face and hands loomed out of the dark; he stuck the candle in a crevice and rummaged in the pack.

Raffi looked around, uneasy. He sensed that the chamber was small, too low to stand in. A roof of stone hung above; somewhere at the back of him was a low passageway, invisible. He let his mind grope into it. There were chambers down there, on each side. Traces of bones lingered in their dust. The last chamber, the one at the end, had something else in it.

He felt for it cautiously. Something very old.

Galen had the box of ointments out; he looked into Raffi's face. "Are we alone?"

"I don't think so."

Nodding, he thrust a small clay pot at Carys. "Then we'll have to hurry. Use this first."

She pulled the top off and dipped a finger in; it was cold and stiff, richly scented. Rubbing it on her hands and scorched face, she felt the seared skin cool; the relief was wonderful.

The Watch, Unsleeping

"What is it?"

"Never mind." Galen slapped it on his own hands, fingers over fingers. "Hurry up, Raffi. There are things to do."

When they had finished he cleared a space, lit seven candles and arranged them in a circle, working quickly. Carys felt uneasy. The new light showed a low passageway behind her, leading farther into the tomb. And though she told herself she was a fool, she felt with a prickling of her skin that there was something down there. "Raffi . . ." she began.

"We know." He looked up. "We know what to do."

He had poured water into a small silver dish, and now pulled out a red leather bag, full of objects. Despite her worry, excitement shivered through her. These were relics.

"Which one?" Raffi had his hand inside.

Galen thought quickly. "The bracelet."

He pulled it out. It was made of some smooth black leather, with a tiny fastening. Threaded on it was a strange flat slab of gold, studded with no stones, but with a gray window. Minute touch-buttons decorated the sides.

Carys edged nearer.

Raffi glanced at her. "Look at this." With his thumb-nail he pressed one of the buttons hard. She stared, as-tounded. For a second, faint numbers had flickered in the window.

"What is it?"

"Who knows. It's almost dead now." Reverently he laid it down among the candles.

Galen had taken one string of black and green crystals from his neck; now he made a circle of it, around the relic. Then he and Raffi began to chant.

She recognized odd words, nothing more. This was the language of the Makers, long lost, except to the Order. It calmed her, made her feel strangely serene. It seemed important, here in the blackness of the tomb, though out-side she would have laughed at it. But in this place some-thing else lived, and she felt the strength of the chant, its protection, warming her, reassuring her. They'll have you believing all this, she told herself wanly. The crossbow lay under her hand, and she was glad it was loaded.

After the last response the silence was huge. Galen picked up the silver bowl and poured the water gently into the ground. "We bring you a gift, guardian," he said. "We're not here to disturb you. We don't break the sacred lines."

Raffi could feel them, the earth-lines. They reached out, one north, two to the west, another, very old and faint, southwest. Invisible, underground. As Galen dug a deep slot in the ground and buried the relic in it, Raffi felt a pulse along the lines, a faint crackle of power.

The Sekoi had taken the gift.

That seemed to be all. Carys sat back against the wall, almost impressed. The ritual had drawn it away, that air of threat in the dark chamber behind her. Or had she imagined the whole thing? Shaking her head, she glanced down at the bag with the journal in it. That and the cross-bow were all she had left. She was really undercover now.

They stayed where they were, not exploring. They drank water, chewed the last of the fish, maybe even slept a little. Raffi wasn't sure. The darkness confused them; they seemed deep, deep underground. Time seemed still. There was no way of knowing if the storm had ended. Maybe it had finished hours ago. And yet none of them moved.

Lying there, Raffi began to imagine he saw scrawls and carvings on the stones overhead, spirals that swirled if he stared at them, so that he looked away, uneasy, and when he looked back they had shifted.

Galen sat huddled, resting forehead on arms. Carys was silent, as if the barrow swallowed her words before she spoke them. Raffi gathered his strength. With a great effort he managed to say, "It may be safe now."

Instantly they all felt hours had been lost. Galen looked up, his face haggard in the candlelight. "What are we doing! Look outside!"

Raffi dragged the stones free. A small draft blew into the chamber; the light outside seemed dim. Late afternoon, Carys thought, rubbing her face. Raffi's head and shoulders blocked the hole. Then he squirmed back inside. "It's stopped. But the seeds are lying all over the ground."

They crawled out one by one and stood stiffly. The tomb rose in a sea of yellow; the scattered seed lay in a clogged mat all around them, as far as they could see on the downland. Here and there swathes of grass were clear, or the fall was light, but in places the poisonous carpet looked almost solid.

The Watch, Unsleeping

"Can we get through that?" Carys muttered.

"We have to." Galen pulled the pack on and gripped his stick. "Follow me close."

Hurriedly blocking the barrow-hole behind them, Raffi took a last glimpse inside. For a moment he felt the sense of something else there, staring at him out of the dark. He jammed a stone in the gap and jumped back.

Galen was stepping carefully through the fallen seeds. He headed west, and went quickly, because there was no knowing how many miles the seedfall stretched, and to be caught in the middle of it on only a two-moon night might be disastrous. But avoiding the densest clots meant they had to circle far out of their way, placing their feet carefully among the seared grasses. Close up, Raffi saw the seeds were fist-sized balls of spikes that rolled in the breeze; sometimes a few gusted up in the air, and the travelers had to stop and watch them anxiously. It was slow, treacherous work, and they knew the corrosive acids were eating into the leather of their boots at every step.

They had walked for two hours and were weary of it when they came to the top of a rise and saw the sunset blazing the sky before them. Something else made Raffi jerk up his head like a fox.

"Galen!" he said.

It was too late. Below, looking up at them in surprise, were three men, two on horseback and one walking.

They were armed, and their horses were painted in dark reds and black. They were the Watch.

13

Even across the dark, even across the loss, even across the emptiness, soul will speak to soul.

Poems of Anjar Kar

CARYS STOOD STILL. She decided to do nothing and say nothing. For a start, she wanted to know how Galen dealt with this, whether the keepers really did have the mind-weapons legends spoke of. And if they escaped, she needed to stay with them.

One of the Watchmen called them down. She was surprised when Galen laughed sourly. Raffi looked terrified.

The Watchman yelled again.

Galen raised a hand and nodded. "There's a village beyond the trees," he muttered, glancing at the smoke. "If they ask, we come from there."

Making his way down between the scattered seeds, he

169

looked sidelong at Carys. "If we're found out, tell the truth. You fell in with us two days ago. You don't know who we are."

She grinned at him, tucking her hair behind her ear. "Oh don't worry about me. I'm good at lying."

"I'm sure you are," he said coolly.

The seed was thin here; they were at the edge of it. The Watchpatrol waited for them. They were well armed, Raffi noticed, wearing a patchwork of body armor. One had a helmet, badly dented. His heart was hammering in his chest; desperately he wished he knew what Galen was up to. He'd learned to fear that cold laugh.

Close up, they saw the men had hardly outridden the storm. They were all burned, and in pain; one had his arm bound up and gripped it tight. And they must have lost a horse.

"Good evening," Galen called out cheerily. Carys glanced at him in astonishment.

The Watchsergeant, the one on foot, looked them over.

"Where have you come from?" he growled. "Out of the downs after a fire-fall?"

Galen leaned on his staff. "There are places to shelter

if you know them. You obviously weren't so lucky."

"We'd have been dead if it hadn't stopped." The man was big, stolid, but shrewder than the other two, who seemed in too much pain to be curious. Carys knew his sort. He'd be suspicious.

"Who are you?" he asked.

"My name is Harn," Galen said recklessly. "These are my children, Raffael and Carys." He put his arm around her and squeezed. She smiled up happily at the Watchman and thought that Galen could tell lies as well as she could. He was far more cunning than she'd thought. She'd have to be more careful.

"You come from the village there?"

"We do," Galen said confidently.

"Then take us there. My men are hurt."

They should have been ready for it. It was a staggering blow, but Galen didn't flinch. He nodded, falling into step beside the Watchsergeant, talking about the seeds as if he hadn't a care in the world. Grudgingly the Watchman listened as he walked. The two on horses trailed behind. Neither would be any problem, Raffi thought; he knew enough to terrify horses. But the third!

They should jump him now. What was Galen doing!

Carys was beside him, her bow slung on her back. "He's mad. What's his plan?"

"I don't know." Raffi stared at his master's back. "He gets like this sometimes. Does reckless things. You can't talk to him. Sometimes I think he's trying to get himself killed."

She stared at him. "Are you serious?"

"He looks for trouble. At least since the accident—" He stopped.

"What accident?"

He shrugged. "A relic exploded. He was hurt."

"His leg, you mean?"

Raffi nodded. He didn't seem to want to say any more.

She looked away, at the seeds on the stubble-field. "Not much of a reason for getting killed."

He didn't answer. She knew there was something important here; something he wasn't telling her, but before she could try again they were in the muddy lane between the first houses. A group of villagers were brushing fireseed into a heap. When they saw the travelers, they stood stock-still.

The Watch, Unsleeping

"Too late anyway," Carys muttered. She unslung her bow, annoyed, glancing back at the stumbling horses. Galen Harn was hers. No one else was bringing him in, certainly no potbellied sergeant. "Get ready."

Raffi shook his head. "You're not in this."

"I am now."

The Watchsergeant strode up to the villagers; most of them fell back, leaving a thin gray-haired man in a patched brown coat as the spokesman. He nodded grimly. "So you're back."

"We said we would be," the sergeant snarled.

"We were afraid the seeds might have killed you." The man's voice was acid.

The sergeant gave him a small sour smile. "Well, they haven't."

"Haven't you had enough from us!" a woman screamed from the crowd. "Where is my son? Where is he?"

"You know where they are." The sergeant drew his sword easily, sensing the rising tension. "In good hands. The Watch will feed them, clothe them, and they'll be taught. More than you could have given them. You should bless the Watch."

"And now you've come for more." The gray-haired man gripped his hands around the rake handle.

"No. You've given your quota. We're only here because the storm caught us out." He half turned. "We met your friends here on the down. They've been lucky as well."

The villagers stared.

Carys gripped her bow.

Galen glanced briefly at Raffi. Carys was close; she heard Raffi barely whisper the word. "Arno."

The keeper strode forward, slapping an arm around the villager's shoulder. "Arno! Good to see you. How have things been?"

Amazed, Carys watched. For a moment Arno was silent, stiff with surprise. He won't do it, she thought. Her fingers slid the bolt in. Behind her, Raffi waited, hands gripped tight.

Then Arno spoke. "They've been fine," he said. His voice was dry; his face held no flicker of astonishment. "We've been expecting you, brother. Here's your wife."

Galen took a step back. He looked wary at once; his face darkened. A woman ran out of the crowd, tall and fair-haired; she flung her arms around him and kissed him. "You're back! And early too!" She came to Raffi and Carys and grabbed their hands. "You both look half starved. I've got some fine chickens roasting for you, just as you like them . . ." Talking and laughing and not letting them answer, she led them briskly between the houses, away from the crowd. Glancing back, Raffi saw the Watchmen dismounting, the sergeant giving orders.

Around the corner Galen stopped the woman. "What's going on!"

She shook her head impatiently. "I should ask you that! How could you just walk in here with them! And why haven't you been answering me? For two days I've been trying to make you hear."

He stared at her, his dark eyes narrowing with delight. "You're a keeper!"

"Of course I am. Now in here. Quickly!"

She pushed them through a low doorway into the house. Straightening, Raffi saw a long room with another beyond it, a bright fire crackling, a complicated arrangement of spits with three chickens being turned by a very old woman who grinned at him, showing only one tooth.

"Is this them?" she asked.

"Yes." The tall woman looked back through the slit of the door. "No one seems to be following. The Watch are back."

The old woman spat. "God curse them."

"Arno will keep them busy. Go and keep an eye on them."

The old hag winked, and pulled a shawl around her head. She slid silently through the door.

"Can we trust her?" Galen asked.

"Of course I can, she's my mother. Now, leave your pack. Sit down. The first thing is to get you something to eat."

Raffi watched her slice the meat. Suddenly he knew he was starving. The hiss of the grease dropping in the flames, the smell of it, tormented him. As she worked, the woman said quickly, "My name is Lerin. I was a scholar of the Order. My master was taken and killed."

"His name?"

"Marcus Torna."

Galen nodded somberly. "I knew of him."

"I escaped. I don't think the Watch knew he had any pupils with him. I had nowhere to go, so I came home.

The Watch, Unsleeping

Here. Ten years ago now. The people here are my family. They despise the Watch, more so now than ever. Those men were here three months ago. They took ten children, all under five, for their filthy Watchhouses. God knows what will happen to them."

She thrust a plate of meat at Raffi. "Think of it! Our own children, drilled and trained and warped into our enemics. The brightest, the cleverest!" She paused, staring at Galen. "What future do those children have? Their mothers are distracted with grief."

He shook his head heavily. Carys sat staring at the fire so hard that Raffi nudged her. When she looked at him, just for a moment, something flickered in his mind, a drift of pain. As he reached for it, it was gone.

She glared at him. "Leave me alone, Raffi."

The woman looked at her suddenly. "Who are you? I didn't know about you."

"We met her," Galen muttered. "On the downs." He sat down on a bench, as if he was suddenly weary.

Lerin glanced at him. Then she stood upright, the knife still in her hand. "Why didn't you answer me, keeper? I have sense-lines—good ones—flung right out into the downs. Two days ago you walked through the first. I searched for your mind. I was nearly a Relic Master—only a few more months with Marcus and I would have made the Deep Journey. I know what I'm doing. Why didn't you answer me?"

Galen lifted his head. He faced her across the room, the fiery shafts of the last sunlight slanting between them. "I think we should talk about this later. Alone. Many things have happened. But I am who you think I am. Galen Harn. Relic Master."

For a moment they looked at each other, and the sun faded. Then the woman's face changed; Carys thought she seemed astounded, and then horrified. "Can it be . . . ?"

"Later!" Galen looked away into the dark. "I'll explain later."

Journal of Carys Arrin
Karnosnight
11.16.546

> I thought Raffi would burst, he ate so much.
> Mind you, so did I. Now he's asleep and so is Galen.
> After the meal everyone was too tired to talk.

The Watch, Unsleeping

Tomorrow, the woman said. The Watchpatrol may have moved on then. She's out, but the old woman is somewhere about.

Something's wrong. He has to ask Raffi for information. The villager's name. Why didn't he know it? Why not answer the woman's mind-call?

Maybe he's a fraud. Maybe the powers of the Order are nothing—and yet she would know that.

Maybe he suspects me.

He's a harsh, strange man, and sees far. And yet he went deliberately into danger. I don't understand what's happening here. But I'll find out.

All right. The real reason I'm writing is that I can't sleep. Why did she have to say that, about those children? Did I come from a village like this? Was my mother distracted with grief? I always thought, before, that Watchchildren were orphans . . . I never thought . . .

This is stupid. I'm going to sleep.

Note: Information about Lerin would be useful to the Watch. I don't think I'll send it.

14

What does the keeper know?
The secrets of the world.
To whom does the keeper speak?
God and the Makers.
What does the keeper fear?
Nothing but despair.

Litany of the Makers

"TASCERON!"

Lerin stared at them in amazement. "Galen, you can't go there! It's madness!"

He brooded across the firelit room. Outside, the cold rain fell heavily, splatting the pocked track into mud. Washed, full of food, and after the best night's sleep he'd had for months, Raffi watched the keeper anxiously. Galen was gaunter these days, his hair long and ragged, his hawk-nose jutting, eyes dark with obsession. Now he turned the cup of ale on the table, tracing the pattern on the leather.

"Maybe it is. But there are reasons for it. The first is the girl's father."

Carys blinked. For a moment she had forgotten her own story.

Lerin looked at her and shook her head. "I'm sorry, but that's . . . well, you have to face facts. He may well be dead already."

"I don't care," Carys said. "I'm going to find out!" She glanced at Galen. "Tell her your other reasons."

He drank, and set the cup down. Then he said, "I'm looking for a Sekoi. Brindled fur, with a zigzag under the eye. A man called Alberic wants him."

"Why?"

"Alberic has a relic of ours. A crystal box that emits light. That can kill."

Carys tried not to stare. She leaned back in the soft comfort of the chair, hoping he'd say more about it, but Lerin didn't seem very surprised. "And he says he'll give it back in return for the Sekoi?"

Galen shrugged. "So he says. I doubt it."

"Then why bother looking for the creature at all!" She came and sat on the bench opposite him, her long red skirt trailing in the soot. "Keeper, you can trust me. Tell me your real reason. No one goes to the Wounded City for nothing."

For a long moment he looked at her.

"I think you should," Raffi blurted out.

"No one asked you, boy."

"They never do. But I'm the one who'll have to go with you!"

Galen was silent. Then he looked over. "Carys. This is not for you to hear. Wait outside."

She glared. "I'm going to Tasceron too!"

"For your own reasons. This doesn't concern you."

She shrugged, and looked at Lerin. "It's a bit wet to wait outside."

The tall woman nodded. "Go in the other room. My mother is there."

Reluctantly Carys got up. As she crossed the room and turned to close the door, Raffi had a glimpse of her face. To his astonishment, just for a moment, he saw that she was furious.

When the door closed, Lerin leaned forward. "Now," she said. "What happened to you?"

Galen was silent; when he spoke his voice was strained. "Ten months ago the boy and I were called to a settlement in the forest, well east of here. They had come across a relic, a huge, strange thing, and had kept it hidden from the Watch. When I saw it, I was astonished. It was tall, tubular, and had once stood upright in the ground. Now it lay fallen. A great rusted mass.

"I knew at once that power was still in it and that it was dangerous. After the Makers had gone, many of their devices ran out of control. This one was evil. I told the boy to move the people away. I opened my mind to it, saw it, all the colors and lights about it, all the threads of power. Then I came closer. Carefully, I touched it."

He sat back and laughed bleakly. "That's all I remember."

She glanced at Raffi, wide-eyed.

"It exploded," he said quietly. "The noise! It was incredible. The forest burned; the villagers fled, most of them. I ran back, though my nose and ears were bleeding. Galen was lying there. For a moment I thought he was dead . . ."

"I was dead." Galen's voice was harsh. "I still am. It's

gone, keeper, all of it. I have only two eyes like other men, and see nothing more than they do. When the wind blows in the trees I hear only the wind. Nothing more. The traces of the Makers are lost. My mind is a great silence."

"Nothing?"

"No bird-speech, no earth-lines, none of the world's million voices. No mind-speech. No dreams."

She watched him closely, full of horror; Raffi could feel it seeping from her like a musky scent. "How do you survive?" she whispered.

"Prayer," he said bleakly. "And whatever the boy can do."

She was silent, plaiting the folds of her red skirt with her fingers. "And you think in Tasceron there might be someone left to help you?"

"More than that." He glanced at the door. "Where are the Watch?"

"Saddling up. They don't suspect anything. They don't know everyone here, and these two are too old for their Watchhouses." She pulled a face. "I hope they'll have forgotten you by next time."

Galen nodded. He shuffled a little closer, the flames edging his face with shadow. "Twice," he said quietly, "we've had word of something very strange. Both messages were the same—that the Crow is alive, and in the city."

"The Crow! Impossible!"

His face darkened with anger. "Don't call me a liar! Marcus Torna couldn't have taught you that."

"I'm sorry." Lerin shook her head ruefully. "I'm sorry, keeper, I was wrong. Nothing is impossible to God. But the Crow! I thought . . . nothing of the Makers is left whole. Why should he be left?"

"Why not?" Galen got up abruptly, as if he couldn't sit still any longer. He prowled to the window and stared out at the rain. "Why not? The Makers have gone, but they knew the future. They may have foreseen the destruction of the Order. They may have left us their messenger, buried deep under the ruins, for us to find him when we need him most!" He turned urgently. "It's an omen, Lerin, I know it is! The Crow can cure me, maybe, but more than that, he can cure the world. He can rid us of the Watch!"

A tiny sound at the door made Raffi stiffen. But Galen hadn't heard it and Lerin was thinking deeply and gave no sign. Raffi could feel Carys close. Perhaps she was listening. But he wasn't bothered about that, the relief was so great. Now someone else knew. And surely Lerin would try to talk him out of it. She had to.

After a while she looked up.

"You think I'm on a fool's errand," Galen said drily.

She shrugged. "Perhaps I do. On the other hand I can see why you have to go. If it could be true . . ."

"It is! I'm sure of it."

She frowned. "But keeper, think of the immensity of Tasceron! There are a million streets, whole warrens of ruined districts. Flames burst from the ground; the air is always black. It would take a lifetime to search, even to stay alive."

"We'll be told where to look." Galen was obstinate. "There will be messages. We just need faith."

She nodded, rather sadly. Perhaps she realized, as Raffi did, finally and hopelessly, that Galen had made up his mind and nothing would change it. Perhaps she knew he could only stay sane if he had some hope.

She stood up, the green and blue awen-beads slipping against her neck. "You'll need a ship. We trade with a village on the coast—a day's walk from here. There's a harbor there; ships cross the Narrow Sea. We'll get you on one."

"The Watch."

"Don't worry. As I said, the people here are my family."

"I'm grateful," Galen said with a grim joy.

"One thing." The woman faced him. "I have a feeling of foreboding on me, keeper. Dark dreams came to me all night, and I fear you may be walking to your death. So I give you this warning from the Makers. Your life is sacred. The knowledge you have is sacred. You have no right to throw it away in defiant risks. Above all, you have no right to risk the boy's life. There have been enough martyrs. Hear this, Galen Harn."

Her voice had changed and darkened. Raffi shivered. All at once she seemed full of some authority that made her face grave and beautiful, and yet was gone in an instant, as if someone else had been there.

"I hear." Galen bowed his head, shaken and uneasy. "I hear you, lords."

The Watch, Unsleeping

THEY STAYED IN the village for two days, eating well and sleeping late. The Watch had gone, taking three goats, some chickens, and the curses of the villagers. Now they nodded to the travelers with quiet respect. Raffi was used to this but it amused Carys.

"They really think you're special."

He looked at her, surprised. "So they should. Most people still have respect for the Order."

Cursing herself, she nodded. "I know that."

They walked on among the houses, the hens squawking away. She thought back to the mumbles of conversation she had heard through the door, once the wretched old woman had finally dozed off. The Crow again. But more, some things she'd missed.

"Raffi," she said suddenly. "How did you know Arno's name?"

He was watching three children play in a puddle. Their mother came out and smacked them. "Names are easy," he said. "They lie on the surface, like a tiger-flower. Bright, with deep roots."

"So why did Galen have to ask you?"

He glanced at her angrily. "You don't know much

about keepers, Carys. He's always testing me. I'm his pupil." He looked away. "Let's climb the hill. I'll race you to the top." And he ran, clambering over the rocks, jamming his feet in the rabbit holes, not waiting to see if she followed, because he hated lying to her, and was ashamed of it.

The weather was sunny, with sudden autumnal crashes of rain. Galen spent much time meditating, and once Lerin took him and Raffi to her relic hoard, in a secret cave in the chalk-country.

In the evenings they talked around the fire, and the keepers took turns to tell stories of the Makers: the adventures of Flain in the Land of the Dead; Kest's great fight with the Dragon of Maar, whose tail tore half the stars from the sky.

Half asleep, warm against the back of a cushioned chair, Raffi dreamed, seeing the scenes of the stories vaguely in the flames and flickering light—the caves and hollows of the underworld, the Sekoi ghosts, the passageways and treasure rooms. Once he watched Carys listening, and was caught by something in her face, some far-off look, till she saw him and frowned.

The Watch, Unsleeping

Part of him wanted to stay in the village forever, but on the third day Lerin told them everything was ready.

"You go tomorrow, with the trade goods. Fleeces, barley, honey, apples. Arno will go with you. The ship is called the *Sigourna*, and she'll be waiting at Troen—that's the harbor. She's sailing to the Morna River—the nearest place to Tasceron we can get you."

Galen nodded. "Good, Lerin! Excellent."

She glanced at Raffi, who just shrugged. He knew that what he thought didn't matter.

15

*One day Flain walked in the Forest of
Karsh and he was thirsty. Coming to
a stream, he drank, and such was his
strength that the ground sank lower.
He went on his way. The sea rose and
drowned the forest.*

   *Though the Sekoi have another story
about this.*

Book of the Seven Moons

THE ALLEYWAY WAS DARK and there was something else in it. Jammed against the damp wall, Raffi heard it swoop out of the darkness. He turned and ran, through cobwebs that webbed his face and hands as he brushed them away.

The floor rose; he tripped, fell flat. The thing was on him, its sharp claws raking his back, its stinking breath on his neck. He yelled and squirmed and was up again, running blindly into the blackness till the wall smacked against him and he crumpled, breathless, fighting, struggling, kicking off blankets, his coat, the strong fingers that grabbed at him again and again.

"Raffi! Keep still! It's me. For Flain's sake, get yourself under control!"

The roar was Galen's and it woke him instantly, just before Carys came hurtling around the door into the cabin, her shirt hanging out. "What's the matter? Is he seasick?"

"No." Galen let him go and sat back. "I don't think so."

"Of course I'm not! It was a dream." Raffi rubbed sweat from his face. "A nightmare."

Under them the ship dipped and sank. His stomach lurched, and a tray of cups and plates slid slowly down the tilted table.

"All dreams count," Galen said, grabbing the edge of the chair. "Tell it to me."

Raffi shrugged. "I was in some sort of street . . ." He explained briefly, bringing the dream accurately out of memory as Galen had taught him. When he'd finished, Carys grinned. "It was that cheese you ate."

Galen frowned at her. "It may be important. Remember it."

The ship rose suddenly; the oil lamp swung, sending

wild shadows over the low ceiling. Carys sat down and laced her boots.

"Still lost."

They had been at sea for two days, and the weather had gotten steadily worse. Halfway over, the fog had come down. Now the tiny cabin was dim with it; it drifted down the steps, making the lamp a cloud of haze; the rough blankets smelled of its damp.

It was late morning, but morning and night all seemed the same.

"Have they asked again?" Raffi asked quietly.

"They will," Galen muttered.

Almost as an answer there was a bang on the open door; Arno came in, bending his head. He looked harassed and soaked. "I'm sorry, Galen."

He stood aside; behind him the skipper blocked the door, a small, black-bearded man, his cap in his hand. He twisted it nervously. "Keeper, the men are scared. The fog's too thick, we don't know how near the shore we are. The Watch patrol this strait, and if they come on board . . ."

"I know," Galen said heavily. "We're bringing you into danger."

"It's just that some of the older men . . . they say the Order had weather-warding skills. I don't know. But if there's anything you can do . . ."

Galen was silent a moment. Carys watched him curiously. Then he said, "I'll come on deck. First I have to prepare."

The two men backed out respectfully and Carys went with them, climbing the steps to the deck and pulling her blue coat around her. The fog was iron-gray and hung close; it tasted metallic and salty. She could barely see the ship's rail till she bumped into it; above her the masts dissolved into dimness. Even the sea, invisible below, was silent, rising and falling as smooth as oil, the only sounds a tarred rope dragging, canvas creaking, the murmur of voices in the gloom.

Then Galen and Raffi came up. The keeper had a small object in his hand; it looked like quartz crystal. Raffi looked nervous, she noticed. Galen shoved a coil of rope aside and laid the crystal on the soaked planks of the deck; with some chalk he drew strange signs around it, some of which she recognized from her training. A bird, the seven sigils of the moons, a slashed circle, a bee.

The Watch, Unsleeping

Behind her the sailors gathered, like wraiths in the fog.

Galen straightened. Then he beckoned, and Raffi came forward. He looked pale in the dimness.

"Aren't you going to do this?" the captain asked anxiously.

Galen stared at him in surprise. "Weather-warding is a task for scholars," he said curtly. "Not masters."

He nodded to Raffi, who took a deep breath, closed his eyes, and spread out his hands. Below him the crystal lay wrapped in fog.

Carys watched closely. For a while nothing happened and she told herself it wouldn't. The whole thing was nonsense. Someone whispered behind her, and Galen growled "Be quiet" without looking over. She saw he was staring at Raffi intently, as if willing him on. The ship sailed silently into darkness. And then a tiny thrill of fear tingled in Carys's spine; she clenched her fingers, breathing in sharply.

Around the crystal, the fog had gone.

A tiny circle of empty air hung there, the white stone glinting, the knots on the shaven planks clear and sharp. Raffi opened his eyes and grinned. He looked dazed and delighted. The circle grew; the fog rolled back, was pushed apart, and men murmured and whistled in subdued awe. Now they could all see one another, then the wide deck, now the opposite rail with a gull that flew off with a shriek of alarm, and still the circle of power swelled. Carys stood rigid, watching. There was the mast, the rigging, the ship's cat in the high spars; they were all appearing in this great bubble of clearness. Turning to the rail, she looked down and could see the sea, the green splash of it, out to the receding wall of the mist. She shook her head, bewildered. "Oh, Jeltok. What would you say about this?"

"Who?" Raffi stood behind her, smiling.

"No one. You look pleased."

He laughed. "I feel it! I've never done it so well!"

"Brilliant!" The skipper had crammed his cap on and seized Galen's hand. "Brilliant!"

Galen snatched his hand away. "Not me. The boy."

"Of course!" Clapping Raffi carelessly on the back, the man stared at the sea. "How big will it grow?"

"About half a league around the ship will be clear. Beyond that the fog remains." Galen crossed to Raffi and looked down at him. Stiffly he said, "Well done."

The Watch, Unsleeping

Raffi was astonished. "The way the power moves through your hands . . ." he murmured.

Galen almost flinched. Then he said, "I know."

"I didn't mean . . . I'm sorry . . ."

"Quiet!" The keeper turned on him fiercely. "That's enough!"

Carys watched them. Then she turned and looked out at the circle of fog, a clear rim. And she saw, growing out of the sea, a forest of huge blackened trees, straight and bare, their branches high above, arching like tunnels over the green swell.

"What's that!"

Galen glared at it savagely and didn't answer. At her back, Arno murmured, "The drowned forest. The Forest of Karsh."

She had heard of it. The great black trees rose like pillars, their roots deep underwater, and as they sailed close to one she saw the hardness of the wood, fossilized and ridged, like rock.

"Are they alive?" she whispered.

"They must be. I can feel them," Raffi said. Then he winced, as if he'd been stung.

"What's the matter?"

"Sense-lines. Something's coming!" He spun around to Galen. "Behind us. A ship. Very close!"

"Watchpatrol!" The skipper turned and leaped up the steps to the upper deck, yelling frantic orders. A new sail plumped out. The ship shuddered and slewed.

"You'll never outrun them," Carys muttered. She stared back. "I can't see anything."

"They're there." Galen slammed the rail in fury; then he turned and yelled, "Into the trees! Take us into the trees!"

"Keeper, I can't!" The skipper stared down at him, aghast. "No one sails in there! There are no soundings— no one has ever mapped all the shoals and currents, the channels . . . And God knows what lives in there!"

With a mutter of fury, Galen raced up the steps and caught him by the coat. "And what happens when the Watch sail out of the fog? Do you think they won't know a weather-warding when they see it? Get in there before they see the name of your ship! Or do you want to be rammed out of the water!"

The man stared at him, white-faced. Then he twisted.

The Watch, Unsleeping

"Hard aport! Get that topmast gallant down! Do it!"

Slowly, unwillingly, the ship turned; sliding toward the dark gap between the two nearest trees.

"Wouldn't it be easier to bring the fog back?" Carys said uneasily.

Raffi shook his head. "Can't. Not now. The spell will last for hours."

"Then they'll always be able to tell where we are."

"If they come in after us."

"Oh, they'll come in," she muttered.

The gap widened. As they entered it, a green dimness fell over their faces; high above them the stark branches stirred and they saw that dim leaves hung in strange clusters. In here it was dark, the only sounds the grunts of men furling the heavy sail and, looking behind them, Raffi saw the open sea beyond the entrance to their tunnel, the ship's wake sending ripples and swell slapping and clooping against the black rigid columns of the trees.

And then, just where the mist ended out there, he glimpsed the prow of a ship breaking out into the sunshine, the great silver eye painted on its side staring at him over the green water, and he shuddered, as if something had seen right to the heart of him.

Then they turned among the trees, and the daylight was blocked.

"Did they see us?"

"Who knows," Galen growled. "If they did, they'll come."

It was eerily silent, but for the wave-slap, the echoes. On each side of them the trees rose like black pillars in some gloomy, flooded hall; a forest waist-deep in dark water, stretching into dimness, stinking of decay, the crisp leaves rustling overhead. How strong they must be, Raffi thought, still growing as they had a thousand years ago, as if they'd never noticed the sea that drowned them.

The ship was deep inside now. The light was a green gloom; strange birds whistled. The branches over his head swished, as if some invisible creature leaped and followed. The skipper hung over the water, watching, afraid of a crash. The ship moved on mysterious currents, without any wind they could feel. Raffi saw how the crew clustered together, staring in fear into the depths of the still, drowned trees. Of the Watchship they could see nothing, and no daylight either. The deeper in they went, the darker the trees became.

Galen stirred. "How near are we to the coast?"

The skipper shook his head despairingly. "Who knows! Almost aground, maybe. The forest comes ashore south of Tasceron, according to the charts, but whether we can get the ship that close . . ."

"You'll have to," Galen said. He turned to Raffi. "Well?"

"They're still coming. Maybe getting closer."

"Right. Get below and get our things. You too, Carys, if you're coming."

"Of course I am!"

Below, in the cabin, jamming her journal deep into her bag she said, "What's he going to do?"

"I daren't think." Raffi checked the relic bag gloomily.

Abruptly, the ship shuddered. The sudden jarring shock sent them both crashing; cups and plates and a lamp slid and smashed on top of them.

Carys picked herself up painfully. "She's gone aground! Come on!"

On the deck, uproar had broken out. Men were running, yelling orders, the ship tilted at a bizarre angle, one side high out of the water. Scrambling up to the rail, Raffi clung there and saw that a huge splintered tree trunk was jammed under them; beyond it a tangle of roots, immense, a gloom of mudbanks.

"Here will do," Galen said. He slung the pack on his shoulder and jammed his staff across it; then he climbed up onto the rail.

"We can't just leave them!" Raffi yelled. "Not like this!"

Galen glared at him coldly. "They don't need us. We're just a danger for them. Do you want the Watch to find us on board?"

Poles were out; the sailors had them over the side and were heaving on them, the small ship shuddering and grinding.

"Now!" Galen said. "While we can." He swung his legs over, steadied himself and jumped onto the black, slippery mass of wood, almost fell, then pulled himself quickly upright. Carys followed carefully, then Raffi, letting himself down by his arms. Just as he let go, the ship juddered free. Arno's white face came to the rail. "Galen, there's no need . . ."

"This is as far as we go." Galen looked into the forest quickly. "Get away from here. Tell Lerin I'll remember what she said."

Arno nodded. "Good luck. Keep safe." He leaned closer. "Give us your blessing, keeper."

Galen spoke the words softly, his hand stretched out. For a moment they watched the ship drift away between the black trees. When he turned, the keeper's voice was quiet. "The bravery of the faithful. Remember it, Raffi."

The three of them had to crawl and slide along the huge trunk, the rounded surface slippery but wide as a track. Halfway to the jutting roots, Carys flattened herself. "Get down!"

Alarmed, Raffi jerked, grabbed, and slid hopelessly off into the water, trying not to splash. Chin-deep he hung on, scrabbling for a hold, finding to his astonishment that his feet touched bottom, sinking into deep mud. Small gnats whined about him; the water stank and he closed his lips tight not to swallow any.

The Watchboat came through the drowned forest in silence, a sleek, black-painted ship, sharp-prowed, her silver eye glinting in the green light. She moved quickly, drawn by the current; on board Raffi could see men in the rigging and on the decks, leaning out, looking anxiously down.

Still as leaf-shadow, they watched the enemy pass, the wake sending tiny waves to lap against Raffi's lips. He turned away.

Finally, when she was gone, Galen sat up, his stare full of hate. "I hope they outrun her." He leaned over and grabbed Raffi's arm; tugging his feet free, Raffi gasped, "I can't get up. Too slippery. I'll wade."

Splashing as little as possible, he struggled along the side of the trunk; to his relief the water quickly became shallower until it was down to his waist. He shivered, rubbing off green slime, water running from his clothes.

Underfoot, the mud was hard to tug out of; the disturbed water was brackish; twigs floated in it, and sediment rose in clouds.

He splashed the whining insects off, and saw that Galen had slid into the water with him, and that what had been sea was swamp.

It took them over an hour to come ashore properly, and by then the sun was almost setting. They stopped to eat a little and change their clothes, and then started off, stiff with tiredness, walking west.

Galen hurried them on. He knew that if the ship was caught the crew would talk, and if the Watch found out their destination they were in trouble. But more than that, the hunger for Tasceron drove him like a pain; all his blinded senses longed for it, to feel the secrets that were there, the power that might be hidden. Silent, he climbed and scrambled relentlessly over the salt-marsh and through the rough scrub, Carys and Raffi struggling to keep up. No one spoke. The journey became a nightmare of cold, cut hands, breathlessness. For miles they walked into a darkness that seemed to grow thicker before them, even though all seven of the moons rose one by one to form the great Arch, each strange and eerie in its own light, the pearl-pale Karnos, red Pyra, the crescent of Agramon at the zenith.

Then, on a low hill, Galen stopped suddenly. Raffi

sank down, too sore to be glad, doubled over the stitch in his side. It was a while before he lifted his head, breathing deeply.

Below them lay Darkness. A valley of night. Tall spires rose out of it here and there; far, far in the distance strange domes were shadowed with steams and vapors. The blackness was heavy; it stretched as far as he could see. Behind him Carys brushed back her muddy hair; Galen stood upright, saying nothing.

They all knew this was Tasceron.

The Wounded City

16

Tasceron, O Tasceron.
I mourn you, my city.
Your great halls are broken open;
The Darkness has come over you.
Rats eat the finery of your kings.

The Lament for Tasceron

CARYS CRAWLED BACK around the tangle of thorns and sucked a scratched hand. "Useless," she muttered. "They're searching every pack and wagon, looking at everyone's papers. I got close enough to listen. We'll never get in this way."

If anything, Raffi was relieved. He peered through the branches at the city gate. It was a gaunt, dark turret, jutting from the wall, and through the gloom that seemed to seep from it he could make out muffled men and a short line of wagons waiting to pass through.

"Bringing food?" he wondered.

"Probably." Galen stared out, his eyes moving along

the line. Then he glanced up at the walls. The double ramparts of the Evil City were huge and black, smooth, Maker-built. There was no chink or window in them; the great stones stretched away into the eerie dark, and Raffi guessed they ran like that for miles, endless miles. The travelers might walk along them for weeks and not find a breach.

"And if we did it would only be guarded," he muttered aloud.

Galen turned, squatting. In the murk his face was only an edge of shadow, but when he spoke Raffi knew that harsh, determined tone, and felt uneasy.

"I have an idea. It's dangerous, but it seems the only way. These wagons—"

"We're not going to hide in one!" Raffi caught his arm. "Galen, they search them! Stab the flour sacks!"

"Not inside." Galen shook him off irritably. "Underneath."

They were silent. He went on quickly. "They're strong, and small. The axle bars don't look too far apart, and there's a wooden brace between them. We should be able to crawl above it and lie there, just under the planks."

The Wounded City

"It's crazy," Raffi breathed.

"What about your leg?" Carys asked.

The keeper glared at her. "I'll manage. Once we're all through the guard-post, we drop off and meet." He nodded at a tall spire that rose in the darkness. "That building. Or as near to it as we can get. Understand?"

Carys thought, then nodded, reluctant.

"Raffi?"

Shaking his head, he said, "There's got to be a better way . . ."

"There's not." Galen gave him a sharp look. "Trust me, Raffi. I'll take the pack. Let's get nearer."

They worked their way through the scrub to the road, opposite the third wagon in the line. Two men leaned on the front of it, talking. Their voices were clear in the stillness. Far back, a dog barked. Galen touched Carys on the shoulder. She gave one exasperated look at Raffi, then dropped to a crouch and sprinted soundlessly out to the wagon. She slipped under it like a shadow.

"What if they find her?" Raffi whispered, appalled.

"Then they'll find all of us. You next."

The wagons jolted forward; the pack-beasts, mostly

mules, plodding a few weary steps among shouts and one whip-crack. Galen touched Raffi and he ran, stooping low. Halfway there he froze, heart thudding, as the wagoner walked by, kicking the wheels, but the man's back was to him, and in seconds Raffi was ducking underneath, the stink of mule droppings close to his face. Grabbing the front axle, he hauled his chest up over the brace, jamming his feet wide against the planks at the back.

Above him the wagon base was bowed with its load—Galen hadn't thought about that. It lay heavy on his back now, and in a moment of terror he imagined the Watchmen climbing on board and crushing him, and he gripped the greasy axle tight, his cheek lying sideways, the stink of dung in his nostrils.

It was a long time before they moved.

The first jolt almost shook him off; he grabbed tighter, feeling the axle slither and turn. Wrapping himself around the narrow brace, he clung tight, arms and legs aching, hoping he wouldn't slip under it. Then they stopped again and he could loosen his hold.

Gradually the cold seeped into him. After an age of stopping and starting he felt exhausted; on top of the long walk from the ship the strain made his muscles knots of pain, and he was terrified of falling. Splinters of sharp wood jabbed his hands, and the puddles on the muddy roadway splashed his face. Then the wagon stopped again. They were still for so long this time he almost slept; only a wild grab kept him up. After that, a long progress. Looking down, he saw the wheels were crunching in gravel, leaving deep ruts over earlier ones.

They stopped.

"Papers," a voice snarled.

Raffi gripped tight. The man was close. Boots splashed in the grit; he caught the word *barley* and then *a couple of sacks of birds.*

The footsteps moved to the back. Hens squawked right in his ear, and the shaven boards on his back seemed heavier. Gritting his teeth, he waited for the man to climb on, tiny grains of flour and chaff drifting on him in clouds from the opened seams.

The silence was the worst. Axle grease was all over his hands by now, they slipped constantly, and he had to cling on with knees and fingertips, praying to Flain to send him strength to last out. The stiffness of his own muscles tormented him; he sweated, despite the cold, to think he might not be able to unclench them if he needed to run.

A sound, to the left. Cautiously he twisted his head. The boots were back. They stood close by the left front wheel, one up on the rim, the other turned aside. With a hiss of breath, Raffi gripped so tight his hands ached.

The Watchman had dropped something. A coin.

It lay there in the mud. For a terrible second, Raffi stared at it; then the man had bent and was groping for it, his face close to Raffi's, the long straggly hair falling over his eyes. His hand reached under the wheel and touched the coin.

Then he was gone, like a nightmare.

Icy with sweat, Raffi clung on as the wagon began to move, lurching and swaying. The shadow of the gate fell over him; briefly there were paved stones, the hollow echo of hooves in a covered place. Then more mud.

He breathed a prayer. He was in the city.

RAFFI CLUNG TIGHT till the wagon came to a corner and slowed; then he let go and slid down with a thump, unable to stop himself. The street was dim; the wagon rolled noisily over him, its great wheels creaking high on each side. He lay there till it had gone, then picked himself up painfully, his hands so rigid he could hardly open them. Standing upright made him gasp, his knees weak.

"Raffi!"

The hiss was from a doorway; briefly Carys's face showed in a patch of light. "Over here!"

Limping across, he slid in beside her, down to a crouch.

"All right?"

"Half dead." Rubbing his aching arms, he looked up. "Curse Galen to the pit, and all his ideas!"

"It seems to have worked." She sounded amused; looking at her he saw she was filthy, her face smeared with grease. He must look as bad.

"Where now?"

"The building with the spire. It must be close."

They were in a narrow street, evil-smelling, the houses leaning overhead. There was no light, not even from the moons. He wondered if their light ever reached down here, through the blackness of the blighted city. He could glimpse drifts and wraiths of smoke around him, as if the wind could never blow it away. The vapors rose from drains and sewers; anyone who lived here in the rotting city had long forgotten the warmth of the sun. Deep underground, Tasceron was burning. That was its punishment, and for them, its safety.

A rat scuttled down the street. Raffi caught hold of Carys and they ran close to the walls of the dim buildings, stumbling over rubble and holes. A peculiar low screech made them stop and look up in terror, and they saw above the house tops a great dark shape float across the gloomy gap.

"What was that!"

Carys shook her head. "I daren't think."

When they found it, the building was ruined. A great hole gaped in the wall; above them the spire crumbled into darkness.

"Looks like it's going to fall down," Raffi muttered.

"Maybe." Carys glanced around. "Is he here?"

"I don't know." Raffi rubbed his face. He was so tired, and already the city confused him, the smoke fogging his sense-lines. Nothing felt clear. He climbed in through the hole after her.

The Wounded City

It was pitch-black. They edged forward a step.

"Galen?" Raffi whispered. "Galen, are you here?"

The crack of the tinderbox answered him. In a far corner a flame grew; it showed a dark face turning toward them. Carys grinned and took a step in, but Raffi grabbed her, rigid. "It's not him."

The face was filthy. A great burn-mark seared one cheek and, as the man raised himself up, they saw that half of his hair was gone, and the burned scalp was painted with a hideous snake, its great fangs wide. He uncurled himself; stained blankets fell from him; he muttered something and to his right another sleeper groaned and sat up.

Suddenly Raffi saw they were all around him; huddled, uncurling shapes. "Out!" he said. "Get out! Now!"

She was already moving. As he fled he heard shouts; in corners faces rose up and stared at him, grotesque faces without eyes, scarred, skeletal with hunger. Leaping the wall, he flung spell-binds behind him, but it was hard to think; the horror of the uncurling creatures made him race into the darkness heedless, around a corner, down a street, until a shadow stepped out in front of him and grabbed him with both hands.

"Keep still. Keep still!"

"Galen . . ." He was shuddering, breathless.

"I know. They're not following." The keeper dragged him to a dim corner and crouched, while Raffi drew long shuddering breaths, sick with fear, listening to Carys explain. She wasn't afraid, he thought bitterly. And yet he was the one with all the powers. All the defenses.

"Beggars," Galen said grimly. "Or worse. We must get farther in. Right away from the gate. Then we can rest." He looked down at Raffi. "Can you walk?"

Ashamed, Raffi pulled upright. Without a word, Galen turned away.

They traveled down three long streets, then a network of narrow alleys where the rats scrabbled, across wide squares, empty and silent, where only a broken fountain trickled. Deep into the city Galen led them, without direction, looking only for somewhere safe. On each side the doorways were black and sinister. Broken shutters creaked. For Raffi it was a nightmare of weariness and pain; the darkness was foul and in it moved voices and ghosts that strained at his senses, and beyond them was the memory of some great disaster, a horror that seeped and smoked from the very walls and ruins.

Finally, Galen stopped. He searched among the shadows and found a small room in the back of a building; once a house, with a courtyard of black weeds. They searched the place twice and found no one, but Galen wouldn't be satisfied until he had blocked the doorway the best he could with splintered wood. Then, without a fire or bothering to eat, they lay down and slept.

Deep below his ear, deep in the earth, Raffi felt the city smolder and crackle.

17

Many lies have been told about the fall of Tasceron. The truth is that whatever weapon of chaos the Order tried to use against us blew up in their faces. As will all their follies.

Rule of the Watch

Journal of Carys Arrin
Time unknown, Cyraxday(?)
18.16.546

It was a crazy plan. As soon as Galen came out with it, I knew we were bound to be caught, so I made sure I went first.

The Watchmen on the gate were thorough, and knew their job. I was out from under that wagon and dragged into the turret in seconds, and it took a great deal of argument to convince them who I was. I knew the passwords, of course, the name of a Watchlord, and I have my agent's insignia on a chain under my clothes. Still, I had to bribe them in the end. And I didn't tell them who Galen was, just that I was working undercover with two spies, who should be allowed to think no one knew about them.

It worked; we're in, and Galen and Raffi don't know. And yet the gate guards will have sold their knowledge on to someone higher, without doubt.

They're both still asleep. The encounter with that nest of horrors scared Raffi—the shock of it, I suppose. The keeper works him too hard; he can't be ready for all this yet. And on the ship it was Raffi who did the weather-warding.

That unnerved me. It's quite clear the Watch have lied to us, and that makes me angry. The Order do have powers and they're real. It makes me wonder how much else I don't know. The Watch wants all relics—to destroy them, according to our teachers—and yet, I wonder. What if someone high up wants this power for themselves?

This is heresy, of course. If anyone reads it I'll be finished. There was a boy once, in the Watchhouse, I forget his name. We were about seven, and it was in the courtyard, the grim stony place they used to let us play in for ten minutes a day. Three of us were under one coat for warmth. He said, this boy, that his grandfather had told him that the Makers were real men, and that their power was enormous. And that he thought the Watch had been wrong to kill so many of the Order.

Someone must have reported what he said, because a week later he was taken away, and he never came back. Like a lot of others . . .

"I DIDN'T KNOW you could write."

Carys closed the journal with a gasp, and spun around. Galen was sitting up against the wall, watching her. For a moment she was lost for an answer. Then Watchtraining surged up in her; she shook her head and laughed. "You scared me!"

"I'm sorry."

She slipped the journal into her bag. "My mother taught me, a long time ago. I don't know how she learned— probably with one of the Order. There were many keepers when she was young."

"Indeed there were." Galen frowned, rubbing his stubbly chin. "But it seemed to be in a language strange to me."

For a moment she looked at him. Then she said, "It's in code."

"Code?"

"I made it up myself. In case the Watch should ever get hold of it. It's the story of my search."

"Then we're in there—the boy and I?"

"Only briefly." She shook her head. "I've changed your names. No one would ever be able to read it."

"I hope not." He pulled the pack over and began to rummage inside. "They say the Watch have men skilled in codes and secret signs. If they caught you with it they'd force you to explain it."

She nodded. "You mean get rid of it."

He passed her some bread. "It would be wise."

Wanting to change the subject, she said, "Shall we wake Raffi?"

"No. Let him sleep."

They ate in silence, listening. A long way off something banged, and once Carys thought she heard voices, but the city was as dark and silent as before, the only sound a faint rushing, as if water ran nearby. She knew it must be late in the day, but outside the blocked doorway the blackness still hung.

"Does it ever get light here?"

The Wounded City

Galen shook his head. In the tiny candle flame his hawk-face looked tired and drawn; he tugged the string out of his hair and raked his fingers through it. "Not since the Destruction."

"What happened?" she asked, chewing the hard bread.

"You know. Or you ought to."

"Tell me again." She did know, but she was curious to hear how the Order told the story.

Galen gave her a hard look. Then he said, "The Order had its most holy sites here. Somewhere in the city, buried deep under layers of other buildings, were the secret places, the houses of the Makers. The House of Trees, the Nemeta, the Hall of the Slain. Where exactly they were is not known now. The Emperor's palace was here too. In the last hours of the siege, when men were fighting in the streets and the Emperor knew the war was lost, it's said he sent a message to Mardoc Archkeeper, to warn him. That was late on Pyrasnight, about eight o'clock. Two hours later the palace fell. The Emperor was killed at the Phoenix Gate—you know about that?"

She nodded, silent. The Emperor had been killed by

accident, by some fool of a Watchsergeant. The Watchlords had thrown the man into the demon-pit at Maar in their fury. They had wanted the Emperor alive.

"And then," Galen went on, his voice dropping, "late in the night, with the hordes of the Watch looting and spoiling the city, there was a great trembling of the ground. Buildings fell. Whole districts crumbled. Fires erupted underground. And from somewhere deep among the alleys and courts of the old palace, the Darkness came. They say it spread like ink over a map, blotting out the moons and stars, filling alleys, doorways, oozing out from cellars and pits and manholes in the streets, up sewers and drains.

"What it was, how it was released, no one knows now, or whether it was meant to happen. So much is lost, Carys!" He sighed, scratching his cheek. "The Archkeeper escaped. He was caught three months later and died under torture, but I don't believe he told them where the Houses were. If he had, they'd be in ruins, and the Watch would be gloating. They want all the power they can get." He spat, savagely, to one side.

Carys was silent. She took some more bread. "The

Watch say Mardoc tried to bring the Makers back. That he had some relic which was so powerful that its explosion would make the city burn forever."

"They would!" Galen watched Raffi stir and roll over. "But Mardoc got out. Something that big would have killed him."

"And what about the Crow?"

She said it slowly, deliberately. Raffi, half awake, stared at her in astonishment; Galen slid his eyes to her.

"What about him?" he asked, after a cold moment.

Carys smiled, but Raffi knew she was uneasy. "All right. I suppose I should tell you. I listened at Lerin's door."

Galen's hand clutched his stick; for a moment Raffi thought he would use it on her and scrambled up, gasping, "No!" but Carys only laughed scornfully. "I'm not your scholar, Galen. Don't think you can beat me into silence."

He stared at her, and Raffi caught the strange taints of anger and despair that wreathed him. Finally, in a voice choked with wrath, he said, "How much did you hear?"

"That the Crow is here in Tasceron. That you'd had messages. That you thought, if you could find him, he could destroy the Watch."

She leaned forward, her hair glossy in the flame light. "That was all. I'm sorry, Galen, but I had to know what was happening! I'm here to find my father, and I don't know where to start. But the Crow! With him we could do anything!"

The silence was terrible. Raffi pulled the blanket around himself and rubbed his face nervously with a filthy hand. Galen sat absolutely still, watching Carys with a bitter stare that made her hand creep toward the crossbow. When he spoke his voice was hoarse. "Never spy on me again, girl. Never."

The threat was cold, and real. Chilled, she nodded. It took all her courage to say, "I want to stay with you. I want to help."

But Galen got up abruptly. Taking his stick, he flung the wood from the doorway. "Stay here. I'll be back."

"Where are you going?" Raffi asked.

"Out!" The keeper stared at him grimly. "To breathe!"

When he was gone, they both relaxed. Raffi drank

some water from the flask and passed it across; kneeling up, he felt for the bread in the pack.

"Was I wrong to tell him?" Carys asked quietly.

He shrugged. "I don't know. We'd have had to explain to you soon, I suppose. And he would have found out. He's a keeper."

"He hadn't yet," she said drily.

Raffi glanced at her, then away. "How could you listen at the door, Carys! We thought we could trust you!"

Looking down at the flask, she said, "You can. Of course you can."

GALEN WAS A LONG time away. When he finally came back he said nothing about Carys or the Crow. Crouching, he crammed the blankets into the pack. "There's a fountain not far from here, still running. The water's tainted, but drinkable. And you can wash."

His own hair was wet and his face clean.

"Then what?" Carys asked.

He gave her a bitter glare. "You'll find out."

They crossed a maze of small lanes, following the

splashing sound, then turned into an open space among tall buildings, whose tops were lost in dark smoke. The fountain was astonishingly hot, the water steaming from spouts and holes among stones that had once been white, but were now streaked with soot. Carys and Raffi drank and washed their arms and faces, while Galen kept watch, eyeing the narrow streets intently. The water was pungent and sour, despite the green lichens that grew out of it.

When they'd finished and were pulling their coats on, Galen said, "Now listen to me. We're making for the old citadel and the ruins of the palace. They should be somewhere to the south, deep within the city. It may take us days. The farther in we go, the more dangerous it will be. Watchpatrols for sure, but I suspect they'll keep to the wider streets. Even the Watch will be wary of the others here."

"Is there anyone?" Carys muttered, looking at the dim openings.

"Don't be a fool. There are thieves, footpads, murderers, all the dregs of the world. And madmen—this place is haunted by them. Other creatures too—beasts swollen and warped by the great Destruction, made savage by the dark. It's not called the Evil City for nothing."

Carys pulled a face, then checked her crossbow. Galen drew Raffi aside. "Sense-lines. As many as you can."

Raffi nodded unhappily. "The trouble is, the buildings—or the dark—something's confusing me. There are too many echoes here."

"Try! We're depending on you now!"

Carys was watching them. Galen picked up the pack and slung it on. Then he stood upright, a tall shadow in the steamy gloom. "Keep close. And keep silent."

They set off into a narrow alley that stank of decay and skeats—the packs of small wild dogs Raffi had seen once before. Halfway down, it was blocked with fallen timbers; crawling under these they found themselves at a crossroads. Six black lanes led away into gloom like the spokes of a wheel. Everything was silent.

With a quick glance at Raffi, Galen strode into the farthest left. A very quick glance. But Carys had seen it.

Through the next few hours, she came to see that it was Raffi who was leading them. Sensing direction in the eternal gloom of Tasceron was almost impossible—there were no moons and no sunrise, and the labyrinth of buildings was intricate and unknown. But a keeper's soul was linked with the earth, deep with stone and tree and soil, and they felt the magnetic lines deep inside themselves. Or so they said. So Raffi knew where the south was. But did Galen? Once, when he walked straight past a turning and Raffi had to call him back, she saw something in his face that puzzled and chilled her. A wretchedness. Almost despair.

There was no time to think about it. They soon found that Tasceron was inhabited. Coming around a bend, they heard voices, and pressing back quickly into shadow, they watched a group of armed men cross between the houses. They wore remnants of armor, ill-patched and rusted; some covered with ragged surcoats and jerkins of what looked like skeat fur. Two wore helmets.

These were the Watch. Close up, they were a ragged rabble, but they moved fast, with discipline; their swords were bright and when Raffi saw the grim knot of prisoners they dragged behind, tied wrist and waist, he shivered and pressed back into the doorway.

For a long time the tramp of feet echoed in the ruins. Finally Galen said, "We were lucky they didn't have hounds."

After that they moved more carefully. The maze of dark courts and tunnels bewildered Carys; she knew she'd never find her way back. They walked for hours; the world shrank to brick, rubble, stairs, the sad remnants of gardens, blackened and fire-scarred. Once they heard a great roaring far off and stood rigid, but it didn't come again. Often rats scattered among the broken houses; clouds of biting insects infested some areas, and everywhere the owls hooted: great sooty-gray owls that swooped down the murky alleys silently.

Twice they crossed rivers on bridges that were crumbling to pieces, and between their feet they saw the black oily water racing below the holes. At the second bridge something leaped out and caught hold of Raffi, mumbling snarling words; Galen gave it a swift blow with his staff and it scuttled, crouched low, into the dark.

They ran then, till they were clear of the place.

"What was that!" Carys gasped.

Galen scowled her into silence, listening to their own echoes, endlessly pattering.

"Are you all right?" she whispered to Raffi.

He nodded wearily. "What a place. Can the Crow really be here?"

But Galen was gone, and they hurried after him.

Later they paused briefly to eat, but soon moved on, always keeping to the clearer streets if they could. Some alleys were so evil-smelling, so filled with stench and black mist, that Galen avoided them, despite the time lost.

Then, under one overhanging house, Carys paused. Her boots were coated with slimy weed, making her slip; she scraped it off hastily. Darkness closed over her. She glanced up and stared, paralyzed with astonishment. The thing was black, huge and winged. Its evil face had tiny eyes; hooked talons slashed at her.

"Get down!"

Galen's yell made her drop. With a whistle of stinking breath the thing swooped over her, its call eerie and wild. Rolling, she jabbed a bolt into the bow. The thing flew back, its claws raked her face; she kicked aside and fired. The creature shrieked, a blot of darkness against the gloom.

"Run!" Galen was yelling. "There are more!"

The Wounded City

Scrambling up, she limped after him, fumbling for another bolt, leaping a shattered wall. Looking up made her skin crawl. The sky was infested with the things; they dropped noiselessly, flapping, screeching, so fast she could hardly make them out.

Ahead, the street turned a corner. Racing around it, she caught up with Raffi, ducking with a yell as one of the things screamed low, its claws snatching at her hair. Then she slammed into a wall, hands flat. Turning, she slid to a crouch, jerking up the bow, hearing Galen yell with fury.

The alley was a dead end.

They were trapped.

18

Out of Darkness shall come Light.
Pilgrims shall walk on the Roads of
the Sky.

Apocalypse of Tamar

RAFFI BUCKLED AGAINST THE WALL next to Carys. She had her bow up; for a second he saw the bolt, then it was gone. But there was so much screeching overhead he couldn't tell if any of the things had been hurt.

Galen fell beside him, ducking, arms over head. "Lights!" he yelled. "Mind-lights!"

Raffi was appalled. "I can't!"

"TRY!"

He tried. He searched for his inner eye; it was buried deep in his mind, closed tight. Opening it took an age; dimly, far off, he heard the shrieks of the attacking beasts and Carys yelling with anger. Then he saw a tiny purple light and caught hold of it, made it swell and brighten. It was in the darkness before him, wobbling, expanding; now it was glowing and crackling, and briefly he saw Galen turn, and Carys's eyes wide in amazement. The pale globe pulsed in the alley, it gleamed on the black wings that drove straight at him. He leaped back, cracked his head on the wall, and staggered, half stunned.

The globe popped like a soap bubble.

Darkness swallowed them; the sky shrieked.

"Do something!" Carys was crouched over Raffi, looking up, her face cut. "You're the keeper, Galen!" she yelled, furious. "Do something!"

Their eyes met. In that instant she knew, without doubt, that there was nothing he could do. He was powerless.

Then he stood up recklessly, stepping out from the wall.

At once the light came. It came suddenly, a great slot of it streaming out, bright yellow light, the first light they had seen for days, and it dazzled them as it swung open across the filthy alley, spilling on black walls and dead moss, and over Galen, as he spun around, his face sharp with thrown shadow. Above it the black night-things screamed in rage, flashes of talon and wing. Then they swooped and were gone.

Carefully, in the sudden hush, Carys picked herself up. Raffi followed, one hand flat against the wall.

"Am I interrupting you?" a dry voice asked from the doorway.

None of them answered. The man gave a strange bark of laughter and stepped out, and Raffi forgot the pain in his head.

Because it wasn't a man. It was a Sekoi.

It was a little taller than Galen, and thin, with the starved look they had. A long, seven-fingered hand held the lantern up. On its sharp face a tribe mark zigzagged under one eye; the short fur was a brindled gray. It wore old patched clothes of green and brown.

"Come inside," it said. "Come inside."

After a second Carys obeyed; the others came behind her and the Sekoi bolted the door.

Galen shook off his shock. "We should thank you," he murmured.

"Indeed you should. You owe me your lives, keeper."
It pointed a thin finger at Galen's chest and smiled.

Galen growled. "What makes you think . . ."

The Sekoi put its small mouth very close to Galen's ear
and whispered solemnly, "An owl told me." Its eyes were
bright; a strange purr of amusement came from its throat.
Galen looked disgusted.

"What were those things?" Carys wiped the blood
from her cheek.

"We call them draxi." The creature looked at her
closely. "Half bird, half beast. Hideous and dangerous—
one of Kest's mistakes. But they don't like light."

"Useful to know," she muttered.

Swinging the lamp, the Sekoi turned. "Up now."

They were in a tiny dim hall, with a spiral staircase in
one corner. The creature ran up quickly and they hurried
after it, the lantern light bouncing off the walls ahead.
After five minutes they were breathless and their legs felt
like lead; Galen was limping heavily. Finally, turning a
corner, they found the Sekoi waiting for them, leaning
against the wall biting its nails.

It smiled kindly. "Tired? A long way to go yet."

"To where?" Carys demanded.

"Safety." It picked up its lantern. "Careful now. There are holes."

It led them through an arch to an uneven chamber, where wooden planking seemed to have been laid over a sloping, swelling floor. The roof above was so low they had to crawl. Raffi guessed that the floor itself was the roof of some vault or dome below; once he put his hand through a hole and felt nothing but emptiness. The dust was so thick that he made handprints in it, and the lantern, hanging around the Sekoi's neck, threw wild, swinging shadows.

They crossed three vaults like this, each one more cramped. In the last the roof scraped their backs. Galen slithered to a halt. "Where are you taking us?" he growled.

Ahead, they caught the Sekoi's grin in a swing of the lantern.

"Safety lies in secrecy, keeper. You know that." It turned and crawled on. Galen gripped his stick and swore.

Finally the Sekoi came to a tiny door in the wall and opened it. "If you fear heights," its voice said, rather muffled, "don't look down."

Coming through the door and straightening up with relief, Raffi found himself on a curved balcony; a rail was to his left, and to his right a wall that glinted here and there. He saw remnants of faces, giant hands, gold, scarlet, and blue. Galen caught the Sekoi's arm roughly.

"What are these?" His voice echoed, hissing in far distances.

Impatiently the Sekoi glared at him, then held the lantern up. "Mosaics. Images. Of the Star-people. The ones you call the Makers. This, look, is Flain."

Galen, astonished, made the gesture of peace; Raffi did the same. In the weak light the enormous face of a man gazed down sternly at them, pieced together from marble, porphyry, precious stones. Parts of it had been hacked out. Staring at the vast eyes, all at once Raffi sensed echoes; lost sense-lines. Turning, he caught hold of the rail and leaned over.

"Be careful!" the Sekoi hissed.

The darkness was immense. A gust of wind blew against him; he glimpsed appalling distances, the floor so far below that he gripped the rail tight with cold fingers, feeling the world swing away under him. Dizzy, he hung on.

The Wounded City

They were above some vast empty place, once a temple. The wind howled through its shattered windows. In the darkness he made out glimpses of pillars, fallen altars, smashed statues. Awed, Raffi gazed down, feeling Galen beside him.

"One of ours."

"Once." The keeper was chilled; the destruction filled him with bitterness.

"Hurry now." The Sekoi tapped their backs. "And keep away from the rail. It breaks."

Tiny in the immense curve of the dome, they followed the star of the lantern, clinging flat to the wall in places where the rail had gone and only emptiness hung. Once, far down in that blackness, something small clattered. The Sekoi whipped its coat over the light; breathless, they waited in the pitch dark.

"Rats," Carys breathed finally.

The Sekoi sniffed. "Maybe," it said quietly.

They went on more carefully. Another endless set of stairs, this time between two tight walls. At the top, the Sekoi blew out the lantern.

"What are you doing!" Galen roared from the dark.

They heard a door unlocking. A slot opened in the wall, and to their immense astonishment, sunlight blinded them. With a yell of delight Carys jumped down into it, onto the broad expanse of a roof that spread far and flat into the sky. The sun shone; faint clouds drifted. It was about three o'clock in the afternoon, and one of the moons hung high and still like a smudge of chalk dust.

"We're above the Darkness!" Raffi stepped down, awed.

The air was clean and cold. Far, far off, the mountains were green in the sun. All the colors exhilarated Raffi; he ran to the parapet and gazed down. Below him, he saw only the smoke and darkness of Tasceron; a black vapor, out of which rose spires and domes, high roofs, spindly towers, and joining them all, a fantastic rickety structure of ladders and bridges, walkways, ropes, high in the sky.

"What is this?" Galen asked.

"The way the Sekoi travel. None of us likes the Darkness, keeper, any more than you. So we live up here, when we come to the city. Which is not often." It turned graciously. "My tribe built this. At the moment I'm the only one here."

On the roof was a scatter of tents, patched and sewn, and some bigger huts, made from wood nailed inexpertly together. The Sekoi took them to the nearest, went in, and tossed out some cushions.

"Be comfortable," it said, and disappeared inside.

Suddenly worn out, Raffi crumpled onto the silk and lay back in luxury, closing his eyes in the sun's warmth. Galen sat beside him, easing his sore leg. Carys watched.

The keeper looked at her; she felt awkward and uneasy. At last she muttered, "You should have told me."

Raffi opened his eyes. "Told you what?"

"Not you. Him."

Galen's eyes were black, like a bird's; he eased the green and jet crystals from inside his coat and ran his fingers over them. "Nothing to do with you," he said fiercely.

Raffi sat up. Anxious, he watched them both.

"Of course it is," she snapped. "We're in this together. If I'd known you'd lost all . . ."

His glare stopped her. Raffi looked away. "When did you find out?" Galen murmured.

"Down there. In the alley. Though I'd thought before that something was wrong." She kept her eyes on Galen. "No wonder you want so much to find the Crow."

Before he could answer, the Sekoi was back, carrying a great platter of fruit. "This is all my people eat," it said, "so it will have to do."

"Where did you get it?" Raffi asked, taking a dew-apple.

"There are ways. Some I brought with me. There are places to buy in the city, but they're brief, furtive, dirty. Knife-in-the-back. Not safe."

Carys took some fruit and ate it hungrily; Galen was slower, and silent. There was clean water to drink, flavored by a sweet sugar that made Raffi realize his thirst.

It was only when the plate was empty that the Sekoi said, "And how is dear Alberic?"

Galen looked up. "How do you know so much about us?"

It purred again, the long fingers brushing its neck-fur.

The Wounded City

"The Order have many secrets, keeper; so do we. Certainly I knew Alberic would send someone after me. He knew I would bring his gold here. And as I said, the owls told me you were in the district." It smirked, showing small sharp teeth. "I gather I'm not your main interest though. Did I just hear the word *Crow?*"

Galen gave Carys a vicious stare. "It appears you did."

The Sekoi shook its head sadly. "You're foolish, keeper, ever to have come here. Nothing of the Makers is left. We'd know."

Raffi looked at Galen, but the keeper's face was hard. "I think you're wrong. Tomorrow, I want you to take us where we might find some of the Order."

The Sekoi scratched the fur over one eye. "The Order!"

"There must be someone left."

It seemed to be thinking. "Maybe. It will be dangerous."

"Good." Morosely Galen watched the sun sink into a red cloud. "All the better."

Journal of Carys Arrin
Date unknown

Galen meditates. For hours. His prayers are all that keep him going. I don't feel glad that I found out about this. It makes things easier for me, and explains a lot, but . . .

Well, I feel sorry for him.

I must be getting soft.

19

You will find that the Sekoi can often be bought—their greed for gold is well known. What they do with it and where they hide it have never been discovered. Their storytelling is some form of hypnosis and may affect the unwary. Keep away from them. They are of no importance.

Rule of the Watch

WHEN RAFFI WOKE, the Sekoi was sitting next to him, its long hands curled under its chin. "At last," it said. "You're awake."

Carys was pacing impatiently, Galen saying the morning litany cross-legged in one corner of the roof. As he stood up, the Sekoi said, "I'm afraid I have no breakfast for you. Should we leave now?"

"Wait." Galen took the last of Lerin's food from the pack and shared it around. The Sekoi took a small piece of cheese and nibbled it daintily, pulling a few faces. It swallowed, bravely.

"Exquisite."

"Stale," Raffi muttered.

"Really?" The creature's fur was fine over its face; Raffi noticed the yellow brightness of its eyes. Abruptly it said, "I should tell you that the Watch know you're here."

Galen almost choked. "Here?"

"In the city."

"How?" Raffi gasped.

"Someone must have told them."

"But no one's seen us!"

The Sekoi purred, amused. "Don't be fooled, small scholar. Many will have seen you. You may not have seen them. The city is full of eyes and spies. I've heard there are patrols out looking for you."

Galen looked bleak. He ran a hand through his black hair. Carys glanced away. Her heart was thudding but she kept calm. It had to be the Watchmen at the gate. Rapidly she thought it out. Now someone higher up knew she was here—but not who the others were; not yet. This would make it harder, though. Everywhere would be watched.

As if it read her thoughts, the Sekoi stood and stretched

lazily. "But no patrols where we go, masters." It turned and waved a web of fingers airily. "We walk in the sky."

The sun glittered on the highest tips of the city, rising from the dark mists below. The Sekoi led them to a corner of the roof and leaped elegantly over a narrow gap to a small bridge that swayed under its weight. Raffi followed; clutching the rope to hold himself, he glanced down and saw the gap between the roofs was filled to the brim with the swirling smoke. Just as well, he thought, imagining how high up they were.

"Move!" Galen yelled. "Hurry up."

Raffi frowned. The Relic Master's temper was getting worse the farther they went.

ALL MORNING THEY FOLLOWED the Sekoi over the intricate sky-road. It was cobbled together: a chain of bridges, rope-swings, planks, and stairway on stairway of trembling, wind-battered steps, around precarious domes and steeples, nested on by birds, stained by rain and the stench from the murk below. They climbed among chimneys, broken tiles, balustrades and balconies, belfries where the cracked bells still hung, filthy with bird droppings, silent since the city's fall. It was cold up here, exhilarating; Raffi found himself almost happy, just being in the sun again. He could see here, he knew where he was. He sent sense-lines spinning into the clouds.

Finally though, he saw the road was running out. Fewer and fewer buildings pierced the dark, and some of the aerial stairways were broken. Twice they had to turn back. When the Sekoi stopped, on the parapet of a small dome, it helped Raffi up with a furred hand.

"Not dizzy?"

He shook his head. "Though I would be if I could see the ground."

"Ah." The creature leaned out and looked down. "So even Darkness has its uses. Worthy of your Litany, that idea." It glanced back at Galen. "I wonder if that's true of all darkness."

Raffi stared at the Sekoi, but it winked at him and said no more. After a moment Raffi said, "You didn't tell us your name."

"We don't tell our names, little scholar. Not to outsiders." It tapped the zigzag mark under its eye. "That's my name. It would just sound like a snarl to you. Didn't teach you much about us, did he?"

"The Sekoi hate water and the dark," Raffi quoted quickly. "They imperil their souls with riches; they tell intricate lies."

The creature winced. "I see." It made a small face. "Well, it's accurate. Gold is precious to us. The sorrows of Kest come to everyone, even us, who were here before the Starmen. But now, I'm afraid, this is as far as we go. Come and see."

Without waiting for the others, it walked around the dome, balancing easily on a narrow flaking ledge of stone, putting one foot delicately before the other. Raffi inched after it, arms wide, holding on to moldings and carved faces that crumbled in his hands. Breathless, the wind plucking at him, he sidled around to a wider part and found the Sekoi sitting, its legs dangling over the abyss.

"There," it said softly. "The great wound."

Before them, as far as they could see, the Darkness lay unbroken. Remote in the distance, the sun caught the tops of other towers, but the heart of the city was black and drowned, with nothing left high enough to pierce the eternal murk. Here the Darkness was vast; it steamed and churned, almost thick enough to walk on.

"So we go back down, then?" Carys said. She had come around silently; now she watched Galen balance, the staff strapped to his back.

"Down and down," the Sekoi said mournfully. "That is, if you still want to."

"We do," the keeper said at once.

"Pity. All the dangers lie down there."

"That's nothing to me," Galen growled.

The Sekoi raised an eyebrow at Raffi. "If you say so."

A door in the dome led them to a stair, and they followed it down. After only minutes the light faded away; by the time they'd passed the third cracked window, darkness was back around them, and the Sekoi had to light its lantern and hold it up. Rats scattered all down the stairs.

Raffi felt his heart sink back into gloom. The sense-lines dimmed. From somewhere down below, the stench of something rotting made him retch. At the bottom of the stairs the Sekoi put the lantern out and hid it. Following through twists and turns of walls, they found themselves in a ruined courtyard. Picking its way through broken pillars and the leaning column of a sundial, the Sekoi paused under an archway. Beyond it the alley was black.

"Where now?" Galen muttered.

The creature eyed him. Then it said, "A few streets away is a story-house. A place where my people gather. We may find someone there who can help. Remember, keep silent."

They moved close together. After the sunlight above, Raffi felt he had gone blind. But gradually walls re-emerged from the gloom, dim outlines. They walked silently down a long street past what had once been shops; now they were drafty holes where rubbish gusted. The street felt cobbled, narrow between the high walls of grim buildings; a shutter banging in the silence; a fountain clotted with dead leaves.

Halfway down the Sekoi turned right, into a blacker crack; a strange archway spanned the entrance and under it Raffi caught a few words carved beautifully in stone: "Street of the Arch," still clear after centuries.

Galen had stopped; he made a rapt sign with his hand. "Look there, Raffi."

Above the street name was a niche with the remains of a statue. Fragments now, but Raffi knew in an instant what it had been: Soren, her arms full of flowers. A carved lily was still perfect in the stone.

"Hurry," the Sekoi hissed from the dark.

Moving after it, Raffi tried to imagine the city as it had been once, filled with sunlight, full of shining statues of the Makers, its fountains rippling pure water, its streets thronged with pilgrims. For a moment he believed it, but it made the Darkness seem worse.

He almost walked past the others; Carys caught him. They were gathered in a narrow doorway. The Sekoi knocked twice, varying the pattern. Then it knocked again, four times.

They waited, nervous, in the inky street. Glancing back, Carys knew if a patrol was watching them it would be impossible to see. She fought off the sudden panicky thought and turned back.

Without a sound, a small grille in the door had opened. The Sekoi muttered a few sounds into it. Seconds later, the door was unlocked.

They never saw the doorkeeper. The Sekoi hustled

them in down a lightless passage; the door locked behind them as they crossed a courtyard to an inner door. The Sekoi turned, blocking the way. "It's best if you say nothing. They won't speak to you anyway. Sit and watch. Try not to listen."

With that strange remark they went in. The room was small, and lit with green candles that gave a wonderful light. To Raffi's joy, it was full of Sekoi; about a dozen of the creatures, lounging on cushions around a fire. They all turned and looked as the strangers came in; then, as one, they looked away again.

"Sit down," the Sekoi whispered. There were empty cushions in a corner; Carys perched on one, knees up. The storyteller, a female Sekoi sitting by the fire, did not pause; it went on speaking in their language of strange purring consonants, one hand moving as it talked, throwing deft shadows.

Fascinated, Raffi watched. He had never seen so many of them; he noticed the different colors and patterns of their fur, the small tribemarks. There were no young ones, though. No children. Each had an absorbed look, as if they dreamed or were in some trance as they listened, and they took not the slightest notice of the travelers.

Finally, the story came to an end. There was no applause, just silence, and then the creatures talked excitedly to one another.

"Why are they ignoring us?" Carys asked, annoyed.

The Sekoi smiled. "My people are honest. If the Watch question them they can say they've talked to no keeper, no Starmen."

It uncurled itself and crossed the room and, taking the storyteller by the arm, began to whisper.

Galen fidgeted. "Are we safe here? How does it feel?"

"There's nothing. I can't read Sekoi."

"I could." The keeper's hawk-face darkened. "But then, they're usually safe. They despise most Starmen, especially the Watch. But not the Order."

"Why call us Starmen?" Carys asked.

"Because the Makers came from the sky. The Sekoi say they watched them come. They have stories about it." He laughed harshly. "They have stories about everything."

Behind the quiet talk another teller had begun; an old-looking Sekoi mumbling almost to itself. As he sat there, Raffi felt the pattern of words; at first they meant nothing to him, but as Galen and Carys talked, their voices faded out and the room rippled, as if it were an image in water. He closed his eyes and opened them, but the rippling went on; he turned to speak to Galen about it but the keeper had gone; all around him was a dark hillside under the stars, brilliantly frosty, and the seven moons beyond, making the Ring.

Standing there, Raffi shivered in the cold, feeling his fur thicken, seeing the night in new colors, colors that had no words but Sekoi words, and he said them to himself, quietly delighted.

In the sky, a light moved. It was a star that grew; it came closer to him, and the hum and glitter of it shook the frosted tops of the trees, and he saw how vast the stars were. It came down and landed. The whole world shook with its weight.

The star opened and the man walked out. Flain was tall and his hair was long and bright. But the sight of him made the fur on Raffi's neck shiver; he rubbed at it and someone's hand caught his and said, "Raffi! Raffi!"

Galen was crouched over him. Behind, the Sekoi was smiling. "I told you not to listen," it purred.

Galen glared at it. "Is he all right?"

"Perfectly. Aren't you?"

Raffi nodded, confused. He looked over, but the story-teller mumbled on, and now the words were impossible to understand.

"Listen," the Sekoi said. "I've been advised that you should try the Street of the Wool-Carders. Apparently there may be a contact there. We should look for the name Anteus."

Galen nodded. "Where is that?"

"Not too far. But near a Watchtower. I could show you."

Galen looked at it curiously. "Why are you helping us?"

The Sekoi narrowed its yellow eyes. "Because the Watch think we're worthless animals." It grinned. "And in memory of our mutual friend, Alberic."

"Have you still got his gold?" Raffi asked.

The Sekoi drew itself up, affronted. "My gold. He should pay his storytellers."

Carys laughed. She wished she knew where the Sekoi hoard was. That would be useful information. But the Crow was better.

The Wounded City

Back out in the black city, they headed for the Street of the Wool-Carders. All the streets seemed the same, but, crossing one huge empty square, Raffi sensed the space all around him, and eyes at his back. Spinning around, he saw only darkness.

When he told Carys, she took the crossbow off her shoulder and loaded it. "I've been afraid of that."

"If only I could sense something clear!"

"I thought keepers were good at that."

"Not here."

The street, when they found it, was very short and bounded by a low wall with some sort of neglected garden on the other side; dead branches snapped under their feet. They walked up and down it twice, but there were no houses, no doors.

Galen leaned on his stick. "So much for the Sekoi," he snarled bitterly.

The creature rubbed its fur thoughtfully. "We may be looking for the wrong thing."

"How?"

"Does not your Order have secrets, keeper? Signs, symbols? Things not known by outsiders?"

Galen straightened. "Raffi. Go with him. Search every inch of this wall. Girl, come with me."

In the dimness they had to peer at the bricks, feel with fingertips. Halfway down Raffi stopped. "This is it," he breathed.

The Sekoi stared curiously at the mess of scratches. "It means nothing."

"Yes it does." He turned. "Galen!"

The keeper came at a run, shoving him aside. "Good, Raffi! Good!"

On the wall was a broken inscription plaque, with the words ". . . memory of Anteus, who . . ." all that remained. But under that were new scratches, strange and meaningless. Galen's fingers outlined them eagerly. A tiny bee, a circle of six dots and another inside, a group of enigmatic slashes and squiggles. Carys tried to get closer. "What does it say?" she hissed.

Galen glanced at her. Then he said to the Sekoi, "Where's the place called the Pyramid?"

It looked surprised. "An hour's walk south. Why?"

"That's where we go."

All the way there Galen said nothing else, but Raffi

could feel the pain in him, the desperate rising hope. Some of the way they ran, as time was running out; even Carys felt eyes on her, the scurrying of shapes in the shadows. She constantly glanced behind her at the darkest corners. Once she laughed at herself—she was the Watch, after all—but in this place everything seemed full of doubt. She knew she was beginning to look like an outlaw, to think like one. She had almost forgotten herself, and the knowledge shook her.

Overhead the draxi flapped, looming out of fog; Raffi glanced up at them with a shudder.

Crouched under walls, against buildings, they ran deeper and deeper into Tasceron's heart. Finally the Sekoi stopped by a smooth sloping wall. "Well, keeper," it said, breathless. "Your Pyramid."

The top was lost in gloom. They walked around it. Four walls, with no opening. It was blank and smooth.

"Now what?" Carys muttered.

Galen put both hands on the brickwork. He began to speak, words that not even Raffi knew—fierce, secret sounds—so that Carys stared and the Sekoi put its long hands together and chewed its nails nervously.

The spell ended. But nothing moved.

In a rage of fury, Galen slammed his hands against the wall, kicked it, beat at it. He moaned and cursed, his voice an agony in the silence. It chilled them all. For a moment Raffi wondered if Galen's mind had gone. Then Galen turned. He looked over Raffi's shoulder into the dark and there was a look on his haggard face that terrified them.

But all he said was, "We're going to have to improve your sense-lines, boy."

Carys spun around.

The Sekoi snarled.

Behind them, a row of armed men was waiting in the gloom.

20

There will be one who will return from the black pit.
And yet he will not be the one who went.

Apocalypse of Tamar

"MY NAME IS NOT FOR YOU YET," the old man said. He nodded to the nearest swordsman. "Search the pack."

They were inside the Pyramid, though Raffi still wasn't sure how it had opened. The scuffle in the street had been brief; the men had dragged them in and flung them down there in a heap. The Sekoi had a torn ear, and Carys's crossbow was in a swordsman's hand.

Now Raffi watched in fury as the pack was tugged open; one by one their clothes were tossed out, the water flask, the tinderbox. Finally the relic bag. The swordsman tossed it to the old man, who held it a moment.

"What might be in here?"

Galen was silent. Raffi's heart thumped.

The old man smiled. His face was small and narrow, his hair gray as ash, clipped short. He wore black gloves. Opening the bag, he took out the relics, laying them carefully on the table. "A device for far-seeing! I've heard of such a thing."

He laid the Maker-gifts in a row, and Carys stared at them. She had no idea what most of them were: a green tube, a box with buttons on it, a flimsy see-through cube. The old man's hand paused in the bag. Raffi felt a sharp tingle of emotion from him, a shock of surprise. Then the black glove came out; it held the glass ball they had found long ago on the island.

"What's this?" The old man looked up intently. "Where did you get this?"

Galen's voice was grim. "I've never seen it before."

The old man stared at him for a moment, then he sat on a wooden bench. "Shean," he said after a little while. "My name is Pieter Shean. I'm a Relic Master of the Order of keepers, as you are, Galen Harn."

Galen's face didn't change. "Prove it."

The Wounded City

Shean shook his head. "What harm have they done us, my friend! But hear this." He said nothing, but Galen's eyes widened briefly; he sat upright and Raffi felt the sudden surge of joy in him.

"I have not heard a voice in my mind these three months," Galen muttered hoarsely.

"I know it. I feel all the pain of it." The old man nodded to the swordsmen. "All is well. Go back out."

The men went. One of them grinned at Carys and handed back her crossbow with a flourish. Annoyed, she snatched it. He wouldn't smile if he knew who she was. Then she squashed the thought. This Shean hadn't lost his power. She'd have to be careful. And take a good look around.

The old man waved them to seats. "I'm sorry for your treatment. My men needed to be sure you weren't Watchspies. Of you, keeper, I'm sure, and your boy, and the Sekoi have rarely harmed us. But who is this girl?"

"Carys Arrin." Galen kept her quiet with a look. "We met her far from here, on the downs in our own country. The Watch took her father."

Shean studied her carefully. "Did they? When?"

"Months ago," she muttered. "I thought they might be bringing him here."

"I know of no prisoners brought from so far. It would be more likely they would take him to Arnk, or the Pits at Maar." He turned to Galen. "Are you sure of her? The Watch have so many spies."

Galen was silent. Then he said, "I know her by now."

"We trust her," Raffi put in unexpectedly. "She wouldn't betray us."

Shean nodded slowly. "Is that so, girl?"

Carys looked at him, trying to keep her mind empty as she'd been taught. She felt strangely miserable. "Of course," she murmured.

"I hope so."

"Keeper," Galen said urgently, "can you do anything for me?"

Shean looked uneasy. Finally he said, "I will try. It depends on how deep your hurt was. Eat first. Then you and I will meditate, and try the healing." He looked at the others. "We will be some time, but there's plenty of food here. In the room beyond are beds, and water for washing. Make yourselves comfortable. You have come home, keepers."

The food was good. Raffi felt he hadn't eaten properly since leaving Lerin's village, and though Carys was quiet, she ate well too. The Sekoi picked delicately at fruit, spitting out pips and looking around the room curiously.

Later, when Shean and Galen were gone, they all slept, on small comfortable couches near the fire, and the Sekoi in a nest of cushions it had piled in one corner. Deep in the night, Raffi opened his eyes. Galen was standing in the warm darkness, looking into the fire.

Raffi propped himself on one elbow. "Did it work?"

But already he knew the answer. Galen gave him a look that went right through him; the keeper's face was drawn and exhausted.

"What does the keeper fear, Raffi?" he muttered hoarsely.

"Despair," Raffi whispered. "But Galen . . ."

"I know despair," the keeper said. "Despair and I are old friends."

"It's not your fault!"

"It must be. I have failed in some way. I have to pay and this is the way God chooses."

Raffi shook his head hopelessly. He felt like crying. "We'll find the Crow. The Crow will cure you."

Galen didn't answer. He sat in the chair, knees huddled up, staring into the flames. When Raffi went back to sleep, he was still there.

Journal of Carys Arryn
Date unknown

What's happening to me?

First I feel sorry for Galen, and now the old man's got me feeling guilty. This place doesn't help. It must be one of the last strongholds of the Order anywhere, and I should be glad that I've found it, but the whole thing seems . . .

CARYS STOPPED. Then she crossed out everything furiously and started again.

They have a Relic-chapel here. I saw it this morning, though Galen spent most of the night in there. It is really very beautiful; Raffi was almost moved to tears. There are superb statues, so real they might almost be Flain and Tamar and the others. Candles burn before them. Relics are kept in boxes of gold—the Sekoi was squirming with jealousy. The windows are pieced together from broken fragments. Seeing it was strange. Old Jellie would have hated it, and so should I. It's just . . . the statues looked too real. I almost thought Flain was looking at me.

Superstition is easy to catch.

Now we're waiting for Shean. I think he has some idea where the Crow may be. If there is such a man.

SHE CLOSED THE BOOK and stuffed it away quickly as the old man shuffled in with Galen. They sat down. All at once it felt like a council of war, and Raffi's nerves tightened as the tension gripped him.

Shean began. He laid the small glass globe carefully on the table, his hand trembling slightly. "Galen has explained how you came to find this. I'm not sure, but I think I know what it is. I have spoken to him about it; that knowledge lies only between us, for now. It is a great relic, and if it is what I think, then it will lead you to the Crow." He looked uneasy. "If that is where you still wish to go."

Galen looked up, astonished. "Of course it is."

The old man paused, moistening his dry lips. "The House of Trees, keeper, if anything remains of it, is under the darkest, most dangerous part of the city. Those who have gone there have not returned."

"So you know where it is?" the Sekoi asked drily.

"We have . . . some idea. There is an ancient list of ways—a list of streets. It dates almost certainly from before the fall of the city. Others have copied it and, I presume, followed it. As I say, none have come back."

"You haven't tried?" Carys was surprised.

The old man's gloved fingers twisted together. "No. I feel it's important I am here. We must gather, find our scattered brothers, rebuild the Order. This will be our center—the heart of the network. We need you here, Galen. Stay with us."

Galen stared at him. "What about me? I need the Crow!"

"My son," the old man said softly. "Have you ever thought that there may be no Crow?"

"NO!" Galen leaped up, his face dark and wrathful. "Never! And how can you say that! Even think it! What has happened to your faith, old man? Has this city of horrors smothered it?"

Shean sat silent. Finally he said, "You may be right to rebuke me. I've lived here too long in the dark, Galen; seen too many martyrs, too many children dragged away. Under this room so many of their bodies lie, bought from the Watch, secretly buried. And maybe I've become weak. Maybe I've thought, if the Crow was here, would he not have saved us from this? Would he not have risen up and saved the city?"

"You sound like a Watchman!" Galen prowled in disgust, then turned swiftly. "Even in darkness, we have to believe! I've learned that. It's we who have to rise up, Shean, us, the remains of the Order! The Makers left the world to us, and if it's lost, then we are the ones who lost it! We have the power! We still have it! And he's waiting for us to find him, to come to him!"

In the silence that followed, the Sekoi said quietly, "Indeed, many of our stories say the same."

Shean shrugged. "Then I hope you find what you want. Because it tears at you so much I won't hold you back. I can give you the List of Ways, though you must swear not to let it fall into the enemy's hands. But think hard, keeper." He stood up and gazed across the room at Galen's grim face. "Are you doing this to save the Order? Or to heal your own loss? Would you be so eager to face death if you didn't think the Crow could cure you?"

Galen glared at him bitterly. "I hope so," he breathed.

"Of course he would," Carys snapped. They all looked at her in surprise; she felt a bit surprised herself, but she folded her arms and looked Shean in the eye. "He hasn't come all this way for himself. I've seen that. Nor has Raffi. They believe in this Crow, and if you'd had their faith you'd have gone to find him yourself, years ago. Keep the questions for yourself, keeper. Mightn't it be that you hide in here because you're too scared to go out?"

Raffi was grinning; the Sekoi smiled slyly. Galen's look was hard and strange.

Shean nodded slowly. "The Litany says the keeper is wise who knows the voice of truth. Maybe what you say is so." He sat down again, looking suddenly tired and older. His black fingers caressed the glass globe. "You go with him then, girl?"

"I've come this far."

"But you don't believe in the Crow?"

She hesitated, uneasy. "Maybe. I don't know. I'd like to find out."

The Sekoi nodded. "And so would I." It rubbed the fur on its face with one sharp finger. "It would interest us. We have our own ideas about the Makers."

"And heresy, most of them are," Galen growled. He came over to the table. "Let me have a copy of this list," he said quietly. "My friends and I will leave tonight." He paused, and the black and green beads glinted at his neck. "With your blessing, keeper."

Shean stood. "You have it, keeper. And maybe you

will be the one the prophecy speaks of. The one who will come back."

THEY LEFT AT NIGHTFALL, though in Tasceron night was eternal. Now they traveled light. Galen had left all the relics in the safety of the chapel; he took only the glass globe and the chart. They each carried a little food; Carys had her bow. The Sekoi went empty-handed, as before. It seemed able to go for a long time without eating; when Raffi asked how it would manage it just purred at him, "I could eat you, small keeper."

Raffi laughed, but uneasily. There were some nursery rhymes he'd heard from his mother . . . As if it knew, the Sekoi laughed too, a small, mocking, barking sound.

Shean's men went with them as far as a corner of a terrace, where a great set of wide steps led up into the dark. There one of them said, "This is as far as we go. Good luck, keepers."

Galen gave them the blessing; they melted into the shadows expertly. Watching them go, Raffi said, "Now we're on our own again."

The Wounded City

"We're never on our own!" Galen glared at him. "You've been neglecting your lessons, boy. While we go you'll repeat the whole Book to yourself, from the beginning to the death of Flain. Every verse, every prophecy."

Raffi pulled a face at Carys. She laughed.

But he could hardly concentrate on his task. They moved through inky streets; twice steam hissed up from under their feet, scattering them in terror. Sparks lit the sky far to the north. No one spoke. Galen led them, guiding himself by the small scrap of paper Shean had pressed into his hand, rubbing soot from the walls, hunting the shattered name plaques of the ancient streets.

When they came to the tunnel he was ahead of them.

"Down there?" Raffi came up and looked at it dubiously.

"Through it and left, somewhere. Do you feel any danger?"

"I told you, I can't feel anything here. Just the dark, and heat somewhere, something smoldering . . ."

They looked into the brick archway; inside it was black, with small gray lichens blotching the damp walls. Galen stepped in. "It seems empty. I can see to the end."

He took one more step and, with a sudden slash and clang that terrified each of them, an iron gate crashed down from the roof behind him, cutting him off from them. The tunnel rang with echoes. Somewhere ahead an eerie screaming rang out, wild and urgent. Raffi flung himself at the bars of the gate; he felt the Sekoi strain beside him.

"It won't move!"

Fiercely, Galen was tugging and heaving at the metal grid. Behind him came shouts; the wailing rose to a howling of skeats.

"Get out!" he yelled. "Take these! Quickly!"

Hastily he thrust his hands through the bars; Raffi snatched the chart and globe, but then he couldn't move, though the noise was piercing every nerve. "Galen . . ."

"Run!" the keeper raged. "Get away. Get him out of here!"

The Sekoi's fingers grabbed him. "He's right, Raffi!"

"We can't just leave him!"

"You have to." Galen's grip caught his. "You're the

keeper now, Raffi. Find the Crow. That's all that matters. Find the Crow!"

The darkness behind him was moving; men, hounds, a crack of blue light.

"The Watch!" Carys yelled.

"Don't worry," Galen said. He pulled upright, his hawk-face hard in the glimmer. "The Makers are with me, Raffi. We'll meet again. Now, get him away!"

Carys and the Sekoi had to drag him, sobbing and yelling. Behind them, blows and howls rang in the black tunnel.

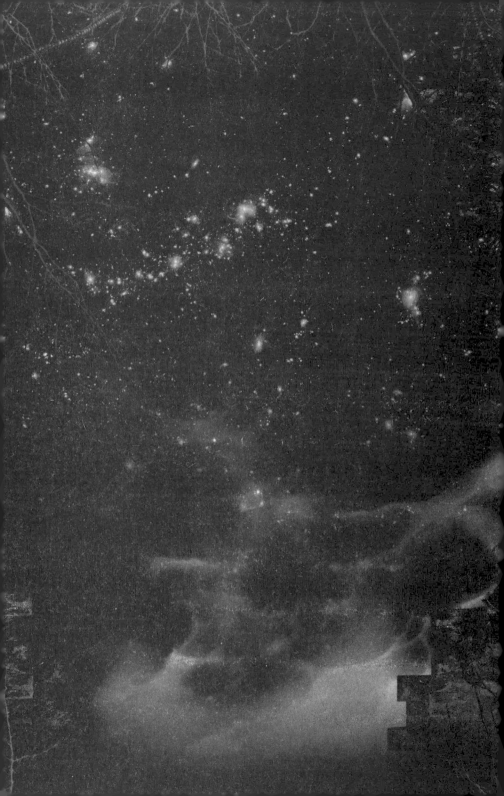

The House of Trees

21

The Makers turned to Kest in despair.
"What have you done?" they cried.
"How have you betrayed us? Your
distorted birds, your hideous beasts
have marred our world." So they took
him and locked him underground for a
hundred years, without food or light.
And each time they looked in on him he
was silent and unsmiling.

Book of the Seven Moons

"HOW DO YOU FEEL, SMALL ONE?"

Raffi shook his head hopelessly. He was shaking and felt sick, though they had run through the streets till they thought they were safe. The Sekoi sat down by him. "Galen is a brave man," it said kindly.

"Yes." Raffi's voice was fierce. "I've seen him yell at a skeer-snake in the forest till it couldn't face him. That was before . . . But he can do anything. He's not afraid of danger." Choked, he closed his fists.

Its back against the ruined wall, the creature nodded. "It seemed to me that he sought death. He had a great

loss to bear. Now he will be a martyr for the Order. That
is a good thing, is it not?"

Raffi nodded. "So the Litany says." But his voice was
small and reluctant, and the silence after it bleak.

Carys flung down the pebble she'd been fingering.
"That's it. That's enough!"

"What?"

"I said, that's enough." She stood up and marched over
to them, kicking the rubbish in the cloister aside. "How
can you sit there and talk like this! Galen is no use to
anyone dead!"

"They believe . . ." the Sekoi began patiently, but she
waved at it angrily. "I know what they believe! 'The blood
of the Order benefits the earth'—all that nonsense! But I
don't! I say we should do something, not just sit here!"

"We will," Raffi said. He looked up, his face determined. "We'll find the Crow. Just like he said."

"But what about Galen!" She dropped to crouch by him.

"We can't help him. The Watch will torture him."

"They will if we don't get him out!"

The Sekoi stared. "From a Watchtower? Don't torment
the boy. It can't be done."

"Do you think I want to leave him?" Raffi muttered, despairing. "If there was any chance, Carys, any chance at all. But there isn't! No one can get into those places!"

She got up abruptly and walked to the edge of the cloister. Pinned on a row of broken pillars, a dead vine rustled. Owls hooted, far off in the stillness. Standing with her back to them, she said, "I can get him out."

After a second Raffi looked up. "What did you say?"

"I can get Galen out."

Raffi stared at the Sekoi in bewilderment. It stood up. "Explain," it said dangerously.

Carys turned around. She forced herself to look at it, but its eyes were yellow and sharp, and she couldn't face Raffi either.

"I work for the Watch. I'm a spy, and I have been from the beginning."

There was a second of intense silence. Then Raffi said, "Don't be ridiculous," but his voice was cold and he stared at her in growing horror.

She forced herself to meet his eyes. "I'm not. It's true."

"You can't be!" He jumped up so quickly the pile of

stones behind him slid down. "You've been with us all along! Your father—"

"I haven't got a father." She glanced at the Sekoi. "I was brought up in a Watchhouse. I came with you because . . . well, at first because I was hunting Galen."

"And then the Crow. You wanted us to get you to the Crow!"

"Raffi—"

"Don't speak to me!" He turned away, then helplessly swung back. "You used us! All that time you lied to us? All you told us about your father . . . ?" Choked with anger, he gripped his fists; to her astonishment tiny green filaments of light flickered around his fingers. "Carys . . ." Then he laughed harshly. "I don't even know if that's your name! I don't know who you are anymore!"

She bit her lip. He looked as if his world had crashed to pieces. "It is my name."

"Did you betray Galen?"

The Sekoi's question was icy; the fur of its nape had swollen and thickened.

"Of course not!" she snapped.

"But someone did."

The House of Trees

"No. It wasn't like that."

"So you did betray him?" Raffi gasped.

"I had to get us into the city! Let me explain!"

"Why should I let you!" he raged. But then he sat down suddenly, as if his legs had given way, and his voice was bewildered. "I just can't believe this is happening."

Carys sat beside him. Her voice was dry and hard. "At the gate, when we hid under the wagons, I was caught. It was a hopeless plan. I told them who I was, that you were spies. They let us in. I swear I never said anything about relics, or keepers. I wouldn't have. I wanted the credit of your capture for myself."

Ignoring his look, she went on. "The news was passed on. But listen, Raffi, I'm sure they don't know who Galen is. That rat-trap was just bad luck; there are probably hundreds like that around the old citadel—aren't there?"

She glared at the Sekoi; it nodded, reluctant. "So we could get him out, Raffi; get him out before they realize who they've got!"

"But why? Why do you want to get him out? Why don't you go back to them and give them all the things you know—where the Sekoi live, the sky-road, Lerin, the Pyramid!" He sounded harsh, like Galen. "Haven't you gotten enough from us, Carys!"

"That's not it. I don't want Galen tortured."

"Might that not be because he may give them all the information you've worked so hard for?" the Sekoi asked acidly.

"NO! Why won't you listen! I like Galen. Like a fool I've gotten to like you all!"

She stood up, pushing back her hair, angry with herself. "I know you can't trust me now. If you want, I'll go away. But first I'm going to get him out, Raffi, and if I have to, I'll go by myself." Picking up the crossbow, she checked it over, her hands shaking.

Raffi stared at her. He felt bewildered, and utterly betrayed. He wished he could hate her, that it was that simple, but she was still Carys, still the same.

He looked at the Sekoi. "What should we do?"

"Your choice, small keeper. I'll stay with you, whatever you decide." It rubbed its furred face with one long finger.

"She may be able to get him out," Raffi said with difficulty.

"She may. Or she may just be taking us back to them. More prisoners to her credit." It gazed at her, narrow-eyed.

Raffi stared down at his hands. He prayed, asking for knowledge, for the way to go, but his mind was as dark as the cloister, and the Makers were silent.

Then, without knowing he'd decided, he stood up.

"All right. We'll take the chance."

Carys smiled at him but he ignored that; he looked away, furious with her. "If you betray us . . . I still don't know if I should be trusting you."

"You never will know," she said, "until you do. Galen would tell you that."

He took out the chart. "Where do we go?"

"They'll have taken him to the nearest Watchtower. Is it on there?"

"There's one marked."

"That'll be it. Lead on, Raffi."

With a glance at the Sekoi, which shrugged, he turned uneasily away and crawled through the hole in the wall.

THE STREETS WERE A NIGHTMARE of dark smoke. Neither Raffi nor Carys was as alert as they should have been; if the Sekoi hadn't hissed a warning, the flock of draxi swooping over the turrets of one villa would have had them.

Confused, struggling to think, Raffi found himself going back over everything that had happened, trying to see Carys as a spy—on the downs, on the ship—but it hurt him like a pain and he blanked it out, concentrating only on the streets, their crumbling names.

Behind him, Carys was silent. She was angry with herself, defiant, reckless, hot. She didn't care what they thought. But she'd show them. Only she could get Galen out, and she'd do it, because she wanted to, because no one would bring him in except her.

In the alley opposite the Watchtower they crouched. At the end of the dark lane there was light, some hanging lanterns and a great fire that blazed on the cracked paving. Men were gathered around it; shadows, talking. Behind them, the great walls of the tower rose up into darkness, without windows.

"Now what?" Raffi said.

Carys eased the bow. "I go in. By myself. I'll tell them

some story—that Galen is vital to my mission, that I have to follow him to get . . . well, something important. I won't mention the Crow."

Raffi laughed bitterly, but she went on. "The trouble is, even if they believe me, they may not let me bring him out alone. That's where you come in."

"Us?"

"If Galen and I get out, we'll come down this lane. Hide somewhere, down under that broken arch. Let us go by; but if anyone follows, deal with them."

"Deal with them? We're not the Watch."

She grinned at him spitefully. "You know the Order's secrets, not me."

He didn't smile. But as she walked away up the alley he blurted out, "Be careful," as if the words hurt him.

"And be discreet," the Sekoi murmured.

She turned and looked at its sharp yellow eyes and laughed. "Oh, I will."

GALEN EASED HIS LEG a little more and felt the heavy chain clink. He was dizzy and bruised; blood had dried on his face, and his shoulder was a mass of pain. He looked around carefully.

For a long time he had wondered if they had blind-folded him, but gradually he had begun to see; there was a tiny window up a long shaft in the wall, and the gloom that came through it was barely light, but his eyes strained through it. He was in some enclosed space, not large. Stretching out his feet, he could feel the opposite wall; his back was against another. Carefully he tugged up the heavy chains and ran his hands over the stone; it wasn't straight. Curved, as if the dungeon was circular. Above him was blackness; he said some words softly and they echoed, as if it was high enough to stand. The darkness smelled of rats, ordure, filthy straw. The stones felt slimy and cold.

Galen smiled grimly to himself. He hurt, but he'd told them nothing, and he was sure they didn't know who or what he was. And yet this was only the start. He knew enough tales of the cruelty of the Watch, but he wouldn't think of them now. That would be foolish. Instead he straightened his back and closed his eyes. Simple chants came to him first, then all the prayers and litanies; he spoke them softly till it seemed to him the darkness was filled with words, as if they hung in the air like spirits. "And Kest was in the darkness a hundred years. How slowly sorrow entered him, how he mourned for the evil he had done, all the things of darkness he had brought into the world."

Galen stopped. The story was not the one for now. And he knew, suddenly, that he would need every ounce of strength and will to stand up to them, not to tell them all the secrets of the Order. Wincing, he dragged his fingers up to touch the awen-beads; the smooth surfaces rolled under his fingers.

"I am as empty without as within," he muttered grimly. Then he nodded. "Though maybe I have one chance. One chance Kest never had."

"WHAT'S GOING ON HERE?" The Watchsergeant pushed his way through the men. "What is it? Another prisoner?"

"She says she's a spy." The men stood back, and the sergeant's eyes narrowed. He saw a girl of about sixteen, brown-haired, dirty, a crossbow on her back. She fixed him with a straight look. "Are you in charge here?"

He grinned. "Who wants to know?"

Putting her hand down her neck, she pulled out something on a chain; tugged it over her head and gave it to him without a word.

He held it to the light; she saw his face change. "Come inside," he said somberly.

Going in under the main arch, she noticed the defenses: armed guards, three metal gates, floor-spikes. If they didn't let her walk out she'd be here forever. But she set her shoulders and held her head up. Why should she worry? She was one of them.

They made her wait a few minutes in the courtyard. Then the sergeant came through a small arch and beckoned. He led her down a stone passageway and knocked on a door.

"Come in."

The sergeant looked at her. Carys took a deep breath, put her hand on the latch, and went in.

It was a small room with a crackling fire in the hearth, and the castellan was perched on the edge of the table.

"You brought this?" He held the insignia up so that it glinted.

"Yes," she said, coming up to him.

"What house?"

"MarnMountain, 547."

"When did you leave?"

"Three months ago."

"Your spymaster?"

"Jeltok. Old Jellie, we used to call him."

He nodded, wheezing a laugh. "Oh, I know." Getting up, he strolled to the fire, glancing back at her curiously. His sparse hair was graying; he was older than most of his rank. Shrewder too, she thought, with sudden misgivings.

He coughed and spat into the fire, rubbing his chest. "Your mission?"

"Surveillance. On a man called Galen Harn. A keeper."

His face glimmered with interest. "And?"

She sighed, sitting suddenly in the only chair. "Watchman, I've come a long way. I'm hungry and cold. And I'm on your side. You don't need to treat me like a prisoner."

For a moment he was still. Then he nodded, went to

the door, and yelled. Carys took off the crossbow and laid it carelessly on the floor. It was no good to her here anyway.

The man came back. "Food's coming. I'm sorry—force of habit. Welcome home, Carys Arrin."

She looked up at him and smiled.

22

We have been used by one of our own.
He has mocked us all this time.

Litany of the Makers.

RAFFI CROUCHED DOWN behind the remnants of the wall. "No sign of her."

The Sekoi was silent, biting its nails.

Raffi put his hand in his pocket and touched the globe; it was almost warm and he pulled it out in surprise, but the glass was dull and dim. He held it to his eyes and stared in, trying to see something; then tried with his inner eye, but saw only darkness. It was the first real chance he'd had to examine it; Galen always kept it close. But it told him nothing.

The Sekoi looked up abruptly. "Listen, small keeper. I think we should go."

"Go?" Raffi was blank. "Go where?"

"Anywhere. Out of here." It knelt up, and he saw the pupils of its eyes were black slits in the dimness. Its hand caught his arm, the seven long fingers clutching tight. "All my instincts say this is a trap! She's gone to them. She'll bring them here! For us! Don't you see, Raffi, I don't think we dare trust her."

A tiny pang of terror went down Raffi's spine. He said hoarsely, "I can't believe she'd—"

"She already has! Long before she met you!" It sprang up, a lean, agitated shape. "My people know of these Watchhouses. They take children young, feed them, teach them, train them. For years. How can all that be taken out of her? She is the Watch, she thinks like they think, hunts like they hunt. She'll have seen things you can't imagine—have practiced cruelties and spite. Her sorna— her soul—will have been changed by that! Don't trust her, Raffi!"

Raffi sat still, though its fear terrified him, made him restless. "Yes, but what about Galen?"

"Galen is lost! And they'll make him talk."

"He wouldn't."

The Sekoi sat down. "He will," it said softly. "Everyone does, in the end."

Raffi couldn't answer. The helplessness and doubt swept over him again; he had no idea what to do. They should go, should run, and yet . . . part of him wanted to stay, to believe she'd come.

"We need to get to the Crow," the Sekoi urged. "The Crow was a great power. If he lives, he can help us. But we need to go now, Raffi, before she brings the Watch and they take the map and the globe! That's all they need!"

Raffi stared at it. Then he got up again and gazed down the dark, empty street.

"THIS IS ALL VERY INTERESTING," the castellan said, refilling her cup. "So this man Harn has knowledge of this relic . . . you didn't say what it was, by the way."

Carys smiled. "No. I'm not completely sure, and besides that—"

"You want to keep it secret."

"My orders are to be as discreet as possible."

He nodded. "I see. But look, Carys, we can get any information you want out of this man by our own methods. Not that he'd be much good to you afterward, of course." He sipped the sweet wine and looked at her. "Wouldn't that be easier?"

She pulled a face. "In a way it would. But it would break my cover—I've worked hard to be accepted by them, and now I think they trust me. No, I think it would be best if I helped him to escape." She raised an eyebrow. "If you agree, of course. He's your prisoner."

He paused a moment, stoking the fire with fresh coals, then turned and picked up the insignia, dangling the silver chain over his fingers. "Who am I to stand in the way of the Watchlords?" He handed it back to her, and she slipped it on, feeling the cold discs slide against her skin. "But there'll be a price."

She looked up sharply. She'd been expecting this.

"How much?"

"Half. Half of the reward for the keeper, and the others, and half of whatever they give you for finding this relic."

She thought briefly. "All right. I've no choice."

"Nor have I. We need to work together." He rubbed

a hand through his stubbly gray beard. "Now. This escape will need to be convincing." He thought for a moment, then stood up and went out, and Carys finished the wine in one gulp. Picking up her crossbow, she loaded it quickly and swung it under one arm. Then she picked some bread off the tray and crammed it into her pocket. When he came back she was waiting by the fire.

He looked pleased, and she knew he had his own plans ready. "The Watch must watch each other first." That had been Jellie's first lesson—all her life she had seen it; even in school, child had spied on child, reported anything, competed for the honor of it. She'd been one of the best. Now they'd be watching her, but that was all she had expected.

"We're ready. Here are the keys." He handed her a small ring. "I'll show you a postern gate which will be guarded by one man—shoot at him and he'll fall. It would be helpful if you missed; I'm short of men as it is."

She took the keys. "How did I get these?"

"You'll have to serve up that story. After all, you've been trained for it." He coughed again, a raw bark. "I'll be glad to get out of this rat-hole. The smog gets to you."

"You're leaving?"

"I hope so. I hope to buy promotion to some comfortable village. Somewhere the sun shines." He laughed harshly. "When I get the money."

Their eyes met. She smiled wryly. "Thanks for the food. Now show me the way."

GALEN PULLED HIMSELF UP as the key rattled in the lock. With both chained hands he pushed the long hair from his face, and winced as the light fell over him.

"Galen!"

She was inside in seconds, crouched by him. He stared at her. "Carys!" Then, convulsed by fear, he grabbed her. "Is Raffi here? He's not been caught?"

"No. No, he's fine. Keep still!" She was unlocking the chains; they slithered off and he rubbed his bruised wrists with relief.

"But how did you get in here? What's been happening?"

"I'll explain outside." She tugged the chains through the straw and grabbed his arm. "There's no time now.

The House of Trees

Follow me close; don't speak. Do what I do. Please, Galen!"

He looked at her as if he would say something, then nodded. She helped him up, but he pushed her off. "I can manage."

"Good." She put her head around the door. "Come on. This way."

The steps led up, around a damp wall. She climbed soundlessly, Galen a tall shadow at her shoulder. He was stiff and sore, but he moved carefully and, glancing back, she saw his eyes were alert. At the top of the steps was a dim corridor, pungent with smoke; from a guard-room nearby the sound of voices and the rattle of dice echoed. They edged carefully by; Galen caught a glimpse of the men inside, their backs to him. Then he was running down a passage, into another, and all the time neither of them spoke.

Then Carys stopped. Finger to lips, she jerked her head and, stepping forward, he saw around the corner a man sitting on a bench eating lumps of potato from the tip of his knife.

Beside him was a small, half-open door.

Galen glanced at Carys. She raised the bow. He gave a harsh smile and shrugged. Carys was surprised, but she turned at once and braced herself. He saw the bolt quiver; with a sound like a crack it was gone. The man sprawled on the floor.

Leaping over, Carys had the door open; she turned back and gasped, "Leave him!"

Galen straightened from the body. He pushed past her to the door and peered around it. The night was black, the narrow alley stinking with refuse.

"Where?"

"Straight on!"

He followed her up the lane, leaping piles of rubbish, the rats scuttling before them. Ducking around corners, they came to a low arch and raced under it; in the shadow she swung around and racked the bow again hastily.

"You think they'll be coming."

"When they find out." She glanced back, then tugged away from the wall. "Down here."

Turning into a ruined courtyard, they crossed it and scrambled through a hole in the wall to a wider street. She turned left. "Hurry!"

The House of Trees

They ran close to the wall, through the fog of darkness and the soft hooting of owls. Once Galen stumbled; picking himself up, he glanced back. Shadows moved in the entrance to the lane. He ran after her, his face dark.

They climbed over a roof-fall, then under a wide arch of stone.

"Come on!" She ran ahead but he caught up with her and grabbed her arm. "Wait!"

She looked back. "We can't! They're coming!"

"Where's Raffi?" Galen hissed. "Where is he?"

"I don't know!" She stared into the darkness under the arch. "He should be here! It was here I said . . ."

They could hear the Watchmen now; soft feet running.

"In the doorway." Galen pulled her in beside him and peered out.

Instantly the side of his face was lit with color; a vivid green flash that dazzled them both.

"What was that!" Carys gasped.

The keeper grinned wolfishly. "We call it the third action of the inner eye. Don't tell him, but he's quite good at it."

Gazing past him she was shocked to see the archway

spitting flame and sparks; for a few moments it fizzed and crackled and then went black, and she could see the bodies of two Watchmen lying still.

"Are they dead?"

"Stunned."

"How can he do that?" she marveled as the shapes of Raffi and the Sekoi came slithering up the broken street.

Raffi raced up to Galen and stood staring at him. "She did it," he said in a choked voice.

Galen smiled grimly. "Indeed she did."

Raffi touched the keeper's arm hesitantly. "We thought you were lost . . ."

Galen shook his head. "Always keep the faith, boy," he said gruffly. "Sometimes the Makers act in ways we could never imagine. Have you got the chart?"

"Here."

"Then let's go from here. Before more of them come."

Following the list of streets, they twisted between houses and past palaces whose windows were empty, and through whose halls the wind moaned uneasily. Rain began to fall; a black, oily drizzle. The city was changing; they were coming to the oldest part, the citadel, and the ruins here were of great temples and palaces, shattered by the terrible destruction. The darkness grew deeper, and more silent; even the rats and owls were left behind, and all they heard now was the sound of their own running, soft footsteps pattering in alleys and doorways, as if the city was full of ghosts that fled endlessly.

After half an hour, Galen stopped them. "Here," he gasped. "We rest here."

It was a small window; climbing through they found they were in the kitchen of some villa. An empty hearth was black with soot, and one table still stood, huge and immovable in the center of the room.

Galen crossed to the wall and sat down, easing his leg with a groan.

Raffi crouched beside him. "Did they hurt you?"

"Not much. They were just warming up."

Carys sat too, more slowly. She looked at Raffi, who bit his lip. The Sekoi stretched its legs out and scratched its fur. "Are you going to tell him, or shall we?" it said severely.

"I will," Carys muttered.

Galen looked up at her. "I should thank you, Carys.

I owe you my life. Maybe more, my honor as a keeper."
Gathering the black hair from his face, he knotted it in
the dirty string and looked at her, his hawk-face grim and
dark. "It's a debt I'll pay, if ever I can."

"You may not want to," she said.

He frowned. "Why not?"

She was silent, looking down. Raffi rolled the glass
globe nervously in his pocket.

"I've got something to tell you." But Galen looked at
her so sharply that she couldn't say it; for the first time in
her life she felt afraid to speak. Lies leaped to her mind,
convincing stories, excuses; fiercely she drove them away.

When she did speak, her voice was defiant. "Galen,
I've been deceiving you. I'm not what I said. I'm a spy.
For the Watch."

It was out. His face did not flicker, his eyes black and
keen. She looked away, but his answer made her jerk her
head back in astonishment.

"I know," he said.

23

*Kest's creatures attacked them. But
Flain had a maze built before the House,
and the beasts and birds of nightmare
wandered in it and howled.*

*Then Kest arose, and wept. "The
damage I have done," he said, "I will
make good. The monsters I have made I
will destroy."*

*And he took up his weapons and
walked through them all into the dark.*

Book of the Seven Moons

THEY ALL STARED AT HIM IN AMAZEMENT.
Then the Sekoi gave a low purr of laughter.

"You knew?" Raffi gasped.

"From the beginning." Galen rubbed his leg calmly. "From the first time we saw her at the tree."

Carys was staring at him. "You couldn't have!"

"And as we went on I grew more certain. She writes an interesting journal, Raffi. You should read it."

"You . . ." She shook her head, disbelieving. "You deciphered it?"

"A few times." He smiled sourly. "I'm sorry, Carys, but you were the one who was deceived. I kept you with us because I knew you'd be useful. You could keep the Watch away from us; get us where we needed to go. So it proved. At the gates, for instance."

Bewildered, she sat down. The Sekoi was purring in ecstasy, all its fur bristling. "Wonderful," it murmured. "Wonderful."

"I made sure you went under the first wagon. I knew there was no real way into the city, but I thought you'd persuade them. I also thought you might be useful if any of us were caught." He rubbed his sore neck. "Luckily for me."

There was nothing, nothing she could say. The shock of it was like a cold downpour; it left her shivering. All this time she thought she had been so clever . . . She shuddered with the thought of her pride. All that time. Now she knew how Raffi must have felt.

He looked furious. "Why didn't you tell me?"

Galen glared at him hard. "Because I'm the master, boy. I keep the secrets. And besides, you'd have given it away a hundred times. You can't lie well enough."

Astounded, Raffi collapsed into silence. Galen leaned forward. "But I'm surprised, Carys, that you've already told these two. When I saw you in that cell I presumed you'd have pretended to be caught. So whose side are you really on?"

She was silent. They all watched her. Then she said quietly, "I'd only ever known the Watch, Galen, until I met you. I'd never spoken to keepers before. You did some things . . ."

He nodded, his long hair falling. "They told you it was all illusion."

"But why?" She looked up at him, face flushed. "I'm beginning to see some of the things they told us aren't true. I'm not sure anymore what I should believe. And then, when you were caught . . ." She shrugged. "I just wanted to get you out."

Galen looked at her, and something in his eyes softened.

The Sekoi squirmed uneasily. "Very touching," it muttered. "Forgive me for saying this, but, keeper, you realize this may all be lies. She may still want us to take her to the Crow. That's why she got you out."

"I do," Carys said.

"Yes, but only to solve your doubts? Or might you not

turn on us all when you find him? To capture the Crow would bring you a great deal of gold, no doubt." Its eyes gleamed yellow.

"For myself," she snapped.

"Prove it," Galen said quietly.

"How?"

"Leave your weapon here."

She stared at him, astonished. "That's madness! The city is full of dangers; we'd have no protection."

"Do it as an act of faith." His dark eyes watched her carefully. "Keepers carry no weapons."

"They do," she retorted. "Invisible ones."

"I have none, Carys."

She glanced away. "Yes, but just to leave it here! It's so stupid!"

"It will show us that you mean what you say."

She turned; for a long moment she stared at him, then at Raffi, who said nothing. Finally she pulled the bow off her back and threw it down. "I must be totally insane!"

Disgusted, she flung the spare bolts after it. "No wonder the Order's been wiped out!"

"It hasn't. Not yet." Galen took the globe from Raffi and fingered it. "And it never will. Not while we have faith."

As he said it an enormous crack burst in the sky outside, making them all jump. The Sekoi slithered to the window; as it looked out, they saw its face was rippled with red light.

"You'd better see this," it hissed.

Raffi pushed in. Another whooshing sound shot up; he saw a burst of red flame high in the dark; it fell in flakes behind the high walls.

"What was it?"

"Watch-flares." The Sekoi pulled its head in. "They've found the men under the arch. We need to move."

"Carefully though." Carys followed. "They'll double the patrols."

She slid out behind the Sekoi, but halfway through the window Raffi saw her look back at the crossbow; a hopeless, bitter look. Then he climbed after her.

Galen hurried them. They moved through broken palaces like shadows. But soon the buildings were left behind; they came to a desolation of smoke, rising and hissing from cracks; shattered walls broke up the way.

There were no streets here; the destruction had left only tumbled masses of stone. They hurried by the smashed pieces of an enormous statue; Raffi saw a hand as big as a room, lying pointing to the sky and, still in its original place, a huge bare foot, so vast that the toes were like small hills they had to scramble over.

The stench grew. Shadows of draxi swooped overhead, their screams keen. Raffi slipped and slithered behind the others, glad that Galen had the globe; he had fallen so often he would have broken it.

Now they ran over a wide square, their feet scuffling on the stones, and in the middle came to a pillar so tall its top was lost in the black sky. Galen stopped to look at it; every side was covered with cryptic letters.

Raffi caught his arm. "We can't stop."

"Look at it. Centuries old. The secrets it has."

"Hurry!" the Sekoi hissed from the dark. "I can smell them. They're close!"

They raced across the square. On the far side was an inky stillness; plunging into it, Raffi heard Carys shout, then he felt the steaming water soak his knees. He scrambled back.

The House of Trees

"Flooded," the Sekoi spat.

They gazed at an eerie landscape. An archway and some broken pillars rose from the water. Vapor hung above the surface and some leathery vegetation had managed to sprout here; it grew over the broken walls like a creeping rash. Steam gathered around them; where they stood, the ground was reverting to marsh, stinking of sulfur and the invisible heat.

Raffi tugged his feet out.

"We'll have to go around." Galen glanced back. "Take care. The ground may not be safe."

They had reached the heart of Tasceron, and it was a morass of ruined halls. Here and there carvings rose, half a body, a broken face; strange obelisks and doorways that led nowhere, standing on their own in the dim lake. Carefully they made their way around the edge of the swamp, climbing over walls and through gaps and holes.

Finally Galen stopped. He bent over the chart. "We're close. We need to find a tree."

"Here!" The Sekoi looked around, wondering.

"Yes. A calarna tree."

Raffi stared at him. The calarna was the first tree, the

tree of Flain. It had given its branches for the House of Trees. Were they that close?

"Spread out." Galen crumpled the paper. "Quickly."

Turning, Raffi ducked under the wall into a blackened garden. Brambles were waist-high; he forced his way into them, arms up, dodging the swinging, slashing thorns. Then a stifled yell stopped him.

"Galen! Over here!"

Tearing his coat in his hurry, he backed out and found Carys at the stump of something warped and ill-shapen. Galen shoved her aside and bent down to it. He gave a hiss of satisfaction.

"This was it."

"Keeper." The Sekoi's voice was quiet and cold. They looked up at it; its yellow eyes were narrowed.

"We're being watched."

"Sense-lines, Raffi!" Galen growled. "Now!"

Silent, he sent them out, and touched the flickers of men, many of them, running silent as ghosts through the ruined arcades. Galen was on hands and knees, groping on the ground. "Hurry! It's got to be here! An opening of some kind!"

The House of Trees

A slither of stones behind them. The Sekoi's fur prickled.

"No time to look, keeper."

"We have to find it!"

Carys crouched beside him. "Should have kept my bow," she whispered.

Desperate, they groped hurriedly in the dark among the smashed wreckage of rooms; broken pots, cups, tiles, brick and mosaic, shards of glass that glinted in the steamy haze.

Digging a splinter from his skin, Raffi felt the senselines snap, one by one. "They're here!" he gasped.

"I don't care!" Galen roared. "Find it!"

Sweating with worry, dizzy with the effort of keeping the lines out, Raffi swept a clutter of rubble aside and saw with a leap of his heart a face in the mossed floor. It was a mask of beaten copper, a huge thing, riveted down, and on its forehead, almost trodden out, a ring of six small circles, and in the middle, the seventh.

"The moons!"

"What?" Galen was there; his firm hands on the mask, fingers stretched flat, feeling for marks and symbols Raffi couldn't see, pushing and prodding.

Behind them, a whistle sounded; another answered, far to the left.

Then a voice rang out, loud in the darkness. "Galen Harn! Listen to me!"

Carys's head jerked up.

"Galen Harn!" the voice roared again. "This is the end for you! My men are all around you, keeper, so come out and bring your friends with you. Don't try anything. We're all armed."

Galen's fingers stopped. Under his hands the slab had moved; with a hoarse whisper it lifted, just a fraction. Out of the black slit came a dry, musty smell.

"Get something," he muttered. "Heave it up!"

The Sekoi jammed a branch under; it splintered but was enough to heave the stone wide; below it they saw a hot steamy darkness that daunted them all till the castellan yelled again.

"Come out, keeper! Or we come in!"

"Down," Galen said.

Raffi slid in first, feeling Carys follow. There were steps; his feet found them and he went down fast, afraid of falling. Above him, bodies slithered, dust fell.

The House of Trees

Then the slab came down, and shut tight.

"Keep silent," Galen hissed. "Don't move!"

Around Raffi, the silence breathed. He could feel Carys's elbow in his chest; looking down he saw only blackness, but far down, something plopped into a pool, a tiny, far-off sound.

Muffled yells came from above. Something scuffed on the slab; Raffi had a sudden vision of a Watchman standing on it, and then he saw the man as if he was looking up from the ground through the eyes of the copper mask. He swayed, giddy; Carys grabbed him. She said nothing, but her clutch was tight.

The shouts and scuffs faded.

After a while Galen's whisper came down. "Go on, Raffi, as quick as you can. They'll find the entrance soon enough."

Spreading his hands, Raffi felt for the walls. He could only find one, to his right, so he kept his hand on that and shuffled down. It was hot and airless. The steps seemed wide, their edges broken and unsafe; as he went down and down, he waited for his eyes to get used to the dark, but all he saw was blackness.

His foot met floor. He slid it out carefully. There were no more steps.

"I'm at the bottom." His voice rang hollow, as if in a great well.

He waited till everyone was down, unable to see at all.

"We should have brought a light."

"Maybe we did." Galen's voice was close; he sounded pleased.

A glow loomed over Raffi's shoulder; he turned in surprise and saw Galen was holding up the globe. It glimmered faintly, a pale light that showed him Carys and the Sekoi's sharp face, lit with delight.

"How can you . . . ?" he breathed, but Galen shook his head. "It's not me. It will show us the way to go."

Something thumped, far above. Galen pushed past him. "Hurry! This way."

They realized they were in an extraordinary corridor, so narrow that the walls brushed them on both sides, so high the roof was lost in darkness. Galen walked ahead with the globe; it brightened as he went, throwing huge shadows on the walls. These were of some soft earth, and in them were deep slits, marked with plaques and carved symbols. Some were so high that Raffi realized the corridor floor must have been cut away, year after year.

"What are they?" Carys said.

"Graves," he said in awe. "The earliest Archkeepers were buried near the House of Trees. Think how old they are, Carys."

She nodded, but all at once he remembered she was one of the enemy, and was angry with her, and himself, and everything.

They came to a side tunnel; an identical corridor. Ahead, the way forked into two.

"This is the maze," Galen said abruptly. "Chapter fifty-six, Raffi."

He said the words aloud, without thinking. "For the way to the House of Trees is a maze of ways and choices. Let the wise man tread it carefully. He knows not where the last wrong turn may take him."

"And I always thought that meant something else." Galen shook his head and the green beads glinted at his neck. "But it's a real maze."

"How do we get through it?"

"The globe." Galen held it gently in the opening of each

tunnel; in the one to the left it seemed slightly brighter. .

"We'll try here."

Following them down the slit, Carys muttered, "We ought to leave some trail. To get back out again."

The Sekoi snorted. "Yes, the Watch might like that.

"I suppose they might." It sounded as though she was laughing; Raffi glanced back and she winked at him. Behind her, the Sekoi looked unhappy. Troubled, Raffi hurried after Galen.

The maze was complex. They went as fast as they could, but the passageways grew even narrower, and there were so many of them leading off that Galen had to go a little way into each, watching the globe intently. Twice they took the wrong way, and had to go back as it dimmed.

Then from the back the Sekoi hissed, "Listen!"

Something moved, far above. A murmur of sound echoed. "They're in." Galen strode on quickly. "There's not much we can do about it."

Feeling the soft dust under his feet, Raffi knew the Watch would follow their tracks easily. All they needed was a lantern. He wondered if Carys had known that, and had been teasing him about leaving a trail. He didn't know. He didn't know anything about her.

Then he walked into Galen's back. The keeper lifted the globe. It was brilliant now, pulsing with white light. And they saw that the walls around them were no longer made of soil; instead they were strangely woven together; and as Raffi rubbed the dust off he saw that these were branches, hundreds of branches of different trees that had grown and tangled together. Galen held the globe high and they saw a vast doorway in front of them, its doorposts and lintel made of living calarna trees, black with age, and the mark of the Makers, the seven moons, was carved deep in the scented wood.

After a moment Galen began the words of blessing. Slow and sonorous, they sounded here; the old Maker-words, their meanings almost lost. Raffi made the responses, and the tunnels behind seemed to whisper the sounds back at him, as if all the dead remembered them. The Sekoi fidgeted restlessly, glancing back, and Carys stared up at the doorway as if inside it all her worst nightmares might come true.

Deep under the city, they had found the House of Trees.

The trouble was, Raffi thought, taking the globe from Galen, that they had also shown the Watch exactly where it was.

"Hurry," the Sekoi murmured.

The keeper went forward quickly and put both hands to the doors. He pushed hard, as if he expected them to be locked or swollen, but to their astonishment the wooden doors rolled smoothly back with a swish of sound.

And out of the House came light.

Blinding light.

24

We cannot undo his treachery. For once evil has entered the world, who can ever root it out?

Litany of the Makers

GALEN STRODE INTO THE BLAZE; coming
after him, Raffi stared around in amazement. The
great room was brilliant with cubes of light, standing
on plinths against the walls. Everything was made of
wood; the floor of smooth planks, and the walls of the
branches of living trees that had grown and tangled in
fantastic sculpture. How it had been done, he could not
imagine. The scents of the wood were sweet and strong.
He breathed them deep; they soothed him, like the forest
at night.

All around, in strange arrangements, were relics; boxes
of every size, dishes and plates of smooth strange materi-

als, statues, pictures, books; a set of small shining discs that glimmered with a rainbow sheen as Galen held one up. Everything had been arranged, put on display, and among the relics were hundreds of half-burned candles with the mark of the Order on them. It was a shrine, untouched since the secret of it died with the last Archkeeper to have closed the great doors. And behind, coming from everywhere, a faint whine, almost too thin to hear.

"What are all these things?" Carys touched a plate.

"The belongings of the Makers," Galen said. She looked at him. His face was unsmiling, but inside he was exultant; it cracked his voice and lit his eyes. "This is where they lived. Flain's own house. The Order kept it as he left it, for always. This is the most holy place." He rubbed his face uneasily. "We profane it by bringing outsiders here."

The Sekoi glanced back. "Keeper, we need to close those doors."

As Galen took no notice, it ran back; Raffi went too. "Galen is overcome," the creature muttered. "He doesn't care. But I can't forget the Watch. Hurry, Raffi!"

Together they rolled the great doors closed, but there

seemed to be no way of locking them. Looking around hastily, the Sekoi caught hold of a heavy table and began to drag it. "Help me!" it hissed.

For a second Raffi paused, terrified to disturb anything; then he too tugged at the dark wood. After all, if the Watch got in, nothing would be left.

They jammed the table tight against the doors. Galen was watching. "It won't stop them." Then he turned. "Come and see this."

It was a picture in a book. Not a painting. A picture that was real. Raffi stared at it, his skin crawling with delight. He was looking at another world.

The sky was very dark, darker than possible, and in it hung a moon, only one, but enormous, with dim smudges of land and splinter-rays of bright craters. Around it, the stars shone in unknown patterns, frosty bright.

Hands trembling, Galen fumbled in other books. Images of animals, trees, birds, some like owls and bee-birds that they knew; but there were others that made Carys gasp aloud—great gray beasts, striped night-cats, a myriad of odd species bizarrely shaped, intricately colored, completely unknown.

The Sekoi chewed its nails. "Galen . . ."

"Another world," he said, rapt. "The world of the Makers!"

There was a crash at the door. The table shuddered.

Galen took no notice. His eyes had fixed on a small silver device on the table in the center of the room. He crossed to it and touched it in awe. There were five touch-panels, like Raffi had seen on relics before; these would operate it. Each had an unknown symbol, set in a circle, and above them were words: COMMUNICATIONS RELAY—OUTER WORLDS.

They were set on a panel, the shape of which made Raffi forget the pounding at the door and the hammering of his heart. A sign that was the most secret, guarded image of the Order; a black bird with spread wings, holding a globe.

The Crow!

Staring at it, he breathed, "But the Crow is a man!"

Something crashed against the door. Carys spun around.

"No. The Crow is a relic." Galen was still for a split second; then he grabbed Raffi and sent him sprawling back. "Block that door! Keep them out! Do whatever it takes!"

Feverishly his fingers danced over the panel.

Raffi and the Sekoi threw themselves against the table; they jolted it back and piled everything they could find against it.

"More!" the Sekoi yelled.

"There's nothing big enough!"

"Then do something." Carys grabbed his hand. "You can, Raffi!"

Closing his eyes, he threw force-lines around it, bound it tight with all the energies he could summon. As if the Makers lingered here, he found it easier than before; the very earth in this place was sacred, it gave him power, fed him, and he laughed aloud.

The door shivered; someone outside yelled in anger.

He ran back to Galen. "Is it working?"

"Not yet! Not yet!" Galen's face was tense; his fingers stabbed each symbol, working out sequences frantically. Behind him, the Sekoi crouched, its fur bristling.

Carys gripped the table. "Perhaps it doesn't work. It's too old . . . !"

"Be quiet! Pray, Raffi. Pray."

Galen didn't have to tell him. But the Crow was silent. No spark came from it, no flicker of life.

And then the room was humming. Amazed, they stared around. It was coming from everywhere and nowhere; it lay in the air and was full of distance; small crackles and hisses, a listening sound.

"Makers. Can you hear me?" Galen asked in a whisper.

Something spoke. It was the voice of a ghost, garbled, distorted in bursts of static. All they knew was that it had asked a question. Galen was shivering, pale with dread and joy. He gripped his hands together. "Hear me," he breathed. "We need you! Hear me, lords!"

Far away, eons away, the Makers answered. "*We hear you. Who is this? What frequency are you on?*"

Galen's voice was unsteady. "I am Galen Harn, of the Order. Masters, come back to us! The world is slipping into the dark. Tasceron is fallen; the Emperor is dead. Do you know what's happening on your world, lords? We need you! Come back to us."

A hiss of static. Behind them the door was jerking

open; chairs crashing down. Only the Sekoi glanced back.

When the voice came again it was broken, the words fuzzy and slow, as if spoken distinctly and urgently, over and over.

"*What . . . world? What world?*"

Galen made the sign of blessing. "Anara," he breathed. "Are there others?"

The answer was a crackle of noise. "*Wait . . . light-years. Are you . . . colonists?*"

Galen gripped the table. "Say it again," he pleaded. "What did you say? Will you come?" But the hissing faded out and died.

The Crow was silent.

Galen bent over it, his face dark, and then slowly he straightened, and his eyes met Raffi's.

"They said they would come. They said, 'Wait.'"

"I'm not sure . . ."

"They will, Raffi! I know they will!"

With a crack that turned Raffi sick, the force-lines exploded; the doors crashed wide, men leaped across the table.

Galen turned, standing in front of the Crow. The

Watchmen stared at him, then around, curiously; each had a loaded bow and they were all pointing at Galen. Dizzy, Raffi pulled himself up and watched the castellan shoulder his way through.

He was a gray, bearded man. He folded his arms and looked at them all in silence.

"This is a great day for the Watch," he said softly.

It was Carys who moved. She came out from behind the Sekoi and said irritably, "You took your time! Where have you been?"

Raffi stared at her with horror.

The castellan smiled. "We had some trouble. Been wishing we were here, have you?"

She shrugged and crossed to him. "They know about me. Things were getting a little difficult."

"So what have I missed?"

She turned around and looked at Galen, her face set and hard. "The keeper will tell you. Show them the Crow, Galen. Show them now."

25

The leaves of the trees shall cry out for joy, for behold, the stars have spoken.

Apocalypse of Tamar

GALEN STARED AT HER; their eyes met. He stepped back, until the Crow was on the table between them, and he spread his hands over it. For Raffi it was a moment of black despair. She had told them. It was all over.

Then the light went dim. The Watchmen looked around uneasily.

"Take your hands off that device," the castellan called sharply.

Galen looked up. His face was wild and triumphant. "Too late," he said.

The thought-bolts burst from him like fire; they

exploded among the Watchmen, who yelled and scattered and dropped their bows. Two turned and ran. The doors slammed tight.

"Pick those weapons up!" the castellan raged. He grabbed one, raised it, and shot the bolt straight at Galen. Raffi gave a strangled yell, but the bolt had already burst into brilliant flames of green and black; then it shattered, sending pieces crashing across the hall.

Astonished, the Watchmen stood still.

"Take their weapons," Galen said harshly.

After a second, the Sekoi pushed past him. It snatched the bows quickly from the men's hands, gripping them with its seven fingers, a wide, happy smirk on its face. Then it dumped the pile against the wall and stood over them.

"What . . . who are you?" the castellan muttered.

The lights flickered, turned green. Galen was standing upright above the device; power from it filled him, flowed from him; he was flooded with it, Raffi could feel it, a wild, exulting joy that surged out of him.

"*I am the Crow*," he breathed. His voice was raw and strange; in the brightness his eyes were black.

362

The House of Trees

Raffi found himself trembling, shaking with fear, his hands clutched in the sign of blessing. The Sekoi crouched beside him, one hand on his shoulder.

It was Carys who answered, tense with excitement. "How can you be?"

Galen was taller, his face dark and hooked. Energy surged through him in crackles and sparks of color; Raffi saw blue and purple and silver threads of it flicker through the dark. Immense shadow loomed behind him, seeming to rustle and flap.

"I am the Crow! I have been buried too long in the dark," he cried, and his voice was harsh, both Galen's and yet changed. "Now I arise and look, Anara, I have summoned your Makers back to you; through the darkness and emptiness I call them! In ships of silver and crystal they'll come, Flain and Tamar and Soren of the trees—even Kest will come—and they will dispel the darkness and scatter the towers of the Watch. This is the prophecy I make! This is the truth I speak! They have told me they will come, and no one will stand against them!"

He flung out his hands; the shadows jerked wide. All

around him the walls were hissing and sprouting; Raffi saw that the trees were alive, growing, slithering out leaves and fruit. The Watchmen called out, some of them crumpled on the floor, terrified, and behind them the great doors thrummed with a strange electric hum, and the symbols on them glowed green and gold.

And then with a yell of delight, Galen made the seven moons, and they came to him with sparks of power out of the dark; Pyra and Agramon, Atterix, the pitted face of Cyrax, Lar, Karnos, the craters of Atelgar. And they moved in their right patterns—the Web, the Ring, the Arch—and Raffi laughed aloud to see them, and the Sekoi purred behind him, its hand clutching his shoulder tight.

As if he could never tire of it, Galen poured out his newfound power; he made sense-lines that snaked and tangled, brilliant flashes of scents, rivers and rainbows of energy that spurted and crackled and lit every one of the thousand candles with one enormous roar of flame.

And then suddenly he was still, and the room shimmered and glinted into silence. The lamps flickered, grew brighter. They saw they were in a room of leaves; millions of fresh green leaves that smelled like spring, and yet fruit hung there too, and great helios flowers.

The Watchmen were lying crumpled up against the door. Carys sat near them. She seemed too astonished to speak, but she was awake, and as Raffi came toward her, she staggered up unsteadily.

"Are you all right?" he asked.

She nodded, silent.

Galen followed them. He looked tired, the crow-black hair hung to his neck, but the very air about him still seemed to crackle.

"How did you know?" He gripped her hands. "How did you know, Carys?"

Her eyes widened, as if his touch burned. "I don't . . . I'm not sure. I just . . . felt that you could."

"But you went over to them—" Raffi began.

"Don't be ridiculous. I had to do something. Did you think I meant it?"

"I don't know." He stared at her. "I don't know what you are anymore."

She glared back, furious. "Well, neither do I, Raffi! Everything was simple before I met you! Everything was clear! The Order were frauds and fanatics and the Watch were my family and I wanted Galen Harn, dead or alive!"

She stared down at her hands. "That's all gone now. Nothing's the same. If the Order's powers are real, the Watch has lied to me, to all of us. I've got friends there, good friends. I won't leave them to be made fools of."

"If you go back," Galen said quietly, "they may see your doubts. I think you should stay with us, Carys."

She looked at him, a long, hard look. Then she hugged herself with her arms and said, "I can't."

"Keeper, you can't let her go back," the Sekoi put in, getting up from its corner. "Her or any of them. They've seen where your holy place is."

"I have the power," Galen said softly, "to wipe that from their minds." Ignoring Raffi's stare, he said, "And for the men I'll do that. But for you . . ."

Stepping forward, he faced her. "Now it's my turn to make an act of faith. Keep the knowledge. It will work inside you, Carys. It will draw you back to us. One day."

Wanly, she smiled. "Always trying to convert the fallen, Galen."

He nodded. "But come soon. The Makers will arrive, and I'd hate them to find you with the Watch."

"The Watch are my father and mother." She shook her head. "Or I thought so. But I can't wipe that training out. I need to think about things, find out what's true."

"You never will. But ask your questions carefully. If they think—"

"I know." She pulled a face. "I've seen people disappear. I know what happens to them, better than you."

He looked at her for a moment with a look that was new to him, then turned away. Bending over the Watchmen, he said something, and to Raffi's surprise they all stood up, but there was no consciousness in them, no memory.

"Lead them through the maze," he said to the Sekoi. "They'll follow you.

"Keeper . . . !"

"Don't worry. They're not dangerous."

With a wry grimace at Raffi, the creature shrugged and turned. The doors opened and the Sekoi walked through, the Watchmen following in a cowed, obedient huddle. None of them looked back.

Galen glanced around. "No power is left here. But the House will be sealed, and the secret kept." He glanced at Carys. "No one must know."

"Oh, don't worry," she said, picking a crossbow off the pile. "They'll only get it out of me on the rack."

"It might come to that," Raffi muttered.

He followed Galen through the doors, with one look back at the room of leaves, and then trudged thoughtfully through the maze. At one corner he turned and waited for Carys.

"I wanted to say I'm sorry." He felt awkward. "But I'm confused. Whose side are you really on, Carys?"

She caught his arm, swung him around, and pushed him ahead of her. "My side. And that's where I stay till I've decided." He felt her grin at his back. "You'll have to be satisfied with that."

He turned, blocking the way. "If you betray him, I'll hunt you down myself. I'd never forgive you."

Silent, she nodded. "I know," she whispered.

He walked on, grim, wondering if it was true, or if she would go straight to the Watch and tell them everything. Galen thought not. Galen with all his powers back—and

more. Galen, who had been the Crow, and had proph-
esied the future of the world.

"We'll have to write this down," he muttered.

"What?"

"Nothing." Coming to the stairs he ran up in the dark,
suddenly happy. "Nothing."

Outside in the dim square the Sekoi sat impatiently on
a low wall, chewing its nails. The Watchmen stood near,
an eerily silent group.

It leaped up in relief. "What have you done to these
men, Galen? Are they alive?"

Without answering, Galen faced the Watchmen.

"Go back to your tower. Remember nothing of what
you've seen. Forget me, forget these others, forget the
name of the Crow. Remember only that in your hearts
you fear the Makers."

They simply turned and walked away, the castellan
among them; for a long while the echo of their footsteps
rang in the empty alleys.

When they were gone Galen closed down the stone,
and then he and Raffi threw every hiding-spell they knew
around it, binding it tight, darkening it, until even Carys

realized that when she looked at the stone she could no longer quite see it, as if some blind spot hovered behind her eyes.

Finally Raffi looked around. The ruins of Tasceron were dark with smoke. Streets away, an owl hooted. "I almost thought all this would be changed."

"Not yet." Galen dragged his hair back irritably. "But when they come, we can rebuild this. We can rebuild everything."

The Sekoi stroked its fur. "You seem very sure of that, keeper."

Galen stood a moment, as if looking deep inside himself. Then he said, "I am."

They walked slowly over the broken stones to a splintered archway. The alley beyond was silent and black.

Carys turned suddenly. "I'll go on from here alone."

"Change your mind!" Raffi urged abruptly.

She grinned at him. "Look out for me. If the Makers do come, put in a good word." Taking the small pack off her back, she tugged something out and pushed it into his hands. "You'd better have this. You can keep it to remember me."

The House of Trees

And she was gone, a flicker in the shadows of the alley, and they could hear her feet running after the tread of the Watchmen.

Raffi looked down; it was a small blue book full of scrawled writing. "Good-bye, Carys," he murmured, and then sent one long sense-line curling after her.

"I can't help thinking," the Sekoi said drily, "that she's gone back there knowing everything she set out to know. I hope you're sure of what you're doing, Relic Master."

Raffi was silent. It was Galen who answered. "Faith is a strange tree. Plant the seed and somewhere, sometime, in the right weather, it will grow. We also have done what we came for." He turned to the creature. "We go back to the Pyramid. Then we need to get out of Tasceron. Can you help?"

The Sekoi's sharp face smiled. "I'm sure it can be arranged."

"Good."

"And then what? Do you drag me kicking and squealing back to Alberic?"

Raffi looked up. "Alberic! He's still got our blue box!"

Galen and the Sekoi gazed at each other with a strange glint in their eyes. Carelessly the Sekoi kicked a loose stone. "I suppose we could always steal it back."

"I suppose we could," the keeper said grimly. Then he grinned. "I think it's our duty really, don't you?"

The Lost Heiress

To Maggie and Roger

Contents

THE STRAIN ON HIS ARMS was agony. Clutching the rope, he hauled himself up, hand over hand, gripping with aching knees and ankles.

"Hurry up!" The Sekoi leaned precariously from the tower ledge above, its seven fingers stretching for him. Behind it the Maker-wall glimmered in the light of the moons.

Raffi gave one last desperate pull, flung his hand up, and grabbed. A hard grip clenched on his; he was dragged onto the ledge and clung there, gasping and soaked with sweat.

"Not bad," the creature purred in his ear. "Now look down."

Below them, the night was black. Somewhere at the tower's smooth base Galen was waiting, a shadow with a hooked face of moonlight, staring up. Even from here Raffi could feel his tension.

"Now what?"

"The window." Delicately the Sekoi put its long hand out and wriggled it through the smashed, patched pane. A latch clicked. The casement creaked softly open.

The creature's fur tickled Raffi as it whispered, "In you go."

Raffi nodded. Silently he swung his feet and slithered over the sill, standing in the still room.

In the moonlight he sent a sense-line out, feeling at once the tangled dreams of the man in the bed, the sleeping bodyguards outside the door, and then, as he groped for it, the bright mind-echo of the relic, the familiar blue box.

It was somewhere near the bed.

He pointed; the Sekoi nodded, its yellow eyes catching the light. Raffi began to cross the room. He knew there was no one else here, but if Alberic woke up and yelled, there soon would be. The tiny man seemed lost in the

4

vast bed, its hangings purple and crimson damask, heavy and expensive. Beside the bed was a table, a dim shadow of smooth wood, and he could just see the gleam of a drawer-handle. The relic box was in there.

Galen's box.

Inch by inch, Raffi's hand moved toward the drawer.

Alberic snuffled, turned over. His face was close to Raffi now; a sly face, even in sleep. Soundlessly, Raffi opened the drawer, pushed his fingers in, and touched the box. Power jerked through him; his fingers clenched on it and he almost hissed with the shock. Then it was out, and shoved deep inside his jerkin.

Glancing back, he saw the Sekoi's black shape breathless against the window; behind it the stars were bright. He backed, carefully.

But Alberic was restless, turning and tossing in his rich covers; with each step back Raffi felt the dwarf's sharp mind bubbling up out of the dark, a growing unease. As he turned and grabbed the window he felt the moment of waking like a pain.

Alberic sat bolt upright. He stared across the dark room; in that instant he saw them both, and a strangled scream of fury broke out of him. In seconds Raffi was out, slithering down the rope after the Sekoi, so fast that the heat seared the gloves on his hands, and as he hit the bottom and crumpled to his knees he heard the dogs erupt into barking and the screeching of Alberic's wrath.

Galen's hand grabbed him. "Have you got it?"

"Yes!"

The dwarf's head jutted from the high window. "Galen Harn!" he screamed, his voice raw. "And you, Sekoi! I'll kill you both for this!"

He seemed to be demented with rage; someone had to haul him back inside. "I'll kill you!" he shrieked.

But the night was dark. They were already long gone.

Flainsdeath

1

*As the Makers shaped the world, Kest
began to brood in his secret place,
remembering the scorn of Flain's and
Tamar's jokes. And in a cave under the
ice he began his experiments, making tiny
beasts from parts of others, giving them
forbidden life. And these things he kept
hidden from Flain's wrath.*

Book of the Seven Moons

"Are you sure you've got everything?" Rocallion asked anxiously.

Raffi finished arranging the black and green beads and looked around. "Maybe a few more candles."

"I'll get them sent up. Will the keeper be ready?"

They both glanced across the dim room. Galen was sitting by the fire, in an upright chair. He seemed to be daydreaming, staring deep into the flames, but when Raffi reached out for the keeper's soul, he couldn't find it; it was walking far away in some place he hadn't yet learned to reach. "He'll be ready in his own time."

Rocallion nodded, pulling berries nervously off the

holly. He was a young man to be franklin of so big a manor, Raffi thought, but he seemed to run it well. The fields they'd traveled through yesterday had been well-plowed, the cottages in good repair. And now Rocallion was worried; it made Raffi worry too.

"No more news of the Watch?" Raffi asked.

Rocallion perched on the edge of the bench. He nearly put the holly berry in his mouth, then tossed it absently into the fire. "Only the rumor of that patrol out at Tarnos. That was two days ago. Before the leaf-fall." He gazed out at the darkening sky. "It should keep them indoors. But on Flainsnight, you never know."

Raffi nodded, crossing to the window and leaning his hands on the sill. He knew that whatever the weather, the Watch would be prowling tonight. In the damp chill of the autumn twilight the countryside beyond was misty, the far hills faint blurs. In the cloud-ragged sky the moons were bright, all seven of them, with Pyra a fiery-red point in the east. There were no other lights, anywhere.

"Raffi!"

He turned instantly.

Flainsdeath

Galen was standing, tall and dark, his hawk-face sharp in the firelight. Power was moving around him; Raffi could see it, the blue tingles and sparks. It made him shiver.

"I'm ready," the keeper said softly. "Let them in."

The room was dark, as it should be, with no light but the fire. As the door opened Raffi saw the shapes of Rocallion's tenants slip into the room, twelve or so men, the ones he could trust, with their wives and a few children. In the dimness they were nervous shadows, the creak of a bench, a whisper.

The air of the room was sharp with sorcery and fear. All of them knew that if the Watch caught them they'd pay heavily. Money, cattle, even their children might be taken away. Rocallion would lose most. But they wouldn't die, Raffi thought bitterly. Not like he and Galen would die. Slowly.

He shivered. But Galen had begun.

"Friends. This is the night of Flainsdeath. Tonight we do what the faithful have done for centuries, since the Makers themselves were here." He frowned. "In these days of evil we have to meet in secret; I salute the courage

15

of each of you in coming. Tonight the Watch will ride out. But if you have kept the secret, we may be safe."

His black eyes watched their tense faces. So did Raffi.

They were scared. That was natural. Or he hoped it was.

Galen paused. Then his voice lowered. "Before we start, I have some news for you. Two months ago the boy and I came out of Tasceron, the Wounded City, the City of the Makers. While we were there we saw and heard things I couldn't explain if I wanted to. But this is the point. The Makers, at last, have spoken to the Order. They've sent us a message. They've promised us they will return."

The silence was complete, as if no one breathed.

Then someone said, "Is it certain?"

"I heard the voice myself, across space and time. The boy heard it, and others. They told us to wait." He rubbed the edge of his hand wearily down his cheek. "How long, I don't know. We must all pray it will be soon. Kest's creatures multiply, and the Unfinished Lands still spread. The Watch grows in strength. We need it to be soon."

They were astonished. Their amazement was so strong

Flainsdeath

Raffi felt he could almost have touched it; it was sharp as the holly hanging from the roof, bright as the berries the fire scorched. But they believed.

The keeper turned abruptly, ignoring the sudden buzz of whispers. "Are your sense-lines out, boy? I may be too busy."

Raffi nodded; he'd already checked them, a net of energy lines around the house, stretching out as far down the moonlit lanes and trackways as he could manage. If anyone crossed them, he'd know.

"Then we'll start," Galen said.

He sat, waved a hand, and Raffi climbed to his feet, nervously waiting for the whispers to quiet.

Finally they were all looking at him.

He had only done this once before, though he had heard the story of Flain's death most years since he was small. Now he would recite it, from memory, from the Book of the Seven Moons. After that the keeper would enter the Silence, maybe for minutes, maybe for hours. Until he woke, like Flain had woken, bringing them the secret Word. And then the candles would be lit and, at last, they'd eat. Raffi was desperate for food. He'd been fasting all day, and now his stomach rumbled quietly. Gripping his fists, he began quickly.

"The soul that had been Flain traveled deep into the Otherworld, always seeking the way back. After hours and years and centuries he came to a low place, no higher from the floor than his knee, and he crawled among the veins and wormholes of the Underworld. Through the mines and tunnels of Death he crept, to a wide cavern lit only by red flame. In the center of the cavern lay a casket, made of gold and calarna wood, and the soul of Flain crossed the soft sand to the casket and opened it.

"In the casket was a Word. And Flain saw the Word, and as he saw it, all the secrets of the world came to him, and he knew the way out from Death, and the future; and far off and very faint, he heard the voices of the Makers— Tamar, Soren, Theriss—calling for him.""

Raffi stopped. In the silence the fire crackled, smelling of pine and furzewood. Faces were red glimmers, sharp angles of shadow. As he sat down, all eyes turned to Galen.

The Relic Master sat upright in his chair, his black hair

glossy in the dimness, his eyes catching the flame light. He sat easily, without moving, his face gaunt and calm. And as they watched, in the smoky hall, through the wood crackle and the soft patter of hail on the shutters, they saw something begin to form, in the air before the fire.

A bench creaked, bodies leaned forward. A child said something and was hushed.

It came out of nowhere, out of the dark, and though they had all seen this happen before, the eerie chill of it was always new. Even Raffi felt the ice of fear touch his spine.

The casket was large, and strange, made of gold and calarna wood: Flain's casket, with its hinges gleaming. Slowly it became solid, until it was heavy, on a small table, the wood richly oiled.

Raffi stared. Every keeper made the casket differently; he had seen Galen perform the Flainsdeath summoning before, but never like this. It was so quick. Something was strange. Something was different.

Outside, the rising wind beat at the shutters. For a long moment Galen waited. Then he stood up, his hands on the lid.

"I open this," he said, his voice hoarse, "as Flain did. Let the Word speak to us, let it teach us the secrets."

It was back, the power that had possessed him before; the power that was the Crow. Dizzy with it, Raffi felt it crackle and rustle around the room like dark wings, making his fingers jerk and tingle, blurring some deep uneasy nagging in his head.

Now Galen was opening the lid, and as he lifted it all the people gasped, because light came out of it, a widening slit, stabbing up into the smoke, throwing a brilliant glare onto Galen's face as he stared down into it, undazzled.

Raffi stood up. Something snagged in his mind, some warning. Outside, the wind howled and rattled.

With both hands, Galen was reaching eagerly into the casket. There were things he should have said, parts of the Litany. He wasn't saying them. Uneasy, Raffi shifted. "Galen. The Responses."

There was no sign he was heard.

"Galen?"

No one moved. Turning his head, Raffi saw why.

Shapes and swirls of energy were everywhere in the room, sparking up paneling, the folds of hangings, spitting along the tables. Amazed, the tenants stared around them. Small blue coils unwound, snapping back on themselves around Galen, leaving a faint smell of burning. Raffi had never seen anything like it before.

Then Galen spoke abruptly. "I see the Word!"

He lifted his eyes. They were black, as if blinded. Rocallion was standing; everyone was. A boy called out; there were noises from outside, horse hooves, running, a banging on the door. With a guilty shock Raffi dragged his mind back to the sense-lines; they were snagged open, torn wide.

"The Watch!" he hissed, but the keeper was rigid, the box in his hands pulsing with light.

"Would you hear the Word?"

"Speak it!" someone murmured, remembering the answer.

"I speak it." Galen breathed sharply, as if a knife had stabbed him. "The Word . . ." He sought for it, hands gripped tight, until suddenly his eyes cleared in shock. "The word is . . . *Interrex*."

The whole room stared at him in astonishment.

Then the casket vanished soundlessly.

Raffi moved. "Rocallion, the Watch are here!" Shoving through the crowd he grabbed Galen's arm. "They're here! At the door!"

"What!" The franklin stared at him in horror. "But I've got men out."

"They're through that! Listen!"

Voices were loud in the courtyard. A horse neighed, hooves clattered over the cobbles.

"Flainsteeth!" Rocallion leaped across the room and grabbed Galen. "With me, keepers, now! Hurry!"

He dragged them through a door in the wall. Behind them Raffi could hear the table hastily pulled out, candles lit, the hurried children being pushed into seats. A Flainsnight supper was not illegal. Not yet.

They raced down a tiny stair, Raffi stumbling in the sudden dark. "Your friends . . ." Galen gasped.

"Don't worry. They won't talk. Just a party."

"Unless the Watch know we're here," the keeper growled.

At the bottom was a corridor. Rocallion looked up and down it, then opened a door opposite, hustled them through, and bolted it behind him.

"Stillroom," he hissed.

It was musky with herb smells, bunches of them hung from the ceiling. A bench was littered with glass vials and bowls. Someone was calling, far off in the house, but, ignoring it, Rocallion crouched and pulled a hidden catch near the hearth. Instantly a small panel slid open in the wall.

Galen crawled in, Raffi scrambling after him.

Rocallion's white face filled the gap. "No one else knows about this. I'll get you out when I can. You'll be safe."

The keeper nodded. "Good luck," he said.

But the panel was slammed tight.

2

*Tamar dragged the thing before the
Council; a six-legged lizard, moaning in
pain, studded with spines.*

*"What abomination is this?" Flain
demanded.*

*"This, lord, is what Kest has done in
secret."*

*And all eyes turned to me, in my
corner.*

Sorrows of Kest

THEY WERE CROUCHED in some black, damp-smelling place. Raffi stretched out his hand and touched a cold wall.

"So." Galen's voice came grimly out of the dark. "They timed that well."

"Will they find us?"

"It depends on how suspicious they are. Can you see them?"

Raffi tried, opening the third eye, his mind's eye. "Six?"

"More like ten." Galen sounded distant, as if his mind was listening to the uproar in the house. "Hard to tell. There's a lot of confusion." He must have eased his leg then, because he hissed with the ache of it; Raffi felt a faint echo of pain.

"Make a light, boy. Let's see where we are."

It took Raffi an effort; concentrating made him dizzy. But finally he managed a weak globe of light in the air before him, wobbling.

"Hold it still!" Galen snapped, looking around.

They were in a tiny cell, hardly tall enough for Galen to stand. The walls were damp brick—plastered once, but most of that lay in lumps on the floor. There were no windows. A crack in one corner let in an icy draft. In another corner was a basket, with a pile of blankets on top.

The globe faded. Raffi sweated with the effort of keeping it.

"Leave it." Galen had the basket open, rummaging inside. A tinderbox sparked; Raffi saw the faint glow of kindling being blown red.

"Save your energy. We may be days in here."

If we're lucky, Raffi thought. He let the globe go out. Then he asked, "Any food?"

"Some. Rocallion seems to have been prepared."

"Unless he knew they were coming."

Flainsdeath

Galen looked up sharply, his face dark. "You think so?"

Raffi shrugged. "No."

"In that case, keep quiet, and don't slur a good man. Take the blankets. They're damp, but thick."

Raffi tugged one around himself and shivered. Galen handed him bread, an apple, some strips of dried meat. "Flainsnight feast," he said.

Raffi stared at it in disgust. Then he ate. He was used to being hungry. Any food was something.

"We have enough for about two days." Galen crunched an apple absently.

"Will it be that long?"

The keeper shrugged. "If the leaf-fall is too thick the Watch will stay in the house."

"He could bring us food."

"He'll be followed. Everywhere." Stretching his legs out, Galen considered. "If no one else knows about this hiding place, we're dependent on him. At least his housemen can't betray us. If he has—" He stopped instantly. His hand shot to his neck.

"Oh God!" he said.

"What?" Raffi knelt up. "What is it?"

Galen had flung the apple down, was searching his pockets, inside his jerkin, desperately. "The beads! The awen-beads!"

They started at each other in blank horror.

"Did you pick them up?"

"No, I . . ."

"God! Raffi!" Galen slammed one hand furiously against the wall.

"There are other things too," Raffi realized miserably. "Your stick. Our bags."

"Those are well hidden. The beads were there—in that room!"

Guilty, sick with fear, Raffi sat rigid, seeing the strings of jet and green crystals in their interlocking circles. He should have grabbed them! He should have remembered them!

"I'm sorry," he breathed.

Galen turned on him sourly. "I suppose I should beat you black and blue."

"No room," he joked feebly.

"Nor any need. The Watch will do it for me."

In the silence each of them imagined a gloved hand

snatching up the beads, a yell. Any Watchman would recognize them at once.

"Maybe one of the tenants found them."

"Listen!" Galen caught him.

Footsteps ran down the stairs above, loud, heavy boots. Galen snuffed the candle instantly. The stillroom door banged open. Someone came in and paced around.

They know, Raffi thought. His hands clenched, he huddled in the dark.

They were searching. Cups crashed over. Something made of glass fell and shattered. A foot kicked impatiently along the paneling.

It'll sound hollow, he thought, clutching his arms as if he could make himself smaller. Galen was a still shadow against the wall.

It did sound hollow, but the searcher seemed not to notice. Someone called him; he yelled back, "Down here," in a voice so close it made Raffi sweat. Then he was pounding up the stairs again, the door banging behind him.

Silence. A long silence.

Finally, tight with terror, Raffi made himself uncurl. He drew a deep ragged breath.

"Sit still," Galen said. "They'll be back."

They were. All evening, late into the night, the house was alive with bangs and shouts, thudding doors and footsteps. Every time Raffi finally dozed into uneasy sleep under the moth-eaten blanket, some crash or voice jerked him awake; cold with sweat, his hands clenched. He was sick and giddy with fear. Galen never spoke, perhaps didn't even hear. He stayed where he was, knees drawn up, quite still in the dark. Raffi knew he was deep in prayer, lost in a rigid meditation, and how the keeper had the discipline for it astonished him. Once or twice he tried himself, gabbling the Litany and the Appeal to Flain, but the words dried up, or he found himself repeating one phrase foolishly over and over, all his attention fixed on the clatter around the house.

Not knowing was the worst.

Had they found the beads? Were they tearing the place apart? Was Rocallion under torture? Had he talked? When would the smoke start curling under the panel, choking them, driving them out into the swords and crossbows of the Watch?

Flainsdeath

He tossed and curled and uncurled hopelessly until, without even realizing he'd been asleep, he was awake, staring at the crack of cold daylight, the sudden sharp stink of a midden somewhere.

He rolled over and sat up.

Gaunt in the dark, Galen was watching. After a moment he said, "Take something to eat. One swallow of water from the jar."

"Have you . . . ?"

"Hours ago."

Guiltily, Raffi broke a stiffening crust and ate it, with a tiny piece of cheese. The water was cool and fresh; he tried not to take a big swallow. "Did you sleep?"

Galen glared, the grim look Raffi loathed. "I prayed for forgiveness. So should you."

"I don't—"

"The beads, boy!" Galen shook his head in disgust. "I let myself fear—I forgot that the Makers have us all in their hands! We have to trust them. They won't let the Watch find us unless they wish it, and if they do, so be it. Who are we to be afraid?"

Raffi chewed the bread. "It's hard not to be."

"You're a scholar. I'm a master and should know better."

Galen was always harsh, harshest of all with himself. That moment of terror would irritate him; it would be a long time before he would forgive himself for it. Raffi sat back, thinking of the Crow, the strange power of the Makers' messenger that had entered Galen in Tasceron, filling him with unknown abilities. Since then there had been little sign of it. Galen had been normal—grim, short-tempered, fierce. Until last night. Raffi licked the last crumbs from his fingers. Last night, it had come back. In a whisper he asked, "What happened, at our Summoning?"

Galen raised dark eyes. Dragging the long hair from his neck, he knotted it in a piece of string. Then he said, "I'm not sure. The casket . . . I made the casket as I always do, but when it came, it was different. Bigger. Then the light . . . If I made that I don't know how. And I've never felt a word so surely. It burned through me like fire." He glanced up. "Did I say it aloud?"

"Yes. You said 'Interrex.'"

Galen scowled. "Maybe the Watch should have come sooner. Some messages are not for everyone to hear."

Flainsdeath

"Don't joke about the Watch." Raffi wriggled under the blanket. "What does it mean?"

"Interrex? It's a word from the Apocalypse. It means one who rules between the kings."

"But what—"

"Enough questions!" Galen sat upright abruptly. "If we're going to be cooped up in here we'll use the time. I've neglected your studies, so first we go over the Sorrows of Kest. From the beginning."

It was an endless day.

Galen drilled him in every chapter of the Sorrows; then they worked through the Litany, the Book of the Seven Moons, the Sayings of the Archkeepers, even the eternal life of Askelon with its forty-seven Prophecies of the Owl. He learned the last twenty wearily, repeating them after Galen in a whisper, the keeper impatiently correcting.

They dared not speak aloud; four times someone came into the stillroom. Once, an animal—a dog, Raffi thought—scratched at the panel, but Galen made a thought-flare that sent it squealing. Each time, Galen went back to work grimly. Raffi knew it was just to keep them both busy, to stop the fear, but in the end it was agony; all he wanted to do was scream. By the time the keeper let him rest, his voice cracking with thirst, the daylight in the corner was long gone. So was most of the food.

Raffi took an agonizingly small sip of water. "He must come tonight. He won't let us starve in here."

"Maybe." Galen slumped against the wall. "Maybe not."

Pulling himself up awkwardly, Raffi limped about. He was stiff with the cold, a bitter cold that felt like snow. Bending down, he tried to see out, but the crack was too narrow. He jammed a rag into it, and instantly felt Galen's hand grab him; a warning grip.

The panel was sliding open.

The candle guttered. When the flame steadied they saw Rocallion crawling in. He looked tired and haggard, tugging food and another jar of water from under his jerkin. "Eat this," he gasped. "Quickly. I've got to get out."

Galen caught hold of him. "Did they find the beads?"

"What beads?" Then his eyes widened. "Have you lost them?"

"We left them in the room."

Flainsdeath

The young man rubbed his hair frantically. "I don't know! The fat man hasn't mentioned them!"

"Then they're safe. One of your friends must have them." Galen sat back in relief. "How did you get away?"

"Don't ask."

Stuffing bread into his mouth, Raffi muttered, "How many of them are there?"

"A full patrol. They've searched the house, questioned everyone. I hope it was just a random visit."

"No one gave anything away?"

Rocallion looked strained. "No. But they—" He stopped.

Raffi swallowed hard.

Outside, in the stillroom, something had shifted. A tiny movement, a creak of floorboard, but they all knew what it meant. Someone had followed him.

Rocallion closed his eyes in despair. He almost spoke, but Galen shook his head fiercely, snuffing the candle with one swift jab. Raffi felt the power gather in him, in the darkness around them.

Slowly, the panel opened.

Someone stood there, shadowy. Then the figure

crouched, and to Raffi's astonishment, a small hand stretched into the cell, and he caught the glint of the green and black beads that swung from the fingers.

"You know, you shouldn't leave these things lying around, Galen," a voice said, amused. "Anyone might find them."

3

*Between the kings the Interrex shall
come; come from the dark and to the
darkness go.*

Apocalypse of Tamar

"CARYS!"

The girl grinned at them in the dimness. "Hello, Raffi. Still hungry?"

"You know her?" Rocallion was staring in astonishment. "But she's one of the Watch!"

"Her name is Carys Arrin. As for what she is, only God and the Makers know." In the half-light Galen reached out gently and took the beads from her fingers. "So it was you who found them."

"Luckily for you." She glanced back at the door. "But we haven't got time to talk. The Watch commander is called Braylwin. He's fat and lazy, but he's got a mind like

a razor and he's sure there was a keeper here for Flainsnight. I'm not exactly the apple of his eye, either. So I
want you out of here."

"You think we'd betray you?" Galen said quietly.

"Under torture, yes." She stared hard at him, her short
brown hair swinging. "Look, I can get you out if you
come now. I'm guard leader for two hours, and everything's quiet. The patrol will stay here at least a week,
Galen. You might not get another chance."

Galen blessed the beads, pulled them on, then stiffly
crawled out of the cell and stood up. "Of course we trust
you," he said, as if she'd asked.

Bewildered, Rocallion stared up at him. "Are you sure?"

Raffi grinned. "We think so."

"Think!"

"Hope."

Carys was already at the door, peering around it. In the
darkness she seemed taller, her hair shorter. The crossbow
was slung at her back. She said, "We go down the corridor, then the cellar stairs. Can the cellar door be opened
from inside?"

Rocallion shrugged. "The Watch have got the keys."

Flainsdeath

"I've got the keys. There's a guard in the courtyard; I'll talk to them while you get by. Down the lane is a byre, by the gate—it's been searched already. We'll meet there. Agreed?"

She's used to giving orders, Raffi thought.

Galen nodded. It was hard to see his expression in the dimness. Glancing back, she said suddenly, "Make sure you wait for me, Galen, because I've got something to tell you. Something important."

As he stepped forward into the lamplight from the corridor, they caught his wolfish smile. "I know that."

"You would!" For a moment she grinned. Then she was out the door. Galen pushed Raffi after her, then came himself, with Rocallion silently at the back.

The corridor was empty, lit with one lamp. Far off in the house someone laughed. They clustered at the end while Rocallion took his keys from Carys and fumbled for the right one; as soon as the door opened they slipped through.

It closed behind them with a click.

"Be careful," Rocallion's voice echoed. "There are steps in front of you leading down."

Raffi found them, edging cautiously. He knew they
were in the cellar—it was bitterly cold and smelled of
beer casks. Twice at the bottom he walked into barrels.
Finally Rocallion pushed through from the back. "Let me
go first."

There was no light and Galen made none; it would
have been fatal if the door above had opened.

When Raffi caught up with Rocallion, the back door
was already unlocked. Infinitely carefully, the franklin
opened it and looked out. Under his arm Raffi saw the
dim courtyard, dark gables, a single star overhead.

A murmur of talk came from somewhere nearby. Carys
pushed her way silently to the front. "Take care," she
breathed. Then she squeezed past them and went out into
the night.

They waited. Raffi felt the cold drift of the leaf-fall
on his face, heard the hiss of it against the roofs of the
manor-house. The night was unusually still, as if held
in frost, though far off in the woods an owl called, and
nearer something squeaked, like a jekkle-mouse.

The voices had gone. Instead only Carys was talking,
loud and furious. He could hear the anger in her voice,

and was amazed again at the way she could lie, and pretend, and act.

"Go now," Galen whispered. They slid carefully out into the blue shadows, edging along the wall.

The leaf-drift had fallen all day. Here in the lee of the wall it was a bare sprinkling, so that their feet cut dark prints; Galen scuffed them out hurriedly. They sprinted between buildings, under the low eaves of a barn. As they flitted through a gate, Raffi glimpsed the red glare of a fire, heard Carys's sharp orders. She wanted a sharper watch kept. And she wanted those dice! Now! Raffi grinned, his fingers slipping over the cold of the gate bar.

In the lane they could run, but the ruts were full of frosted puddles that tilted and splintered, wheezing as they broke. The ground was rock hard and even the firethorns had leaf-dust all over them; the storm had brought a sudden sharp frost, the first this year. Raffi shivered, his breath smoking in the sudden glint of two moons that drifted from the clouds.

Galen pulled him into the hedge-shadow. "This byre. How far?"

Rocallion caught his breath. "Just ahead."

They could see the low edge of its roof, among branches. This end of the lane was banked with leaves; a great wall, well-trampled, as if cows had forced a way through. The pungent smell of fireberries was rank.

Rocallion put his hands on the door-bar, but Galen stopped him. "Wait."

In silence the keeper stood, one hand on the wall. They both knew he was sending sense-lines inside.

"I thought you trusted her?" Rocallion whispered.

"We do. And we don't."

Then the keeper nodded, and they lifted the bar and hurried in. The byre was empty, deep with old straw. A rat rustled away. Breathless, they crouched in the cold; Raffi buried himself in straw.

"Maybe I should go back," Rocallion murmured.

As he said it the door creaked; Carys slipped in and stood there. She folded her arms and grinned at them. "I'm glad you stayed."

"I wouldn't have missed it," Galen said gravely. "But won't they miss you?"

She came over and sat by them, taking the crossbow off and tossing it down. "Them! They'll be glad to see the back of me." She hugged her knees. "So what have you both been doing? How did you get out of the city?"

"The Sekoi have ways," Galen said carelessly. "After that the three of us came north and paid a little visit to a thief-lord named Alberic."

She laughed. "We know about that. He's after you."

"Is he?" Raffi was alarmed.

"Some of our spies have reported that he's sent men out, asking questions. You should be careful."

"I intend to be," Galen said drily. "Did you hear how Raffi climbed up the wall of his tower?"

She giggled. "I didn't think you had it in you."

"Neither did I," Raffi muttered, remembering the terror of the swinging rope, his raw hands.

Carys was silent a moment. Then she looked up, her eyes bright. "I've got some information you'll find . . . interesting. It's highly secret." Her glance flickered to Rocallion.

He caught it, and stood up. "Your packs are hidden in an old well out near here. I'll get them for you."

When he had gone she got up and checked the door, then came back and crouched. Excitement was streaming from her; Raffi could almost see it, and he struggled up in the straw, his skin tingling.

"Listen," she said. "Last month, up in the hills, an old woman was being questioned."

"Questioned?" Galen looked at her grimly.

"I can't help their methods. In any case, she suddenly came out with some amazing information, probably to save herself. She told them she once worked in the Emperor's palace. When the Emperor was killed at the fall of Tasceron, the young man next to him, whose body was too badly burned to be sure about, was assumed to have been his son. According to the old woman, this wasn't so. The son, the Prince, escaped. He lived for many years in hiding in a village named Carno. He married, and seven years ago he had a child. The old woman lived with them. Her name was Marta. No one else knew who they were. But then a Watchpatrol came for slave laborers for the mines at Far Reach. They took the parents, and the old woman, though she was no good to them. No one seems to know what happened to the child."

"And the Prince?" Galen said.

"Dead. We checked."

Flainsdeath

They were silent. Then Raffi breathed out slowly. "So the Emperor had a grandchild."

Galen pondered, his eyes glinting. "This is excellent news, Carys, if it's true . . . Boy or girl?"

"That was one thing she wouldn't say."

"A new Emperor!" Galen stood up and limped around in excitement. "It's a miracle! And it fits. When the Makers come back everything will be restored."

"You're still sure they're coming?" Carys asked quietly.

"You were there. You heard them."

She shook her head, rueful. "I heard something. A voice. But look, Galen, if you want this Interrex of yours—"

"What did you say?" The keeper whirled around, staring at her, his eyes black. In the shadows his face was suddenly hooked and sharp. The Crow's face.

"I said Interrex. It's Braylwin's joke. It's from your Book."

He glanced at Raffi. "Once again."

Carys frowned. "What do you mean, again?"

"It was the Word. On Flainsnight. The word the Makers sent."

For a moment she looked at Galen so still and strangely

49

that he felt something flame up in her, some doubt or anger. Then she said bleakly, "Well, anyway, if you want this Interrex you'd better find him fast. Or her. Because we're already looking."

"We?"

"The Watch. And the reward is big, believe me."

Galen came close to her, suddenly. "Leave the Watch, Carys! Come with us."

"I've told you I won't. You could be all wrong, Galen. Mistaken about everything."

He smiled coldly. "Was the Crow wrong? When you saw the House of Trees break into leaf, when you heard a voice from the stars, was all that a mistake? You know it wasn't."

The silence was bitter.

Then, abruptly, the door banged open and Rocallion backed in, two packs in his arms and Galen's stick thrust through his belt. A gust of leaf-dust swirled in with him.

Carys stood up. "I've told you. You must do what you want about it. If the Watch find the child they'll kill it, that's for sure." Then she laughed at them, eyes bright. "I'm not really with the Watch, Galen. I'm for myself,

Flainsdeath

I told you that. There are things I want to find out, and being on the inside is the best way. Braylwin's lazy; he spends every winter in the Tower of Song, and I want to go with him, because that's where all the Watch records are kept. I need to know who I am. Where I came from. But you must find the Interrex. That word was for you."

She was at the door, but she stopped when Raffi blurted out, "You haven't told us how you've been."

"Under suspicion." She kicked the straw absently. "I put in a report about Tasceron. It was a masterpiece of lies—you'd have loved it, Raffi. But someone must guess I'm holding back. I was hauled off surveillance and assigned to this Braylwin. For the time being I'm stuck with him. He's as sly as they come. And odious."

"Be careful," Raffi muttered.

She nodded.

Galen gave Rocallion a hurried blessing; the young man knelt hastily in the straw.

"Go back with her," Galen told him. Then, turning to Carys, he said, "Get him into the house. I don't want him in trouble for this, Carys. He's done nothing but save our lives."

"Don't worry."

Rocallion shook Galen's hand, then Raffi's. "Good luck, keepers," he said.

"And you," Galen answered. "Both of you."

From the door Carys gave them a strange look. "I'll survive. But if you find this child, Galen, will you let me know? Will you trust me enough to tell me where it is? You'll need the Watch kept away."

For a moment he stared at her darkly. Then he said, "You'll hear from me, Carys."

4

It is impossible for the agent to be over-cunning, or have too little conscience.

Rule of the Watch

BRAYLWIN POURED half a flaskful of Rocallion's best wine into a glass and sipped it, licking every drop from his lips. As Carys came in, his hand hovered over the dish of spiced chicken, picking out a succulent piece.

"Well?"

She went over to the fire and stared down angrily into the flames, leaning her forehead on the chimney-piece. "You're scum, Braylwin. Odious, stinking scum."

He smiled an oily smile. "Ah, poor Carys. How hard she takes it! And not even to have any reward at the end of it—because all that will be mine. Anyway, it was your idea." He spat a bone elegantly to one side and mopped his lips. "Tell Uncle all about it."

"Galen's gone. And the boy."

"You got them past the guard?"

"Only too easily."

"And they had no idea I knew about them? None at all, Carys?"

She twisted, glaring at him. "Not from me. But Galen's . . . Well, he's got ways of knowing. I can't be sure."

"Mmm. Well, it will have to do. Because if I thought you were playing your little tricks on me, sweetie, your uncle would be annoyed. Very annoyed."

She hated him. At that moment, staring down at his sleek skullcap, she longed to put a crossbow bolt through him, and was shocked at herself. Gripping her fists, she kept her voice calm. "I told them about the Interrex—all the information we had. I'm not sure it'll work. He won't know where to look any more than you."

"He won't. But keepers have ways of finding things out. It's said they talk to trees." He giggled.

"As a matter of fact," she said savagely, "they do."

The small, sharp eyes fixed on her. "Ah, I'd forgotten

you know all about them. One day, Carys, I'll find out exactly what did go on in Tasceron." He scratched his cheek and selected another piece of meat. She watched him, cold with fury, his fur-trimmed coat and the tiny black skullcap he wore to keep warm. "They'll find the Interrex for us. What keeper could resist it?" He licked his thumb. "And as you say, it saves us doing any of the work. We get them, and the child, and a nice fat sack of gold. Or at least I do. Probably promotion too."

"What about me?"

He wagged a greasy finger at her. "You get away with your life, sweetheart. And Uncle doesn't tell about that business at Carner's Haven."

She turned back to the fire, knowing he was smirking behind her. "Galen is worth ten of you," she snarled.

"He is, is he? That remark is enough to get you two years patrolling ice. Or worse. If you play games with the Watch, Carys, you pay the price." She heard him clink his glass thoughtfully. "Does it hurt so much to betray them—the keeper, the boy, the cat-creature? Perhaps it does. Long ago I might have felt the same."

"I doubt it."

He glanced over. "High and mighty. But underneath, you and I are just the same, Carys."

Suddenly her disgust was too much. She turned and stalked past him, slamming the door, pushing two of Rocallion's house-girls aside. Upstairs, in the small room she'd taken for herself, she flung the crossbow down and herself after it, onto the bed.

How could she have brought herself to this? Been so stupid?

Rolling over, she stared up at the ceiling, thinking back to Carner's Haven.

It had been the first time she'd seen the Watch take children, and it had shaken her. The patrol had ridden down to the village early, Braylwin on his new green-painted horse, but somehow the villagers had had warning. The place was in total confusion. All the children under ten were in hiding, the men yelling threats and the women screeching with anger and fear. "Search the place!" he'd roared, and she'd been the one to go into the barn in the last field and see the little girl wriggling halfway out of the straw.

Thumping the mattress, Carys got up and went to the window, tugging it open. Leaf-dust drifted against her lips.

Flainsdeath

Carefully she remembered that moment. The girl had been about four or five, crying, her face contorted with terror. The mother had burst out of hiding between them.

"For God's sake," she'd breathed. "Let her go! Let us go!"

It was only then Carys had realized the crossbow had been loaded and aimed; she'd lowered it abruptly, astonished.

Why had she let them escape? Even now she wasn't sure. Was it that the little girl with the brown hair might have been herself, all those years ago? Had she cried when the Watch took her? She couldn't remember. She couldn't remember her mother or father, her village, anything before the grim stone rooms and snowy courtyards of Watchtower 547, Marn Mountain. Maybe that was why she'd lifted the baby and pushed her hurriedly through a gap in the back wall to the mother outside. Thinking about it made her feel uneasy, even now. Galen would have been pleased. Why did it matter what Galen thought?

She looked up unhappily for the moons, but they were lost behind cloud; pale strange edges and nebulous glimmers. It would have been all right, but when she had turned around Braylwin had been standing inside the barn door, looking at her. He'd seen enough; she'd known instantly that he would use it against her. All he'd said was, "Oh, sweetheart!" in that mock-surprised, stupid way he had. But he'd seen.

All he had to do was report it.

Things were tricky enough already. They'd certainly have her in for questioning, and she knew too much. The House of Trees, the Order's safe house in Tasceron, that Galen was the Crow, they'd get all that out of her—she dared not let them question her. Moodily she stared at the windowsill and cursed Galen to the Pit for letting her remember it all. Braylwin had her in his power, and how he loved it. Carys do this, Carys do that, all the worst work, the wretched endless reports. She was sick of it.

And then he had found the awen-beads.

His fat hand had picked them delicately from around the candles and she'd recognized them with a cold stab of dread. She knew Braylwin would tear the house apart to find a keeper. It had been her plan to let Raffi and Galen go and urge them to find the Interrex—the only thing she could think of on the spot.

60

Flainsdeath

But Braylwin had liked it. It was clever, and meant no work for him. He was lazy. That was one weakness she could use.

Perhaps she should have told Galen. Warned him. Or maybe not. He had to find this child in any case, and when he did . . . Well, she'd worry about that when it happened. At least they were free.

Out in the cold night Agramon loomed suddenly from behind a cloud, outlining the dusty buildings and the fields beyond, their hedgerows dark and spiny, the trees branching against pale sky.

It had been good to see them both again. Raffi looked a bit taller. Where were they now, she wondered, out in that leaf-littered land? Where would they go?

For a brief, bitter second she wished she was with them, that she was walking down the muddy lanes away from here, away from the Watch, laughing with Raffi. Then, fiercely, she banged the window shut and turned her back on it.

Braylwin was going to the Tower of Song.

And she was going with him.

Games of Chance

5

*Flain's anger made the sky shudder. Stars
fell; the new seas boiled.*

*Before them all, Kest swore he would
make no more creatures; he abjured his
poisons and philters and alchemies. But
his heart was full of resentment. And he
lied.*

Book of the Seven Moons

THE HEDGEROWS WERE RIPE with berries, swelling russet and red in the long five-month autumn of Anara. As he walked, Raffi picked handfuls, eating some and tossing the rest into a small sack on his back. Far ahead, Galen leaned impatiently on a field-gate.

Tall fireweed blazed scarlet; the leaves of hawthorn and elder and strail clogged the ruts, and from somewhere not far off the smell of smoke drifted—a stubble field burning, or from the chimney of a house. Raffi pulled a maggot from a fat blackberry and tossed it aside, into a patch of withering white-lady that glinted with dew.

"Come on, boy," Galen growled.

They were two days' walk from Rocallion's manor, and deep in the network of tracks and lanes called the Meres. This was flat, marshy country, wet underfoot, the rich grasses sprouting from saturated peat. All day the two of them had squelched through it, Galen morose, brooding, striding relentlessly for hours and then sitting silent while the mists and fen fogs gathered around him.

Picking a last berry, Raffi walked down the lane. The day was waning. Fog was thickening on the fields; in a copse on the horizon, woses chattered. Galen stared out grimly at the wood. "Hear it?"

Raffi nodded bitterly. He'd hoped they'd spend the night under those trees, but not now. Woses were filthy and noisy, and savage in packs.

"We'll keep moving," the keeper said.

The fog gathered, swirling out of ditches and dykes. As they trudged on farther it closed in, and they lost sight of what was behind, pushing through a rich bruised smell of berries and hawthorn, the wet branches swinging back into their faces, stumbling in hidden ruts and puddles.

Games of Chance

Halfway up a long slow climb, Galen stopped. He turned his head. "Listen."

Glad of a rest, Raffi hitched his pack up, breathing hard. A bat squeaked in the twilight just above him.

And then he heard it: the slow, wet clopping of a horse's hooves. It was behind them, coming up the hill.

Galen turned, the drops of fen fog glinting in his black hair. On each side the hedge was dim, spiny, unbreakable.

"Quick!" he breathed.

They climbed hastily up through the mist, moving in a strange luminous grayness. One of the moons must be out—Cyrax, perhaps—and her pearl-pale shimmer blurred the haze.

As he hurried, Raffi sent a sense-line back, feeling the hot breath of the horse, the sweaty strength of it, the heaviness of its rider.

Then Galen grabbed his arm, tugging him into the fog. Bushes loomed up and at their base a hole, wormed by some animal. Even as he fell on his stomach and wriggled in, Raffi knew they were taking a risk, and he tore his coat recklessly off the thorns. The hedge cracked and snapped; he breathed prayers of silence at it, apologies, feeling the trees' reluctant, displeased hush.

With a hiss of pain Galen was in too. He raised his hand and Raffi saw, with a shiver of fear, that a Kest-claw clung to him. Galen flung it off and stamped on it, over and over. Blood ran between his fingers.

"It's bitten you!"

"I'll live. I've had it before." But Raffi knew this was bad. A Kest-claw bit deep, poisoning the blood, sending dizziness and sickness, sometimes for days. It could kill.

Galen wrapped the wound tight, crouching.

Hooves thumped close on the track. From here, deep in leaves, his ear next to the ground, Raffi felt the heavy thump in his head like a pulse. A harness jangled. The horse blew and whickered and a man coughed.

Carefully Raffi parted the leaves. He saw the horse's legs. It had stopped.

There was no doubt it could smell them both, hear them too. Galen was still; Raffi knew he had sent a thought-line out to the beast, was soothing it, speaking words of comfort to it. Inching to one side, he saw the rider.

A man, muffled in coats and a hood. Difficult to see;

a misty figure, its head turning to look around, until a wraith of fog drifted away and the moon glimmered suddenly on armor, a heavy crossbow.

The man turned. Raffi glimpsed eyes, beard, wet hair.

Then the horse clopped on, vanishing strangely into the mist.

For a long time they crouched, hearing it toil up the invisible hill, until the harness creak faded into silence, and only the smell of its droppings hung on the air.

Galen leaned back. "Well, well."

"What?"

"Didn't you recognize him?"

Raffi scrambled around. "No. Who?"

"Godric. Remember him? One of Alberic's men."

A drop of dew slid into Raffi's ear; chilled, he shook it out. "Alberic!"

"Who else?" Galen eased his legs out, flattening nettles. "I'm not that surprised. Carys warned us. And when a thief-lord screams out that he'll kill you, he usually means it. He must have men out on all the roads. They'll ask in every village too. We'll have to go twice as carefully. And we'll have to get to the Sekoi before they do."

"How far to the meeting place?" Raffi asked anxiously.

"About a day. We'll spend a few hours here and travel on before dawn. You can get the food out."

Raffi nodded, unhappy. "But what about your hand?"

The keeper glared at him. "Leave that to me."

As Raffi pulled some dried fish from the pack and ate it, Galen worked. He took leaves from the pocket at his waist: salve-all, Flainsglove, agrimony. Some he chewed, others he steeped carefully in cold water, binding them tight against his palm. The water should have been hot, Raffi knew. "Look," he said, "we could make a fire. The fog will hide it."

"No time. A few hours' sleep, that's all. Then I'll wake you."

Raffi lay down. It was useless to argue. Carys might have tried, but he knew better. There was something in Galen that was dark, untouchable: a grimness that all the unhappiness of his life had bred—the destruction of the Order, his hatred of the Watch. "A driven man," the Sekoi had remarked once, and Raffi knew what it meant. And since Tasceron, since the Crow had possessed him, it was stronger.

Games of Chance

He began the night prayer wearily and fell asleep in the middle of it.

When he woke he was stiff and cold and damp. It was still dark. Nettle-rash itched all down his cheek.

Galen was gone.

Instantly, Raffi was alert. He sent sense-lines sprawling and touched the keeper, close, scrambling out of the hole anxiously. In the lane it was deep midnight. The mist had gone; huge and still over the black land hung six of the great moons—Atelgar, Agramon, Pyra, Karnos, craggy Lar, distant Atterix. Fingernails and crescents of pink and blue and pearl.

Galen was standing in the blended light, his arms folded, staring up. As Raffi splashed a puddle he turned, and for a second there was something other in him that looked out, sharpening the blackness of his eyes, his long glossy hair, the muddy coat.

Then it was just Galen.

Raffi swung his pack on reluctantly.

"Slept enough?" The keeper strode off without waiting for an answer, down the moonlit track. "Sleeping and eating, boy. All you're good for." He swung his stick down from his back. "Now we step out. We're meeting the Sekoi at Tastarn, and we need to get there fast."

"Then what?"

Galen looked at him sidelong. "Then the Interrex."

"Where do we start looking?"

Galen laughed, that sudden laugh that always turned Raffi cold. "You'll be surprised," he said.

ALL THE REST OF THAT NIGHT, as the moons swung slowly above them, they walked, silent; out of the dark and into the morning, the sun breaking through infinite veils of haze over watery fens. Herons rose and flapped; acres of bleak rushes moved and stirred, their seed rising in clouds. The long track led down into hollows and marshy swamps, through endless plantations of spindly willow, and as the sun rose so did the midges, biting and stinging.

At midday, worn and thirsty, they stopped. Galen was sweating, his coat hanging open, and as he ate, Raffi took a sideways look at him. The keeper was ashen, dark hair plastered to his forehead. The Kest-claw's venom was working in him.

"You should rest."

Galen rubbed his face with the back of his hand. "Two hours from here," he said hoarsely, "is Tastarn. I'll rest there."

But they went slower, all afternoon. It grew warm, even sultry; far off in the hills thunder growled and cracked. Galen stumbled, as if the energy of it had struck him like a wave. They left the track and crossed a stream, keeping east, through woods of delicate silver sheshorn trees that threshed in the faintest stirring of air. Munching berries, Raffi watched Galen anxiously, but the keeper walked fiercely, relentlessly. It was only when the roofs of Tastarn rose up among the trees that he staggered, crumpling against a great oak by the track.

Raffi raced up. "Sit down!" he said. "Take a rest."

Galen slid down the tree till he was sitting, and leaned his head back. He looked gray; his hands shook as he dragged the water flask to his lips, then poured it over his face.

Raffi crouched next to him. "Listen. You can't go into the village, not like this. It's not safe! We could both be caught too easily."

The keeper shivered. "Are you trying to give me advice?" he snapped.

"Yes. Stay here. I'll go in and fetch the Sekoi. He'll be easy to find."

There was silence. A soft warm rain began to fall on them, pattering lightly on the leaves overhead. Galen dragged his hair back. Raffi knew he was struggling to think; the fever was confusing him.

"I won't be long. You've got plenty of water. You could sleep."

"I don't need sleep."

"Well, rest. Can you manage some sense-lines?"

Galen glared at him. "Just about."

"And you'd have the box." The box was the relic, the light-weapon of the Makers they'd stolen back from Alberic. Since then neither of them had used it. The dwarf might have emptied it of power, Raffi thought suddenly. But no. He wanted it back.

Sweat or rain ran down Galen's chin. "All right," he

whispered at last. "All right. But be back by dark, Raffi, or I'm coming in to find you."

Nodding, Raffi slipped off the pack and pushed it into the bracken.

"Wait," Galen said. "Leave your beads."

For a moment Raffi hesitated; then he slipped off his two threads of blue and purple beads and put them in the keeper's hot hand. Without them he felt strange; as if some protection had gone. But Galen was right. It would be safer.

He stood up. "Will you be all right?"

Galen glared at him, furious. Then he said, "Nightfall. Remember."

With a grin Raffi turned and ran down the track into the soft rain, and only when he got down to the stream did he glance back.

Galen was gone. Only a quivering of branches showed where he'd moved. For a moment Raffi felt guilty, leaving him, but there was no choice. And it should be easy to find the Sekoi.

Oddly happy, he jumped the stream and crossed a field of sheep, climbing a wall into a narrow road. Small houses loomed out of the rain, a goat chewing thought-fully outside the nearest.

He walked warily into the village. It was busy. A small market was going on in the main street; he heard and smelled it even before he turned the corner. Pens of squall-ing hens and slow black cattle bellowing their discomfort; men standing around a great bull; stalls of hot bread and cooked meats, clothes, garish rings and belts. He wished he had some money, just to buy something. Not wanting to speak to anyone, he wandered around, hands in pock-ets, watching carefully. Above the marketplace rose the ominous black Watchtower; he could see men on its roof. A group of them moved through the market too, wearing the usual dark motley of worn armor, whips tied around their waists. The crowd opened for them, no one looked around.

Raffi backed away, behind a food stall. An old man was there, his arm deep in a barrel puling out apples.

Raffi decided to take a risk. "I'm looking for a Sekoi," he said quietly. "Tall. Brindled, a zigzag under one eye. Have you seen it?'

"Seen it!" the old man grunted, straightening. He

looked at Raffi curiously. "It's been cleaning everyone out for days. In Marcy's, it'll be."

"Marcy's?"

The old man wheezed. Then he turned Raffi around and pointed. "Marcy's, son. Not for the likes of you."

It was a low, squalid building, the roof patched and the windows all but smothered in ivy. One dim door hung open; even from here he could smell the stink of the place.

"Take my advice." The old man leaned back into the barrel. "Keep your hand on your money."

"Thanks," Raffi muttered.

Squeezing between cattle, pigs, sausage-sellers, jugglers, he made his way up to the broken hanging shutter of a window and peered in.

The room was smoky; fires burned there, and lamps were lit. It was crammed with men, a noisy, jostling, uproarious crowd. In the middle was a table and around it some players were gambling at cards. Large piles of gold coins were stacked in front of them. Three of the players Raffi could see, the other was hidden by the passing crowd.

Then he ducked back with a sudden indrawn breath.

The horseman, Godric, was standing by the hearth. He had a gray tankard in his hand, its lid open, and he was drinking from it now, his eyes fixed on the card game.

Someone laughed. Men moved away.

And through the gap Raffi saw the fourth player, chatting and shuffling the cards with its seven fingers, a great stack of yellow gold heaped in front of it.

It was the Sekoi.

And Alberic's man was watching its back.

6

I watched him, day by day.
Suspicious, I followed his eyes,
the movements of his hands.
I knew my brother plotted.
What his plan was I could never see.

Apocalypse of Tamar

CROUCHING UNDER THE TANGLE OF IVY, Raffi watched the smoky room in despair. How could he warn the Sekoi?

The creature was enjoying itself. Its seven long fingers rippled the cards expertly, flicking them out into rapid fans and shuffles. It was laughing, its yellow eyes bright as the gold stacked in front of it, the fur on its sharp face tense with excitement.

Carefully Raffi rustled the ivy. No one even looked. He glanced at Godric; the man had his great scarf open, showing his black stiff beard and the glint of the rusty breastplate. He had found somewhere to sit—the end of a bench full of bargaining market-men—and he leaned there, a threatening shadow, his eyes always on the Sekoi's back.

It was hopeless.

Raffi turned away and stared out into the rain. What would Galen do?

Pray.

The answer came at once as if someone had said it, and he nodded, sending his mind out in the long call to the Makers: to Flain the Tall, Soren, Lady of Leaves, Tamar, Beast-bringer, Theriss, Halen. Surely one of them could send him some idea.

He turned back, rain dripping on him from the tattered thatch. The Sekoi's fingers whisked in a few more coins. The other players looked disgusted. The shadow that was Godric drank in silence.

He would have to try some sort of Rapport. It was probably too hard for him. And it meant going inside.

Desperate now, he went around to the door and cautiously edged down three steps into the noise. The stench and smoke made him cough: a smell of beer and bodies and sizzling food. Before he even began, he knew he couldn't do it. There were too many people shoving him, too much shouting and laughing. Someone grabbed his arm; he turned in fear and saw a woman, her face painted green and blue, holding him with sharp nails.

"Lost, darling?" she simpered, her voice slurred. "You're not Tomas, are you? Tomas looks like you."

He tugged away and ran, pushing through the crowd, fighting his way between bodies up the steps and out into the cool rain.

Soaked and shivering, he kicked the wall furiously. Galen needed him! He *had* to do something.

All at once the idea burst in his mind.

Soren must have sent it; she had made the trees, put seeds in the earth, sap in the veins. He breathed his thanks to her in relief.

Then he went back to the ivy.

He had to work a long time to wake it. It was sluggish, sleepy; it twisted away from him. It had forgotten the keepers, had been asleep too long, was too tired now . . . Patiently Raffi squatted by the gnarled stem, fingers in the cracks, telling it over and over what he wanted it to do, explaining every detail as if to a tiny child. It was young, he knew, and the power of the Makers was weak in it; it had no memory like the old yewman that had once talked to him. But something was there. He argued with it, coaxed it, ordered it, went on repeating the task.

The leaves sighed, as if a breeze moved them. It moaned and complained and then, reluctantly, a tendril began to creep in through the broken window.

Breathless, willing it on, Raffi gripped the sill and watched it, the thin bine with its tiny glossy leaves slithering jerkily down the wall, along the floor, between benches, boots, table legs, behind settles, dragging through the filthy straw. It stopped once, and the drowsiness of forgetting came to him, a great wariness and confusion, but he insisted and it moved again, rustling, tapping, ten years' growth in ten minutes, a mighty outpouring of its green effort.

Now it was under the Sekoi's chair, blocked by people passing from its right. Raffi moved impatiently.

A corkscrew of leaves was climbing up the chair leg.

A roar of laughter burst out somewhere in the room. Raffi held his breath. The ivy curled, slithering up, out into the air, feeling its way. Delicately it wrapped a frail bracelet around the Sekoi's wrist.

For an instant, the creature went rigid. Then it picked up a card, put another down, and dropped its hand below the table. It glanced around swiftly, then to the left, then across the room till its eyes came to the window and met Raffi's. He made a quick slash with his finger across his throat and jabbed it toward the Sekoi's back.

With a wry smile the creature looked down.

Raffi ducked under the sill, cold with relief. The creature's sharp, striped face had made not a flicker of surprise—no wonder it won at cards, he thought happily. But the fur on its neck seemed thicker, even from here. He prayed Godric hadn't seen him.

Already the ivy was falling back into sleep. He thanked it gravely and peeped in at the window again. The Sekoi said something to the player on its left, put down its cards, and spread them with a wicked grin. The groan of the others was loud enough to hear outside. As it gathered the money, it stood and flashed one look into a mirror on the wall, instant and sharp. But that was enough. It would have seen Godric.

Raffi crept away. He was soaked to the skin and tired; the ivy had been harder to wake than he'd thought. And it wasn't over. When the Sekoi came out, Alberic's man would follow. He needed to think of something else now. The man was armed, after all.

Wearily he crouched by the door and tried to plan, seeing all at once how late it was, how the sun had nearly gone. Moths danced in the smoky entrance; above the dim roofs flittermice squeaked and flapped. Galen would be getting worried.

After a few minutes he realized, stupidly, that no one had come out—and that all the noise in the room had stopped. Only the bang and clatter of the closing market came to him.

Suddenly afraid, he went to the steps and peered in. The room was dim. Fires crackled. Pipe smoke hung in thick blue layers. The Sekoi was sitting on the card table, its long knees bent up over a chair. It was telling a story.

Everyone in the room was silent, listening intently. Only the jugs of ale moved, up and down as the men drank, absorbed in watching the creature's strange, spread hands, its keen yellow gaze. It spoke quietly, but with an odd hypnotic purr in its voice, and as he came down closely enough to hear it, some vague anxiety drifted out of Raffi's memory like smoke, and all that remained was the story.

It was dark, and he was in a forest that spread endlessly all around him, and he knew his left arm was torn and bleeding. Far down between the trees evil things moved; they were creeping closer, the horrors that Kest had bred, things that slid and slithered and lurched through the wood. His skin prickled; he scratched his face and it was furred. A great sword hung heavy from his seven-fingered hand.

Out of the forest came a screech so savage it made him shiver. He lifted the sword and waited, seeing the starlight gleam on the cold metal, the fur on his neck prickling, and he snarled, his eyes watching the approaching shapes that crackled through the undergrowth. The darkness was thick, poisoned with steams and smoke; he strained to see through it, every crisp leaf breaking, a glimpse of slithering tail, scaled claw.

Then, out of the leaves the thing rose. A wyvern of Kest, huge, its wide wings blotting out the moons, the cold triplet of its eyes high above him, its scaly neck oozing blood and pus from the wounds the Cat-lords had dealt it. They were dead, his own sweet princes, and it still lived, and his anger at that was so raw that he raised the sword with both hands and swung it at the beast, screaming, but it put out a great claw and caught his shoulder and said, "Raffi. Raffi! For Flain's sake boy, listen to me!"

Gasping, tears running down his face, Raffi stared at the Sekoi.

It grinned smugly. "You're back."

Slowly, bewildered, he lowered his empty hands. "What was . . . Who . . . ?"

"You call him Kalimar. Last survivor of the Battle of the Ringrock. You know the story." It glanced around darkly. "Come on now, before they stir."

Gripping his sleeve with its long fingers it hurried him away from the inn—he realized suddenly they were outside—and between the houses. The market was gone, the muddy ground trampled with straw and scraps of vegetables.

Raffi shook his head. "The story didn't finish . . ."

"Didn't have to. They all knew it. Start them off and

leave them to it, small keeper." It looked pleased with itself; it walked with a strange satisfied swing through the shadows, the fat purse bulging an inside pocket. "Could have been sticky though. So Alberic's looking for us, is he?"

Raffi nodded. He still felt stunned; waves of anger and grief flooded him and he felt sick. The Sekoi glanced down curiously. "You were far in, small keeper. Too far."

"I hadn't meant to listen."

The Sekoi grinned. "They all say that. Where's Galen?"

"Galen!" Raffi stumbled. "He's sick. A Kest-claw bit him on the hand."

The creature made a spitting noise in its throat. "Ack! Then we should hurry. He'll need keeping warm. Is he delirious?"

"No. He's had it before."

"Maybe, but it's always serious, Raffi. We should—"

It stopped abruptly. Then it turned its head.

A man was standing in the gloomy lane behind them, dim against the trees. A burly man in a dark coat. He held a loaded crossbow, and it was pointing straight at Raffi.

"I didn't mean to listen either," he said gruffly. "I've

heard your stories before, Master Graycat. It was hard, but my hood was up, and one ear pressed against the settle drowned out most of it."

The Sekoi hissed a spit of annoyance. It glanced around quickly. The village was silent. No one was about.

"Now what?" Raffi whispered.

"No spells, boy. No keeper-tricks, or this bolt flies. I won't kill you, but Alberic won't mind damaged goods." He leered. "He's got plans to do a little damage of his own. Now, against that wall."

The Sekoi backed, and Raffi followed. He still felt dizzy, and glimpses of the story kept flashing back at him—the wyvern, the forest, the sudden weight of the sword—as if this was all part of it, or he was in two places at once.

Then the field wall was hard against his back.

Godric stepped closer. "Where's the other one?"

Neither of them told him. He shrugged. "We'll get him. Alberic has patrols out; the little man's spitting venom for you three, and the magic box of tricks." But his eye was on the Sekoi, and Raffi knew all at once something else was on his mind.

"Tell me where he is or I tie you up and we move out now." But the man didn't move, and he was looking at the gold. Raffi felt a sudden quiver of hope.

Godric edged forward. "Won a lot, didn't you?"

The Sekoi's fur rose silently around its neck. "I was lucky."

"So I saw." Suddenly he lowered the bolt, just a fraction. "All right. Listen. Give me the gold, and you and the boy go free. I never even set eyes on you. Agreed?"

The Sekoi gave an eerie low hiss—a terrifying sound.

"Never," it breathed.

"I mean it."

"So do I." The creature's eyes were slits, dark as chasms.

Raffi's heart sank.

"Suit yourself. I'll take it anyway."

But like lightning the Sekoi moved; it turned and was gone into the dark. With an oath of fury Godric leaped in and grabbed Raffi; a great arm tugged his hair back, the crossbow bolt pressed horrifyingly into his neck.

Raffi froze; only the slightest of pressures would have set it off.

"The gold!" Godric roared. "Put it down in the road or I kill him!"

There was a long silence. Then the Sekoi's voice came, strangled and odd from somewhere close. "I'm sorry, Raffi," it said.

"You can't just leave me!" he yelled, appalled.

He could almost feel the Sekoi squirm. "The gold," it hissed. "I have to keep the gold!"

"You scum." Godric spat in disgust. "What do you people do with it all? Alberic would love to find the Hidden Hoard. Does it exist, Graycat? Is it real?"

"Alberic could drown in it," the creature purred.

"Could he!" Godric sounded tight with anger. The crossbow quivered; Raffi gripped his hands together.

But the bolt that shattered the darkness was blue; an enormous flash that burst in his head like a flame, and as blackness crashed back he felt the wyvern again, roaring and falling down upon him, into some endless pit.

7

Let the keeper own nothing but his faith.
For the Sekoi hoard gold
and men desire goods,
but the dew on the early grass
is a treasure beyond price.

Litany of the Makers

WHEN RAFFI WOKE UP he found himself wrapped in his own coat on a damp bank of dead leaves; they rustled and crisped as he uncurled. Above him, smooth trunks of beech trees rose into darkness, stars glinting through their tangled branches.

For a moment he lay still, staring up; then a crackle of sticks made fear break out of him like sweat. He rolled over.

Galen was sitting by a small bright fire. He was shivering as if he couldn't stop, huddled over some cup of steaming drink, but when he looked across, there was the flicker of a grin on his face.

"So you're back with us, are you?"

Raffi propped himself up. He felt strange. One side of his head and one shoulder were numb. His left hand tingled.

"Did you fire the blue box?" he asked slowly.

Galen nodded. "Nothing else I could do. But he was holding you too close—you caught some of the blast." He laughed grimly and spat into the flames. "A good thing dear Alberic didn't use it all up."

"Did it kill him?"

Galen threw him an irritated glance. "I'm not the Watch, boy. He's over there."

Turning, Raffi realized that the fire was burning in a hollow among beech trees. Propped against one, well tied at the ankles, was Godric. The big man's head lolled to one side, and a few dead leaves had fallen on his hair and chest. But he breathed evenly.

Next to him, picking elegantly at a plate of berries, was the Sekoi.

"You!" Raffi jerked upright, suddenly furious. "What were you doing! You would have let him kill me!"

The Sekoi spit out a pip. "Nonsense."

Games of Chance

"Did you see what happened?" Raffi turned on Galen.

"No. What?" he said quietly.

"Godric offered to let me go if that . . . creature gave him the gold. A great bag of gold. And it wouldn't! It just said 'Sorry, Raffi'!"

Even now he could barely believe it.

Galen was silent.

The Sekoi wrinkled its nose and waved a hand. "Small keeper, work it out! What if I had given him my gold? Do you really think he'd have trotted back to Alberic saying 'I haven't seen them'? Nonsense. We'd have lost you and it."

"Well, you wouldn't have cared about me!"

"Raffi . . ." Galen growled.

"The Sekoi wouldn't! It was the gold, that was all that mattered! I knew! I could feel it!"

The Sekoi glowered, its fur puffed out, but it folded its long arms calmly across its chest. "Oh you could, could you?"

"Yes."

"Clever. Not many keepers can read the Sekoi."

Galen scowled. "That's enough." He tipped the dregs

of his drink angrily into the flames. "I don't know what went on. I only know Raffi feels betrayed and you"—he glanced at the creature darkly—"you feel some sort of regret."

The Sekoi shrugged. "I have nothing to regret."

"Thanks to me. However, the boy is right. We need to know where we stand. In my experience, the Sekoi have always hated the Watch."

"They enslaved us," it spat.

"They did. But the Order . . ."

It waved a hand irritably. "We have no quarrel with the Order, Galen. We are friends, you and I. And the small one. I would not betray you."

"Nevertheless." Galen pushed the damp hair restlessly from his face. "I know the Sekoi. About gold, you can never be trusted. Your loyalty to that goes beyond any friendship with us. I understand that. The boy is too young to know yet."

The Sekoi squirmed. Finally it said, "It may be. Some things are too sacred to speak about." It looked up, its yellow eyes sharp in the flame light. "I'm sorry, Raffi, Galen is right. I am your friend and always will be, but we have our own beliefs, and gold is . . . vital to them. I can't explain why. Galen says we cannot be trusted. I would say, regretfully, that may be, but we are all of us on the same side."

"And if the Watch offered you enough gold to give us up?" Raffi snapped, rubbing his arms savagely. "What then? You'd do it, would you?"

The Sekoi was silent. It scratched its tattooed fur thoughtfully. At last it said, "Let me put it this way. If I was in trouble, you would help me, yes?"

"Of course I would! I'd never—"

"Yes. Yes. But if the price of rescuing me was to give up the secrets of the Order? All the hidden knowledge? To betray your master, all the Makers? Would you do that, Raffi, just to save me?"

Raffi felt foolish, confused. Glancing at Galen was no help. He ran his hands through his hair, dragging out leaves. "I don't know," he said at last.

"No, you don't. It would be a fearsome choice. Always, you would try for some other way out." It leaned forward, toward the flames.

"You must understand that we Sekoi also have our secrets, our beliefs, and the purpose of the Great Hoard is one of them. It may only be a metal to you. To us it is more, much more. It is our deepest dream. And every one of us is sworn to add to it, coin by coin, ounce by shining ounce until . . ." It stopped and smiled. "Well, I can say no more. But you understand? For a second, back there, when he asked me for the gold, I was on the edge of that fearsome choice."

Raffi was silent.

The flames crackled, glowing against the smooth brown boles of the beeches. And quite suddenly, out of his confusion and annoyance, he saw Carys, walking up some endless stairway, around and around, carrying a torch of pitch that dripped and crackled. She looked at him sideways, and she was scared, her eyes alert. "The Interrex!" she hissed. "Keep your mind on the job, Raffi!"

And then all he was staring at was a beech tree.

"What was it?" Galen had hold of him already. "What was that! That was Maker-sent."

Raffi took a deep breath. The Sekoi watched them both with interest. "Some vision?" it murmured.

"I saw Carys. Climbing a stair. She reminded me about the Interrex. That was all."

Galen bowed his head. "My fault. We should have been moving faster!"

"But you couldn't. And where, anyway?"

"At least I know that. The only way to find out where the child is, is to make a pilgrimage to the well. Artelan's Well."

He touched the black and green beads at his neck. "I hear your rebuke, Flain." Suddenly he looked exhausted. He leaned back against a tree and said, "Tomorrow. We leave tomorrow."

"You should sleep." The Sekoi came and laid its long hand over his forehead, and then at his wrists. Galen shook it off, but it grinned. "My cure is working. You're less hot."

"I wish I were even a little hot, Graycat."

The growl came from the darkness; turning, they saw Godric was awake and watching them. The Sekoi snarled, "That's not my name."

But it threw Godric his cloak, a firm bundle that he had to catch hastily. Unruffled, he shook it out and wrapped it around himself. "Much better. And something to eat?" He rubbed one hand over his beard, watching Galen closely. "You owe me that, keeper, after nearly killing me with your relic."

Galen gave a weary nod.

Raffi took the last of the berries over and dumped them down.

Godric gazed at them in disgust. "Flainsteeth! Is this all you people eat? Alberic's dog gets more than this!" He looked up. "You should have let me take you prisoner, lad."

Raffi tried to look uncaring. "Keepers have higher things to think of than food."

"Ha!" The big man roared noisily. "By God, Galen Harn, your boy's either well-beaten or an idiot. Pass me that satchel, Graycat. It looks like I'll have to start feeding my captors. It's a new one, I'll admit—Alberic will love it."

With a scowl at Galen, the Sekoi rummaged through the pack for weapons, then hurled it over. Godric pulled out some fruit and small packages. They were wrapped in fresh calarna leaves and smelled superb.

"Venison. Smoked and stuffed. From the market." He filled his mouth and pushed a package at Raffi. "Go on, boy, eat some. You're just skin and bone."

Raffi shook his head doggedly, but Galen's voice muttered, "Do as he says."

Astonished, Raffi looked around. Galen was still leaning against the tree. His shivering seemed to have stopped, but he looked gaunt and weary. "Go on. Eat."

Godric wiped grease from his beard with the back of one hand. "You too. And you, Cat."

"We don't eat meat," the Sekoi said haughtily.

"I'd heard that." The big man hauled out a wine flask and drank noisily. "Afraid you'd like it too much, eh?"

Raffi was barely listening. The meat was delicious, rich and tender and sweetened with herbs and salt; he swallowed every mouthful slowly, savoring the taste, licking every scrap off his fingers.

Godric watched him in real wonder. "Here," he growled, "have more." He glanced over at Galen and said grimly, "I'll tell you this, keeper, we may be thieves, but we take more care of our own than you do."

Galen watched, his dark eyes level and unmoved. All

he said was, "We move on tomorrow. We'll leave you tied here, your weapons in that bush. You're near the road. You can shout. Eventually someone will hear you."

"Probably the Watch!"

Galen nodded gravely. "Your problem. Tell Alberic that he won't find us and that he will never get the box back."

Godric snorted. "It's you he wants!"

"Tell him. And next time he won't find his men left for him."

"Next time he'll come himself." Godric drank heavily and stretched out his legs. "You've made a bad enemy in the dwarf, keeper. Alberic has a puny body but big ideas. He rules because everyone's afraid of him. He'll ride out here with the whole thief-band when he knows you're here. And he won't go back without you." He laughed loudly. "In pieces, probably."

"We're used to being hunted." Galen rolled over, wrapping the coat around himself. "Will you watch?" he said to the Sekoi, sounding bone weary.

"I'll watch. Go to sleep."

As Raffi swallowed the last scrap of meat, Godric

leaned toward him, clutching the flask. "Do yourself a favor, lad," he whispered, his breath stinking of ale. "Leave this lot. Both of them care more about their dreams than about you." He clapped a great hand on Raffi's hair and ruffled it. "Clear out with me. Be a thief. If you like to live well, that's the life, boy." Drunkenly he leaned back, closing his eyes. "After all, what have you got to lose? You're an outlaw already."

Jerking back, Raffi glared down at him bitterly. "Thanks," he said. "Thanks a lot."

The Tower of Song

8

For Flain, the city of Tasceron, gold and sunlit;
For Tamar, Isel's mountain, cold and high.
For Soren, the Pavilion of Song in the Green hills;
For Theriss, the blue chasms of the sea.
For Kest, the plain of Maar, abode of horrors.
Above them all the seven moons
and the Crow, flying between.

Litany of the Makers

IT HAD BEEN RAINING ALL DAY, and there was no sign of it stopping. Carys had given up; her hood hung useless and her hair streamed, trickling and dripping inside her soaked clothes. Shivering, she urged her horse on, seeing how the water oozed and bubbled out of the leather of her gloves.

Ahead, under a stand of black-leaved saltan trees, Braylwin and his three men were waiting. Wearily her horse splashed up to them, and she saw how the beasts' red paint had smeared and dripped into the puddles below.

"Problem?" Braylwin asked absently. He was dressed

in a vast black traveling cape that hung down below his stirrups; the rain pattered off it in torrents. It was stiff with wax.

"He's going lame." She slipped off, knee-deep in water.

Braylwin shook his head. "I've told you before to get yourself a better horse," he said crisply, above the downpour. "And clothes, Carys! I like my patrol to be well turned out."

Crouched over the horse's hoof, she snapped, "I'm not as rich as you."

"Ah, but that's your fault, sweetie. Prize money is only the half of it. The small gifts of the people, the bribes, the little inducements. Your trouble, Carys, is being too long among keepers."

She dropped the hoof and slapped the horse's flank, then glared up. "That's my business."

His round face smiled down at her. "Is it?"

"How far are we from this wretched place?" she asked sullenly.

"How far?" He took a plump hand off the reins and pointed. "We're here."

She stared out. She saw a vastness, a rising shape, indistinct in the rain, gray in the misty drizzle. At first she had thought it was a cloud, a great bank of fog drifting up over the mountains, but now she realized with a cold awe that it was real, a vast building climbing the mountainside, rising in a countless series of rooms, stairways, balconies, and galleries, far away and immense, its topmost roofs white with snow. And up there, like a needle sharp with ice, one uttermost pinnacle flew the remote black pennant of the Watch.

The Tower of Song.

How Galen would have loved this, she thought, the rain running into her eyes and down her face, the heavy downpour hissing from the low gray skies. How it would have amazed Raffi. They'd have prayed, she thought wryly. Looking up at the vast, rain-clouded walls of it, she almost wanted to pray as well.

Braylwin had been watching her. Now, as the rain began to crash with a new ferocity, he turned his horse hastily. "Come on," he called irritably. "Before we drown out here."

She walked, leading her horse up the steep mountain track. The tower loomed above; she saw how it had been built over centuries, been added to, repaired, ruined, neglected, renovated. All the Emperors had spent their summers here, far from the heat of Tasceron, building their palace of luxuries around the lost core of Soren's pavilion, the place she had chosen for her own when the Makers divided the Finished Lands between them, long ago. Now the Watch held it, one of their greatest fastnesses, and here were stored rooms of confiscated tribute, loot, treasures. And the records, the vast bureaucracy of files and papers and reports of its millions of agents. If she really wanted to find out about herself, about the Watch, about the Interrex, this would be the place. But she'd have to be careful. Very careful.

Hauling the horse up over the slippery pebbles, she wiped her face and scowled at Braylwin's back. He came here every year for his winter quarters, warm and dry. Here they'd stay—until she had word from Galen. Irritated, she shook her head. She should have warned Galen.

It took an hour to clamber up to the outer barbican, and another half hour to satisfy the searchers, fill in identity forms, get their papers and permissions and passes to the inner courtyards.

The Tower of Song

Trailing behind Braylwin across the cobbled yards and under the porticoes, she was amazed at the crowds of people: scribes, clerks, scriveners, translators. There were men dragging great trolley-loads of papers, long lines at doors, crowds around notices pinned to hundreds of boards. Most of them were sleek and well-fed; only a few were field agents or post-riders, looking far more weatherworn. Climbing one vast staircase, she looked down and saw an endless miserable line disappearing under one porch—not Watch, but tired-looking men, haggard women, a few lounging Sekoi.

"What are they?"

Braylwin paused long enough to glance down. "Petitioners. People looking for their families. Criminals. No-hopers."

He climbed on clumsily. After a minute she ran after him.

His apartments were about a mile into the labyrinth of rooms and corridors they called the Underpalace; she realized after a while that even with all her training she was hopelessly lost. When they got there he went along a narrow passageway, banging doors open, tutting over dust, fussing at ornaments that weren't where he'd left them. She knew the men-at-arms would sleep outside his door when on duty, otherwise in the endless dormitories all Watchholds had. She was expecting that for herself, but Braylwin beckoned her coyly to the end of the corridor and flung a door open. "For you, sweetie."

She peered in.

A tiny room, with a bed and an empty hearth and a chest, and rain dripping into a pool, but when she'd crossed to the window and looked out she smiled, for the room was high in some turret, and it hung out into the sky over the tangle of lanes and courtyards and alleys far below.

She was glad it was up on its own. She was already beginning to dislike the Tower of Song.

"It'll do," she said, turning.

Braylwin smirked from the door. "Yes. For keeping an eye on you, Carys."

It took her three days even to find a map of the place. In the mornings Braylwin would dictate long reports of the summer's tax-gatherings to a harassed clerk who had been ordered to work with him.

The Tower of Song

The man deserved a medal, Carys thought darkly, watching the sleek Watchleader tease and flatter and make a fool of him. Harnor, his name was. Once she saw him give her a quick, exasperated glance, but he never lost his temper, and Braylwin smirked and preened and invented endless imaginary accounts until he tired of the game and sent one of the men-at-arms to fetch his dinner. After that he spent the long, wet afternoons sleeping, or entertaining the gaggle of unpleasant cronies he called friends.

Carys was rarely needed, but he kept her hanging around; only in the afternoons could she vanish without suspicion. "Take a tootle around," he said once, filing his broad nails. "This place is a labyrinth, Carys, you'll never find anything you need in it. Your friend Galen will love it, when we bring him in." And he winked at her, so that she wanted to spit.

One thing she realized soon was that the rain here was eternal. The weather must have changed since the Emperor's time, because now the tower loomed constantly in its cloud of drizzle; all the long afternoons rain trickled in runnels and gutters and spouts, spattering through gargoyles of hideous beasts and goblins that spat far down on the heads of hurrying clerks. Always the roofs ran with water; it dripped and plopped and splashed through culverts and drains, or sheeted down, a relentless liquid gurgle that never stopped, until she started to imagine that this was the song the tower sang, through all the throats and mouths and pipes of its endless body.

At first she wandered without direction, just trying to find her way back to the nearest courtyard, but she soon realized that was hopeless; once it took her three hours to find Braylwin's rooms again.

As she climbed the stairs wearily, Harnor was coming out.

"How do you find your way around this warren?" she snapped.

He looked at her in surprise. "The maps. How else?"

"Maps? Where?"

For a moment he glanced at her. Then he pushed the thick folder of paper under one arm. "I'll show you."

He led her down three stairways and along a gallery that had once been painted with brilliant birds. Now only the ghosts of them lingered, and great damp patches of lichen were furring them over. At the end he stopped and opened a small door. "There's one in here."

She went in after him warily, but through the door was nothing but a balcony, and looking down from it, she saw she was above a great echoing hall, full of desks and the murmur of voices. Coins were being counted down there, millions of them. She grinned, thinking of the Sekoi.

"This is the map. There are many, and they're scattered around the Underpalace. Would you like some paper? You could make a copy. It takes a while to find your way around otherwise."

As Harnor riffled through the file for a clean sheet, Carys watched him curiously. He looked pale, as if he never went outside. He found a piece and gave it to her.

"Thanks. How long have you been here, Watchman?"

"All my life." He smiled sourly. "Forty years and more. Once I hoped I'd be a field agent, but not anymore. Too old."

She nodded, looking up at the map: an immense sprawl of rooms and courtyards painted on the wall, each with its name in silver. "This isn't Watchwork."

"It's from the Emperor's time. There are many remnants of those days scattered around. Most have been destroyed, but the place is so huge . . ."

"Have you ever explored it all?" she asked quietly.

He looked up, a strange, almost frightened look. "Of course not. No one has. There are places that are not allowed."

Carys had turned and begun to draw; now her pencil stopped. "What places?"

He looked uneasy. "The Great Library . . . and others. I'm not sure, really."

She looked at him. He was small, his hair graying early, his beard clipped. He looked away. "Is that all?"

She nodded, thoughtful. "Thank you. Yes, that's all."

Watching him hurry out, she knew he was afraid of her. That was normal. Everyone in the Watch spied on everyone else; it was their strength. But there had been something else; she had felt it, that sliver of danger. She'd always been good at that. "Top of the class again," old Jellie had wheezed, back in the cold hall of the Watchhouse on Marn Mountain, and all the others in the class would stare, spiteful and envious and friendly, all the ones who had lived with her there, all the children the Watch had stolen . . .

She bit her lip and went grimly back to the map.

It took her an hour or so to make a copy, and even then it was rough and hasty. The names of the rooms enchanted her: the Gallery of Laughter—what was that like? And the Corridor of the Broken Vases—what had happened there? Even when she'd finished she knew this was only the Underpalace. There was far more than this: secret rooms and whole wings that needed extra passes even to get to. And above that the Overpalace, totally unknown. But it was a start.

Back in her room that night, chewing dainty filled rolls left from Braylwin's latest party, she lay on the bed and pored over the map, ignoring the relentless rain plopping into the filling bucket. Then she leaned back and gazed up at the ceiling. Where to begin? First she needed to find out about herself. And then—she frowned, because this was treachery, and if they knew it she'd be in deep trouble—then she had to find out if Galen was right. He said the Watch was evil.

And what did they do with all the relics they found?

Destroyed them as abominations, she had always been taught; but since then, not only from Galen, she'd heard other things. That the relics were stored here, great rooms of them. That they held real power. She scowled, knowing she'd seen that for herself. And another rumor, never spoken out loud, only hinted at. That the Watch had a Ruler; that somewhere, above all the sergeants and castellans and committees and commanders and Watchlords there was someone else, someone secret, who knew everything. She shook her head. She'd never told this to Galen or Raffi, and even now she doubted it was true. But she had to find out.

Rolling over, she put a finger on the map, on a small corridor that ran north. That was the way. Higher up, there would be fewer people. She had a high clearance, she could certainly get that far. The corridor led to a place called the Hall of Moons. Under that, in Watchletters, was the word *Births*. Tomorrow she'd try there.

It was as she sat up and reached for another roll that she saw the eye. It stared at her out of the wall, unblinking, and for a second an ice-cold fear stabbed her, and she half grabbed the bow, and then breathed out, and laughed at herself.

The Tower of Song

The eye watched her, clear and sharp.

Carys got up and crossed to it. Taking a small knife from her pocket, she reached up and hacked at the plaster; it was damp and fell in lumps.

Slowly the figure appeared, gorgeously painted in golds and reds; a great bearded man, carrying a black night-cub that struggled in his arms. She knew who he was. Tamar, the Maker who had made the animals. The one who had been the enemy of Kest.

She lay back on the bed and gazed at him. Two months ago, in Tasceron, Galen had spoken to these Makers. She had heard them answer him.

Or thought she had.

Long into the wet night, she stared at the figure on her wall.

9

*In the form of an eagle he flew over
Maar, and saw how a great pit had been
dug, its maw smoking, full of strange
cries.*

*Then Tamar felt fear, and he knew this
was in defiance of the Makers.*

Book of the Seven Moons

"GOING SOMEWHERE?"

Braylwin smiled at her sweetly over Harnor's shoulder.

She paused at the door. "For a walk."

"Ah, but where? Tell Uncle."

She scowled, but turned. "I thought I'd do some intelligence gathering. About . . ." She glanced at the clerk's back. "About that person Galen is looking for."

"Ah!" She saw his face change. "Good idea. Why not."

But halfway out he called after her. "I'll hear all about it when you get back."

"I'm sure you will," she murmured, and stalked down the corridor.

Five minutes later she knew he was having her followed. He wasn't using his own people, but a woman in a red dress—that was the one she was supposed to see—and a thin boy, the one she wasn't. She grinned. He was clever, but it was standard stuff. Maybe training was better these days.

She lost the woman in the Square of the Rainbow Fish, where there was a tatty scatter of stalls and food-sellers. The boy was more difficult. She knew she had to pretend she didn't know he was there, that he'd lost her by accident. She tried ducking through doorways and corridors, but he obviously knew the ways of the place more intimately than she did. Then she had a better idea. She'd let him follow.

Finding the Hall of Moons was bewildering, even with the map. She passed through endless halls, one so dark it was lit by candles, another piled with broken chairs, thousands of them, in some bizarre toppling structure, all interwoven, with a tunnel for passersby through the middle. The Passage of Nightmare, which she'd looked forward to seeing, was painted entirely black, and had no lights in it from one end to the other. She unslung her crossbow as she padded through it, and only three people passed her there, as if it was avoided. The Gallery of Tears ran with rain, dripping from the vast golden roof, so that the name still seemed right. She turned and climbed through whole labyrinths of corridors, always upward, and once or twice when she passed through a wide square or long room, she glimpsed the boy far back, clever, never obvious.

The Hall of Moons was barred by two great doors and two guards, the first she'd seen. A few people went in before her; her papers and insignia were scarcely glanced at. Being a Watchspy has its moments, Galen, she thought wryly.

Inside she stood still, utterly astonished.

The Hall of Moons was enormous, so vast the other end was barely visible in the gloomy light. Great windows reached from floor to ceiling on one side; on the other the wall was painted with seven gigantic images of the moons, the features of their surfaces, craters, humps, hills, and valleys. And holding these, as if they were toys, were the seven sisters themselves: Atelgar, Pyra, Lar, all of them, painted ten times life-size in gold and cream.

Cautiously she moved to a desk in the corner. A tall man looked down at her. "Yes?"

"I want to see the records for a Watchhouse. Marn Mountain. Five forty-seven."

"Your clearance?"

She gave him the insignia, pulling the silver chain over her head. He glanced up, surprised. "Your own house?"

"Yes."

"This isn't usually allowed."

"Even for the silver rank?"

He handed it back slowly. "For what reason?"

Carys looked up at him. All at once she was angry. "The reason is secret. If you're not able to help me, perhaps I should speak to your Watchmaster."

The man almost winced. "No need. I'll see to it," he said quietly. "Please take desk two forty-six. I'll bring the record."

She turned and stalked away, keeping her head up. When she found the desk she lounged there, looking around moodily. Maybe he'd report it. Maybe not. She didn't really care.

When the records came, they were in three enormous

red books. She signed her name for them, then leafed through eagerly, but was soon disappointed.

Each year had the name of the children brought in, and their age, but that was all. No villages, no family names. All the children in Marn Mountain that year had the same surname—Arrin. It had been the castellan's name, that was why. Briefly she wondered about *Carys*, but there was no way of finding out.

When she found her own name and number she stared at them coldly for a long moment, as if they belonged to someone else. And in a way they did. It surprised her how bitter she felt then; the Watch had taken everything, her family, even her name. But the Rule said, "The Watch is your name and your family."

She slammed the book shut and tapped her fingers on it thoughtfully. She'd been stupid to think she could find anything here. They covered their tracks too well; they didn't want anyone to know too much. As for the Interrex, that would be hopeless.

Abruptly she got up, walked down the endless hall, passed the clerk without a glance, and went out, into the labyrinth.

Braylwin was not impressed. Smoothing the sleeves of a new coat he watched her closely in the mirror. "The Hall of Moons? I went there myself once, years ago. Were you looking for the Interrex, sweetie? Or something else?" His eyes were sharp in his plump face. "Has little Carys being looking for her mummy?"

She ignored him. Instead she said, "Have you ever been to the Overpalace? To the library?"

He shrugged. "Never. It's not an easy place to get to. And there are no maps of the Overpalace—the place is almost unknowable. The Higher Watchlords may go there, maybe." He grinned at her. "All those delicious secrets, Carys."

She nodded, thinking. "It's guarded, of course."

"Three bastions, each with a metal door. Once you get inside . . ." He turned, interested. "Do you know what I was once told? Deep under the whole of this mountain are tunnels, a great network of them. Kest-creatures lurk down there, and some of them find their way up through to the passageways and corridors of the Overpalace. They're allowed to. They crawl about at night. Eat the odd spy, I suppose, or any fanatical keepers who get that far." He was smirking, enjoying himself.

Suddenly she stared back at him, dubious. "Stories to scare children, Braylwin."

"Ah, but are they? Who knows what goes on in the Tower of Song—isn't that a proverb?" He turned back to the mirror and adjusted his sleeves. "Even we in the Watch, beloved, don't know the half of this place. When it was first taken, patrols often got lost. One group starved; their bones were found days later. Bones, mind. Something ate them. And then there's the legend of the Lost Hall . . ."

"Go on," she said drily, peeling a slim-fruit with her knife. She knew he was teasing her, that it might all be lies.

He examined a spot on his chin. "It's a famous story around the tower. A captain called Feymir was drunk one night, wandered off and got lost. Next morning he put in a report about a great hall he'd found, chock-full of Maker-gadgets. When he tried to find it again he couldn't. No one ever has. Whatever he'd been drinking, it must have been good."

Outside the open window, the rain was crashing on a roof.

Braylwin fiddled with his skullcap and stood back. "What do you think?"

"Charming," she said, eating peel.

He picked a pair of gloves off the table and swished to the door. "Don't wait up!"

When he'd gone she hurled the knife after him in disgust. It embedded itself in the wood, vibrating. Then, head on hands, she stared grimly out into the rain. What was wrong with her? She'd never felt so useless—as if she were some rat in a maze, going around and around and getting nowhere. Calm down, she told herself furiously. Think! The tower worked on everyone like this; already she'd seen how the people who tried to find out anything in it went away hopeless, baffled, dulled into despair.

But it wouldn't happen to her!

For the next two days she read files, pored over reports, waded through endless, useless paper. Next she tried to get into the Overpalace. The first set of guards turned her back, despite arguments and passes and bribes. As a last resort she explored restlessly, walking for hours deep into quarters she'd not seen, once into a district not even on the map, a deep warren of disused kitchens and sculleries, down so many stairs they were probably underground. It was dark and empty, and it was down there, at one turn in a corridor, that she stopped, listening, the crossbow in her hands.

A distant, eerie howl had risen out of the floor, from far beneath. Silent, absolutely still, she waited, and at last it came again, indefinably closer, but muffled, as if layers of stone—rooms, dungeons, cellars—were between her and it. Not human. She crouched down with her ear to the stone slabs. Somewhere down there, unguessable levels below, something prowled. Tucking her hair back, she cradled the bow, her skin prickling with the menace of that wail. Whatever it was sounded hungry, and ferocious. After a while she stood up and walked on, the bow racked and loaded. Maybe Braylwin had been telling the truth after all.

Once more she thought she heard a similar thing, very faintly under the Corridor of Combs, but no one else there spoke about it, or even seemed to notice, hurrying past her with their arms full of papers.

Finally, she went back to her room late on the third afternoon, in despair, but Braylwin's snoring and the overflowing bucket in her room were too much. Furious, she flung the water out of the window and spun around, glaring at Tamor's bright eyes.

"What are you staring at?" she hissed. "Can't you do something! Galen would say you could. Well, do it!"

Storming out, she leaned over a balcony in the Room of the Blue Rose and kicked the ornate balustrade. Crowds milled around her. No one spoke. In all this filthy ant-hill, no one cared about her—no one even knew her. Even Braylwin had given up having her followed. She wished, suddenly and fiercely, that Raffi were there, so she could talk to him, laugh with him. She'd forgotten the last time she'd laughed.

Then, just below her, she saw the clerk, Harnor. He crossed the room quickly, a file under one arm, and she called him, but he didn't hear. Suddenly she wanted to talk to him, to talk to anybody. She darted down the steps in time to see him vanish through a doorway, and she ran after him, pushing through the crowd.

Harnor was in a hurry. He was walking quickly, and

she couldn't catch him until he'd crossed the Walk of the Graves and two courtyards.

By then she knew he didn't want to be seen.

He was going somewhere, and he was uneasy. He looked around too often and, passing the guard-posts, he seemed scared and alert. Carys kept back, interested. She began to trail him, using all the cunning of her training.

He went down a long corridor and through the third door. Opening it gently, she saw this was some kind of store area—great cupboards and shelves overflowing with unsorted papers. There was no one in here. At the end of the room was a smaller door; through that she found steps, leading down into a damp passageway with a dead rat in the middle of it. Water dripped somewhere near.

Ahead, in the dimness, Harnor's thin shape padded.

She was intrigued. What was down here? And why was he so nervous about it? Twice she had to wait, breathless, as he stopped and stared back. At the end of the stone passage was a turning, then another. He walked quickly; he knew the way well. And then, as she peered around the last corner, she stared into dimness, astonished. It was a dead end.

But Harnor had vanished.

Carefully Carys walked down after him.

The corridor ended abruptly; a stone wall with rainwater running down it in green seams. It was solid and firm, and so were the walls on each side; she ran her fingers along the greasy stones in amazement.

So where had he gone?

Suddenly she knew with a shiver of joy that this was important, this was what she had been searching for. Feverishly she pushed and prodded each stone, knelt and ran her hands around the joints and edges of the wall. And she felt a draft.

It was slight, but cold. Putting her fingers to it, she touched a wide crack lost in the blackness of one corner and found a small raised circle, smooth and warm. She knew it was Maker-work; there had been panels like this in the House of Trees. She took a deep breath, and pressed it.

Silently, with a smoothness that amazed her, a section of wall melted. A small doorway stood there, and beyond it a room was pale with light.

Carefully she lifted the crossbow and stepped inside.

10

Promotion must be earned. Be ruthless;
there are many who will be passed over.

Rule of the Watch

SHE WAS STANDING IN A DIM HALL. Light filtered through one window high up in a wall; the rest seemed shuttered or blocked.

The hall was crammed full of objects, piled high, and someone was moving down in the shadows among them. She heard steps, creaks, the bang of something closing.

Creeping nearer carefully, she found she was moving between huge towers of dusty boxes, ledgers, astrolabes, collections of skulls, hanging maps that brushed her face with soft, cobwebby edges. Ahead was a patch of light, oddly unflickering. Silently Carys crouched behind a wooden crate and peered cautiously around.

Harnor was sitting at a tall desk, in a pool of light from a lamp—a Maker-lamp, which lit his gray head and hunched shoulders with amazing clarity. He was reading a great volume of thick pages that turned with small, stiff crackles. There was no other sound at all: The hurrying lines and crowds of the tower seemed an eternity away.

Carys looked around, noting everything. Galen might know what some of these things were—she had no idea. There were boxes, panels, piles of broken wiring, bizarre devices with screens and buttons and dials that she knew were relics, ancient things collected by the Emperors. There were priceless books, marble statues, charts of trees, and the complete skeleton of some small, unknown animal, as well as a globe showing Anara's continents, even the Unfinished ones, strange pieces of paper pinned all over it.

Harnor turned another page.

In the silence Carys scratched her cheek thoughtfully. Then she stood up and walked forward into the light.

He was so engrossed that for a moment he didn't even notice her. When he did, his whole body jerked with terror; he leaped up, knocking the stool away with a smack that was deafening in the silence.

"You!" His eyes flickered over her shoulder, wide with fear. He seemed too choked to say anything clearly. "How . . . did you . . . ?"

"I followed you." She perched on the edge of a table, the crossbow loose in her hands. "You needn't worry. There's no one else with me."

As soon as she'd said it, she realized she might have made a mistake. But he was terrified. He swallowed, rubbing his face feverishly, then took a step toward her. She raised the bow, but he'd stopped already, gripping the desk as if to hold himself up.

"For God's sake," he said hoarsely, "for pity's sake, don't tell them!"

"I'm not surprised you're worried."

"Don't play with me!" It broke from him like a cry of agony. "I've got a wife, two children! What will happen to them! Think about them, please!"

"I'm not going to tell anyone."

"But you're a spy. You work for Braylwin and if he—"

"If he knew, you'd be in chains so fast you wouldn't

have time to blink, but I'm not him. I don't work for him." She grinned. "Haven't you noticed how he has me watched?"

Confused, Harnor clutched his head. "Everyone is watched."

"Except you, it seems. A small, timid man nobody notices." She waved the bow, curious. "How long have you been coming here?"

He shrugged, then stammered, "I—I'm not sure . . . about twenty years."

"Twenty years! Does anyone else know about it?"

"No." For a moment his glance was proud, almost greedy. "This is mine. No one else's. Except . . ." He put a hand to his head hopelessly. "Except you."

Carys smiled. Deliberately she laid the bow on the floor and folded her arms. "Listen to me, Harnor. I'm not investigating you. Finding this place was an accident. Sit down."

He sat numbly, as if he had suddenly become old, his hands clutched together, his thin face drawn. She could see the sweat on him. Leaning forward, she said quietly, "Will you trust me?"

The Tower of Song

"What does it matter! You've found it all now."

"I certainly have." She glanced up at the towers of boxes. "What is all this? Are they all relics? Are there other rooms?"

"Lots." For a moment he stared down bleakly. Then he began to speak, and there was a faint edge of defiance in his voice, almost lost, but she caught it.

"I wanted to be a spy once. Out there, hunting outlaws, free, on my own. But they sent me here to keep accounts; year after year, petty records, endless reports, and I was weighed down by it, it buried me, closed over my head." He stared hopelessly. "You can't imagine that. You're too young. Oh, at first I was hopeful, I put in applications, I bribed people. I waited my life away, but it was all useless. I was too ordinary. Just a number, a small, despairing pen-pusher no one cared about. I lost hope. This place does that to you."

She nodded, swinging her foot. "I'd noticed."

"Well, think of spending decades here. All the years of your life."

They were silent. Then he looked up. "But somewhere, deep down, I wouldn't give in. I thought, if I'm trapped here, I'll make this place my adventure. I'll learn it, as no one else ever has. If there are secrets, I'll find them."

He glanced at her, and she saw his eyes were very bright. "I explored, Carys. I learned every corridor, every gallery. I spent years searching, all my spare time, planning, charting in my head, writing nothing down so they'd never know. And then, one day, I came into the corridor and found the hidden door."

He wasn't scared now. He was trembling, exultant. "There are whole suites of rooms here no one knows about. All the things in them, the Emperors' things, the Maker-things, are mine. I've spent years with them, these statues. Look . . . look at this, how beautiful it is!"

He jumped up suddenly and, picking up a cube, thrust it into her hands. As she turned it she gasped, because trapped inside what seemed like glass was a whole landscape, a place of green fields and strange trees, and the sky there was blue, a deep, perfect blue. It wasn't a flat picture. Somehow it was real.

"That's the home of the Makers, Carys, and there's more here, much more. It would take years to show you all of it; beautiful books, statues you almost think are watching you. I love these things. I've grown to love them." He stopped abruptly and looked straight at her. "I know it's wrong. But I do."

She frowned, thinking how he had suddenly become alive, and then his eyes fell and he was Harnor again, aghast at seeing her there. To give herself time, she got up. "Take me around," she said.

For the next half hour each of them forgot all danger. Even Carys was dazzled by the treasures the rooms contained. Harnor had piled them all here, cleaned the frescoes and wall paintings so that they glowed: bright, colorful scenes of the world's Making that would have silenced Galen. There were wonderful fragments of sculpture, jewels, crystals, strange artifacts, bizarre machines, a whole collection of brilliant and intricate tapestries. Fingering a small device that clicked a flame on and off, she looked up and saw him watching her.

"Did you mean it?" he whispered. "About not telling him?"

"I meant it."

"Why?"

"Because I want you to help me." She put the flame-maker in her pocket and sat herself in a huge, winged chair, feeling like some empress. "You see, I'm a bit like you, Harnor. Not quite what I seem. You say you know the tower. I want you to get me to the Overpalace. To the Great Library."

He stared at her in horror. "But—"

"Do your passages go that far?"

Bewildered, he ran his hand down an exquisite silver figure. "No . . . at least, well, yes they do. There are ways, but—"

"No buts. That's where we're going."

"But why?"

"Because I want to find things out," she said shortly. "About who I am."

To her surprise he laughed, a bitter laugh. "Oh, do you? Well, you won't find anything." Seeing her stare, he looked away. "You wouldn't be the first. Even I tried that. Many years ago. The library is dangerous to get into, but I went there. Once was enough. There are no records, Carys. Each child's first name is entered and that's it. No one cares where they came from. It's not important."

She got up, furious, and stalked over to a box and stood looking down, seeing nothing. What would I have done anyway? she asked herself coldly. Gone and found the village? My parents? They wouldn't have even recognized me.

"We're still going," she growled.

He glanced frantically around. "You're crazy!"

"Listen, Harnor!" She turned on him, blazing with wrath. "You're not the only one who breaks the rules. I know a keeper, well, two of them . . ."

He stared at her, aghast. "A keeper!"

"That's right. And he's made me think. Who is it that runs the Watch? What do they want with relics? Why stamp out the Order so savagely?"

He shrugged. "Everyone knows the Order was evil."

"But the relics! Think about it! They were once full of power, a power we know nothing about. The keepers do. I've seen that. What I want to know is why the Watch teaches us it doesn't exist!"

He shook his head in fear. "I don't want to think about this."

"Get me to the library, and you won't have to." She

came over quickly. "I'll go then. You'll never see me again. And you'll still have all your treasures."

For a moment, seeing his despair, she felt like Braylwin and hated herself. But when he looked up, his face was set.

"All right. But only once." He looked bleakly at the silver fish under his hand. "Be here tonight. And come armed."

11

For a year they held me underground,
bound with chains.
They tried to enter my workrooms, but
the Pit was sealed.
My secrets lay deep. And they were well
guarded.

Sorrows of Kest

THE RAIN WAS HORIZONTAL, crashing in sheets. Lightning flickered, white and silent. As Carys waited for the sleep-drug to take effect, she watched it from the window, hearing all the gutters and waterspouts of the tower gurgle their song. Far below, one dim torch burned in the corner of a courtyard.

The third time she checked, the man was asleep, propped on his bench outside Braylwin's door. She stepped over him, then went back and knocked the cup over with one foot, spilling the dregs. Just in case.

All the way she was careful—doubling back, going by narrow routes, quiet back alleys. No sign of anyone following. When she was sure, she went down into the stone corridors.

It took her a while to find the right dead end, and when she slipped inside, Harnor was waiting. He looked white and agitated.

"Where have you been!"

"Making sure I wasn't followed." She settled the crossbow. "Come on. I need to be back before morning."

He fidgeted, anxious. "Listen. There are things up there. Creatures. They roam the tunnels."

"You said you'd been there before."

"Years ago . . ."

"Well then, you can do it again." She was sharp, irritated. "Now come on!"

He gave her one miserable look and led the way to a door in the corner. She'd need to watch him, she thought. He could lead her anywhere down here. Try to lose her, even. "Remember this, Harnor," she said. "You get me to the library, or I make sure Braylwin knows everything."

For the first hour they barely spoke. He led her along filthy corridors and empty rooms, once across a courtyard choked with weeds, high wet walls all around them.

Glancing up, she saw dark windows. All these empty rooms. The size of the place made her uneasy. Was it possible no one else knew about it?

They climbed stairs, vast wide steps and narrow spiral ones, lit by torches Harnor kept in various places. Halfway up one she stopped, so suddenly that Harnor stared back in terror. "What? What is it?"

Carys stood still, not answering. For a moment she had seen something amazing, as if a panel had opened in her head. Raffi had been there, and Galen and the Sekoi, all around a fire under some dark trees, vivid and close. She could even smell the burned wood, and Raffi had turned and seen her and called something.

"Have you found the Interrex?" she whispered.

But he hadn't answered, and she couldn't see them now.

"What's the Interrex? Is it here?" Harnor stared around in agony.

"No." She shook her head absently. "Forget it. Keep your mind on the job."

As they climbed higher into the warren of rooms and galleries she thought about it, pacing through vast dim halls. Was that the third eye Raffi talked about? It was

amazing. And what did it mean? Had they found the Interrex? Galen had said she would know, but was that it?
So soon?

Then she realized Harnor had stopped. He was waiting by a gate, a grille of rusted metal. A small entrance
had been made by twisting some of the bars. Beyond, the
darkness was complete.

"Once in here," he whispered, "we're in the Overpalace. Or rather, under it. About three floors below the inhabited parts. You should load your bow." He took out
an old curved knife from behind a stone. "I'll have this."

"So what's in there?" She racked the bow quickly.

He shivered, unhappy. "Who knows. I've heard hor-
rible noises, found droppings, chewed food, great holes
torn in doors. Often I've thought I was watched."

She nodded. "But you've never seen anything?"

"Once I thought . . ." His hands shook on the knife.
"Each time, it was harder to come back. Last time I swore
to myself I'd never come here again."

"After this you won't have to." She felt heartless, but
she needed him. "Right. Now lead on."

It was darker here. Dust lay thick on the untrodden

floors. Harnor seemed less sure of the way. Twice they doubled back through long galleries; once at a crossroads of four passages, he hesitated. Carys watched him gravely, and his eyes flickered to her in the dark.

And there were other things here. She knew it, with a growing instinct, all her training warning her. A scuttle in the dark, something that breathed around a corner. They went slowly now, more carefully, and once they were so near the inhabited rooms, she heard voices through a wall and muffled laughter.

After about half an hour, she heard something else. It was in the distance ahead of them, a regular throbbing that echoed strangely in the passageways. "What's that?" she murmured.

Harnor gave a wan smile. "That won't hurt us."

It grew louder as they walked, a cacophony of knocks and ticks and chimes until, as he pulled open a great door, the sound burst out and she saw a vast hall full of clocks. There were thousands of them, candle-clocks, sand-clocks, mechanical clocks in every shape, all ticking at different rates, different speeds, a bewilderment of noise.

Carys stared. "Did you bring these all here?"

He shook his head nervously. "I found it like this. I haven't been here for over a year. As I said . . ."

She glanced at him in instant alarm. "So who winds them?"

He was aghast. He stared at her and went so white she thought he would faint on the spot. "I didn't think of that," he breathed.

"Fool!" Carys snapped. She couldn't help it. She was furious with him. "So much for your secrets! How far to the library?"

"Ten minutes." He was shaken, and he wiped his face with a damp hand. "Should we turn back?" he whispered. Then, "Please, Carys."

"No."

They hurried through the Hall of Clocks. Shuffles moved in the darkness behind them. Harnor was reckless with fear; Carys kept a sharper lookout.

Halfway down one gallery he stopped.

"Here?" she whispered, surprised.

He raised the torch up and she saw a ladder: narrow metal rungs up the wall, climbing into darkness. "Up here."

The Tower of Song

She put the torch out, stamping it with her foot. After a second he did the same. The tunnel was dim with acrid smoke.

"You first," she said.

He seemed to force his courage together; then he was climbing, a thin figure lost in the dimness. Carys put her foot on the lowest rung and her hands up. For a moment she looked sideways, into the dark.

Something slid. She could hear it, for a moment, a soft, scaly sound. Then silence.

Hurriedly she swarmed up after him.

The ladder was high: twenty, twenty-one rungs. Breathless, she clung tight and looked up. "How far?"

Her hiss echoed as if they were in some great shaft or airwell.

"Nearly there." He sounded as if he were struggling with some weight; a slot of paler dark opened above him, swung to a wedge, then crashed back to a great square, and he climbed up through it and was gone.

Coming after him, she hoisted herself quickly through the hole and stood up, dusting her hands.

They were in the library.

It was vast; a series of enormous arched halls leading one out of the other, and down the centers of them, great shelves rising to the roof, each crammed with books. After a moment she wandered along them, seeing thousands of volumes, each one held by a tiny chain, some lying open on the desks below. What secrets there must be here, she thought bitterly. And how could she look through them all? Where should she even start?

She turned on Harnor, a dim, nervous figure, the great windows behind him dripping with rain.

"Where are the most important books kept?" She came up close to him. "Think! They're locked up, probably."

He ran a hand through his gray hair, then turned reluctantly. "Up here."

Beneath the great ranks of books they felt small, uneasy. They walked quickly, conscious of the echoes of their footsteps, the endless patter of rain. Rats ran before them, scattering with tiny scuttering noises. Harnor hurried through three great halls; he came to a dais of three steps and stopped at the foot of it. "Up there," he gasped. "But be quick, Carys. Be quick!"

She saw the seven circles of the moons on the wall, vast

shapes of beaten copper, gold, and bronze. Under them, standing in a long row, were the Makers. They looked down at her with huge dignified faces as she walked under them; and in the center was Flain, his dark hair bound with silver, his coat shining with stars. In his hands he held a box, and coming up to it, she saw there was a real door in the painting, a tiny door with a shining lock.

She grinned and fished in her pocket, took out a long thin wire, and slid it into the keyhole.

"What are you doing!"

"Opening it. I always enjoyed these lessons."

Harnor sank in a huddle on the steps; he seemed too terrified to speak.

The lock was difficult, but suddenly the wire clicked around and she laughed, pulling the door wide and putting her hands in.

Harnor squirmed around, fascinated. There were piles of books in the safe, most of them rich with jewels and carved gems, too huge to lift, and she rummaged hurriedly among them, right to the bottom. She was still a moment; then she said, "Look at this," in such a strange voice that Harnor fought off his fear and scrambled up the steps, and he saw she held a relic in her hands, a very small, gray console with a blank screen. She brought it out carefully, knowing that this was precious, secret, something meant never to be seen. It had been burned once; its edges were black and scorched. Baffled, she turned it over.

"What is it?" Harnor whispered.

"I don't know. But Galen will."

"Who's Galen?" he began, but then he stopped, staring over her shoulder, his face set in a sudden agony of terror.

She spun around.

Far down the halls, up through the open trapdoor, something dark and long, endlessly long, was slithering.

12

*The creatures of the deep, how shall we
number them?
Beasts of nightmare, spun from the dark
mind.
All the spiny, envenomed things of anger.
They infest us, they breed.
Who will rid us of them now that the
Makers are gone?*

Poems of Anjar Kar

IT RIPPLED LIKE A GREAT WORM, its fluid body thick and loathsome. As they stared, the tail slid out of the hole, whipping swiftly behind the dark bookshelves.

Harnor looked ashen. "God," he kept muttering. "Oh God."

Carys stuffed the relic inside her coat and grabbed him tight. "Keep quiet. Quiet! And stay close."

He shuddered; she saw the knife blade quiver in his hand. They stepped carefully down from the dais, every nerve alert. She held the crossbow ready.

Neither of them spoke.

On each side the vast black shelves loomed, the creature winding invisibly among them. Faintly, they could hear it; somewhere it was slithering, its scales making a light, sinister hiss and scrape on the stone floor. The sound seemed to be all around; Carys, her fingers clutched on the bow trigger, glanced nervously behind them.

Harnor jerked her arm in terror. "There!"

She whirled, saw a length of something slide into shadow. Her fingers were damp with sweat; she knew if she fired and missed, it would be on them before she could reload. It was hunting them, whatever Kest-horror it was, rippling around them with its endless coils. Somewhere in the halls the narrow eyes would be watching, behind some tower of books, through some slit.

It stank, too: a sickening, putrid stench.

The black halls seemed enormous; far ahead in the darkness the trapdoor waited, a slanted square. It was their bait.

"We'll never make it," he moaned.

"We're not meant to make it." She was walking backward now, the bolt spanning the shadows.

They came through the first hall, then the second. Small

squirms and ripples of movement slid in the dark, out of sight. Carys's arms ached with tension.

Ahead, the doorway to the third hall loomed. They were almost under it when his choked yell made her leap around and she saw it, towering over them: a great looping, uncoiling serpent, grotesque fins of small bones splaying from its neck, its great head flat like a snake's but crested with spines that dripped poisons and acids in pools on the floor, bubbling and hissing into the stone. Wide green eyes gleamed at her. She jerked back as the scorching saliva seared her face, then she aimed and shot the bolt straight at its throat.

Almost mocking, the head swerved aside; the bolt splintered something in the dark. Cursing, Carys scrabbled for another, but the worm darted straight at her, and with a gasp of terror she squirmed away, fell into a gap between shelves, picked herself up, and ran.

Harnor was ahead, reckless in the dark. They raced the length of one passage, then swung into another before she hauled him down and they crouched, breathing hard, the darkness spitting and slithering all around them.

"Don't get lost!" She jammed the bolt in frantically. "We have to get down that hole!"

"We can't."

"We can! Don't panic. It's a beast—it has no reason."

He was white; the knife trembled as he clutched it. She had to drag him to his feet, but he crumpled again and cowered into the shadows, hands over his face. "I can't. I can't. I'll stay here. I'll be all right."

"It can smell you!" She hauled him up, furious. "For Flain's sake, listen to me! Listen! We get through these shelves till we're opposite the trap. Understand? And don't get lost, Harnor, because I won't come looking for you."

He stared at her in dread. Then he rubbed his face again. "All right."

They paced down rows of books. Halfway along one, Carys paused. The library was utterly silent, except for, far off, the drumming of rain. Nothing moved. The silence was like an ache. And now she could smell the thing, a strong stench of rotting weed, stagnant water. Bending, she felt the stones of the floor. Her fingers touched a thick slime, an acrid smear that crossed before her and ran under the dark shelves.

Hurriedly she straightened and stepped over it. But the hall was crisscrossed with the worm's trail; soon the stench was on their hands and boots, a cold slime they couldn't rub off. By the time they crept to the crack in the shelves they were sick with it, Harnor retching with the back of one hand over his face. Sweating, she peered out.

Everything was still.

"Now," she whispered. "Stay together. We'll need both of us against this thing. Stab deep, but remember there are coils of it, so don't stop. Just get down the ladder."

He nodded, but she saw he was stupid with terror. Gripping the bow tightly, she said, "Now. Run."

He didn't move.

"Run!"

"It's out there. It's waiting." His voice was a breath; he was staring out at the trapdoor like a man in a nightmare, frozen with panic. Suddenly she turned and shoved him, hard, out onto the dark floor so that he screeched and rolled and scrabbled in horror toward the square of darkness.

And instantly the creature was on him.

It swooped, out of some high place, and she was awed

at the rippling speed of it, the glistening coils. Harnor shrieked; Carys fired the bolt hard, and it thumped into the creature's flesh, but the thing didn't stop. It kept coming, and Carys pulled out her long knife and ran, slashing at it. It hissed and spat; it was all around her, moving fast, bewildering, and suddenly she was entangled in it, the firm muscles slithering under her arms, around her knees. As she slashed, some coils loosened but others came, squeezing her tighter, slippery with slime and a cold, watery blood.

"Harnor!" she screamed.

Then she saw him. He was halfway down the hole; for a second he looked up and saw her and she yelled at him again, and caught the furtive glimmer of his face, white as paper. Then he was gone, and she was being dragged, one arm trapped tight, kicking and fighting. She had no breath now; she squirmed and wriggled, and then suddenly, lay limp.

The terrible squeezing slowed. Somewhere in the dark, a long hiss told her the head was zigzagging in.

Carefully, one-handed, she felt inside her pocket and pulled out the tiny firelighter she had picked up earlier.

She felt choked; the cold grip of the contracting worm was suffocating all the anger out of her, but she waited until its head loomed above, spiraling down, the green eyes alight in the dark.

Then she flicked the lighter on.

The head whipped back.

She held it out, as far as her arm would reach; then, with a better idea, she brought it back against the beast's skin. It convulsed into shivers, squeezing her harder, but she held the flame there, relentless, coughing at the burning of the scales and the acrid smoke, the tiny fierce Maker-light flaring blue and green. Then, with a jerk that almost broke her ribs, the creature opened up and flung her out, kinking and wriggling in irritation, and she dived under it into the open square of the hole and fell, swinging with a scream and a crash against the ladder, grabbing again, the knife and bow clanging and clattering down into the darkness below.

Above her the creature searched frantically; as its body looped she hauled herself up and grabbed the trapdoor and with one great heave pulled it down over her, so that the blackness rang with the crash of falling dust.

For a long time she clung to the ladder, shaking, breathing hard. Above her the slither of scales sounded faintly; she was sore and bruised, her legs weak with sickness and relief.

After a while, she felt calmer. Then she thought of Harnor. Where was he? She cursed him silently, calling him coward, craven little rat, and the anger put fresh strength into her; she found herself clambering down the slimy ladder, down the long descent into blackness until her feet met the stone floor abruptly.

She stood still.

"Harnor?"

The whisper echoed; she hadn't expected any answer. Moving cautiously, her foot nudged something. She bent and groped for it, her hands feeling it over. The crossbow. Dented. She took out the tiny fire-maker and flicked it on; the blue flame shone pale. After a longer search she found her knife and stuck it into her belt grimly. So he'd gone, then. And what a squirming panic he'd be in, running back through the silent rooms, sobbing with fear, dodging shadows, imagined slithers down the walls.

She smiled remotely. Poor Harnor. Was this what the

Watch had done to him, or had he always been afraid? Was that why they'd never trained him? How would she be without that training? She frowned. Anyway, he must think she was dead, or if not dead, then lost, hopelessly lost in this labyrinth of rooms and tunnels and halls.

She grinned, pushing the grimy hair from her eyes. Then she lit the torch propped against the wall and began to walk, the bow slung ready.

The first mark was on the corner of three passages; the torchlight fell on it and she reached out and smudged it off, the chalk whitening her thumb. He hadn't seen them, then. She'd made them low, bending in snatched moments when he hadn't been looking, with the tiny lump of chalk she'd brought. If he'd been trained, he would have guessed.

"Always leave yourself a way out," old Jellie would say, pounding up and down the icy classroom with his stick, crunching daydreamers sharply in the back. "Never rely on anyone else to get you out."

She walked quickly, but the way seemed endless and she had no idea how much time had gone by. The rooms and halls were dark, and once or twice she had to search hard for the chalk-marks. Down in the dampest tunnels great slugs had crawled out; the torchlight flickered on them, white, flabby monsters. She ignored them because they were no danger, but sometimes there were other sounds: a creak of wings in a high hall, muffled voices, and once a faint scuttling, as if some immense insect ran up an invisible wall.

The Hall of Clocks was a relief; she heard the tocking from far off and almost ran through the hall toward it, but when she'd squeezed through the twisted gate into the courtyard she was dismayed to see how light it was. Drizzle was falling, but it was well into the morning. Cursing, she kicked the weeds aside and raced for the opposite door, praying that Braylwin would still be asleep. In her hurry she took two wrong turns; it must have been over an hour before she came through the door into Harnor's cluttered secret halls. She dumped the worn-out torch into a corner and ran past the piled-up relics and smooth statues to the hidden sliding panel.

For a moment she thought he had locked it; then she realized she had never opened it from the inside, and it took her hasty, irritated minutes to find the catch.

Once out, she sped through the halls and courtyards. The tower was awake; a clock chimed ten, and she pushed through the crowds of clerks and wagonloads of files with rising despair.

Up the stairs, along the corridor, smoothing her hair, rubbing dirt from her face, and then as she turned the corner she saw Braylwin's door was open and heard his high, plaintive voice whining inside.

"Well, where is she? How long has she been gone?"

Coming to the door, Carys peered in.

Braylwin was swelling with rage, his red silk gown bursting its buttons. The man-at-arms looked sour. In one corner Harnor was working, bent over his desk as if he wished he could disappear into it. He looked tired out and terrified; he still wore the same clothes, and she could see the dried mud on his boots.

Braylwin took breath for another outburst. Then he saw her. "There you are! Where on earth have you been?"

All heads turned.

Carys came in and looked at Harnor. She had never seen anyone cringe like that. For a moment their eyes met and she stared at him levelly, wanting him to feel the terror, the suspense. It was the only punishment she could give him; now she had to save herself, get herself out of the stifling tower before the loss of the relic was traced to her.

"Well?"

She perched on the table and began picking at the remains of Braylwin's lavish breakfast. "Out. I wanted to walk."

Harnor almost collapsed in relief. Braylwin glared at him. "You. Get on." Looking back at Carys he said, "So early?"

"Yes. I had to think."

"About what?"

"About whether to tell you." She looked up and gave him the best lie she could think of. "I've had a message from Galen."

Braylwin rubbed his fat hands. "You have?"

"I have. We need to leave at once. He's found the Inter-rex."

Artelan's Well

13

Always now, we will be hunted.

Third Letter of Mardoc Archkeeper

RAFFI WAITED ANXIOUSLY BY THE DOOR. The cottage was small; he could see the fire crackling inside, the dresser with its pewter plates, a basket of chopped wood. It looked cozy. For a moment it reminded him of home.

Then the woman came back, a toddler clutching her skirt. "Here. Take these." She dumped the rough sacking in his arms hastily. "Cheese. Some smoked fish. Vegetables. That's all I can spare."

"It's very generous," Raffi muttered.

She gave him a hard looking-over, and he felt himself going red. "Wait," she said.

In a moment she was laying a blue jacket on the sack. "That was my eldest's. It's too small for him now. You have it."

He was really red by this time. "Thanks," he mumbled.

"You'd better hurry. My husband will be back and he won't stand for tramps. Which way are you heading?"

Off guard, he shrugged. "West . . ."

The woman turned and gathered the child up onto her hip. "Then be careful. The Watch are always patrolling that way."

He nodded, walked to the gate, and turned to say thanks again. She was looking after him, the baby playing with her hair. Suddenly he saw how young she was.

"Give us your blessing, keeper," she whispered.

For an instant Raffi was still. Then he raised his hand, as he had seen Galen do, and said the Maker-words slowly, carefully. It made him feel strange. Older. She bowed her head, and without looking up, went back into the house.

Three fields away, under a blackthorn hedge, Galen looked sourly at the jacket.

"Keepers didn't use to have to beg for castoffs," he said bitterly.

186

Artelan's Well

Raffi didn't care. He tried the jacket on. It was dark blue and warm, and even the patches were better than his old, worn coat, full of holes.

"She knew what you were?" the Sekoi asked quietly, nosing in the sack.

"She guessed. She said the Watch are about."

Galen snorted. The burst of fever was over, but it hadn't improved his temper. He bit into a carrot. "You said nothing else?"

"No." But the memory of that word, *west*, stung him. Galen stopped chewing and stared harder. Then he leaned over and caught Raffi's arm. "What else? What did you tell her?"

"Nothing . . ." But that was useless. He frowned and took a breath. "That we were going west."

For a moment he thought Galen would hit him. Then the keeper flung him away, his eyes black with fury.

"I didn't mean to! She caught me unaware!"

Galen gave a harsh laugh. "Never mind. Too late to start being careful now."

"She won't tell anyone."

"Let's hope not," the Sekoi said uneasily. It spat out the

pips of a dewberry and stood up. "Still, it would be best to be gone. How far is this magic well of yours?"

Galen flashed it a vicious glare. "I don't know."

"You've never been there?"

"No one's been there for years. It's lost."

"Lost?"

"In the marshes."

They both stared at him, but he flung the pack at Raffi and stalked off, his tall stick stabbing the mud.

The Sekoi gave a tiny mew of disgust. "I should have taken my chances with Godric."

For two days they trudged through fields and scrawny pastures, always upward. The weather was warm, and Raffi tied his new coat to the pack and watched the vast flocks of migrating merebirds flying over, always west, their loud cries breaking the evening hush. But the nights were cold; once they lit a fire in a copse of oak trees that Galen said still had much Maker-life and were prepared to allow it.

By now they were high up, and the pasture was poor, full of hollows and humps, studded with boulders, cropped by hungry sheep. Four moons, wide apart, lit the sky.

Artelan's Well

For a change, Galen was in a milder mood. He was wrapped in his dark coat, the firelight making shadows move on his sharp, hooked face. The Sekoi asked its questions carefully, flipping a gold coin over in its fingers.

"So what is this lost well?"

The Relic Master smiled. "It's a long story. Once there was a keeper; his name was Artelan. He had a vision and he saw Flain. Flain told him to travel far to the west, to the edge of the Finished Lands, and he would find an island called Sarres, where fruit grew all year, where there was no snow, no strong winds, a place out of the world. And on the island was a well, and whoever drank out of it would have his questions answered."

"So he went?"

"He went. The story of his adventures is a long one, but finally he climbed these hills and on the other side saw the Moors of Kadar, green and fertile. And rising out of them was a strange hill, remote and eerie, looking like an island in the mist, and Artelan traveled there, and they say he found the spring and the fruit trees, just as Flain had said. I've often thought it odd, though, that Flain should say it was an island."

The Sekoi smiled, scratching its zigzag tribemark with one finger. "You people waste your stories. I could tell this so that we would all seem to be there now."

Galen nodded. "Our gifts are different. But the Makers gave them all."

"They did not!" It sat up fiercely. "Not ours!"

Galen frowned, but Raffi said, "Never mind all that. Tell us more about the well."

This time they both glared at him, but he didn't mind. He was warm in his new coat and a blanket, and the soft crackle of the fire soothed him. Galen dragged his hair back irritably. "It became a place of pilgrimage, a holy place. The Order built a great house there, and a custodian lived there always. People came, looking for peace, some of them for healing. When they came back they were different. The well had given them wisdom."

"And you think it will tell us where this Interrex is?" The Sekoi looked politely dubious.

"Me. It will tell me." Galen was silent for a moment, then shifted, so the green and black awen-beads glinted. "If it still exists. Because the Watch have destroyed us, and who knows what happened there. Artelan once wrote that the spring would never fail, and never be foul. Let's hope the Watch never found it."

"What would have stopped them?" Raffi asked sleepily.

Galen gave him a strange look. But he didn't answer.

Raffi was silent too. He'd had a sudden mind-flicker; it was water, the shimmer of it under leaves. Just a glimpse and it was gone. He turned over and checked his sense-lines, but the countryside was empty except for the numb minds of sheep, and the faint intelligences of the listening oaks, too deep and too old for him to reach.

Next day, for hours, they climbed the relentless ridge. Each time Raffi was sure they had finally sweated to the top, another fold of hill would rise up before them, and the bitter wind flapped their coats and rippled the long wet grass. The hills were empty; few animals lived here and fewer trees, only stunted shreds of old hedgerow, sheep-gnawed and bare, and the immense burrows of ridge-rats, the fat females scattering from under their feet.

Clouds swept over, some dragging showers. Soon they were soaked; Raffi was glad of his coat. Turning the collar up, he smelled suddenly, as if it were real, a scent of soap, of wood smoke. Ahead of him Galen limped grimly, finding ruts and tracks in the slippery grass; the Sekoi stalked far behind, its fur drenched, miserably silent.

Just below the ridge, Galen stopped. He turned quickly and stared out at the gray country below, blurred by showers.

The Sekoi walked past him. "Come on, keeper."

"Wait." Galen was alert, his eyes dark. "Do you feel that, Raffi?"

Raffi opened his third eye, groping into distance. Far at the edge of his mind-set, something rippled. "Men?" he said doubtfully.

"Men. Following us."

The Sekoi had stopped; now it came slithering back in alarm. "Are you sure?"

"Certain." The keeper glanced around hastily. "Over there. We're too exposed."

They ran to the hollow and slid in; the bottom was muddy and sheep-trodden. As Galen rummaged in the pack, Raffi kneeled up and stared out; the land seemed empty, but he knew Galen's sense-lines were stronger than his, reaching far into stone and soil. The keeper had tugged out the seeing-tube, one of their most precious relics; as he murmured the prayer of humility and gazed through it, the Sekoi looked on with interest. Its yellow eyes flickered to Raffi.

"A relic?"

"It makes far-off things seem nearer."

"Got them," Galen muttered. He was rigid a moment, the tube pointing northeast into a brief moving patch of sunlight on a distant slope. "Ten. Eleven. All on horseback."

"The Watch," Raffi said.

"I don't think so." Galen's voice was sour; he lowered the tube. "Take a look."

Eagerly Raffi took the relic and held it to his eye, touching the red button so that the blurred circle suddenly shriveled into focus, and he saw trees, small in the distance, and between them horses running, red-painted.

"Alberic?" the Sekoi said to Galen.

"Without doubt."

"But how could he be so close?"

"Godric must have been meeting him nearby. He wasn't worried about having to take you any distance, was he?"

Across the circle a shape flashed: Raffi steadied the tube, brought it back carefully. The rider was tiny, muffled in coats; turning, shouting something.

"It's him," he muttered.

"Besides," Galen said acidly, "they probably asked at some cottage."

Raffi scowled, watching the minute horseman vanish behind trees. He gave the tube back curtly, and after a second's hesitation, Galen offered it to the Sekoi.

The creature's eyes glinted; it held the tube carefully with its fourteen long fingers, then lifted it and looked in, and its whole body quivered with surprise.

"I see them," it said after a moment. "They're riding fast. They'll be here in less than an hour." It looked around anxiously. "They'll catch us."

"Maybe." Galen took the relic and stowed it away. "Come on."

They hurried to the ridge-top. The gale increased, pushing them back; Raffi felt he was struggling with a great invisible force, coming out of the land ahead, a hostile force, something he had never felt before. "What is it?" he gasped.

Artelan's Well

Galen gave him a sideways look. "We're coming to the end, boy."

"The end?" For a moment he thought that the ridge was the edge of the world, that there was some vast giddy chasm on the other side, but as Galen hauled him up over the rocks and the full rage of the wind crashed against them, making him stagger over the skyline, he saw what the keeper meant.

They had indeed come to the end.

For in front of them were the Unfinished Lands.

14

*Out of the Pit came disease. For leagues
around, the trees died; grasses curled.
Unseasonal frosts split the rocks. The
Makers abandoned their works. In
Tasceron they brooded on the treachery
of Kest.*

Book of the Seven Moons

IT WAS THE WRECKAGE OF A WORLD.

The hill that Raffi stood on descended into swamp, a green decaying morass stretching as far as he could see, humped and hollowed, dissolving into poisonous yellow mist. Thunder cracked and rumbled; at the horizon were vast jagged ranges, as if mountains had surged up and shattered into sharp slopes. Even the weather was evil, an icy, spitting rain.

The Sekoi shivered. "Chaos creeps in on us."

"Indeed it does." Galen stood upright in the chill wind, staring out. "Year by year the Unfinished Lands creep back, undoing the Makers' works. Spreading like a disease."

"I see no island out there, keeper."

Galen looked over. "Nor do I."

"Will it not have been destroyed, like the rest?"

"Maybe." He stared again into the mist. "But I believe it is there, somewhere. Hard to find. Dangerous. If you don't share that faith, I won't blame you if you don't come."

Raffi watched them both. The Sekoi rubbed sleet from its furred face. It glanced back up the hillside. Then it shrugged, unhappy. "I'll come. For the moment."

"We'll find it." Abruptly Galen stalked off down the slope.

The Sekoi stared after him. "I'm glad you're so sure," it said.

Half an hour later, the stink of the mere choking him, Raffi leaned on a rock to catch his breath. They were at the bottom of the slope. Already the ground was soft, oozing with water. "I thought this was moorland?" he gasped.

"Swallowed up." Galen stabbed the mire with his stick. "Kest's work, all of this. Once he began to meddle with the world, changing things, no one could stop it. Only the

Order fought to keep the balance, kept it so for centuries. But since the Watch destroyed us, all that's lost."

"It makes you wonder," Raffi said suddenly, looking up. "What if the Watch is Kest's work too?"

Galen's glance turned him cold, stabbed him. He felt the shock of it, the tingle of power that he knew was some stirring of the Crow. For an instant the scream of migrating birds rang like alien voices. Galen's eyes were sharp and dark. But all he said was, "I sometimes think so."

"Relic Master!"

The yell made them turn.

A row of horses stood on the hillcrest, high above. From the central one a small figure was grinning down at them. "How are you, Galen Harn?" he called, his voice ringing among the rocks.

The Sekoi spat, and snarled something in its own language.

"Keep still," Galen muttered. Then he called back, "I'm well, thief-lord. But you're too far from home."

Alberic's war-band smirked; one of them said something and they all laughed. Raffi let his sense-lines play over them; he felt weapons, a ruthless confidence. They weren't worried.

Alberic waved an arm at the marsh. "You seem to be running into trouble." He was wearing a coat of quilted blue satin and bearskin, his small, clever face mocking. "Nowhere left to go."

"I go where I'd planned to go," Galen growled.

"Really? Well, I'd hate to see that little blue death-box of mine sinking in a swamp. Why not leave it behind for me?"

"Come down and get it."

Alberic shook his head. Even from here Raffi could see the glint in his bright, hooded eyes. "I intend to. Or at least my boys and girls here will come down. I don't like blood on my clothes."

Galen folded his arms. It was a small action, but Alberic's grin faded. He frowned out at the marsh. "I hope you're not going to be stupid."

Galen laughed, his rare, harsh laugh. It terrified Raffi, and he knew at once it had worried the dwarf.

"I'm walking out into chaos, little man," the keeper said grimly. "And if it drags me down, all the relics go with me. I'd rather the swamp have them than leave them with you. You're a disgrace to your kind, thief-lord. Your soul is shriveled like a plumstone. You're forgetting how to feel, how to know joy. You're tired of all the world, Alberic, and the more you get, the more it turns to ashes in your hand."

For a moment they watched each other, unmoving, the dwarf's face set and cold. Then Galen turned. "Come on."

They scrambled into the soft, yielding swamp. Behind them Alberic stood up in his saddle, furious. "Keeper! Don't be a fool!"

"Keep going," Galen snapped. "Don't look back."

An arrow slashed the reeds. The soft ground vibrated with hoof-beats; Raffi felt them as he thrust aside the tall reeds.

"Boy! Are you going to follow him to your death?" Alberic's yell was raw with anger; Raffi tried to ignore it, but his foot sank suddenly into the mud and he plunged with a gasp, up to his waist.

Galen tugged him up. "Keep hold of me!"

"It's deep!"

"It'll get deeper!"

In front of them the Sekoi slithered in, its face squirming with distaste. Raffi floundered, his boots deep in the mud, the green stinking mire giving off reeks and vapors that made him dizzy. Great weeds clustered over him, giant scumwort with its hairy leaves like hands on his hair and neck. As Galen moved ahead, Raffi slipped and fell, this time right under the murky water.

He yelled, then choked. Hands hauled him out; a sudden swirl of the mist showed him Godric's face, grinning, and he squirmed and fought, but they had him, they were dragging him away, three of them, and somewhere Alberic was shouting orders, his voice pitched high.

"Galen!" Raffi screamed. He kicked, but his legs were grabbed. A muddy hand slammed over his mouth, but he yelled again with all his mind-power, at the keeper, at the Makers, and at the same time a blue shaft of light slashed past him; the knot of men leaped apart in terror.

"The box!" Alberic raged. "He's using my box!"

Raffi picked himself up. A horse's hooves almost trampled him; looking up through a sudden tear in the fog, he glimpsed the girl Sikka, her snake-armor glinting. She saw him and shouted; then he was up, floundering, and Galèn was somewhere close pulling him by some strong mind-tug so that he hurtled into the marsh in a shower of arrows and sank deep, only his face above water, splashing, drowning, till a hand grabbed his tightly and Galen's voice said, "Quiet!"

Instantly, the night was very still.

Two slow bubbles oozed from below and plipped, one by one, under his ear.

Silence slapped in ripples against the scumwort stalks.

When Alberic spoke, they were shocked at how close he sounded. "All right, Galen. You've made your point. It's noble, but what good are drowned bodies? Is that what the Makers want?"

Harnesses creaked in the fog.

The dwarf's voice was calm, reassuring. "Come out. We'll talk terms."

Galen's mouth came close to Raffi's ear. "Walk. Slowly. Don't splash."

"Where?" Raffi breathed.

"Out there."

"There's nothing for you out there, keeper!" It was as

if Alberic had heard them. Now he was barely controlling his fury. "You'll drown, or the fog will choke you! There are horrors out there, Galen, fish that will eat your fingers away, steelworms, leeches, grubs that burrow into the flesh. Nothing else! And you, Cat-creature, water-hater, you know I'm right! The Great Hoard will never have that gold that's weighing you down!"

Nearby in the fog, the Sekoi sighed. "The worst thing is, he's right."

"Ignore him." Galen led the way, carefully brushing through leaves. They waded after him, trying not to make a sound.

"Gnats will lay their eggs in your hair, keeper! Germs, hideous fevers, that's all you'll get. I want that box! Give me that and you can go, all of you!"

He was raging now, desperate.

In grim silence Galen waded always deeper, the scumwort dark above them. Insects whined. On a sudden open stretch of water Raffi saw the pale moon, Agramon, like a coin on black cloth.

"Galen!" Alberic's roar was distant now. "Are you that scared of me?"

Artelan's Well

But they were far out, and the swamp was up to Raffi's chin, so that if he stumbled, it washed into his ears and he swallowed it, coughing and spitting. He gripped tight to the keeper's coat, and the night closed in around them, until they were struggling and hacking their way through the stiff growths, gasping for breath, bitten by innumerable flies.

In no time at all he was exhausted. His drenched clothes dragged him down; the relentless suction of the mud made every step an effort. He was coughing, half choked by the marsh vapor. So was the Sekoi, its thin, bedraggled shoulders barely visible, shuddering uncontrollably with the bitter cold.

The water swirled. Something nibbled Raffi's knee; he panicked, jerking and splashing, yelling in fear.

Galen grabbed him. "What!"

"It was biting me!" He held on, shaking.

"There's nothing there."

"It'll be back!" The Sekoi's snarl shocked them; it was a hiss of despair. Looming up in the mist they saw its yellow eyes, the short fur swollen with bites and tics. "For Flain's sake, Galen! We have to go back!"

Stubborn, the keeper shook his soaked hair. "We're close," he gasped. "I know we're close."

"There's nothing out here!" The creature came close to him, clasped his arm with its spindly, dripping fingers. "Nothing! It's all gone. The Unfinished Lands have spread over it. Even if we get to the island, it will be overgrown, stinking, poisoned. Listen to me. All this is folly. We can get back, avoid Alberic, get clear. We can still be safe . . ."

Its voice was low, hypnotic. Tingles of warning hummed in Raffi's mind; he knew it was putting them under the story-spell, but he didn't care; he wanted that, to convince Galen, to get them all out before his strength went, before . . .

"NO!" Galen's roar was savage. A sudden burst of energy sparked in Raffi; he stumbled, flung an arm out wildly to stop himself going under. He struck something hard. Solid.

"It won't work on me!" the keeper yelled.

"Galen," Raffi breathed.

"Go back if you want to! Take the boy! I'll walk to my death before I give up!"

"Then walk to it!" the Sekoi snarled. "This isn't faith. It's stupidity!"

Raffi put out his other hand and felt the structure. It was real. Marshlight flickered cold phosphorescent flames under it.

"Galen."

"*What?*" the keeper roared.

"There's some sort of trackway . . ."

In the hush an eelworm rippled by his face. Then the water surged, and Galen pushed him aside.

It was a mesh of branches, woven tight, rammed down between uprights. Old, oozing into decay. But in the green fumes of the fog it was a godsend.

Galen hauled off the sodden pack and dumped it in the Sekoi's arms. Then he climbed, tugging himself up in a great heave of water. Branches cracked; mist closed about him. Something bit Raffi's cheek and he slapped at it, his whole body shuddering.

Then Galen was leaning down, eyes bright, dark hair falling forward. "Come on."

Dragged up, Raffi felt himself dumped on the mesh of branches; he collapsed there, lying still, letting the water run from him endlessly, pouring out of his hair and sleeves and pockets, out of his eyes, out of his mind. He didn't know he had blacked out until Galen grabbed him, propped him up, rubbing his soaked arms briskly. "No time to sleep. You'll freeze."

Shivering, he nodded. Now that they were out of the water the cold was unbearable; he couldn't stop shaking.

Galen pulled him upright. "This trackway leads somewhere," he said harshly, "and we need to find out where."

He was elated. Numbly Raffi felt it, and wondered why. In all the stillness of the fog, all the endless miles of marsh, there was nothing his mind could touch, no one, no Maker-power, nothing but a nightmare of swimming, slithering things, and all the threads of power that should have been in the land were tangled, broken, deeply drowned. But Galen was fierce with hope; he hardly waited for them, forcing his way through the leaves, then walking swiftly, carelessly over the creaking, splitting mesh of the trackway.

The Sekoi pushed Raffi on. "I sometimes think his mind's gone," it said bitterly. "That business in the city. It scorched him."

Raffi shook his head, dragging himself over a hole. "He's always been like this. Even before he spoke to the Makers. This is why they chose him."

The Sekoi was silent. The trackway led them deeper into murk; at times they could hardly see each other. Galen was a shadow far ahead. Raffi was stumbling; he felt sick and ill, hot and thirsty and bitterly cold all at once.

And then he saw that Galen had stopped.

The keeper stood still. Very still. Crowding behind, Raffi saw they had come to the end of the trackway. It broke off abruptly, and beyond it was nothing. Nothing but fog.

The Sekoi gave a hiss of despair, Raffi clutched his hands to fists. He wanted to sink down and cry, but he wouldn't, he wouldn't. He was a scholar of the Order. He had to have faith.

Into the silence the Sekoi said, "What now?"

Galen didn't answer. He was alert, as if he listened.

"Perhaps it's at the other end," Raffi said hopelessly.

"No, it's not." Galen gripped his stick tightly. "It's here."

Before they could stop him he stepped out, into the marsh.

Raffi yelled, grabbed, but to his amazement the keeper didn't sink; he stood there, on the scummy surface, as if it were solid, something real and hard.

And instantly everything changed.

A warm breeze blew the fog apart. He smelled grass, and apples, and to his astonishment the moons came out one by one above him, as if they had been waiting there all the time.

Before them, dark grass sloped in the moonlight, and a figure was sitting under the apple trees. When she stood up, they saw she had two shadows, each an echo of herself.

"Welcome, keepers," she said, and smiled. "I was afraid there was no one left to come."

15

There no trouble will be;
There the summer will linger.
There I will speak to my people
with the water's tongue.

Flain to Artelan, *Artelan's Dream*

RAFFI WAS AWAKE BUT he didn't open his eyes.

Instead he lay curled in the warm heavy fleeces, completely relaxed, hearing somewhere outside the trickle of water over stones, an endless liquid ripple. Behind that was birdsong, a robin or pine-finch, and beyond that, silence, a tranquil silence with no worry.

He dozed again, but the oily wool tickled his bare shoulders. Scratching, he rolled, yawned, opened his eyes. Then he sat up.

The house was large and pillared, swept clean, the door open, letting sunlight in. Raffi fingered the bites on his face. It was afternoon; he'd slept too long.

Getting up he found his clothes, washed, amazingly soft; as he pulled them on he tried to remember the last time they had been clean, and couldn't. He splashed in a silver bowl of water, soaking his hair and neck. As he dried himself, the Sekoi's shadow darkened the doorway. "So you're awake!" It looked cheerful, despite a swollen eyelid.

"Where's Galen?"

"Near. He hasn't slept much. Spent most of the morning talking with Tallis."

Raffi frowned. He had only glimpsed the woman last night, had felt a great sense of age, a bent figure in the dark. "Is she the only one here?"

The Sekoi grinned and winked at him. "She's the Guardian. Whether there's only one of her I haven't worked out yet." And it went back out, bending under the low door.

Puzzled, Raffi followed it.

Outside, he stared around in a sudden warmth of delight. The house stood among green lawns, studded with ancient oaks and calarna trees, and beyond were apple orchards; even from here he could smell the ripening fruit. Near him were phlox and high banks of overripe daisies and some red gentians still in flower, and foxgloves with the fat bees fumbling in their speckled bells. The sky was blue and warm. Beyond the trees, a strange hill rose up almost to a point, an eerie humped outcrop with a buzzard circling over it, just as Artelan might have seen it in his dream.

The Sekoi was grinning at him. "Hard to believe, little keeper?"

"How is it here? How has it survived?"

It shrugged. "Ask the Guardian. It seems the Order has more power left than my people thought."

Galen was sprawled on the grass, under a calarna tree. He looked oddly clean too, wearing a green shirt, and on his face was the look of grave content that Raffi had not seen there before. Beside him was a woman. She stood up stiffly, and he saw she was very old; a small, bent woman in a russet dress, her hair white, her face shrewd and wrinkled.

"Welcome, Raffi. Have something to eat."

"Thanks." He crouched down at the half-empty plates, littered with cuts of ham and cheeses and crusty bread that broke white and soft. There were different fruits too, currants and pears, and hot pies full of blackberries and jugs of cream. Relentlessly he began to eat.

They watched him for a while. Then Galen said, "When will I begin?"

"Tomorrow." The woman's eyes, palest blue, watched Raffi in amusement.

"Begin what?" he muttered, swallowing.

"The Ordeals." She looked out at the orchard. "Galen has told me why you've come. To find out where this child, this Interrex, is, he will have to drink from the spring, and that needs preparation if it is to be safe. A time of fasting, of prayer, the pilgrimage of repentance around the island, a night alone on the peak. Then, when he's ready, he will drink."

Raffi cut himself a big slice of pie. "How long will it take?"

Galen shifted, the awen-beads shining. "That depends on the Makers."

"And on you," the woman said softly.

He nodded. "Yes. On me. We may be keepers, Guardian, but life outside has changed us. The teachings are in fragments and we've lost so much. Too many days spent running and hiding, not in prayer. Too few relics. And the Maker-life in the trees and leaves and stones curling up, harder to reach."

For a moment she watched him. "It hurts you," she said.

He glanced up, eyes dark. "Yes. But this place . . . Here the life is strong. How have you kept it?"

The Sekoi came and sat down, its long fingers picking at the damsons. She nodded at it. "Our friend here has a belt full of gold coins wound about his body."

The Sekoi almost choked.

Raffi laughed aloud. "How did you know?"

"Oh, I know. But he keeps his treasure hidden, under the surface, and so do we, here. Flain made this island holy. The ground has deep lines of energy, the water strange properties. While the swamp spread around us, year by year, we worried, but the island has stayed untouched. Some keepers still came in the troubled years, we heard what was happening: the Fall of Tasceron, the Emperor's death. But the swamp thickened and fog rose out of it and we were lost. The Watch never found us."

Raffi rubbed a finger around his empty plate. Into the silence he said, "Us?"

Tallis looked at him, her smile sharp. "Did I say us? There's only me."

She tried to stand then, and Galen had to help her. When he crouched to collect the dishes, her gnarled hand caught his shoulder. "No. You prepare yourself, keeper. The boy will help me—in return I will give him his lessons, while you're busy."

Galen nodded gratefully. "He needs it. Work him hard."

She met Raffi's eyes and smiled. "Oh, I will."

But after the dishes were clean she let him go exploring, wandering through the long grass of the orchards. The branches were heavy with apples, russets and pippins and medlars falling into rotten, wasp-tunneled softness in the grass. The air was rich with scent and the buzz of honey-bees. At the end of the fields was a gate, and coming through that he found himself on a track, green and overgrown, the tall umbels of burrwort and hemlock and hare's-ear turning to heads of seed and fluff that drifted in the slightest breeze. Birds whistled; from the

elm trees a few leaves pattered, caught on webs, spinning. It was so warm he took his jacket off and hung it on
the hedge and walked on, humming, wondering at how
happy he felt. It was as if they had stepped out of some
endless heartbreak. Here, time stopped. Nothing could
get in.

He left the track at a stile and began to climb the hill,
quickly at first and then more slowly, the sweat cooling
on him, the breeze whipping his hair. Soon his chest thud-
ded with the steepness; he dragged in huge breaths, la-
boring on, and whenever he looked up, the smooth green
slopes hung out over him, so steep he almost had to pull
himself up with his hands.

When he scrambled over the top he was breathless;
soaked with sweat, he crumpled in the spiky grass. Below him the island lay warm in the evening light. Beyond
orchards and woodland the sun was setting; a great red
globe shimmering in the cloudbanks, the strange shift-
ing veils of mist that hid the marsh. He watched it sink,
breathing deep, fingering the blue and purple awen-beads.
This was how it should be, how it had been. This was the
rule of the Order, all that Galen was fighting for. Odd

memories moved through his mind. Slowly, over hours, the color drained; the island became a purple twilight of moths and owls calling from the distant woods. He stared down at it, still, unmoving.

That night Galen lit the log fire in the house, and the candles were arranged. The Sekoi watched, curious. "Can I stay?"

"If you want," Galen said drily. "You might learn something."

Two of the cats that lived there came in over the window ledge; one climbed warmly onto the Sekoi's lap, curling itself up, the other coming and purring at its ear. The creature purred back, as if it spoke to them. Then it said, "I apologize for my behavior in the marsh. You were right, as we see."

For a moment Galen's hand was still. Then he lit another candle. "This time," he said quietly.

Raffi turned as the door opened. To his amazement a young woman came in, with long red hair braided and loose. She sat down next to Galen.

"Are we ready?"

"When you are, Guardian."

She glanced across archly. "Raffi?"

They were grinning at him, he knew. He tried not to
look bewildered. "I'm ready."

So they sat, the three of them, and Tallis began, because he knew it was she, the same woman, somehow
impossibly younger. In a shimmer of candles and bells
they chanted the long sonorous verses of the Litany, the
praises of the Makers, and it sounded more mysterious
to Raffi than ever before, until Galen and Tallis went on
into chants and chapters he hadn't learned yet, full of the
sorrows of the broken world and the echoes of ancient
words.

Later, when he slept in the warm bed, the words ran
through his head, endless as the rippling water outside.

ON SARRES, DAY BLURRED INTO DAY. Scarlet
calarna leaves fell silently into the grass. Galen fasted,
and spent long hours meditating in the quiet garden, as
still as if he slept. On the second day he walked barefoot
up the hill; from below Raffi watched him, sprawled
in the warm sun. They prayed the prayers together,

morning and sunset, and then Raffi had lessons from
Tallis, or fed the hens, or helped picked the endless crop
of apples and pears.

Tallis bewildered him. Sometimes she was old, and
sometimes a woman of about twenty, her red hair swinging, full of energy, climbing the apple ladders and whis-
tling. And once, as he fished in the narrow lake for carp,
he saw her come out of the trees and call him, and he sat
up, cold, because now she was a little girl, barely ten, her
voice high and petulant.

"It's time to come in for tea."

He stood. She was small, her face plump, her red hair
tangled. The russet dress was short, showed bare legs.

"Who are you?" he breathed. "How can you do this?"

The little girl grinned. "I'm the Guardian," she said.
Then she stuck out her tongue at him and ran away.

He asked the Sekoi about it, because Galen was too
busy. The creature had made a hammock for itself between trees in the orchard; it spent hours there, slumber-
ing in the shade, lazily.

Now it fanned itself with a chestnut leaf, one leg dangling. "You're the keeper."

"But I don't understand! Is she . . . Have the Makers given her this ability? Which age is she really?"

"*Really* is a word with no meaning." The Sekoi closed its eyes. "My people have stories of similar beings. After all, we have our past ages somewhere inside of us."

Raffi picked a stone out of the grass and turned it over. "You mean she's not human?"

"Why not? I'm not."

"Yes, but . . . Well, there's your people and ours. That's all."

"And the Crow?"

He glanced up; the Sekoi was looking at him with one eye open.

"What?"

"What I mean is, small keeper, the Makers remade this world and then Kest warped it. Who knows what beings are here?"

Raffi thought about that for a while. Then he said, "I'd like to live in this place forever."

But either it was asleep, gently rocking, or it had no answer for him.

Next day he was memorizing Artelan's dream when he

looked up at her. She was sewing the tears in his coat, so old now, her face drawn and wrinkled, her hands stiff, knobbly with arthritis. "Tell me about the well," he said. "In all the time we've been here I've never seen it."

"All the time?" she mocked gently. "How long is that do you think?"

"Six days. Seven?"

"Four."

He was astonished. "Is that all?"

She brushed wisps of gray hair off her cheek. He saw how the skin sagged in folds under her chin. "That's all. As for the spring, it's not far. You can hear it, can't you?"

"I've heard it since we came."

"If you want to find it, you can. And Galen will be ready soon." She looked at him, her eyes pale. "Your master is a strange man. Something has entered him."

He looked back at the tattered book in his lap. "I know."

Watching him, she said, "A man hard to live with?"

"He always was." And he lay down on his back in the grass and closed his eyes, the book on his chest.

Later, after supper, he went out across the dim lawns,

following the ripple of water. Behind him in the house Tallis sang in her little-girl voice, and the Sekoi lounged by the fire, joining in tunelessly. He didn't know where Galen was.

The evening was purple, faintly misty. Far off three moons hung, Cyrax, Karnos, Lar, the last a pale crescent nearly setting. Stars glinted in the branches. Everything was so still that his feet sounded loud in the grass, the low branches he brushed aside sharp rustles and cracks.

The ripple was louder. It sounded like a voice now, an endless song of secrets and lost lore. He pushed under a thick yew, and found that its huge ancient trunk grew out from a mass of splintered rock, and beneath it the water ran from a deep crack, falling into a small pond edged with mossy stones. Chained to the brink was a silver cup, lying on its side.

He squatted and touched the water. It was cold, and looked black. A few dead leaves floated on the surface and he picked them off. Then, without thinking, he picked the cup up and filled it, seeing the seven moon-sigils of the Order on its side, almost worn smooth from the wear of hands that had used it.

The water rippled and splashed into the pool.

He knew he shouldn't do this, that he hadn't prepared, but it was only water, only a sip, and he was so thirsty all at once, and if something happened, really happened, then Galen might be pleased that he could do it, that he was fit to be a real keeper.

He put the cup to his lips, and drank.

It was cold.

Once he'd begun, he couldn't stop until it was empty.

16

*To make the Deep Journey the keeper
must be ready, and of age.
He must have completed the Ordeals,
and be wise.
Or else his mind will shatter in the grip
of the Makers.*

Fourth Warning of Gaeraint

H E WAS FLYING.

Though he had no wings.

No body.

Giddily he stared down through the fleeting clouds; they sped under him, and plunging through their rifts and tears he saw a whole countryside spread out below; green fields, hedges, the long unwinding glitter of rivers, then a sudden upsurge of mountains, so that the air iced, and he gasped and soared into cloud, through tiny crystals sharp as needles, and then out again, sun-warmed, the frost on his eyelashes melting.

He fought for control but couldn't stop, couldn't hold

himself steady. Below now were networks of lakes and a great forest; the smell of sap and pine dizzied him, the trees seemed to shout at him. He plunged down, crashing through the treetops and all the birds flew out, screaming irritation; jekkles yelled and chattered. Dragged out, breathless, upside down, he air-tumbled over fields, bare and furrowed, struggling to slow down, until he steadied and looked on the ground for his speeding shadow, and it wasn't there.

He knew what this was. This was the Ride, the first part of the Deep Journey, and it would go on and on forever unless he could control it. A swarm of mere-bees flashed around him; he squirmed, stung, screamed for it to stop. Next he tried closing his eyes, fighting for mind-control, but that was worse; he couldn't breathe, was terrified of flying smack into some hill. Opening his eyes, he gave a stifled screech, and he was sucked into a narrow crack in a mountainside, buffeted along it, dragged through an icy chasm so that the rock walls grazed him, banging and bruising, seeing up close the astonished eyes of a fire-fox in a cave, tiny green lichens, the twist of a snake that fell from its ledge and plunged past him in a rattle of stones.

Artelan's Well

Abruptly a rock reared ahead; he cried out and jerked aside and he was out! He was in a wide blue sky and he yelled in relief and caught hold of his mind, slowing himself, slowing, fighting bitterly for control.

He dropped carefully. Now he had it; then it all slipped away and he was plunging wildly again through endless blue air. He couldn't keep it up. Panicking, he held on, praying for help, gabbling the Litany in terror over and over.

He was above the Unfinished Lands. They were more terrible than he had dreamed. Below were vast plateaus where nothing grew, where great cracks had opened in the ground, and plumes of filthy smoke hissed up and choked him. Flames and sparks spat from ravines; ahead a cone of ash erupted scorching lava, its gray cinder-field spreading destruction for miles. Briefly he saw ruins, crushed houses. Beyond that the land heaved and buckled as he watched, as if the very atoms of rock and soil were coming undone; convulsions cracked mountains, new rivers gushed out, sinister lichens crawled over every rotting growth. He began to think he was soaring over some great disease, as if Anara were pocked and pustuled with abscesses, as if the planet burned and tossed in fever, and then below him, coming suddenly into view, was the worst of it, a great wound, a vast open sore in the planet's side, and out of it crawled creatures so disfigured that even from this height they filled him with horror.

These were the Pits of Maar.

Seven great holes, like some obscene reversal of the moons.

They were in every story he'd ever heard, and the sight of them filled him with dread. The nearest was pulling at him. Desperately he struggled to tug away, but it had him, it dragged him and he tipped over and fell, head-first, mile after mile, arms out, screaming. Below, the Pit gaped, spiraling down in immense terraces, thousands of them, one beneath the other, and as he fell into it the darkness closed around him, and swallowed him in one gulp.

HE WAS STANDING IN A ROOM.

It was very dark; there were no candles. A small fire burned in a brazier, and as Raffi looked he saw that in front of it was a desk, and at the desk, far back in the shadows, someone was writing.

Bewildered, he stared around. He felt sick and giddy, battered, sore, and for a moment the room seemed to sway around him, and then it was still.

There was no sound but the pen, scratching.

He was glad of the fire; awkwardly he stretched out his hands to it and saw with a shock that they were frail and ghostly, and he could see right through them.

The figure that was writing never turned its head, but quite suddenly the scratch of the pen was an ominous sound, as if the words it formed were evil, and Raffi knew that the writer had sensed him, or heard him. He kept still, his heart thumping.

It was too dark to see the figure properly, but there was a wrongness about it, a slither of soft mesh or scales, something abhorrent in the shape. Slowly it stopped writing and put down the pen.

Raffi stared, astonished, at the hand that lay in the firelight. It was long, ridged. Unhuman.

And then he knew, suddenly and surely, that he was in the very depths of hell, in the Pits of Maar, and that for mile upon mile above him the unimaginable horrors of Kest bred and spawned and crawled.

The figure spoke. Its voice was low, reptilian. "Who are you?" it hissed.

Rigid with terror, Raffi couldn't answer.

He could see the edge of its face: long, too long. If it got up and walked into the firelight he knew he would collapse, crumple in on himself, that it would destroy his mind like a searing flame. But he couldn't take his eyes off it.

Close your eyes, he screamed at himself. Close your eyes! But they were fixed. The eyelids were heavy sheets of steel; he couldn't do it, couldn't force them down.

The figure stirred.

"A keeper!" it said, wondering. It began to stand.

And then, abruptly, Galen was there, Galen was helping him. Together they forced down the iron blinds, blotting out the room, fire, the nightmare narrow turning face. But Raffi was screaming, or someone was, far off, over and over, and for a second he saw himself lying in a dark bed, and the tall shapes were holding him down and calling him, calling him.

Artelan's Well

There was a hundred years of silence.

Water dripped into a pool.

"Raffi?"

Ages later, Carys was standing with him. They were alone in a golden place. She looked around, bewildered. "Where are we?"

He was sitting on a stone, huddled up. When she spoke, he found he could move, stiffly, could rub his face with his hands. His skin felt strange, his hands like an old man's.

"I don't know."

She knelt and caught hold of his arm. "Are you all right?"

"I'm glad you're here."

"But where's here? And I wish that screaming would stop!"

Vaguely he thought he could do something about that. Far off, he let it ebb into silence. Then he said, "This is all a dream. A vision. I drank the water of the well, Carys. I shouldn't have done that. It was so stupid! And now I'm lost. I don't know where I am; I've been here too long. And I can't get back!"

She looked at him closely. "You look older. You *are* older."

He knew that, could feel himself aging, as if month by month all his years were speeding up inside him. His chin felt stubbly, his hands too big.

She caught hold of him, and her hands were warm. "Concentrate, Raffi! What did you come here for?"

"What?"

Impatient, she shook him. "What are you looking for? Is it the Interrex?"

"Yes!"

Suddenly the word shone in front of him; he reached out his hands and caught hold of it and it was solid, heavy. It was a box, and he opened it and climbed inside, and walked down the long stairway. Behind him, Carys stood on the top step.

"Hurry up!" she said. "Time's running out!"

He could see it too, time trickling down the stairs past him like water, rippling and dripping, the sound loud and close, a spring that never ran dry.

By the bottom of the stairs he was old; his hair was white and he couldn't straighten; a pain throbbed in his side. But as he limped on, a sense-line came out of the dark and wrapped itself around him, and instantly he was young, only about ten, and he opened a door and walked into the classroom.

IT WAS A HUGE ROOM. BITTERLY COLD.

About fifty children sat there in rows, writing in utter silence, and he realized with a shock they were all wearing around their necks the insignia of the Watch.

He slid into a desk at the back, picked up the pen, and read what was on the paper. It was Galen's handwriting.

Which one of them is the Interrex?

Glancing up, he saw a tall lean man patrolling the lanes between desks, a splintered stick under his arm. Every now and then he would stop and bark out a number. A child shot up, chanted a section of the Rule, and sat down.

Something cold touched Raffi's chest. Feeling inside his shirt, he pulled out a small metal disc on a chain and read the number on it: 914.

Then he noticed, on the opposite side of the room, a small girl, her red hair hacked short. She was no more than six or seven, and was watching him slyly. He smiled at her.

Instantly her hand shot up.

"What?" the Watchmaster roared.

"He isn't writing."

"Who isn't?"

"Him."

She pointed. Every head turned to Raffi. He swallowed; the Watchmaster was already striding down the aisle like a great long-legged stork.

"Stand up," he hissed.

It really was a stork now, a black one with a viciously sharp beak. "Speak the Rule," it snapped, but Raffi didn't know the words.

The bird's beak jabbed his chest. "Speak!"

"I . . . I can't."

"Can't?"

"I don't know it," he shouted, desperate. Then he glared across at the girl. "Why did you tell him?"

She giggled. "The Watch must watch each other first, stupid."

Raffi. Can you hear me?

"He's a spy!" the stork hissed.

They were all around him now, crowding, prodding. They held him tight, he couldn't move, and though they were children, they were changing before his eyes, slithering, growing tails, mutating with nightmare speed.

"He must be punished!" The stork beak stabbed at his eyes; he jerked aside in terror. "Where is this?" he yelled. "What Watchhouse? Tell me!"

Raffi.

The girl smirked, her ears pointed like a cat's. "Keilder Wood seven seventy."

Raffi! He's coming. He's coming!

Hands scratched at him; he fought and bit and struggled, but they had him, and the vicious beak stabbed at his forehead till the pain exploded in him and the blood ran down, and a voice was saying over and over, "Raffi. Don't fight us, Raffi. Open your eyes. Open your eyes."

And finally, hopelessly, though he knew they were open, he opened them.

The Sekoi sat back, weary and gaunt with relief. "It's all right, Galen," it said. "He's back."

17

They questioned me. "What have you done?" they raged.
I was silent. I dared not tell them the worst of it.

Sorrows of Kest

"I CAN'T BELIEVE," Galen growled, "that you were stupid enough to do it."

Tallis and the Sekoi exchanged glances. "Never mind that now." She pressed the warm cup into Raffi's hands. "It's all over, at last."

The room was dark. They were sitting around the fire, Tallis in her young-woman shape, the door behind her open, so they could see the moths in the soft moonlight over the lawns.

Raffi sipped the warm ale. He still felt tired and guilty and dizzy. Yesterday they'd told him he'd been in the dream-coma for three days and nights. He knew now he'd never have gotten out of it on his own; Galen had come in for him, in deep, into the journey, because that's what it had been, the Deep Journey that only Relic Masters should make. It would have killed him soon. Even now, a whole day later, he barely had the strength to make a sense-line, and fell over if he stood up.

The ale was honey-sweet. It made him feel better.

When he had woken, all he had wanted to do was be sick, and then sleep. But Galen had been relentless. He had forced him to tell the dream, all of it, every detail, before he had let him collapse into nausea. Now the keeper sat grim, his hooked face dark and shadowed.

"I'm sorry," Raffi muttered. It sounded weak, and stupid. "I just . . . I didn't think anything would happen to me."

"You didn't think at all." Galen was haggard and weary; his fasting had made him thinner, and Raffi knew he had prayed over him and fought with him for control all the time of the dream-sleep. "It was a mess, boy," he said fiercely. "You could have ruined everything."

"But he hasn't, it seems," Tallis put in smoothly. She sat down on the floor, her back against the bench. "And now we must discuss these messages the Makers have sent. However they came."

The Sekoi put a bony finger into its ale cup and stirred thoughtfully. "Odd messages too. And dispiriting." It looked up. "The last part seems the most important for us. Do you agree that it seems to tell us that the Inter-rex is a small girl-cub, and that she is in the hands of the Watch? In a Watchhouse?"

Galen nodded gloomily.

"You mean that girl who put her hand up?" Raffi went cold. "She's the Emperor's granddaughter? But she's one of the enemy!"

Tallis shook her head. "It may be her. It may be the number round your neck will be more important. Nine fourteen. Remember it. At least we have a clear idea where to look. Keilder Wood is not far from here."

Galen was sunk in his bitter mood. "We know where to look. But it's worse than we thought. They may know who they have. If they do, we're finished."

"They'd have already killed her," the Sekoi put in.

"Maybe. But even if they had no idea who she is, the child's mind will already be twisted against us. This won't be a simple rescue. She won't want to come. It will be a kidnap."

Thinking of the girl's spiteful grin, Raffi thought Galen was more right than he knew.

"And anyway," he said aloud, "how do we get in?"

Galen smiled strangely. "You know how. Carys must get us in."

Tallis looked up. "Who is Carys?"

The Sekoi pulled a face. "That would take some explaining, Guardian. She's a Watchspy. She may, or she may not, be a friend of ours."

"Of course she is," Raffi said hotly. He banged the empty cup down, annoyed. "She helped me. I saw her."

"The Makers helped you," Galen snapped. "And they appeared in forms your mind would recognize. But certainly Carys is our only way into a Watchhouse, so she must be told."

The Sekoi looked uneasy, but it said nothing.

Tallis stared into the fire. "And if she betrays you?"

"She's had that chance before." Galen glanced at her, his face edged with flame. "I believe the Makers want her. They are stronger than she is."

For a moment, in the silence, an owl hooted softly outside. Then Galen tugged a string of the green and black crystals from around his neck and began to wind them absently around his hand, something he only did when he was really troubled. "There is one thing in the vision that concerns me even more," he said at last.

The Sekoi edged forward. "And me."

Raffi had been dreading this. "You mean the thing in the Pit."

"Yes. The thing writing in the dark room."

They were silent. Even here the mention of the Pits of Maar chilled them. No one had ever gone into them and come back; whatever horrors Kest had begun were still there, in all his workrooms and laboratories, breeding and mutating out of control.

Tallis too looked grim. She got up and closed the door, and when she came back they saw she was an old woman again, her hands frail. Carefully she lowered herself into a wooden chair. Then she said, "Tell us what worries you, keeper. All secrets are safe here."

Galen wrapped the beads around his fingers. Finally he said, "I've never told anyone this. Ten years ago, when he was dying, my master told me a great mystery. He told me that many who had been high in the Order had suspected something so terrible that they dared not record it; it had never been written down. It was based on an ancient lost text of Tamar's, and on rumor, dark talk, the gabblings of a few, barely sane, who had claimed to have seen it in visions."

"It?" the Sekoi breathed.

Galen looked away. When he spoke again his voice was harsh. "The rumors were that Kest had not tampered only with animals. His last experiment, they say, was on a man."

Raffi stared. He felt the terror of the dream sweeping back over him; for a moment the Pit gaped under him and he felt himself falling into it, snapping his eyes open as the Sekoi hissed.

The room seemed much darker. Raffi was afraid now, wished Galen had never spoken of this. Fighting to stop trembling, he edged closer to the fire.

Tallis said, "I have never heard this. Could even Kest do something so monstrous?"

Galen took some time to answer. Finally he said, "Who

knows. These are whispers and dreams. But if Kest had meddled, if he had taken a man and made something else out of him, something grotesque, a creature that could live long lifetimes, that had an evil intelligence greater than any animal's, what an enemy that would be."

"Living in the dark," the Sekoi muttered. "Letting others do its work." The creature's fur was swollen around its neck; it looked tense and distant.

"Your people know about this?" Galen asked.

The Sekoi's yellow eyes blinked. It put its cup down slowly as if choosing what to say. "There is a name," it said, "in the darkest of our stories. A being. Not a man, not Sekoi, not a beast. A creature of evil. Immortal, too hideous to look on. We call it the Margrave."

The fire crackled, splitting a log in a shower of sparks. The Guardian tapped the chair arm. "If you feel able, Raffi, can you tell us more about what you saw? Was it a man?"

"I don't know." He couldn't, he didn't want to think of it clearly; the memory dodged away, was a cold terror. His hands shook and she noticed and put her own over them. "Don't be afraid, not here."

He looked up at her. "I think . . . it had been a man. The shape of the face was too long . . . I didn't see it properly."

"If you had, you would not be speaking." She turned to Galen. "You think he saw this thing?"

"I think the Makers are warning us," he said bleakly. "We've always wondered at the Watch, how it grew so fast, how it defeated us, and all the time none of us knew where it came from. If this is the mind that rules the Watch, then it's still the legacy of Kest . . ."

No one answered. Galen rubbed his face wearily. It was the Sekoi who stirred, kneeling suddenly and piling new logs on the fire, so the dry wood crackled cheerfully. "None of this concerns us now," it said firmly. "We have to find this girl-cub. And I suppose you're right about Carys, keeper, though you know I have doubts about her. How will we send to her? Shall I go?"

Galen glanced back, his eyes black and sharp. "Thank you, but no. I'll tell her. The Crow will tell her." Tallis was watching him, intent. He smiled, and at once the sense of weariness among them broke; Raffi almost felt the warmth creep back into the room. Until the keeper said, "We leave tomorrow."

Artelan's Well

The Sekoi looked doubtfully at Raffi. "Will he be ready?"

"He'll have to be." Galen turned to Tallis. "It's been good to live in this place. Even though we have to leave it, it cheers me to know it's still here."

The Guardian smiled at him. "For those who hold the faith, keeper, it will always be here."

STANDING ON THE WET LAWNS in the morning, looking back at the house, Raffi knew what she meant. He thought that Artelan's Well had put something in him that hadn't been there before, something so deep he could hardly feel it. But it was there, a small hard gem at the center of him. He touched it with his sore mind. It was no use wishing they could stay; it would be too hurtful even to think of that.

Before them the wicker walkway stretched into mist; beyond it the Unfinished Lands steamed and hissed. Tallis kissed each one of them and stood back, her arms at her sides.

"May Flain go with you. May Tamar be at your back

and Soren smooth your way. And when you find her, bring the child to us. For anything the Watch can do, we can undo."

Bleakly Galen nodded. Then he turned and led them into the fog.

Standing in Line

18

*I saw my brother suffer a hundred years
of remorse.
He had worked with evil and fought to
be free of it.
I saw how despair turned cold in his
heart.*

Apocalypse of Tamar

CARYS STEPPED BETWEEN the two oak trunks warily.

In the deep hollows, crisp leaves were piled; she stood knee-high in the forest's debris. Above, the gnarled branches rustled in every breeze, a new gilt shower tinseling down. Under the slow pattering, she waited.

The wood was silent, its pathways lost behind trunks and branches.

But she knew they were here.

Careless, she leaned back against the oak trunk, squatting down in the fork between immense sprawled roots. Her crossbow was loaded. She could wait.

The dream had come two nights ago, just when she was running out of lies to tell Braylwin. A great black bird had perched on the end of the bed, some village girl's bed she had borrowed for the night, and it had spoken to her with Galen's voice.

"Keilder Forest," it had said. "Near the Watchhouse." And then it had gone, flapping out of the window as if it had really been there.

She turned at a cracked twig. A skeat eyed her coldly, then padded off among the bracken. As she watched it, she glimpsed a sharp face looking at her between branches and glanced away to hide a grin. It was the Sekoi.

Galen came out first, brushing between ferns, Raffi a shadow at his back. They squatted.

"Took your time," she said coolly.

"We had to make sure you were alone."

"The Watch are never alone."

"Neither are the Order." Galen looked sharp, as if power moved in him.

She grinned over his shoulder at Raffi. "You look older."

Standing in Line

To her surprise that startled him, even scared him. "Do I?" he breathed.

"Well, don't worry. Not that much."

The Sekoi had ambled over; it crouched in the deep leaf-drift. "All together again. How cozy."

She made a face at it.

"We've found the Interrex," Galen said quickly. "At least we know where she is."

"She?"

"We think so."

"In this forest?"

He looked hard at her, then tipped his head to where the distant edge of the Watchhouse roof showed beyond the trees. "There."

Carys stared, astonished. "In a Watchhouse!"

"We think so," he said again.

She whistled, then shook her head, pulling a leaf out of her hair absently. "No wonder you want me! How do you know she's in there?"

"The Makers told us." He was watching her steadily; she knew he suspected her, that he guessed something. Abruptly she laughed. "I never know what you mean when you say that, Galen. Well, if she is in there, you've got your work cut out. She'd probably slit your throat rather than let you take her."

That stung him. His face darkened, and she saw suddenly how he hated this, that even the heir of the Emperors should have been tainted and corrupted by his enemies. And she hated it too. So much, she even surprised herself.

She tucked a stray hair behind one ear. "So what's the plan?"

"I thought I'd leave that to you. You know these places."

Indeed she did. Grim, bare classrooms, icy courtyards, the stark dormitories, the punishments, the ones who sobbed in the dark, who disappeared one day, never to be seen again. The guards, the passwords. Nowhere to hide. No way out. And what it did to you.

She looked up at him suddenly. "Listen, Galen, get out of here. Go now! Go quickly!"

At once the Sekoi hissed, its yellow eyes narrowing, "What do you mean?"

"She means," Galen said softly, "that we're surrounded by the Watch."

Standing in Line

The creature leaped up with a snarl. Galen never took his eyes off Carys.

"I can explain," she said.

"I'm sure you can."

"If you knew, why did you come?"

"Because I wanted to find out why."

Harnesses clinked in the wood. Raffi was on his feet, feeling the sense-lines shatter, praying that Galen knew what he was doing.

Ten men on horses faced them. Each crossbow was firmly aimed. The horses were painted red; the men wore the black patrol-helmets of the Watch, their eyes bright in the slits. On the end of the line sat an extraordinary figure, a fat man in a great waxed coat, his puffed face rimmed with black, oily hair, perfectly curled. He smiled, his swollen fingers tossing the reins. "You must introduce me to your friends, sweetie."

"Drop dead," Carys said. Her face was hot and angry.

Slowly Galen stood up and turned. He stood, feet apart, staring calmly across the clearing. "I'm Galen Harn, Relic Master of the Order of keepers."

Braylwin smirked. "Are you now. And I'm Arno

Braylwin, Captain of the Watch, Spymaster, first grade, thief-taker, interrogator of sorcerers."

Raffi felt cold. He couldn't take his eyes off the nearest crossbow. One twitch, he thought, and sweated with the effort to keep still.

Braylwin gave a haughty nod.

One of his men slid down and brought a small set of wooden steps, garishly painted, which he put in the leaf-drift. One hand on the man's shoulder, Braylwin climbed unsteadily down. Then he flicked some leaves off a log with his coattail and sat down.

The Sekoi snarled at Carys. "You betrayed us," it hissed. "I always knew you would."

"I had no choice!" Suddenly it was all too much. She scorched into temper, leaping up and pushing Raffi aside so fiercely that he lost balance and crashed into the thick drift of leaves. Crossbows swiveled after him. He lay still.

"He knows something about me! I thought it would help if I told him about you, and it was a way of telling you about the Interrex! For Flain's sake, Galen, I never thought you'd really find her!"

The Sekoi spat. "Playing both sides, as ever."

Standing in Line

Galen stood listening, silent.

Carys marched up to Braylwin and stared down at him, her hand quivering with fury. "But this slug has brains. He's like a shadow. Whatever I tried I couldn't throw him off."

She turned her head, suddenly not sure whom she was angry with. "I'm sorry, Galen. All of you."

"Impressive." Braylwin looked at her admiringly. "You'll go far. I almost believe it myself."

Stubbornly she glanced at Raffi. He looked away. What was she doing? What was she really up to?

Galen stirred, ignoring the taut bows. He looked coldly down at the Watchlord. "I'll give you no information, no matter what you do."

Braylwin shrugged. "It doesn't matter. The boy will talk." He smiled easily. "Believe me, I know. I've seen them scream and beg to tell me anything, even to die. He looks terrified already."

Leaves pattered in the bitter silence. Braylwin scratched his cheek with a thumbnail. "So. The Interrex exists and is in the hands of the Watch! It seems all your dreams are in ruins, keeper. It also poses an interesting little problem for me, actually. After all, I don't want to tell the school-

master in there why I want her. There'll be a stiff reward
for this one, and I don't intend to share it." He glanced
over. "Except with my loyal staff, of course."

Carys glared at him. She looked so cold and expressionless Raffi was suddenly icy with terror—the sense-
lines wreathed around the backs of his hands, raising the
small hairs. She raised the crossbow slowly, until it was
pointing directly at Braylwin's head.

He smiled, sweating slightly. "Don't you love your
uncle, then, Carys? You ought to, you know. Fire that
weapon and you and these will die in the same shower of
bolts, and that would be a shame, now, wouldn't it. Such
a promising career."

The bow didn't waver. Confused, a few of the horse-
men aimed at her reluctantly.

"He's right." Galen's voice was harsh and steady. He
watched, a half smile on his hooked face, his eyes dark
and sharp. "It wouldn't be worth it, Carys."

She whirled so the bow faced him. "Maybe I should
kill you, then. Profitable for me, better for you. Better
than torture, anyway. I've seen what they'll do to you."

Dry-mouthed, Raffi watched. No one was looking at

him anymore, but he didn't dare to crawl away.

"I think," Galen said softly, "you should remember your own first rule. Isn't it something about the Watch always being watched?"

He moved, walking slowly toward her while the Sekoi fidgeted with terror. Coming close, he put a hand on the bow and pushed it gently down. Taints of purple sparked from the keeper's fingers; Carys saw them and stared.

The bolt smacked into dry leaves.

At the same time, out of nowhere, arrows slashed across the clearing into the Watchmen, sending their horses swirling in a sudden crashing, whinnying panic. A bolt slammed into a tree above Raffi; he rolled, scrambling and wriggling deep under the leaves and away.

When he raised his head and looked back, Galen and the Sekoi hadn't moved. Neither had Braylwin. But the five Watchmen lay still, and the rest were scrambling from their horses' tangled harnesses.

Around them, among the trees, a war-band laughed and mocked; a dirty, gold-decked, gaudy army, dressed and painted in crazy colors, their horses' manes tangled with bright ribbons.

Galen looked at Braylwin. "You may be ruthless, my lord. But here's someone who could give you lessons. I too have my troublesome shadow."

Braylwin stood and stared at the tiny man in the blue quilted robe who was leaping from his horse.

"You may have heard of him," Galen said drily. "His name is Alberic."

The dwarf grinned, immensely pleased. "This is a feast, Galen Harn, a feast! Not only you and that tale-spinner, but a Watchlord! A ripe, fat, money-dripping Watchlord!" He was hugging himself in delight, dancing a few happy steps among the leaves. "Down, boys and girls! Pick up those bows. Whip some rope around our prisoners."

Appalled, Braylwin glowered. "You can't. You wouldn't dare . . ."

"Shut it, flesh-pile!" Instantly Alberic's joy died. His shrewd eyes flicked around the clearing. "Wait!" Then he whirled on Galen and roared the question the keeper had been waiting for.

"Where's your scholar? And where's that girl!"

19

The stupid must be cast aside. Those of medium intellect are of most use. Beware the ones who are too clever. They may be taught to hate us yet.

Rule of the Watch

CLOSE UP, THE WATCHHOUSE was immense, a squat, ugly building of black brick, dumped in the forest. All around stood its defenses; a fence of spiked logs, a ditch, and one drawbridge, lowered now, for the children to straggle across.

From his hiding place under the thorns, Raffi watched them forming up in lines, many staggering under the weight of logs and kindling; even the smallest children had their arms crammed full. There were three guards; two laughing and joking together, the last calling up to someone at a window. None of them were watching the trees.

Carys nudged him sharply, and was gone.

He hoisted the wood bundle up against his face and stumbled out behind her, his heart thudding like a hammer-bird's knock. The sense-lines snagged under his eyelid; he knew Alberic's hunters were only yards behind.

And still he couldn't believe what he was doing.

"Line up!" Someone shoved him; he kept his head down, praying numbly. Children closed in behind. Quickly they began to walk.

The branches were heavy, but they kept him hidden, and the boy next to him didn't even glance across. There was no talking, no pushing. In the silence he could even hear the leaves falling, and the whistle of an oat-piper far off in the wood. Then wooden planks were under his feet; the children's boots rang in hollow echoes. They were crossing the drawbridge.

Glancing up, he saw the archway gaping over him, a great mouth, one lantern hanging from it like a single tooth. This was it. He didn't know any passwords, any rules. Carys would get in, but they were bound to find him, drag him out, beat him. He closed his eyes.

She jolted against him. "Stay close."

Standing in Line

The arch swallowed them. He sensed it over him, felt suddenly small, as if his personality had shrunk, become crushed. Defiantly, miserably, he mumbled the Litany.

The smell of the place was overpowering. Old musty rooms, stale fat, a smell of fear, long-enclosed, as if the windows were never opened. And it was bitterly cold.

As the line shuffled on, he glanced at Carys; to his surprise he saw something like hatred on her face. She moved up to him, but before she could speak the line halted.

Ahead the children were chanting numbers to a bored-looking woman on a stool; then one by one they disappeared through a doorway. Nervously Raffi waited his turn.

"Next," the woman said, not looking up.

He had decided what to say.

"N-nine one four," he stammered, then walked on fast, in case she raised her eyes from the page and looked at him. In seconds Carys was behind him; there was no outcry. It seemed to have worked. In relief he breathed his thanks to Flain.

They found themselves going down a dim stairway; at the bottom was an evil-smelling cellar where the children were stacking the wood. Their silence scared Raffi. They didn't laugh, or joke, or even smile. And he saw how they all watched one another, slyly, as if none of them were friends, or to be trusted.

Carys pulled him gently by the sleeve, then turned and marched out of a different door. Trying to look calm, he followed. She looked as if she knew where she was going. Through a warren of crypts and cellars, up some stairs, then into a corridor where the roof leaked. Opening the first door on the left she peered in, drew her head out, and nodded.

They slid inside, and closed the door tight.

It was a storeroom. Barrels were stacked against a cracked wall. The hearth was a drift of wind-blown ashes.

Raffi breathed out slowly. Then he said, "I can't believe we're in."

She went over and knelt on top of the barrels, rubbing dust from one pane of a tiny window. "Keep your voice down."

"Will they come in here?"

"It's unlikely."

Standing in Line

He looked at her back. "How did you know about it? How did you know your way?"

Cold suspicions moved in on him like eelworms, but she turned and stared at him contemptuously. "Don't be stupid, Raffi. These places are all the same—if you know one, you know them all. The Watch pride themselves on that. Wherever you go, always the same. One big family."

She turned back to the window, but he still watched her. Quietly he said, "So you knew this room somewhere else?"

For a while he thought she wouldn't answer. Then she said, "It was the one I spent hours in at Marn Mountain. I had it all worked out. The rotas were easy to alter—everyone thought I was in some other class. I kept food here, books, all the things you weren't allowed. I did it for years, till they found out."

"What did they do to you?"

"They promoted me, of course." She turned and grinned at him. "In the Watch, the slyer you are, the better. You look shocked."

"I just . . ." He shook his head. "I always assumed you liked it."

"Liked it!" She spat viciously into the ashes. "These places are hell, Raffi! You've got no idea. Come up here."

He climbed up beside her. She rubbed the spot on the window wider, and looking through it he saw a grim courtyard, with a high spiked wall. Children huddled around. Some sat in groups, others ran to keep warm, but there was still little noise, except from one end of the yard where a group silently watched three boys beat a smaller one, punching him in the face and stomach while he sobbed. Raffi stared in horror. "Why doesn't someone stop them?"

Carys smiled grimly. "It's probably a punishment. Look."

Two Watchmen were standing behind the crowd, their arms folded, laughing. One shouted encouragement.

Raffi turned away. He was white with anger. "No wonder Galen hates the Watch. How can they make the children punish each other?"

"They don't make them. They volunteer." She climbed down and sat beside him.

"Volunteer!"

"You get better food. And credits on your workcard.

Standing in Line

The more of those, the better you do. I'll bet Braylwin collected plenty."

"What about you?" He stared at her. "Did you 'volunteer'?"

"Sometimes." She said it softly, looking away from him. "They teach you how to use people here, Raffi. I never realized that until after. To hunt and lie and lay traps but never to care. And you have to survive, you have to get through it somehow. Have you ever thought of what happens to those who don't?"

Numb, he shook his head.

"Well, they vanish. It's said they're thrown down the Pits. The Watch has no failures."

In silence they heard a bell ring, far off in the building. The scuffles stopped outside. Then Raffi said, "Where do we look for her?"

"We don't, yet. At five bells they all parade in that yard for name-check. Then you'll have to see if she's there. You haven't told me how you know what she's like."

He shrugged. "It doesn't matter. Then what?"

"From where she stands in line I'll know where she sleeps. But listen. If I get caught, you don't know me. Understand? You just walk by. One of us has to get her out."

"I can't," he muttered.

"You can. You'd better. Because if you're caught, that's what I'll be doing."

He didn't know whether to believe her or not.

All afternoon they stayed hidden in the cramped store-room, except that every hour Carys led him out through a maze of corridors, walking quickly, looking at no one, coming back to the room when the patrol would have looked in and passed on.

"The sweep, we call it. Two men check every room in the whole house constantly. It took about an hour at Marn. You have to time it just right."

Bewildered, Raffi sat on the floor. The place upset him. He dared not send out sense-lines; they touched things that made him feel sick. Odd noises and cries echoed in the building; he had glimpses of desolate classrooms, like the one in his vision. He felt trapped, totally cut off. "And if we find her," he said, "how do we get her out? Or help Galen?"

Carys licked thirsty lips. "Galen can take care of him-self. But you're right about one thing. Getting in was easy. I haven't a clue how we're going to get out."

They didn't notice the darkness come. But after a while the room was too dim for them to see each other clearly, and the faintest edge of Agramon was glimmering from somewhere high over the roofs.

A bell rang. Raffi was already sick of them, but Carys stiffened. "Name-check." She jumped up to the barrels. "Right. Get ready."

The courtyard was dark now and lit with flares; garish red flames that crackled and guttered in the cold wind, sending shadows leaping. The Watchchildren were lined up, silent and sullen, in identical rows rigidly spaced, feet apart, arms behind their backs, eyes fixed on the ground. They wore thin clothes; most were shivering. Raffi ran his eyes anxiously along the lines, past thin boys, tall lanky girls, a sobbing infant everyone ignored.

"Well?"

"I can't . . . yes! That's her! Third from the end, in the back row! That's her!"

Carys pushed him aside and put her eyes to the pane. She saw a small stubborn-looking seven-year-old, her hair hacked off, her face freckled, already thin. "Are you sure?"

"Certain. I'd never forget her."

She spent a long time looking, then turned and leaned back thoughtfully against the wall. She was oddly silent, Raffi thought. A tinge of sadness came out of her and touched his sense-field.

"Right." She lifted her head firmly. "We need to plan this. Get her on her own. Diversionary tactics. Something to deal with any pursuit." She grinned slyly. "Just like they taught us."

He looked baffled.

Carys laughed. "Don't worry, Raffi. I was always top of the class. Look, that thing you did in Tasceron, the bangs and flashes, the inner eye thing, can you do it here?"

He shrugged, uneasy. He was cold and hungry, and he loathed this place; the very air was miserable. "There's no awen here."

"Awen?"

"Energy, power. Life."

He shivered, and she felt anxious. "But you'll do your best?"

"Of course I will. But, Carys, it'll take an army to get us out."

Standing in Line

Angry, she shook her head. "One step at a time." Unstrapping her crossbow, she loaded it, then pulled a small pouch from under her coat. Opening it, she took out some fine rope, candles, a tinderbox, some tiny boxes, and a package wrapped in black cloth.

He touched the package and she saw his eyes widen. "This is a relic!"

"Yes." She shoved it back. "I got it in the Tower of Song. It's for Galen. Now come on, Raffi. We've got to be ready in an hour. Before the patrol comes around."

It was exactly an hour and a half later that Carys walked cautiously down the middle of dormitory twenty-seven, glancing at the bed numbers, the sleeping huddles under gray blankets. The bed she wanted was third from the end, near where the night candle spluttered in its lantern. She leaned down and took a deep breath. Then, quickly, she twitched the girl over, clamped a cold hand tight on her mouth, and hissed, "Don't scream. Don't speak. Just listen."

Wide brown eyes stared up at her.

"My name is Carys Arrin. I'm a Watchspy, silver rank." She dangled the insignia carelessly in the child's face. "You've been selected for a special mission. It's highly secret; none of the other children must know. Do you understand?"

The girl nodded. Her body was tense in the bed.

"You must come with me now. Get dressed, and hurry."

She took her hand away and stood back. This was the test; if the girl screamed . . . Carys folded her arms and looked away up the room, as if she was impatient. But the child dressed silently, hastily. She was used to obeying orders, as they'd expected, though once or twice she peeped up, curious, into Carys's face.

"Come on!" Carys growled.

"I am!" the girl said impudently. She pulled on her shoes and went back to the bed. Plunging her hand into the straw, she pulled something out and turned, but Carys had seen. "What's that?"

"Nothing."

"Liar." Carys came and snatched it; the girl glared, furious. "He's mine! And I'm bringing him!" The hiss was loud, but Carys barely heard it. In her hand was a small stuffed toy, a night-cub, so battered one ear was gone, and the dark fur almost rubbed away.

Standing in Line

The girl snatched it back and pushed it into her dress. "I'm not going without him."

Carys was amazed. There were no toys allowed in Watchhouses—for the girl to have kept it this long meant she was cunning. Incredibly cunning.

"All right. Follow me."

She turned and marched down the dormitory, the little girl pattering beside her. In the silence their footsteps sounded loud; Carys felt sweat chill her back. But no one woke.

Once again she hurried, up the steps, then up again to the dim landing. Lamps burned down long corridors. Far below, the endless patrol closed and opened doors.

"Where are we going?" the girl demanded suddenly.

"Wait and see." Carys stopped. "Raffi?"

He stepped out behind them, and the girl stared at him, her brown eyes solemn. "Who's he?"

"He works with me."

"I've seen him before. I saw him in a dream."

Aghast, Carys looked at him. "What?"

Raffi bit his lip. "It's—it's all right," he stammered.

"No it's not. You're from the Evil Order."

"No . . . Listen."

But the girl's voice was louder. "I don't believe you. Where are you taking me?"

Carys clamped her hand tight over the girl's mouth, crouching. "Keep quiet! I told you, this is a secret!"

The child's eyes blazed; she squirmed with anger, then clenched her teeth on Carys's fingers and bit down savagely. With a gasp, Carys snatched her hand back.

The little girl looked at Raffi, a cold look.

Then she opened her mouth and screamed.

20

To open and close,
build and destroy,
move forward and back,
to bless and to curse . . .

Litany of the Makers

"THEY'VE DONE WHAT!"

"Entered the Watchhouse." Alberic spread his tiny hands to the fire, looking up slyly at the stricken face. "It's nice to know I inspire such terror. Sit down, Relic Master, before you crumble."

Numb, Galen crouched. "Are you sure?"

"Sikka's group traced them. Saw them go in—quite cleverly done, they said." He crooked one finger, and a small table was brought and propped unsteadily on the cave floor. A crystal goblet was placed on it, into which Godric carefully poured an expensive golden cordial. Tied in a damp corner, Braylwin gazed at it enviously.

He had already complained so much they had gagged him.

Galen was staring into the flames. Alberic drank daintily, wiped his mouth with his hand, and leaned forward. "I want to know why. What's in there that's so important? If your boy's caught he'll be skinned alive. I've tracked you this far and all the time I've wondered what you were after."

Galen stirred, rubbing his chin wearily. His eyes were black, his long hair glossy as a crow's wing. When he looked up, there was a tension in his face. "Do you remember what I once said to you?"

Quizzically Alberic spread his hands. "Which time?"

"Last time. At the marsh. I told you you've got nothing in your life worth having, despite all your wealth."

The dwarf grinned, sipping the liquid. "Oh. That old yarn."

"No faith. Nothing to fire your soul. You're tired of thieving, war-lord. I can feel it."

"Indeed." The tiny man pursed his lips. "Keeper, are you trying to convert me?"

"I'm trying to save you. Or let you save yourself."

Standing in Line

Alberic winked up at Godric. "He's appealing to my better nature."

"You've haven't got one, chief."

"He has," Galen said.

Alberic turned. "Isn't it nice to know, boys and girls, that our souls are causing such concern! Flain himself couldn't be more worried."

Giggles echoed around the cave. Galen ignored them, his stare unmoving. "Under your laughter you're listening, little man."

"And what must I do, hmm?" Alberic mocked. "Learn the Book of the Seven Moons by heart? Live on bread and water? Give all my money away to the poor?"

A roar of laughter broke out around him. Into it Galen said quietly, "None of these. I want you to attack the Watchhouse."

The Sekoi hissed. Alberic stopped drinking and stared in utter astonishment. The cave was silent.

Finally the dwarf managed to speak. "What?" he whispered.

"You heard. Raffi and Carys will need to get out. I want you to give them the chance. Give the Watch something to think about. A short attack, then withdraw. None of your people need be hurt."

Alberic leaned forward, staring at Galen as if he thought the keeper was insane. He seemed too amazed even to laugh. "And what exactly will you give me for this act of total recklessness?"

Galen shrugged. "The blue box."

"The blue box is mine already." The dwarf pointed to the pack lying dimly in a corner. "As is the Cat-liar's belt of gold. Have you got anything else that would interest me?"

"One thing."

Alberic's eyes were greedy. "What?"

"Your soul."

The silence was profound. Only the crackle of the fire broke it. And then Alberic bent over, wheezing, and when he straightened they saw he was laughing helplessly, crying with laughter, and all his war-band roared with him, the tears rolling down their cheeks, hooting and screaming themselves into an exhaustion of hilarity.

Braylwin giggled too, a dry mockery. The Sekoi closed

its yellow eyes and snarled. But Galen never moved, never flinched, watching the dwarf as if he could see right into him as he gasped and clutched his chest and kicked his legs helplessly against the stool.

Finally, wiping his eyes, Alberic struggled to speak. "Oh God, you're so good for me, Galen," he gasped. "I'm almost tempted to keep you alive. My own tame preacher."

He scratched his cheek and all at once the laughter in his crafty face had gone, and he looked at the keeper hard. "Tell me what's in that Watchhouse," he said. "Tell me. If it's worth getting out, I might think about it."

Slowly Galen stood up. He turned and looked at Braylwin. The huge Watchman smirked and widened his eyes over the dirty gag. They both knew he dared not tell Alberic about the Interrex, knew what a prize she would be. Galen frowned, his eyes black. Then he swung to the Sekoi. "I suppose we'll have to tell him."

"I suppose so," the creature said doubtfully. Its fur was lifting with tension; its yellow eyes stared at him. "He'll want a share."

"Of course he will. Will there be enough?"

It shrugged unhappily. "It means less for the Great Hoard."

Galen's eyes shifted. Alberic hadn't moved, but he was already more alert, the sense-lines sparking around him.

"So now," he said softly, "you're going to pretend this Watchhouse is stuffed with gold?"

Neither of them spoke. Around the cave, talk hushed; most of the war-band not guarding the approaches were crammed inside, keeping warm. Suddenly they were interested.

Reluctantly the Sekoi stood up, its head bent under the low roof. "I suppose I'll have to explain."

"Oh no!" Alberic waved a hand sharply. "No stories! Not that again. Godric!"

The bearded man was there already; he raised his crossbow lazily and pointed at the creature with a grin. "I'm watching you, Graycat."

The Sekoi made a spiteful, spitting noise.

"Right. Talk." Alberic leaned back. "But any hint of a spell and that bolt flies."

Uneasy, the creature looked sidelong at Galen. Then

it spread its seven-fingered hands. "You have no reason to trust us, thief-lord, I know that. I think the keeper is wrong to tell you this, because how do we know that you won't kill us when you learn it, and take the gold anyway?"

Alberic's shrewd face creased into smiles. He swirled the wine in his cup. "Go on."

Galen went and leaned beside Braylwin, half in shadow. The Sekoi's eyes followed him. "The keeper leaves me in a dangerous place."

"Never trust a reckless man," the dwarf said, drinking.

"I'm beginning to believe you're right." It stroked its tribemark warily. "Well, I will tell this plainly. You will have heard, of course, of the Great Hoard . . ."

Alberic was listening now.

"No one but the Sekoi know its purpose. But it is vast, and all our lives we add to it. Last year a tribe near here had all their gold loaded on wagons—ten of them, piled high—and they sent it . . . where we send it. They had to pass through this forest. Normally, we can evade the Watch. However, this time it seems there was some problem."

"Problem?" Alberic said sweetly.

"They were ambushed. All were killed. The Watch took the gold and have kept it inside the house. Among it were some relics, made of precious metals, which are what the keeper wants."

"The boy went into a Watchhouse for a few relics?"

The Sekoi looked uncomfortable. It bent forward and said quietly, "These people are fanatics, my lord."

"So I've heard." Alberic folded his hands. "All this is so interesting! Isn't it interesting, Godric?"

"Thrilling," the big man said, his bow never flinching.

"Ten wagons of gold! Worth doing a lot for. Worth attacking for. More than a small attack, though, wouldn't you say?" He glanced slyly at Galen, who watched darkly. "More like a small war, that would be. People get killed in such attacks. Children. I never liked children."

Galen glanced at the Sekoi, who shrugged. Alberic wheezed a sudden laugh. "Oh, don't get too worried, keeper. You don't think I believe this farrago of nonsense, do you?" He leaned back, stretching out his boots and gazing at them critically. "Not for one second. Cramps your style a bit, creature, doesn't it, my lad's crossbow?"

Standing in Line

The Sekoi smiled sourly.

Suddenly Galen stalked forward. Pushing the creature aside, he stood in front of Alberic, tall and grim. "Will you attack?" he asked harshly.

"No."

Galen nodded. Ignoring the bow, he tugged the awenbeads off and spread them on the sandy floor; seven rings, overlapping.

"What are you doing?" Alberic said suspiciously.

Galen didn't answer. Instead he stood behind the circles and raised his hands. At once, the cave seemed darker. Talk stopped. The fire cowered down before him.

"Stop it!" Alberic snapped. "Sit down."

Galen began to speak. His words were quiet, intense; Maker-words that no one else knew. Around him, in the dark, sudden blue sense-lines uncoiled and crackled. His face was dangerous, edged with anger.

Alberic stood up. "Kill him," he said.

The bow in Godric's hands burst instantly into flame. He threw it down with a yell.

No one moved.

Galen looked up and pointed at the dwarf. "Hear me,"

he said, the darkness rustling around him, his voice shaking with effort. "In the name of the Makers, I curse you, thief-lord. I curse you up and down, from side to side, from front to back. I curse you from fingertip to fingertip, head to toe. I curse you today and yesterday and tomorrow. I curse all you eat, all you drink, all you speak, all you dream."

White-faced, the dwarf stared up at him. The cave was black, crackling with power. The fire went out, and still Galen snarled the words remorselessly, his finger pointed, sparks leaping about it.

"May your possessions be dust to you. May your body tremble and rot. May your hair turn white and fall . . ."

"No." Alberic stepped back, holding up his hands. "No! Wait!"

". . . May all your friends betray you. May water, fire, earth, and air become your foes. May the horrors of Kest worm into you."

"Galen!" The dwarf seemed to crumple abruptly, his hands trembling. "Stop it! Not that I believe . . . You can't do this . . ."

Light crackled from the keeper's hand. It roared into

the spaces of the cave; blue stinging snaps of light around the tiny man, crawling over his limbs, around his neck, so that he yelled and squirmed and beat them off.

"From this instant you will begin to sicken. Pain will fill you. Your food will choke you. Six weeks of suffering I lay on you, and when you die your soul will scream for eternity in the Pit."

"*Enough!*" It was a shriek; it broke from Alberic's twisted mouth like a pain, and he held his hands over his head as if the malice of the words battered him. "Enough. No more!"

There was silence.

The cave was black and smoky, as if something smoldered.

Galen waited. Slowly he lowered his hand.

Trembling, Alberic clawed his way back to the stool and leaned on it in utter silence, everyone's eyes on him. He tried to drink a sip of wine, but the cup shook too violently in his hand.

When he looked up, his face glistened with sweat.

"I don't believe," he breathed, "that even you would wish that on me, keeper."

Galen didn't answer.

"But . . . having considered your story . . ." He swallowed painfully. "Having thought about it . . ."

"Will you attack?" Galen asked, grim.

Alberic looked at him, furious, white-faced, his hands still shaking.

"Yes," he spat.

21

*In the unlikely event that all training
fails, the agent must use whatever
strategies are left.*

Rule of the Watch

INSTANTLY A BELL BEGAN TO CLANG, hard and insistent, appallingly loud. Doors banged open; someone shouted.

Carys cursed bitterly; she grabbed the little girl's arm and twisted it up behind her back with a savage jerk. "One more sound and I'll break it!" she hissed.

White-faced, the girl stared up at her, pain forcing tears into her eyes. Raffi looked around in terror. "Come on!" he said.

They ran down the corridor, through the lamp-shadows. Turning the corner, they saw two men; Carys pushed the girl aside, raised her bow, and fired. One man collapsed, clutching his arm; the other fired back, the bolt embedding in the lintel over Raffi's head. Rolling, Raffi gathered up all his energy and flung it in a flaring explosion down the corridor. There was a bang, and a crackle of light. When the smoke cleared he saw both men were down.

"Brilliant!" Carys hauled the child up and jammed a new bolt in the bow. Raffi ran down to the men and knelt by them anxiously.

"Are they dead?" she asked.

He looked up sharply. "Of course not!"

"Then come on!" As she tugged her away, the little girl stared back. "What did he do? What was that?"

"That was the Order at work." Carys laughed sourly. "You'd better forget all that stuff they taught you about illusions. These people know a few tricks."

They ran up the stairs, around a corner, then crouched, breathing hard. Far off the Watchhouse was astir—voices were yelling orders.

"How long?" Raffi said.

"They'll check the dormitories. They probably already know she's missing." Wrathfully Carys glared down.

Standing in Line

"Why couldn't you have kept quiet! And why didn't you tell me about this dream, Raffi?"

He frowned. "I didn't realize she would . . . It was more like a vision. Anyway, it means she really is the Interrex."

"The what?" the girl asked.

"Nothing."

Silent, the child surveyed them, especially Raffi. "In my dream," she said, remembering, "you were in the classroom."

He crouched beside her. "That's twice you've gotten me into trouble."

Her quick face grinned. "Yes. I'm good at that."

"I'll bet you are," Carys said.

"They'll never let you out." Calmly the girl pulled the night-cub out and smoothed its head. "You'll be killed. I won't care."

Chilled, Raffi reached out and held her thin wrist. "What's your name?" he asked.

She looked surprised. "Felnia. What's yours?"

"Raffi." He turned the insignia on her neck. The number was 914.

They were silent a moment. Impatient, Carys shuffled

down to peer around the stairs. "It's late. I knew that fuse was—" Before she'd finished, a vast explosion deafened them, shaking the walls; then another, far off in the depths. "Now!" Carys breathed. Slipping out, she raced ahead, checking every corner, Raffi pulling the little girl hurriedly after. Halfway around the next bend a small, cold hand slipped into his. He held it tight.

But there were too many patrols, too many people. Twice they were nearly caught; at last they stumbled into an empty classroom as a group of tall women stalked by, banging open every door and looking in.

Crouched under a desk, Raffi waited for the footsteps to fade. "What now?" he whispered.

Carys pushed back her hair. "The front gate is impossible. We won't even get near it." She scowled. "Mind you, I never thought we would."

"Is there any other way out?"

"Not from here."

"So what do we do?"

"Withdraw. Somewhere we can defend ourselves." She turned to Felnia. "The north tower. What do they use that for?"

Standing in Line

The girl stuck her tongue out. Carys shrugged. "We'll try it. It's usually staff quarters—they may not think we'll go there."

They moved quickly, putting out every lamp they passed. Then Carys stopped, so abruptly that Raffi ran into her. "Listen."

"What?" But as he said it his sense-lines swirled; he felt it intensely in a shiver of sweat, a black, swollen thing, some grotesque six-footed beast slavering down the corridors.

"The bloodhound." Carys sounded furious. "We've no chance." She rammed the bolt home and turned to face the dark.

"Not here!" He grabbed her. "Up in this tower. We can wedge the doors. Don't give up, Carys!"

She looked at him strangely; he pulled her away. Around the next bend was a door they tugged open, but inside there was no way to lock it, so they raced and gasped breathlessly up the wooden stairs, pushing the girl in front of them. Up a high flight was a kitchen, full of barrels and stores. Carys flung down the bow and grabbed the nearest cask. "Push them down!"

They toppled the cask and rolled it to the stairtop and over; it crashed down, splintering with an enormous thud against the door below.

"All of them!"

Barrel after barrel they rolled, Felnia pushing with them, all suddenly helpless with giggles, laughing stupidly, as if it was a game, till the stairwell was jammed with splintered wood and sour wine, the reek of cheeses and dried salted fish.

Below, the door jerked, rammed hard, but the barrels clogged it, kept it closed. Someone yelled furious orders.

Carys stopped laughing, clutching her side. "They'll get an ax. Come on."

They burst into the top room. Two beds, the blankets sprawled, a chest, a small table. Nothing else. Raffi ran to the window, tugging it open. Then he stood still. Directly below was the ditch, yawning, rammed with sharp, upright spikes.

All at once, cold hopelessness came over him. He felt sick and tired, as if all the energy had gone out of him with that bolt of light. And he knew what Carys had known since the girl screamed. They were finished. There was no way out.

Carys had jammed the table against the door. Now she sat against the wall, tense, the crossbow aimed.

In the silence he said, "We can't just wait for them!"

"What else can we do, Raffi?" Wearily she shook her brown hair. "Never get into a one-way trap, old Jellie used to say. He never said there was sometimes no choice."

Something clanged below.

Felnia stood by the door, the night-cub still under one arm. Looking at them, she sat cross-legged on the floor and said, "You could give yourselves up."

Carys snorted.

"No." The girl nodded. "I suppose not." Her brown eyes fixed on Raffi. "Why did you want me? Where were you taking me?"

"Out of here." Suddenly he knelt up close to her. "We're your friends. We came to rescue you. We were taking you to a place, a beautiful place, full of trees and flowers, peaceful, even in winter. The Watch never come there. Everything you want is there, food and clothes and people to look after you and love you. Wouldn't you like that? Wouldn't you?"

Expressionless, she stared at him. "No punishments?"

"None."

"I don't know." She glanced at Carys. "Would I like it?"

"Not at first," Carys said quietly. "But I think you'd come to like it."

"Have you been there?"

She looked at Raffi. "No. But I believe it would be a good place."

"But why me? Why not Helis, or Dorca?"

"Because you—" But Raffi stopped warily. Carys had given a quick shake of her head; the little girl saw it.

"I won't tell," she said at once.

Raffi felt a sudden surge of bitterness. Somehow it hurt most that the Interrex might die without even knowing who she was. He knew well enough that when the Watch stormed the room, none of them were likely to survive. "Do you remember anything, before you came here?"

The girl looked surprised. "Of course I do. I remember

an old woman called Marta. She cried a lot. She gave me Cub." She frowned. "Was that my mother?"

Raffi sighed. "No."

"Is my mother in this garden you were talking about?"

He glanced despairingly at Carys. "No. Not your mother."

The girl nodded. She seemed quite satisfied.

"It's a pity we won't be able to go there," she said.

Raffi rubbed his hair. He was so terrified, he felt like hugging himself tight. "I wish Galen was here."

"He'd only end up dying with us." Carys was listening calmly; now he could hear it too, the regular, harsh thwack of the ax on the distant door.

"Couldn't you lie to them?" he said abruptly. "Take me prisoner. Say—"

"Raffi." She looked at him in amusement. "In this situation I'd have no chance. They'll shoot first."

"You could call down."

"I could. Then we'll both be tortured and they'll know all about Tasceron, and the Crow, and the Interrex, and anything else that's in your mind."

He felt foolish.

She looked back at the door. "It's strange," she said,

"but I always had an idea it would be my own people who would get me."

"They're not your people," he said quietly.

The ax splintered through the wood. Warily Raffi sent a sense-line down to it; he could feel a crowd of Watchmen. At least fifteen. All armed.

But there was something else too. Faintly, beyond them, beyond the walls of the house, he sensed it. Without knowing, he raised his head sharply.

Carys glanced over, alert. "What is it?"

Rippling out, he touched them. Wild people, smelling of the forest. Bright with stolen gold. An army of them.

"Alberic?"

"What?"

"*Alberic!*" He scrambled to the window. "Look!"

A shower of arrows was slashing over the fences. Men were running; a few fell. Already the drawbridge was smoldering; as he watched, a blast of familiar white fire shot out of the forest again, roaring the wood into flame. "That's the box! What's he doing?"

Carys gave a yell of joy. "It's Galen! He's gotten them to come!"

Standing in Line

"But how?"

"Who cares!"

The ax-thumps stopped. Then, furiously, they came again, faster. Raffi wrenched the window open. A sudden wild idea had come to him, as if it had shot out of the forest like an arrow, and he had caught it. He turned to her. "Give me that relic!"

"What?"

"The relic!"

She reached into the pouch and threw it. Raffi tore off the black cloth and saw a small gray console, faintly glowing. Holding it tight, he reached into it, felt the Maker-power there, drew it out in long blue lines, sending them spinning down out of the window, long ropes of power, weaving and twisting them into a net, suspended above the deadly spikes.

Below, the door crashed down.

He grabbed the Interrex and forced her up onto the sill. "Jump! You'll be all right. Quickly!"

Footsteps came warily up the stairs.

"I'll be killed!" She looked down at the spikes and grabbed him with both hands.

"You won't!"

"I will!"

"For Flain's sake, go!" Carys screamed. "They're here!"

The door burst open. Instantly she fired. Snatching up the girl, Raffi squeezed himself through the window.

Then he jumped.

The Falls of Keilder

22

*From a high place, Soren looked out at
the Unfinished Lands. "The winters will
be long now," she murmured.*

Book of the Seven Moons

THEY CRASHED INTO THE NET.

It dipped and sank and steadied, the blue lines sparking under his hand. He tried to get up and couldn't; suddenly he felt utterly spent, clutching the relic tightly in case it fell.

Someone was shouting at him and tugging his hair, then the net plunged again and flung him over. He moaned, opened his eyes, and saw just below a terrifying glimpse of the sharp stakes. Then Carys with her shoulder soaked in blood was hauling at his arm.

"Raffi!" she yelled. "Come on!"

He staggered over the edge of the net and collapsed

onto his knees. The forest seemed a hundred miles away.

Arrows slashed the air around him. He felt exhausted, wished they'd leave him alone, let him sleep, let him crumple, but Carys hauled him up with one arm under his, calling him vicious names, and on the other side two small cold hands clasped tight around his waist.

Half dragged, he stumbled away from the Watchhouse, into darkness, into a roar of voices and one strong grip that heaved him up, over its shoulder, and away.

When he opened his eyes it was dark, and warm. For a moment he thought he was back in Sarres, but above him was the roof of a cave, seamed with glittering quartz, red in the low glow of a fire. The rocks around him felt calm and ancient. Briefly, deep within them he touched a song, a drift of music so old it barely existed. Then, gradually, memory crept over him, and an ache in his chest that made him catch his breath.

He sat up.

A tiny lamp burned on the sandy floor. Outside, someone was yelling in anger. Alarmed, Raffi pushed the blankets away wearily and stumbled out, but a long hand

caught him and steadied him. "Take care, small keeper!"
The Sekoi stood, its sharp eyes bright in the moonlight.
"How do you feel?"

"Terrible. What's wrong with me?"

It shrugged. "Nothing I can understand. Your master says you did too much in making that magic net." It winked at him. "He won't say it, but he's proud of you."

"Galen!" Weakly Raffi laughed. He found that very funny.

The Sekoi scratched its fur and bit a nail. "You Starmen," it said. "We'll never understand you."

It was Alberic who was angry. From the cave mouth Raffi could see him now, furiously slamming his hands against a tree.

"What's going on?"

"Come and see." The Sekoi led him outside; he saw Galen standing tall and grim in the dark clearing, arms folded. The keeper glanced across but his face didn't change. Between them Alberic raged, kicking over a stool in uncontrollable fury.

The change in the dwarf astonished Raffi. He looked pinched and gray; his hair seemed thinner, and his temper was foul. A tipped goblet of wine spilled among the leaves; as they watched, he picked up a gold plate full of fruit and hurled it hard at the bushes with a scream. The Sekoi looked after it eagerly.

"Are we his prisoners?" Raffi asked, bewildered.

"I think not. Galen has put some fearsome curse on him. In fact, I rather think he's our prisoner." It slid into the undergrowth quickly.

Suddenly Alberic stopped raging, breathless. Clutching his side, he swung around. "You promised me!"

"I promised you nothing." Galen was remorseless. "I asked you to attack."

"We attacked! We burned the drawbridge! Three of my boys are having bolts picked out of them! I even used up all that damnable blue box. What more do you want? Take the stinking curse off me!"

"Not just yet," Galen said calmly.

Alberic clutched his arms around himself like a man in a nightmare. "For Flain's sake, keeper! Everything I eat tastes like ash!"

"First," Galen went on, "you get us out of the forest. We'll need horses—the boy's too worn out to walk. And you protect us from any Watchpatrols till we get to the marsh. A day's journey, no more."

"The marsh?" Despite his pain, Alberic's eyes went sly. "What's in that marsh?"

"Nothing you'll ever find." Galen shifted the weight from his stiff leg; he looked grim, but Raffi could tell he was enjoying this. "Agreed?"

The dwarf swore. "I've no choice."

"No, you haven't. And if anything happens to me, the curse will never be lifted. Take care of me, thief-lord. Without me, six weeks of suffering . . ."

"I know! Don't start that again!"

Galen grinned darkly. "And if my friends are hurt, I'd see them die before I'd cure you. Believe me."

"I'd believe anything of you." Alberic spat, and watched him sidelong, a murderous look that chilled Raffi. "But what I really want to know is, did I have to suffer all this just to rescue *that*?"

He jabbed his finger out. Raffi looked over.

Felnia was sitting near a campfire, eating a huge slice of melon; there were pips all over her face. She rubbed them off, fascinated, her brown eyes staring at the dwarf.

"Is he crazy?" she asked.

Galen grinned. "I hope not. I can't cure that."

Someone came up behind Raffi. "Feeling better?" It was Carys. She had a different shirt on, and a bloody slash down her jacket sleeve.

"A bit. What happened to you?"

She frowned, shaking her head. Reluctantly she said, "I couldn't jump."

"Couldn't?"

"Too scared."

He laughed, but she looked up quickly. "I mean it. I saw how it held you, but . . . it was only made of light, Raffi!"

He nodded. "But you did it. Galen would say that was a leap of faith."

They watched Felnia. She stood up and came out into the dim clearing, deep in leaves. First she looked at Galen, then Raffi. "Are we going to the garden now?"

He nodded, feeling suddenly happier. Lightning glimmered silently, high above the trees; the girl looked up at it, surprised. "Good."

"You're willing to come with us?" Galen asked harshly.

She pointed. "With him. I'll go with him."

Raffi felt foolishly pleased. Then he realized she was pointing behind him, and turned. The Sekoi lurked there, astonished.

"Me?"

"I like you." The girl took another bite of her melon. "You're furry," she said, indistinctly, "like Cub."

"Thank you." The creature looked dubiously at the moth-eaten toy; moving forward, it thrust something from behind its back into Carys's hands. She hid it expertly, but not before Raffi had glimpsed the golden plate.

"This is so sickening," Alberic spat.

The Sekoi crouched on its long knees and held out a seven-fingered hand. "Shall we go into the cave?" it said quietly. "Because I think it's going to rain."

The little girl nodded. As she passed Alberic, she whispered loudly, "He *is* crazy."

"Indeed?" the Sekoi said mildly. "Then that makes two of us."

That night, in the back of the stuffy cave with the rain crashing outside, the four of them sat on their own, deep among stalactites, with the Interrex asleep in blankets on the Sekoi's lap.

It pulled dirt from her hair thoughtfully. "She'll be a handful. She's as haughty as an Emperor's child ought to be."

Raffi grinned, feeling warm and rested. He'd had plenty to eat, and Alberic's guards prowled the woods for miles around. The Interrex was safe, and they were going back to Sarres, and Braylwin was tied up and guarded somewhere. And yet, he thought sleepily, they were still in the middle of their enemies.

Carys was telling Galen about the Watchhouse. He nodded grimly. "It sounds worse than even I thought. You think the child will be satisfied to stay with us?"

"If she's got any sense."

"What about you?" Raffi said suddenly. "You can't go back now."

She shrugged, uneasy. "Of course I can. No one knows it was me in there."

"Except Braylwin." Raffi stopped. Galen's warning had snagged every sense-line he had; he looked down, giddy.

"There's time to decide. It will take a day to ride clear

of the forest." Galen tugged the hair carelessly from his face and knotted it in the dirty string. "Now one of us stays awake, all night. But first it's time for the Litany, boy. And don't fall asleep."

IT WAS STRANGE BEING on a horse again. He and Carys rode together, with the Sekoi and the little girl on a white horse in front of them. Even Galen rode, a green-painted creature with sidelong frightened eyes. They traveled quickly, in the long straggle of the thief-band. The remaining Watchguards, Braylwin's men, had vanished; Raffi didn't know if their throats had been cut or if they'd been released. Certainly Alberic wouldn't have gotten any ransom for them.

But Braylwin was still there. They'd made him walk at first, but he'd been so clumsy and complained so loudly, they'd found a horse for him too, a great stubborn pack-beast. Raffi stared at the man, repelled by his great bulk. As if he sensed it, the spymaster turned around in the saddle and smiled greasily.

"Fond of the lad, aren't you, Carys?"

"Ignore him," Carys muttered.

But Braylwin slowed his horse, hanging back. "Won't you release your uncle, sweetheart?" he whispered. "It would be wise."

She stared out into the trees icily.

Braylwin scratched his cheek with plump, tied hands. "You see, I was just composing my report. What an epic that's going to be! It's a pity you'll never have a chance to read it."

"What are you going to say about her?" Raffi was worried.

The big man jolted in his saddle and smiled. "Why, everything I should. Betrayal of the Watch, that's a hanging offense. Abduction. Counterespionage. Of course, if either of you should decide to help me escape, that would be different. Very different. You and I could make up some really tasty little story . . ."

"As far as I'm concerned, you can rot!" she snapped, turning savagely.

"But I won't rot." The black eyes were sharp in his flabby face. "I'm rich, Carys," he hissed, "and the dwarf's greedy. I can buy freedom. When I do, believe me, I'll have your name on every hanging-list from here to Maar. So hurry up and decide!"

But she urged the horse on, past him, and for a long time after, even when Raffi spoke to her, she wouldn't say a word.

THE WOOD WAS A MORASS, and the gale had brought all the leaves down. In the afternoon, drizzle began again; every rider became a gray shape, slithering and splashing through mud and over slippery rutted tracks. As he jolted, Raffi let his third eye open and looked out into the wood, feeling it cower under the leaden weather, the gray, dragging rain, all the bare thorns scattering great drops down on his face. Soon he was soaked, holding loosely to Carys's coat, and far off in his dream-sight he watched a skeat-pack splash through a swollen stream, tiny larvae scattering between their paws.

The world was dissolving; he felt the whole hemisphere reeling into winter, the long, bitter Anaran winter of ice-storms and raw gales, each year worse than the last; the time when the grass froze and the carnage-wolves prowled down from the Unfinished Lands, when the seven moons glinted frost-bright among the Maker-stars. He shivered. Last year he and Galen had barely come through it. But this year things would be better; they would be in Sarres. If only Galen would stay there.

Darkness came early, a dank autumn twilight, a rain-gloom gathering between the wet twisted boles of the trees. Boulders and great shattered cliffs of dark rock rose around them. Flittermice came out; owls began to hoot from the caves far above. The Sekoi looked up and listened to them, holding Felnia carefully.

Late in the evening they stopped briefly to eat, but lit no fires; Alberic was determined to press on. He had given up riding; four of his toughest men carried him now in a litter that was gaudily painted and hung with sodden crimson cloth. Godric took him some food but ducked away quickly, the plate flung furiously at his head. Some of the war-band laughed; others looked evilly at Galen. Raffi felt afraid.

In the dismal rain it was difficult to see; Raffi sheltered under a larch tree eating bread miserably, water dripping from his hair and fingers. Suddenly everything seemed wrong: Sarres a hundred miles away, his senses dulled and shivering, all the power-lines drawn into the earth like a snail draws into its shell.

Then Galen came up and grabbed him. "Where is she? Is she with you?"

Bewildered, Raffi stared. "Carys?"

"Felnia!" Galen's hawk-face was anxious, his hair plastered to his forehead. "Have you seen her?"

A rainsquall gusted into their eyes. Among the trees, Carys yelled; Galen raced toward her, crashing through the decaying bracken and fat stumps of puffballs, shoving through an interested crowd of the thief-band. Raffi ran after him, dropping the bread.

The Sekoi lay on its back, eyes wide open, staring sightlessly up. Godric was feeling its limbs over carefully. "Not dead. Some sort of blow to the head."

Galen whirled around. "She must have run off!"

"No." Carys stood stock-still. She was staring at something dim in the rainy wood; Braylwin's great packhorse, cropping lichen from a dead log. Sliced rope hung from its neck.

"Oh God, Galen," she breathed. "He's got her."

23

*Bind a bright web about the doubtful
soul.
If you pull hard, it will come to you.*

Apocalypse of Tamar

"AND WHY SHOULD I?" Alberic was peevish; he shivered in his quilted robe, a fur-lined cloak clutched tight around him.

"Because if you don't," Galen stormed, "I'll go alone and you can burn in your own hell!" The keeper was reckless with black fury; Raffi knew that in this mood he might do anything.

Alberic knew it too.

"All right." The thief-lord waved a sickly hand. "Get the lads out, Taran. Search groups of ten. We want the child alive." He looked at Galen slyly. "And the fat man? He's good for a thousand marks."

"I don't care." The keeper snatched his staff down from the horse, the rain lashing between them. "Raffi, come with me." He glanced at Carys. "You too, if you want."

She nodded, loading the bow. Her face was taut and white. Raffi felt strange memories in her, and anger. Deep anger.

They slipped between the trees. Galen had his own way of tracking; he followed the glints and taints of feelings, the tiny intricate sense-traces. He led them down a gloomy trail between holly and larch, the trees thickening as they went, the ravine's shattered cliff looming somewhere behind the rain.

Shouts rang in the wood. Behind them Alberic came, scowling and limping, Godric a big shadow behind him.

Galen questioned trees and owls, swiftly, silently, bursting straight to their deep consciousness, leaving them dizzy. He was ruthless, and Raffi felt the sore echoes of it. But Braylwin had come this way. Pictures of them flickered in his third eye: the big man carrying the child easily, under his arm.

"I'm surprised he could go this fast," he gasped.

Carys glanced back. "He's fitter than you'd think. He can run when he wants to. All that puffing is an act."

The trail scrambled down, broke into scree and falling rock. It was dark down here, softened with mist, every branch black and dripping. A were-bird screeched, and Galen slipped, jamming his stick into the mud with a curse.

At the bottom, distorted rowans sprouted, their thin boles white and spindly. The track split in two. Galen crouched, hands on the wet rocks, sending his mind far into soil and puddles and clotted leaves. But Carys darted forward and picked something out of the left-hand track. "Don't bother. She's Watchtrained, remember?"

It was the toy night-cub. She threw it to Raffi, who jammed it into his pocket; Galen was already gone, pushing his way among the sprawling branches. Moss and lichen coated everything; down here the rocks and trees were green in the gloom. It all smelled rich and rotten, the path choked with strange ghostly moonflowers that grew too high, grotesquely twisting after the light.

Crashing through them, Raffi heard water; the roar of it, falling from some unguessed height. Then his sense-lines touched it, and were swept away into a moving flow of energy, patterned by rainbows.

"He's close!" Galen yelled. "Get ready!"

They burst out into a clearing; before them the black waters of a torrent glinted over the stones. Down the cliff a great waterfall roared, a deafening crash of water, the foam at its base endlessly breaking and whirling away in bubbled white patches.

It was almost too loud to think; the sense-lines jangled, and Raffi felt suddenly dizzy, as if someone had slapped him hard on the side of the head. Galen looked around too, disoriented. "Can you see him?"

A crossbow bolt thumped into wood behind them; Carys yanked Raffi down among the moonflowers.

"Idiot!" she yelled above the water-crash. "Keep down!"

At least now they knew Braylwin was armed. And just then, as if the Makers had ordered it, the river mist thinned, and through its frail wisps the seven moons shone clear, a ragged formation that was almost the Arch, though Lar was just a crescent and the strange pitted surface of Karnos was too far down among the trees.

The Falls of Keilder

Galen glanced up. He said nothing aloud, but Raffi sensed his prayer, some deep affirmation he couldn't recognize.

"Can you see him?" Carys called.

Galen shook his head. But his eyes were closed; he was feeling with his mind, and on the ground he had laid one ring of awen-beads and a small hazel twig. He turned it gently in his fingers as they watched.

Then it stopped, pointing across the river, to the right of the falls. Raffi strained his eyes to see what was there, but the dapples of moonlight and the energy-field of the water were bewildering. Stripes of pearl and rose filtered down the rock face.

Galen tugged on the beads. Pulling Carys closer, he said in her ear, "I'll get him to concentrate on me. You move up the bank." She nodded; his hand tightened. "Keep the Interrex safe, Carys."

She laughed, and said something Raffi couldn't hear; then she was gone, slithering into the moonflowers. "Go with her," Galen yelled.

Raffi hesitated.

"Do as you're told, boy!"

He turned, pushing between the tall stalks, uneasy. Galen was too exposed. The sense-lines were useless here. Everything echoed and rang. He wondered if Braylwin had known this would happen.

Worming along in the moonflowers, he worried about blue spiders and vesps. This was just the sort of place for them, and he'd never even feel them on him. He shivered. Ahead, Carys crawled, and the moons' light quivered on the crashing water.

Then, just below the fall, a flicker of movement over the river caught his eye. He stopped, straining to see in the dimness. From rock to rock near the cliff base a black figure climbed, bulky but swift.

"Carys!" he hissed, but she was too far ahead to hear.

Turning back, Raffi saw Braylwin wedge himself securely, bracing his feet. Then he whipped the crossbow up and aimed it, his eye looking down the bolt. Raffi leaped up, glancing back. Galen stood between two trees, the moonlight catching his shape.

"*Galen!*" Raffi screamed.

The bolt flashed, the keeper turned, and instantly a small figure leaped up at him and tore him down into a crash of shadows. Oblivious of danger, Raffi raced back, flinging himself down breathlessly as Godric came lumbering up.

Both of them stared.

Alberic was sitting up, swearing savagely, picking clots of mud off his cloak, Galen half lying in the leaves, staring at him. Just above their heads the crossbow bolt had splintered the rowan trunk in half.

"For Flain's sake, you stupid, reckless fool, keep your head down!" the dwarf snarled.

Godric snorted with laughter; his chief glared up at him wrathfully. "You! Brainless! You're assigned to him. If he dies I'll have you skinned an inch at a time and hung out of my tower-top for the crows to pick at! Understand!"

The bearded man nodded, his grin still wide. Galen picked himself up stiffly. "You're a better man than you want to be, thief-lord."

Alberic ignored that. "A keeper for the keeper," he said sourly. "But when this curse is off, Galen, I'll make up for lost time, believe me!"

A shout made them scramble hastily to the river. Looking out, Raffi saw Carys, far off near the falls; she yelled again, pointing.

Braylwin had the girl with him now. In the moonlight they could see how he pushed her ahead of him up the cliff, climbing behind like a vast shadow, and far above in the mist strange birds called, their cries disturbed and wary.

Galen cursed; then he was gone, Godric swiftly behind him. Ignoring the dwarf, Raffi ran after them. They raced along the path, the torrent churning below them. There were huge rounded boulders in the stream; looking up, Raffi saw Carys leaping from one to another, perilously balanced, the waterfall crashing over her.

Braylwin was higher now, the little girl kicking and struggling, sending trickles of stone that rattled down the cliff. The Watchman struck her hard with his fist, but still she fought. Behind them, Carys fired her bow, but deep rocks and springing trees hid them. Shouldering the weapon, she began to climb.

Galen scrambled down to the rocks, crossing recklessly, and Raffi came after him. The roar and speed of the water filled him with fear; one slip and he knew it would whirl him away, crashing him downstream, snapping his limbs against boulders and tree stumps. Cold spray soaked him; his feet slithered every way, he wobbled and leaped through rainbows, and the moon-splashed crash of the fall was heavy as wet snow from a roof. One more jump. He landed on hands and knees in the mud, scrambled up, exhausted.

"Braylwin!"

Carys's yell stopped them all.

Slowly the Watchman turned, crossbow ready.

She was just below him, feet braced, bolt aimed.

"Let her go!" she yelled.

In the moonlight they saw the big man's smile. "You should come with me, Carys. We can share the profits."

"I'd rather kill you," she snarled.

He shook his head, the drops of water falling like silver slashes. "That's better. For a while I thought they'd made a keeper of you. But revenge, that's a Watchman's act."

"Yes," she yelled. The bow didn't waver. "Yes, it is. And this isn't about Emperors or their heirs. This is about me. I don't know who I am, Braylwin. I'll probably never know. All I've learned is hunting and lying, that's all you and your Watchlords want from me, that and never asking any questions. But I don't believe it anymore. I've finished with them and you and your lies, because every time I look at that girl I see myself, and all the things you've done to me."

He laughed, one hand tight on the bow. "Poor, dear Carys. It's hardly my fault."

"And not just me. All the others too."

"The whole world, Carys! For the whole world is the Watch now. You'll never get away from it. It's even in you. Deep in you. And it always will be!" He twisted suddenly, grabbed Felnia and thrust her in front of him. Carys didn't move.

"Don't," Galen said softly, just behind her. "He's not worth your soul."

She flicked a glance at him, amused. "Always trying, Galen. I'll give you that."

A rock shifted, crashed down. Instantly the little girl screeched and bit; he jerked her away and dropped the crossbow and she jumped, ledge to ledge, like a cat.

The bow clattered endlessly down, then splashed.

Braylwin was alone.

He drew himself up, held his arms wide. "Well, Carys," he roared over the falls. "I'm ready now!"

Carys was still.

"You haven't gone soft on me, have you, sweetie? You know what to do. You have to kill me now, Carys. Or you're finished with the Watch."

"No!" Galen said. "Carys, listen to me . . ."

"And you want to, don't you!" Braylwin folded his arms. "Remember your training. Fast and firm. Do it now, girl."

"Carys. For Flain's sake . . ."

"Shut up, Galen." Her face was wet. She didn't even look down.

"It's not the way!"

"Of course it is," she snarled.

Then she fired.

24

Kest raised himself in great pain. "I have done evil and I know it. I went to war on my own creatures; the dragon is destroyed, but I have to follow it, even to the caves of death." He closed his eyes, Tamar lifting him. He spoke only once more. "Beware the Margrave," he whispered.

Book of the Seven Moons

"MY RANSOM!" Alberic's howl rang over the waterfall. "God rot you, girl, my ransom!"

Galen leaped fiercely up the cliff; he grabbed the Interrex and swung her down into Godric's grip. Then he stared up.

"You'll have your ransom, thief-lord."

Braylwin was standing stock-still, his face white. The bolt had split the rock inches from his left eye. He reached up and touched it, unbelieving. When he spoke his voice was only a whisper in the water crash. "So we've lost you, Carys. We've lost you."

She stood silent, looking up at him. Then she turned

and climbed down, past Raffi, into the wood.

It took some time to get Braylwin down and back over the river, Alberic fussing and moaning the whole time, cursing Galen and the clumsy bearers. In the end, Godric had to carry the dwarf back, and all the way the thief-girl, Sikka, mocked him about how much care he was beginning to take of his enemies.

Raffi was shocked, as if some bolt had gone through him too. He had sensed nothing as Carys had passed him; worse than nothing. An emptiness, black and deep and cold. Stumbling on the path, he shuddered. Had she meant to miss? he thought. Or to kill?

All evening, in the hasty camp they made under the rocks, he waited for her to come back. Completely unworried, Felnia had taken Cub back from him and gone to sit by the Sekoi; it had told her intricate rambling stories until she slept and now it lay, long legs stretched out next to the fire, brooding on the pain in its head. Galen was nowhere to be seen, and Alberic was yelling at the grumbling, half-drunken man he called his "surgeon."

Raffi moved uneasily. When he looked up, the Sekoi was watching him, its yellow eyes narrowed to slits.

The Falls of Keilder

"Why don't you go and look for her?" it said quietly.

He shrugged. "Do you think I should?"

"I do, small keeper." The Sekoi chewed a nail thoughtfully. "Someone should. It would be best if it were you."

Abruptly Raffi stood up. He went straight past the sentries and walked back along the river trail, moving quietly in the dark till the noise and stir of the camp were distant.

The forest rustled. Far off, the great falls roared. Sending out sense-lines he touched sleeping trees, their deep consciousness stirring; startled the tiny minds of voles and shrews; woke a weasel that curled back up into weariness.

Then he winced. Something else was there, so sharp it stung him like a black bee. He pushed off the path, through a thick stand of larch trees, forcing his way through the dusty, matted branches until he stumbled into a clearing, brushing needles from his hair.

Carys was sitting on a rock in the moonlight.

She had her back to him, and she made no sound, but he knew she had been crying bitterly; he could feel that, a raw urgency of grief and fury that made his palms sweat.

He stood, awkward.

After a while she raised her head. "Well?"

"Felnia's all right."

"I know that!" She turned, furious, her eyes red and sore.

He nodded. "So is he. You could have killed him, but you didn't."

"I wanted to!" She pushed her hair back; her face was taut and white. "I really wanted to, Raffi. My mind was empty, except for hating him."

"It's all right . . ."

"Don't be stupid!" Ripples of agitation slammed against him. "Of course it's not all right! I wanted him dead. And Galen knows I did. I'm finished now, with the Watch and with you." She laughed bitterly. "How did I get to this, Raffi? I thought I had everything under control."

Quietly he came forward. Standing opposite her he said, "Come with us to Sarres."

"Why? To be punished for my sins?"

"No. To be healed."

Amazed, she stared at him. "What?"

He chewed the ties of his jacket nervously. "You've

been hurt, Carys. You may not know it, but I can feel it. It's like a big emptiness in you. We can help . . . the Order has ways . . ."

"To forgive me?"

"That's not what I mean."

She stood up quickly, brushing her hair back. "You're soft, Raffi, that's your trouble. You'd never survive without Galen. He won't want me along. He probably despises me."

But something had changed in her. Raffi smiled. "You don't know him."

"I know he's hard as nails."

"He's a Relic Master. And it says in the Book that love is as fierce as hatred—as strong, and as reckless."

She looked at him strangely. "Does it? Perhaps that's why they never let us read all of it."

She pushed past him through the larches. He trailed behind, catching the branches that swung back into his face.

At the campfire Galen was talking to the Sekoi, but when he saw them coming the keeper stood, tall and grim, his hawk-face half hidden in the shadows.

Carys walked right up to him and flung the crossbow down.

"You were right. It's not the way."

His silence forced her to look up. "All right, Galen," she breathed. "I missed him. I meant to. But . . ." Hopeless, she shrugged. "I'm sorry."

"You don't feel sorry," he said. "You feel angry. And free."

"I don't suppose you care what I feel."

He laughed then, his rare harsh laugh. "The Order welcomes anyone, Carys. We have no failures either."

She smiled. "Even Watchspies?"

"Especially those."

The Sekoi went to say something, but then waggled its long fingers and was silent.

Carys sat down. The fire glow made her look red and tired. "I would have killed him once," she said. "Before I knew you, I probably wouldn't have thought twice. Now it's all more difficult." She looked up firmly. "Look, I'll give you all the information you want. Everything. Numbers, passwords, details of patrols . . ."

"Carys." The keeper crouched, his eyes dark in the

flame light. "We don't want information. We want you. Will you come to Sarres?"

"Where is that?"

"Beyond your world. The place where the Order will begin again. The heart of the web, where we'll wait for the Makers. Will you come? We want you to come."

She looked at him a long time, then away into the flames. "I'll come. After all, where else can I go?"

Then, quickly, she reached into the pouch at her waist and brought out the relic, thrusting it into his hands. "You'd better have this. I stole it from the Tower of Song. I think it's important."

He stared at it in surprise, then at Raffi. "Was this what you used for the net?"

"Yes."

Galen clicked his tongue in annoyance. "It'll have little power left, if any." He spread his fingers over it. "It feels faint."

"So do I, sorcerer."

The voice was a snarl; Raffi jumped up nervously.

Alberic had to be helped to the fire. Sikka brought a chair for him and placed it down; the dwarf lowered himself into it as if he were an old man. His hair was thin, his face drawn with pain. His chest heaved, as if he had no breath. But he glared at Galen as furiously as ever.

"You've got what you want. Take the curse off."

"And then?" Galen asked.

"Then I take my lads and lasses and clear out. Oh, and the Watchman. He's mine. You can have her." He pointed a tiny finger at Carys. "She won't fetch you much."

"On the contrary." Galen turned the relic over. "She already has."

The dwarf eyed it without interest. "You people and your bits of junk. Well?"

Galen sat still, the moonlight falling on him. "The curse has been on you a long time," he said softly. "How can I take if off?"

Alberic went rigid. "By Flain, you'd better!" he raged. "Or you'll never leave this wood."

Galen grinned. "You mistake me." He stood up suddenly and leaned forward. "You've read the Book, you told me once?"

"The Litany." Alberic waved his fingers painfully. "Rather obscure style, I thought."

The Falls of Keilder

"So you know about the Crow?"

"I've heard of it."

"Now you can see it."

Galen tossed the relic to Raffi; sparks were leaping from it. As he stood there, he seemed strangely taller; the darkness closed in around him. He reached over, caught Alberic's hand, and pulled him upright. The dwarf stared, astonished, and as Galen looked down at him a sudden shiver of energy moved through their linked fingers, and in an instant of breathtaking clearness everyone saw it, the sharpness of the black eyes, the power that looked out of them, the abrupt shift that made the dark figure something else, something charged, out of myth, out of legend.

Alberic swore, snatching his hand away. Behind him his people stared.

Galen grinned.

"God, keeper," the dwarf breathed. "What are you?"

"I'm the Crow." He said it quietly, and the ghost images of seven moons drifted between his fingers. "See it and believe it, thief-lord, because apart from these, you're the first. Things are changing. The Interrex is found, Anara will have a leader again. And the Order has a home;

we'll make it such a powerhouse it will re-energize the world. Above all, I've spoken with the Makers. The Makers are coming back, Alberic."

The dwarf swallowed. He stood up straight now, breathed easy. "Crackpot fanatics," he muttered. "I almost believe it."

"You should. Because I haven't finished with you."

"Oh no!" Alberic jumped back. "Oh no. I came looking for you once, but never again! I've had my fill of sorcerers. From now on I'll avoid you like fireseed, Galen Harn."

Galen nodded darkly. "That's what you think."

He turned, took the relic from Raffi, and held it in both hands. It spat and crackled. Suddenly it hummed, and the dwarf stepped closer greedily.

Raffi stood up. To his amazement he saw the tiny screen had lit, and words were racing across it, minute white Maker-words that Galen hurriedly began to read aloud.

> . . . Things are desperate; it may be we
> will have to withdraw. There's been no word
> from Earth for months. Worst of all, we're

```
sure now about Kest. Against all orders,
he's tampered with the genetic material.
Somehow, he has made a hybrid out of
what was once a . . . Flain fears it has
a disturbed nature, certainly a greatly
enhanced lifespan . . . When it was let out
of the chamber it destroyed all . . .
```

The screen flickered; Galen frowned and shook it desperately.

```
. . . We have flung it deep in the Pits
of Maar. Kest called it the Margrave. We
should have destroyed it. We should . . .
```

The screen went blank.

In the silence only the fire crackled. Then Raffi said, "That was what I saw in the vision."

"It's what rules the Watch," Carys said in disgust.

Slowly Galen turned the relic over in his hands. He seemed slightly dizzy. Finally he said, "This may tell us more. In Sarres, we might be able to restore it in some way." He looked at Raffi.

"It seems the Makers have spoken to us again. How

can they re-make the world if the most evil of its creatures still lurks here?"

Worried, Raffi said, "What can we do about that?"

The keeper folded his arms. "I don't know."

It was dark in the wood now; the fire had sunk. As the Sekoi piled wood on, the flames sparked up and crackled. Alberic yelled at his people, "Get me something to eat! Plenty!"

He sat down by the Sekoi, who said idly, "I suppose there's no chance, now that you're cured, of me getting my gold back?"

"Don't push your luck, tale-spinner. It's not half what you stole from me."

"And do you still want me as your prisoner?"

"Want you!" The dwarf put his face close up to it fiercely. "I fully intend never to see any of you scumbags again."

Carys grinned, and Raffi smiled too. But then he turned and saw Galen. The keeper had a dark, thoughtful look.

Raffi knew it only too well.

It always meant trouble.

Don't miss
CATHERINE FISHER'S
New York Times bestselling duology:

AND

IT GIVES LIFE.
IT DEALS DEATH.
IT WATCHES ALL.

NAMED A BEST BOOK OF THE YEAR BY:

The Washington Post

Horn Book

SLJ

Kirkus

PW

CCBC

YALSA

THE ONLY ONE
WHO ESCAPED . . .
AND THE ONE WHO COULD
DESTROY THEM ALL.

An Indie Next List Top Ten

Kirkus Reviews **Best Book of the Year**

MORE REMARKABLE STORIES FROM
CATHERINE FISHER

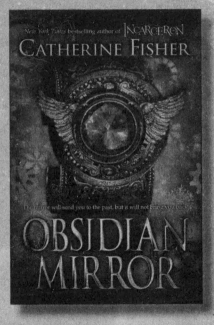